HARPER FALLS BOOK THREE

If You Only Knew

MARY J. WILLIAMS

About the Author

Want to know how to motivate yourself to write a book? Have your favorite football team lose the Super Bowl. On the last play. With an interception. The next day I was so depressed I tuned out all media. No TV, no internet, no newspapers — nothing. And I started to write. I'm still writing. As you can see, a little motivation can do wonders. Football will play a big part in my next series of books due out next year. And since I'm writing the ending? No interceptions. Guaranteed. Happy reading everyone.

Mary J. Williams

Please visit me at these sites and leave a message or ask a question.

NEWSLETTER: http://eepurl.com/bhFPPn

WEBSITE: www.maryjwilliams.net

www.amazon.com/Mary-J.-Williams/e/B00V041ET6/

www.facebook.com/pages/Mary-J-Williams/1561851657385417

www.twitter.com/maryjwilliams05

www.pinterest.com/maryj0675/

www.goodreads.com/author/show/5648619.Mary_J_Williams

More Books by Mary J. Williams

Harper Falls Series

If I Loved You
If Tomorrow Never Comes
If I Had You - Christmas in Harper Falls
(Coming In October)

Contents

Prologue

TYLER JONES HAD a secret. Not easy when you lived with two brothers who wouldn't understand the word private if it kicked them in the rear. Then there were her two best friends and the honesty pact they made the year they turned eleven. They pledged to tell each other everything and up until now, Tyler happily complied. However, sometimes something came along that was so big, so special, you had to keep it to yourself, at least for a little while.

She hid her bike behind a large group of rocks. It still amazed her that anyone in Harper Falls could at this very moment be looking her way and would have no idea she was there. The small cove was a haven, isolated, and all hers. Finding it had been a fluke. One of those happy accidents that when it happened, could change your life. That was how it had been for Tyler.

Sometimes she needed to get away by herself. Rose and Dani understood. They witnessed firsthand the family drama that seemed to be a daily occurrence at the Jones house. Her father had turned into a bitter, discontented man. Life hadn't played out the way he planned and he had no problem taking it out on his family. If he wasn't angry and sullen, he just wasn't there. He used his job as an excuse to be out of town as often as possible. Her mother had no backbone. She was sweet and quiet, and her husband and sons treated her like a doormat. Tyler could only stand up for her so often. As much as she loved the woman, her complete lack of fight could be wearing.

When Tyler reached her breaking point, she would get on her bike and ride. It seemed only natural that one day she would ride across the bridge towards Harper House. Her father would have been livid if he'd known, her mother horrified. Nevertheless, Tyler thought of it as having an adventure in a town that too often offered few surprises.

It was on one of those outings that she found the path down to the beach and *her place*. She didn't go there often but when things at home got so unbearable not even Rose and Dani could talk her down, she came here.

Today wasn't about getting away. Today, she wasn't going to be alone. In fact, for the past few months, her alone place had become something else altogether. Tyler Jones, outcast, rebel, nonconformist, was in love. It was her secret and she was ready to burst. She wanted to shout it to the sky, the trees. She wanted everyone to know. But for now, she would be happy just to tell him. She hadn't, not yet. Neither of them had spoken of feelings, though she was certain he had to feel the same; how could he not? The way he looked at her, the softness of his touch. And his kisses. Only someone in love could kiss like that. So today was the day. She couldn't keep it inside a moment longer.

"Tyler."

She spun around, her face lighting up, her every emotion there for him to see. There he was, the man she loved — Drew Harper.

Chapter One

TYLER JONES HATED what ifs. It never helped to live in a world where you fantasized about how life might be — if only. *If only* I hadn't eaten that entire chocolate cake, I wouldn't have gained five pounds. *What if* I'd turned right instead of left and not hit that parked police car? There was no going back. You did it — live with the consequences. However, she was only human. When her best friends found love and made it work, it was hard not to indulge in a bit of *what if* self-pity.

Hanging out with Rose O'Brian and Dani Wilde used to be about making a simple phone call and meeting up wherever hit their fancies. Three single women free to go where they wanted, when they pleased. Now, there were men to consider. Rose and her Jack, Dani and Alex. Three had become five. Not that they ever made her feel like she wasn't welcome. Sometimes though, like today, being around so much happiness made her long for something she'd once had — love.

She'd had it, reveled in it, and lost it. Or rather, had it ripped from her grasp in the cruelest manner possible. It was hard to forget when it had once seemed so perfect — especially when the source of her heartache stood across the room. If Drew Harper had never come back to town… God, how many times over the past year and a half had she started a sentence like that? He was a nagging ache that had never gone away, but that had been bearable — manageable. She learned to live with it, often forgetting it was even there. But how could she do that when he now seemed to be everywhere she turned?

Today was a perfect example. Rose had invited her to an end of the season cookout. The house she now shared with her fiancée, Jack Winston, was an entertainer's paradise and the couple loved to have their friends over. Dani and Alex Fleming, newly engaged themselves, stood with Alex's sister, Lila, and Boyd Stevens. Boyd worked for H&W Security and looked none the worse for his recent run-in with a mad man bent on killing Dani and Alex. Tyler shuddered whenever she thought about how close they had come to losing Dani. The fact that all three had walked away, living to tell the tale, was a miracle. A miracle, and Dani's ability to take care of herself. Her friend might look like a frail, fairy princess, but under all that white-blond hair and delicate features, was a warrior — the kick-ass kind.

"You look pensive." Rose put an arm around Tyler's waist and squeezed.

Their friendship started when they were girls, all knobby knees, and gangly bodies. Before dreams of the future had taken a firm hold and everything was an adventure. They had weathered the storms of adolescence, family dramas, and personal crises — coming out stronger. Not just friends forever — friends no matter what.

Rose's dark hair just brushed her shoulders, her brown eyes, warm and welcoming. They were close to the same height though Tyler topped her by an inch. Her friend's body leaned more towards curvy — a walking wet dream — some man had once called her and Tyler supposed that fit. Maybe it was because Rose's transition from flat-chested girl to heartbreaker had been so gradual. She never acquired the ego some beautiful women possessed — which made her even more stunning.

"I was just thinking what an eclectic group of friends you and Jack have acquired." Tyler nodded to the people assembled in the large, open living room.

"Do you mean the twelve hulking bodyguards, Jilly Underwood, or Regina Harper's personal assistant?"

Where to start? The bodyguards were a no-brainer. Alex ran that branch of Jack and Drew's business. There always seemed to be one or two, or, in this case, a dozen, of them at the H&W compound. They were either being trained, retrained or just checking in. At one time, Jack and Drew had considered dropping that area of their business. In their younger days hiring themselves out as bodyguards had paid the bills. Once they'd made their first million as software moguls, they kept the personal security side of H&W going out of sentimentality, and a bit of superstition. Since Alex had come on board, instead of scaling back, they expanded. As a result, more and more big, brawny men appeared in Harper Falls.

Which brought her to Jilly Underwood. An annoyance on her best day, the woman had always seen Tyler, Rose, and Dani as her chief rivals. It didn't matter that Jilly was pretty and smart. It didn't matter that her family had money and indulged her every whim. Or that Jilly went to Harper Academy, an exclusive, private high school that neither Tyler nor Dani's families could afford. Rose went there for a few years before circumstances had her finishing her education at Harper High. Yes, Rose had beaten Jilly out of the lead in every musical production. However, was that reason enough for a lifelong grudge?

Tyler gave a mental shrug. The fact was Jilly equaled mean girl. They were twenty-seven years old, for Christ's sake. Time to put any slights, perceived or otherwise, behind them. Unfortunately, Jilly seemed determined to hang on by her fire engine red acrylic fingernails. She would resent Tyler and her friends until the day she died.

"Did we ever discuss why Jilly was here?"

"It seems it isn't every day you find out your perfect new boyfriend is a psychotic killer."

"Which sent her running here for sympathy?"

"No. She jumped into the nearest big, strong arms she could find." Rose clarified. "In this case, Wally Arnot. She hasn't let go of him since they arrived."

"You have to give the woman credit for her nerve." Tyler shook her head, amazed. "Why would she think she would be welcome?"

"I made sure Jack let all the guys know they could bring a date. Jilly was the last person I expected to show up. I didn't want to embarrass Wally, so I let it go. As long as she behaves, I think we can put up with her for a few hours."

If she behaved. At the moment, Jilly was busy batting her eyes at her date while simultaneously flirting with any man within range. Tyler had seen men get into fights over less. She imagined Jilly would love to have three or four muscled hunks throwing punches over her.

"All that bulk could do some damage." Tyler looked over at the piano. A gift from Jack's mother, it was Rose's most prized possession. If it were damaged by three-hundred pounds of falling flesh, it would be devastating all around.

"Maybe you should herd them to the backyard. How badly can they hurt a pine tree?"

Rose watched as Jilly admiringly squeezed the arm of a man who was not her date and decided Tyler was right. Walking across the room, she pulled Jack aside and whispered in his ear. Whatever she said had him nodding. Before anyone was the wiser, he and Alex had the party moved from indoors to out — potential crisis averted.

"Jilly," Dani said with exasperation. She came over to join Tyler, offering a perfectly chilled glass of chardonnay. "She isn't happy if she's not the center of the storm."

"True." Taking the wine, Tyler smiled at her other best friend. "Just remember, the last storm was not of your making."

Dani sighed. "I know. I still feel bad. She could have been physically hurt by Pete Landry; the man was unhinged — to say the least."

Tyler felt a shiver as fear raced down her spine. She hated remembering how close they had come to losing Dani; luckily, the lady could take care of herself.

"As soon as Alex suspected anything was wrong, he had one of his men watching Jilly. We both know there was no way to warn her. She wouldn't have listened if we'd tried."

"True. And, as a result, Jilly Underwood is a guest in Rose's home. How is that for karma kicking you in the ass?"

They laughed, sharing a joke the same way they had since they were old enough to toddle across the few feet of grass that separated their childhood homes. Neighbors since birth, Dani liked to joke that they became friends while still in the womb. Their mothers went to the same doctor, attended the same childbirth classes. They both joked, and cringed at the thought, that they must have been conceived on the same night. They were born less than a week apart, Tyler being stubborn and refusing to come out on her due date.

After that, they were inseparable. They had other friends, but the two girls spent almost every waking moment together. When Rose moved in with Tyler's family the summer they all turned nine, the dynamic duo became the Three Musketeers. The transition wasn't without its bumps — Tyler had never been good at sharing. Rose, though, had made it impossible not to love her. Within a week, they all ran wild, sharing everything. College and life had them going on different paths for a while, but when Dani had told them she was moving home, it was a no-brainer for Tyler and Rose to follow. At seventeen, Tyler never wanted to see Harper Falls again. Now, she couldn't imagine living anywhere else. Full circle — or pretty damn close.

"I think we may have a budding romance in our midst."

"You don't mean Jilly and her muscle man?"

Dani shook her head. "No, if that lasts a week, I'll be shocked. I meant Portia Nessmith and Boyd."

"Queen Reggie's PA and your bodyguard? Talk about an odd couple."

"*Ex*-bodyguard. And as for odd, you'd be surprised how much they have in common. Boyd loves classical music and French food. Portia is willing to learn about both."

"God, they're practically down the aisle."

"Tease all you like. I say they're a good fit."

Maybe, Tyler conceded silently. Who was she to judge? Relationships were a constant mystery that she didn't think she would ever solve. Dani and Rose made theirs work. Her best friends practically glowed with happiness. There had been times — early on — when Tyler had been on alert, ready to knock either man in the head if he hurt her friend. Fortunately, that hadn't been necessary and now she looked at Alex and Jack as what they were — good men who loved without reservation. Dani and Rose were in good hands, and that made her very grateful.

"Any progress on the Drew front?"

"Well, let's see." Tyler used one long finger to tap her chin as though contemplating deep thoughts. "I've been here for over an hour and he's not only spent the entire time as far away from me as he can physically get, he's never even glanced my way. What does that tell you?"

"That my usually observant friend is blind when it comes to Drew Harper."

"What the hell does that mean?"

"Only that his eyes have been glued to you since you arrived," Dani said. "Though admittedly, he looks away whenever you look at him. I swear the two of you act like pre-teens with your first crushes."

"I distinctly remember my first crush," Tyler told her. "That boy had no doubt about my feelings."

"Poor Kenny Henderson." Dani practically bent over with laughter when she thought of the tall, skinny boy. "It took him until junior year in high school to recover from that kiss you laid on him."

"Hmm. In retrospect, it might not have been the best strategy to do it in front of all his friends. But I was thirteen and thought it was high time I had my first kiss. Once I'd decided on Kenny, I didn't see any reason to shilly-shally around. How did I know he would put his head in the sand and not pull it out again for four years?"

"Boys — an unpredictable lot." Dani agreed. "He made up for lost time when he finally got going. I remember him that last year of school. He dated every girl that would say yes. Didn't push it, I'll give him that. I turned him down and so did Rose — no hard feelings."

"It was good to know I hadn't scarred him for life." Tyler thought about it for a moment. "He never asked me."

"Kenny knew you were still getting over Drew. All the guys did."

"I didn't have a single date that year. Another thing I have to thank Drew Harper for."

"You wouldn't have said yes." Dani reminded her.

"I deserved the right to say no."

Tyler would have sent the man a dirty look, but as usual, the second she glanced his way, he seemed fascinated by the view out the back window. Frustrating. He'd been frustrating at seventeen and was even more so at twenty-eight. Things had simmered between them for over a year — lately it escalated to a low boil. Soon the lid on that old pot was going to shoot off with all the pent up pressure. It was just a matter of time.

"I made the first move, now it's up to him."

"Telling him you should hit the sack and get it out of your systems is not making the first move."

"What is it?"

"It's... passive-aggressive bullshit."

"Thank you, Dr. Ruth."

Tyler mumbled the words into her wine glass. Friends. There just might be such a thing as knowing someone *too* well. Especially when that person insisted on pointing out the obvious and had the nerve to be right. It made it almost impossible to argue. *Almost.*

"I know what you are going to say." Dani interrupted Tyler before she could even begin. "All that's left between you and Drew is an animal attraction. Fuck like bunnies, and you'll burn it out."

"Right."

"Ha, I say."

"Ha? You say? Who talks like that?"

"I do," Dani said. "Don't try and change the subject."

"I wasn't. I just wanted to point out—"

"That it's all about the sex. Wrong. I don't know what it is, but I guarantee it's a hell of a lot more than sex. I'm all for the two of you having some. Have lots. But you won't get him out of your system that way."

"Then tell me how." All the teasing was gone. Tyler needed to know. She needed a way. Drew Harper was in her blood and nothing she had tried had purged her of him.

"Oh, honey." Dani reached over and squeezed Tyler's hand. "I know you still hurt. I'd hold him down while you kicked his ass if I thought it would do any good. Maybe it's time to take the direct approach."

"And what would that be?"

"Ask him why he broke your heart."

Chapter Two

TYLER LET HERSELF into her studio, her mind still rolling over her conversation with Dani. *Ask Drew.* Such a simple thing and yet so complicated, her brain felt like it was about to explode. Land mines at every turn; huge areas of quicksand. Neon lights flashing *DANGER, DANGER.* Ask Drew. She had never been a proponent of self-flagellation — she wasn't starting now.

She dropped her keys on the counter of her small, but serviceable kitchen. When she had decided to return to Harper Falls, Tyler knew exactly the space she wanted. She was an artist. Her mother swore Tyler had started drawing before she could walk. Using the walls as her canvas hadn't gone over very well with her father, but Mom encouraged her daughter every chance she had. Anita Jones was not a woman to assert herself. When it came to Tyler's artistic abilities, she at least had tried. Martin Jones hadn't cared enough about his daughter or her talent to waste his energy arguing. "Scrub the damn walls" was his only response. Anita scrubbed.

The abandoned warehouse by the river suited Tyler's purposes perfectly. Large, open, with plenty of natural light. At one time, it was used to store building materials. A huge docking area out front would have been perfect for trucks to back in, unload, and be on their way again. The building boom in Harper Falls went bust and the warehouse sat vacant for years. A restaurant tried its hand for a brief time. Mediocre fare and food poisoning had put them out of business almost before they started.

As kids, she and her friends would ride past the old place on their bikes. Rose thought it was creepy. The overgrown weeds and spider-filled cobwebs made her shudder. Dani thought it might make a good photography studio, but it would be too much work to make it habitable. Tyler knew if she had the money what she would do with it. The plans were in her mind and had stayed there until she was able to implement them all these years later.

She quickly changed her clothes. A glance in the mirror showed her a tall, slender woman. At the moment, she had on nothing but the ridiculously expensive lingerie she loved to wear under her jeans and t-shirts. Her little secret — not Victoria's. Subtle curves, strong muscles covered in silk, satin, and lace. Today, pale lavender. It made her skin look like rich cream, smooth and silky.

Her ancestry was a mixed bag. Irish, American Indian, a hint of Slavic, and a whole lot of *your guess is as good as mine*. The result, in Tyler's case, was straight, near black hair that she wore long, often piled into a messy bun. Her gray eyes could be a clear silver or dark pewter or stormy gunmetal. It depended on her mood. Happy, sad, angry — the shade told the tale.

She pulled on a pair of loose paint-covered cotton pants and an equally stained man's button-up shirt. They were clean but well used and as far as Tyler was concerned, every mark was a symbol of her sweat, toil, and creativity. She would wear them until they fell apart, only then throwing them out, and starting over. Same outfit, same effort. Her art was what got her out of bed at three in the morning, and what kept her up sometimes days at a time running on brief naps and gallons of coffee.

Inspiration was a fickle bitch. Tyler and hers had a love/hate relationship of long standing. Right now, they were in a good place. The

Harper Falls Centennial Statue was coming along at an amazingly fast pace. Every time Tyler touched the sculpture, it almost talked to her — vibrating with energy. Yes, she talked to her projects, and sometimes when everything flowed, they spoke back. This one was creating a soliloquy.

Tyler had to admit that of all her projects, this one had a special place in her heart and mind. Just getting the commission had been a process fraught with more drama than a *Real Housewives* episode — and most of it just as manufactured.

Harper Falls had been buzzing about the centennial celebration since before Tyler returned. The planning stages had been slow and meticulous. What else could you expect from a project headed by Regina Harper? She may have married into the name, but she took her responsibility as matriarch of the town's founding family seriously. As far as Tyler could tell, Regina took everything seriously. The woman had no discernible sense of humor. She'd especially found the idea of her one and only child, the heir to the Harper money and power, becoming involved with Tyler Jones nothing to smile about.

Tyler mentally shook herself. Those memories were not for now. Dani encouraged her to confront Drew. Her friend thought it was time to find out why he had broken — no, check that. Why he ripped out her heart and ground it into tiny pieces. She was still looking for some large chunks of the battered organ — almost convinced they were lost forever. If the day ever came when Drew told her the why of it? Well, that was a conversation he was going to have to initiate. She was ready to fuck him — not spill her guts.

Tyler pulled back the cloth that covered what would be her contribution to Harper Falls. She ran her hand over the unpolished bronze. It didn't look like much at the moment, but she could see it — perfectly. In her mind, the lines were bold, almost stark — but infinitely powerful. It would sit in the middle of town. Visitors would notice right away. How could they not? It was large and dominating. Harper Falls residents would eventually become used to the sculpture. They would pass it on a daily basis getting to the point where they would seldom even notice it. However, there it would be. Created by Tyler Jones. And no one, not even Regina Harper would ever be able to take that away from her.

Of course, if it had been up to Queen Reggie, Tyler's design would never have been in the running, let alone been chosen. The woman did her best to eliminate every entry Tyler submitted, under every alias Tyler used. How had she known? Well, Regina Harper had her spies — everywhere. In the end, none of the intrigue or teeth gnashing had mattered. Regina had stepped away from the committee in charge of choosing a winner and they chose Tyler. Her design — her original design — had been deemed the best.

Tyler was so happy that it took her awhile to figure out who had made it happen. Only one person had that kind of influence. Only one person held any power over Regina Harper. Her son — Drew Harper. Tyler didn't know what he had said or what he had done. She was certain, though, that it had been Drew.

Her stomach knotted. The text she sent him had been so inadequate and had gone unanswered. *Thank you.* Had he cared? Been insulted? Even seen it? How was it possible that once — so long ago — words hadn't been necessary? Tyler only had to look at Drew and everything that was important would pass between them. When had it changed? She couldn't pinpoint the exact moment. Sometime during those last few weeks. The ease between them slipped away — tension grew. Tyler was blissfully unaware that it even happened. That was how he blindsided her. She had been wrapped in a false cocoon. With just a few sentences, Drew burned it away, leaving her raw, and her emotions in tatters.

Work. Her art. That was what she needed — the only thing that mattered. They were about to celebrate the founding of Harper Falls. A century ago, her love for Drew hadn't even been a wisp in the wind. A hundred years from now, it would be a long-forgotten blip. But this. Her hands traced the sculpture again. This would last. This, people would remember.

Tyler picked up her welder's torch, flipping down a protective visor over her eyes. She lit the torch and went to work. Yes, in all likelihood, history would forget. Unfortunately, she never could.

ELEVEN YEARS EARLIER

HER PARENTS WERE fighting — again. No, that wasn't right. Her mother didn't know how to fight. She whispered, cringed when her husband raised his voice. That was something Tyler never understood. Martin Jones was a bully but to her knowledge, he had never hit his wife. He didn't loom over her in a threatening manner or pull his hand back, an instant away from slapping her face. Why then did Anita Jones cower before he even opened his mouth?

Because she was meek — and not the kind that would inherit the earth.

Tyler longed for her mother to stand up for herself — just once. She wanted to scream at the woman to get a backbone, to stop letting not only her husband but also her two sons walk all over her. As frustrating as it was to watch the woman let herself be used as a doormat, Tyler loved her mother. She refused to be just one more person exerting her will on that sweet, timid soul.

All Tyler could do was ease her mother's burdens as much as possible. Right now, that meant keeping her worthless brothers occupied and away from the family drama playing out in the living room. Martin Junior, or M.J., and Kyle loved nothing more than joining in on chipping away at their mother's self-esteem. It must have been genetic — passed down to the male members of the Jones family. If they could catch the scent of weakness, they moved in like a pack of hungry wolves, tearing away until there was nothing left but bloody bones. Or in her mother's case, a too-thin body. Her once pretty face looked perpetually haggard and ten years older than her forty-three years.

Today, thank goodness, Anita only had to deal with her husband's censure. Tyler had slipped both her brothers a twenty. With money burning holes in their lazy-ass pockets, they called their one friend in town who owned a car and headed for the big city. Tyler almost felt sorry for the residents of Spokane, but they would have to fend for themselves.

Who knew, maybe she and her mother would catch a break and the idiots would get themselves arrested. Nothing too serious, just enough to keep them in jail for a few days and out of their mother's hair.

The noise volume from the living room increased. That meant the end was near. Martin Jones would soon storm out of the house, off to drink with his buddies. And Anita Jones would head to church to pray for…? Who knew? Her mother had followed the same pattern for as long as Tyler could remember. Take verbal abuse from her husband and sons — talk to God. You had to admire the kind of faith that had you coming back, seeking comfort, even when you never received any.

Tyler heard the front door slam and sighed with relief. Her bedside clock read three o'clock. Not too soon for her father's first drink of the day — he'd started earlier. Right on cue, only minutes later, she heard her mother's less volatile exit. Martin would have taken the car — Anita would walk. Again, the same moves in the same pattern.

Certain that everyone was gone, Tyler slung her backpack over one shoulder and slipped out of the house. She didn't have a lot, but what she had was always clean. Her sneakers had seen better days. The shorts that covered her long, tanned legs were getting a bit threadbare from all their washings. She had filched one of her father's t-shirts; he liked to keep himself looking good so his clothes were always new and perfectly pressed. It hung on her, but she didn't care. Being a fashion plate had never been a life's ambition and the thought of taking something from her father gave her a twisted kind of pleasure.

Martin Jones made plenty of money. He traveled, selling insurance. And he was good at his job. Charming, persuasive. When he poured it on, her father could get almost anything he wanted. But for some reason, it was never enough. Dissatisfied with the life he led, convinced he had been destined for greatness, he took his frustrations out on his family. He needed a new suit or new golf clubs. His wife and children could get by another year with the perfectly good clothes they already had — clothes that his hard work had put on their backs.

Her father's chintzy ways had been why they had taken Rose O'Brian in as a boarder. Tyler imagined it hadn't taken much persuasion. One little girl wouldn't get in his way and the extra money would keep more of his salary in his pocket.

Tyler had her own money now. She and her best friends, Rose and Dani made a good income doing odd jobs around town. Need your lawn mowed? Your hedges trimmed? Gutters mucked out? They did it all and were grateful for the chance. The three of them worked hard and were dependable.

Word traveled fast and soon they were actually turning down requests, something they all regretted. If there had been more hours in the day, they would have used them to earn more money. Rose used hers to buy instruments, guitar strings, and sheet music. Dani spent hers upgrading her cameras. She would sell the old ones on eBay and use the same website to find a better model at a bargain price.

Tyler wanted things. A pair of silver earrings she'd seen in the window of *Jeri's Jewelry Jamboree*. Molding clay. A set of sculptor's tools that, even secondhand, had a price that took her breath away. But she bought none of it. Her money had one purpose and one purpose only. To help get her out of Harper Falls. She had been saving every penny, every hard-earned dime, from the time she was old enough to dream of leaving.

Now, fifteen years, three hundred and thirty-six days old, she had a very nice nest egg squirreled away in the bank. The loss of the forty bucks she'd used to bribe her brothers had hurt, but it had been worth it. Right now, they were miles away, making other people miserable.

Tyler jumped on her well-worn bicycle and headed out, free for a few hours. She gave a wave at Terry Wilde, happily mowing his front yard. He and his wife, Bobbie, represented everything that was good in a marriage. Loving, supportive, a household full of laughter. Tyler didn't know what the norm was — the Wildes or the Joneses. She supposed it was somewhere in between. Whatever the answer, Dani had hit the jackpot — Tyler had rolled craps. And Rose? Well, her family situation was a whole different kind of messed up.

Luckily for her and Rose, Dani's parents welcomed them with open arms and hearts whenever things got too heated in the Jones household. Terry had even put bunk beds in Dani's room so they didn't have to sleep on the floor. If she were to actually stop and count, Tyler would have bet that as the years passed, the girls had spent more time "sleeping over" than staying where they supposedly belonged. Home, such as it was, never felt very homey.

Any other time Tyler would have sought out her friends. Today she was on her own. Dani and her mother were in Tacoma visiting Bobbi's sister. Rose was at the high school mapping out the school's big fall musical. Barely June and she was worried about something that wouldn't happen until October. But put a piano in front of her friend and she was in her element. For Rose, it wasn't work.

It was one of the many things that the three friends had in common. They all created. Rose had the ability to make grown men weep and the melancholy smile. Music and words, words and music. They flowed from Rose's brain and onto paper with an ease that was stupefying. She had a gift. She might not have the whole world singing yet, but it was just a matter of time.

Dani had vision. She looked at what was in front of her and saw it in a way no one else could. When she picked up a camera, lifted it to her eye, and framed the picture, it came out telling a story. Her images never lied.

Tyler liked to think that the time would come when she would be able to match her friend's abilities. She knew she was talented. She could draw anything, put her own spin on it, and remain true to the subject. Painting came easily. But sculpting was her passion. She had a raw talent that needed honing. She longed to be where she would be taught — encouraged to spread her wings.

Rose and Dani were her biggest fans. They believed in her. Her mother had hope but little else. Her father and brothers, when they could be bothered, put down her dreams. Name a famous sculptress, her father derided. M.J. and Kyle barely knew what that was; they only knew that their sister didn't have what it took to be one. Others in Harper Falls shared those sentiments. If they didn't laugh right at her, they did it behind her back. Tyler preferred the ones who got in her face. At least they were honest.

None of it mattered. Tell Tyler she couldn't do something and it was like throwing gasoline on the fire of her ambition. One day the faith her friends had in her would be justified. One day she would show Harper Falls that Tyler Jones was somebody to be reckoned with.

Today, all she wanted was to get away. Find some air — breathe.

Her first thought was the little cove across the river.

Just thinking about it made her feel lighter. Hidden from the world, no one to answer to. It was her place. It didn't matter that technically she was trespassing every time she set foot across the long, wide bridge that spanned the Columbia River. The only thing on the other side was Harper House and the surrounding land. It all belonged to the family whose ancestor founded the town.

Tyler supposed that if she were caught, the Harpers could have her arrested. She was only fifteen. What was the worst that could happen? What would the Harpers gain by having the book thrown at a skinny girl of no consequence? Maybe make an example of her to keep other kids away?

Tyler didn't know what the Harpers were like; they and her family didn't exactly run in the same social circles. But she had seen them. Every now and then, they actually set foot in the town that bore their name.

Russell Harper III was a handsome man, quiet, dignified. What Tyler imagined a high priced New York lawyer would look like. His wife, Regina, was so regal, just like her name — it seemed like she floated instead of walked. Her clothes were expensive and perfectly fitted. Polly Porter, whose mother had once worked at Harper House, said Mrs. Harper had all her clothes custom-made. Couture only.

Then there was Drew Harper. The heir. The only child. He never socialized outside of his own socially and genetically superior crowd.

Full of himself, Tyler thought. Given every advantage, his every whim catered to from birth. Who wouldn't be at least a bit spoiled by all that money and attention? Rose swore he wasn't that bad. A year older, they had been in some of the same classes.

She loved having her friend at Harper High; they and Dani now walked to school together. Unfortunately, the reason behind the switch was too disturbing for such a perfect day. Rose was safe — that was all that mattered.

Getting Drew Harper out of her head wasn't quite as easy. They had never exchanged a single word — why would they? He didn't know she was alive. When he was in town with his friends, he kept far away from the Harper Falls crowd. No matter what Rose said, Tyler thought he was a snob. Looking down his well-bred nose. The luck of the draw had put him on one side of the river. The better side — in some people's opinion. He seemed to think he was doing the rest of the world a favor by just breathing the same air.

And yet.

Tyler sighed. In spite of all that, she had a bit of a crush.

It was easy enough to justify. In the fall, she would be starting her junior year of high school. Still a girl, but with so many adult thoughts and feelings. Drew Harper was the perfect *teen dream*. Tall, dark-haired. He had an athlete's body. Better filled out than most of the seventeen-year-old boys she knew. Then there was that face. He wasn't pretty. He was…? Tyler didn't know except when she looked, she wanted to sigh.

He could have starred in one of the movies she and her friends watched. Classic. That was the word. Drew Harper had a face for the ages.

Tyler was glad no one was around to see the blush that covered her cheeks. What silly thoughts. He was just a guy. A little better looking, true. But just a guy. If he made her heart beat a little faster when he smiled, so what? Nobody knew, not even Rose and Dani. When the silly crush passed, as it was bound to, she would be glad she had kept it to herself.

Tyler coasted around the slight bend at the end of the bridge. It was an interesting spot, one where she sometimes stopped. Like her little cove, it couldn't be seen from either side of the river. If you stood and leaned over the rail, it was a sheer drop-off. Cliffs to one side, air to the other, and nothing but jagged rocks and water down below. The view was not for the faint of heart or anyone with even a touch of vertigo.

Tyler's heart was just fine. As for vertigo? Just a movie starring James Stewart. When she leaned over, she imagined the bridge gone, that she could fly. She was just in the mood for that and anticipated the feeling when she saw him. Drew Harper. The subject of her late night fantasies. In her spot. Leaning over farther than even she would have dared. Ready to jump.

Tyler felt her stomach drop and her ears ring. Hadn't she read somewhere that you shouldn't startle a jumper? Yelling could precipitate his fall. Calm words, easy movements. That was the protocol. Tyler forgot it all and followed her first impulse — she shouted. Loudly.

"Hey, what the hell do you think you're doing?"

If he hadn't been planning to jump, the loud voice from only a few feet away might have sent him over from pure fright. Luckily, he had a strong grip on the rail and steady nerves.

"Are you out of your mind?"

Drew rounded on the intruder. He was so incensed that he didn't even look; he just grabbed a pair of arms and shook.

"No, I'm not out of my mind, but if you don't stop that, my brain will be permanently rattled.

Tyler could tell the moment his annoyed anger slipped from his eyes and was replaced by... something she couldn't quite identify. His hands softened their death grip. She tried to pull away; he was much too close for comfort. However, breaking free would mean a bit of a tussle and then she wasn't sure she could get out of his hold. It would be embarrassing, struggling with someone stronger, all the time secretly hoping he wouldn't set her free.

Tyler didn't like her attraction to Drew Harper; it was uncomfortable, to say the least. She couldn't let him know he affected her in any way, so she did the first thing that popped into her head —

she kicked him. Hard. It didn't get him to turn her loose, but it did get her another shake. And, Drew Harper, right up in her face.

Not the result she had been hoping for. Having him a hair's breath away, his lips so close she could practically feel them on hers. She would have sworn to anyone who asked that she didn't feel a thing. She would have been lying like crazy — to them and to herself.

"What is wrong with you, Jones?" Drew dropped his hands from her, reaching down to rub his shin. "First you try to scare the crap out of me. When that didn't work, you try to kick it out of me."

Tyler felt a twinge of guilt. She hadn't meant to scare him — or hurt him. Both had been unpracticed reactions. She never had a problem with admitting when she'd done something wrong. She was neither too proud nor too stubborn to apologize when the situation called for it. Drew Harper deserved her contrition; she just couldn't bring herself to tell him.

He did something to her brain. Scrambled it. And that scared her and pissed her off. Drew was out of bounds in every way. Why did he have to be the only boy who had ever made her heart rate accelerate and her usually sensible mind go all fuzzy? Tyler didn't have the answer. She certainly wasn't likely to get one standing here with him so close she could smell a hint of spicy cologne.

"You shave."

Tyler wanted to groan. Why, oh, why, had she said that?

"I'm seventeen." Drew shrugged, but there was a definite defensiveness in his voice.

Oh, boy, Tyler thought. *The male ego.* She knew for a fact that neither of her brothers had needed to shave until they were out of high school, though they had all the paraphernalia needed and made a big production of miming the process every day. Her mother made a big deal about it, feeding their need for validation at every turn.

Well, Drew Harper could stroke his own ego. Wow, that sounded dirty. She might have been just shy of her sixteenth birthday, but she knew a double entendre when it skirted through her head. Thank goodness she had kept that one to herself.

"Congratulations. Next comes eighteen." She spoke as if he were five.

"You are living up to your reputation."

"I have a reputation?" The idea pleased her beyond measure.

"Bitch."

"Bastard." If he were going to start throwing around nasty insults, she would show him that two could play at that game.

"No, I wasn't calling you one, though you deserve it. That is your reputation. Hot, but a real bitch."

"Oh."

Tyler wasn't insulted. If anything, she was back to being pleased.

"You think I'm hot?"

"I also think you're a…" Drew seemed to think twice about using the word again. "Ballbuster."

"Just so you know? Guys might think that's an insult, most girls don't."

"Good to know."

He sounded like he meant it. Like he appreciated a bit of insight into the female psyche. Tyler turned her head slightly to the side, contemplating the young man in front of her. Not boy. She would have to stop thinking of him like that. Drew Harper was on the verge of taking that next step. No longer a child, almost a man. It was impressive. Her brothers were older, M.J. almost twenty-five, Kyle less than a year younger. They were still boys. Tyler often wondered if they would always be.

"I didn't mean to scare you."

"You change the subject fast."

"Can't keep up?"

He looked at her — long and hard. Tyler didn't know what he was thinking, but she liked the way his gaze never wavered. Dark, chocolate-colored eyes assessed her with an honesty she'd never seen before. The boys she knew would have looked away by now, fumbling for something to say. Uncomfortable with silence. She stared back, almost daring him to blink first.

He did, but it was slow, deliberate. Tyler felt a funny tingle in the pit of her stomach. She had read about physical desire — this was the first time she'd felt it.

Panicked, she decided it was time to go. No hidden cove today. Drew Harper was dangerous to her peace of mind. She needed to get as far away from him and his disturbing gaze as possible.

She picked up her bike. In all the excitement, she had let it fall onto the hard surface of the bridge. Giving it a quick once-over, Tyler was relieved to see that her careless action hadn't resulted in any injury to her only mode of transportation outside of her own legs.

"Hey," Drew called out when she would have ridden away without a backward glance. "You never told me why you yelled at me earlier. You sounded worried."

Tyler glanced over her shoulder and shrugged.

"I thought you were about to pull a Billy Joe McAllister."

"A what?" Drew called out after her.

Not stopping, Tyler yelled, "Look it up, Pretty Boy."

TYLER TURNED OFF the torch and stood back. She gave the statue a once-over with a critical eye. It was good, really good. She stopped at great, not out of any misplaced lack of ego, but because she hadn't gotten there yet. But she would. This would be the best thing she had ever done — it would be great.

Her musings about Drew hadn't stopped the flow of her artistic creativity. It had never been a problem for Tyler to do both — work on a project, and work through a problem. Not that rehashing their first real meeting had solved any problems. But it had reminded her of how strong the connection had been from the very beginning. It got stronger and stronger. She had been in the thrall of her first love. The intensity had been breathtaking — overwhelming.

Moving her shoulders in a circular pattern, feeling the pop in her neck, reminded Tyler that she had worked past the two hours she had designated for the evening. All traces of sunlight had left the sky. There was no moon or stars to illuminate the dark night. It would rain before morning if the clouds that started to roll in that afternoon were any indication. Too soon for snow, too cool for a refreshing summer storm. It might not yet officially be fall, but it was in the air and any precipitation they got would have a cold, gray feel to it.

That was fine with Tyler. In fact, in anticipation, she hit a button to open several of the high-placed windows. A nifty feature she had installed along with the automatic blinds. She had them installed judiciously, sporadically. Partly because the price was dear. Mainly because she never wanted her place to be light tight.

She couldn't stand the thought of being in a black box. She was five years old when her brothers locked her in the basement closet. What a great joke. They then proceeded to leave the house for the rest of the day, "forgetting" they hadn't let her out. It wasn't until three hours later when her mother arrived home from work that Tyler was set free. She had cried herself to sleep but her voice was hoarse from the screams that went unanswered and she never again liked the dark. For some reason, small areas didn't bother her as long as she had a light. But the dark — it was her enemy.

Right now, she was fine with the lights by her work area. The cool air from the now open windows was welcome, not too cold, bracing. Tyler breathed in. It could cost an arm and a leg to heat a place with such high ceilings and almost no walls. Insulation had been almost nonexistent. Another expense she hadn't needed. In the end, it had been a wise investment. The electric company had given her a price break and her bills were a fraction of what they would have been without the fiberglass that had been pumped into her walls.

Then there were the solar panels that covered her roof. The bank actually balked at increasing her loan when she'd put in for the money. How could they not see the benefits? Well, Tyler took care of that. She went to her meeting with the bank manager, armed to the teeth with information. Power. The more you knew, the better your research. The more graphs and charts, the better your chances of moving the decimal point on her already sizable debt.

Unlike Rose and Dani, Tyler didn't have unlimited cash flow. She made some good sales, some important ones. But most of that money went into the down payment on this warehouse. The bank, for the moment, owned most of it. She had a plan. If things continued the way they were, it would all be hers in just a few years.

Tyler Jones was an up-and-coming artist. She might not do what she did for a big paycheck; she wasn't a fool. Her commissions were growing and so was her asking price. She would have created for free — luckily, she didn't have to.

Carefully packing away her tools, Tyler gathered up the empty water bottles that were littered all around the work area. She kept a supply handy and drank from them absently. It stopped being a surprise to find so many. She would gulp one down when she was thirsty.

As she piled the bottles into the dark blue container, Tyler noticed the recycling bin was close to full. She searched for what day it was. Still Saturday. The city truck wouldn't be around until Tuesday for their weekly pick-up, but she didn't expect to be adding much more before then. She was just reaching to close the lid when there was a loud pounding on her front door.

With a frown, Tyler walked across her room. She looked through the peephole. Not something she always did, but it was late and weird things had happened lately. It did tend to put a person on guard.

What she saw was so unexpected — startling — that it took Tyler a moment to gather her wits and release the locks on the door. Pulling it back, she was greeted by a sight she had never expected to see.

M.J. And right behind him, holding her brother's arm in a vice-like grip — Drew Harper.

Chapter Three

"TELL THIS ASSHOLE to get his hands off me."

M.J. spat out the words, struggling to pull free of Drew's hold. It was like a piece of lint trying to fight its way out of a wind tunnel.

Drew was tall, muscular. His body was fit and hard. M.J. had never taken care of himself. He had the same build as Tyler. Above average height, a frame that ran to skinny. When he was younger, his face had attracted women with little effort. Handsome, almost pretty, he never had to work to get what he wanted. His mother indulged him, his father left him to be whatever he wanted, and his girlfriends stupidly picked up the tab — whether it was at dinner or a department store. M.J. had ridden the genetic gravy train from birth.

But now, well past thirty, his looks were on the downswing. Too much alcohol, drugs. Too many high calorie, nutritionally void meals. And the closest he got to exercise was walking from his front door to his car. His once rangy body had developed a pronounced pot gut that he tried to hide with baggy t-shirts and oversized jeans.

Even with five feet separating them, Tyler thought he smelled only slightly less objectionable than a garbage dump. Greasy, matted hair, patchy beard — it never did grow in right — and bloodshot eyes completed the none-too-appealing picture. M.J. had never cared that much about his appearance, but this was bad even for him.

He was on one of his post bender run-offs. Brain fuzzy, looking for a place to crash, and if lucky, something to steal to put a few bucks in his pocket.

"Your alarm went off about ten minutes ago. Didn't you hear it?"

Tyler shifted her gaze to the man behind her brother.

"I turn off the sound when I'm working."

"Well, what the fuck, Tyler? There's a reason you have the thing."

"I'm well aware." She almost called him by name, something she had avoided for over a year. It was silly, but *Drew* stuck in her throat.

"Do you mind?" M.J.'s whine broke the silent messages she and Drew passed with their eyes.

"What are you doing here, M.J.?"

"I need an excuse to visit my sister?"

"He was trying to jimmy the back door. Luckily, it's well locked up. Not that he was going to get in with this."

Drew used his unoccupied hand to hold up a straightened coat hanger.

"Really, M.J.? This is a building, not a car."

"It worked before." He mumbled under his breath. But it was loud enough for Tyler to hear. Unfortunately, if she could understand her brother so could Drew.

"He's broken in before?"

Drew tightened his grip, ramming M.J.'s arm up into the middle of his back.

"Hey, that thing breaks."

"Don't tempt me."

"This is ridiculous." Tyler stood back and motioned for Drew and her brother to enter. She closed the door behind them and stood with hands on her hips. God, what a pair. You would never know that M.J. was ten years older — he looked twenty.

"Why are you here?"

"Who are you talking to?" Drew asked. "Cause if it's me, you already know the answer."

"Actually, I was talking to both of you." Tyler turned to Drew. "But since you're the first one to speak up. It was agreed that either Jack or Alex would take care of my security system. You shouldn't be here."

H&W security, owned by Jack Winston and Drew, was a billion dollar software empire. They had earned every dime the hard way — through working long, tireless hours and their own brains and ingenuity.

When Drew had left Harper Falls, the day after high school graduation, he hadn't taken a dime of the Harper fortune. He'd been blessed with a good, sharp mind. It earned him a scholarship and he worked to pay for what that didn't provide. Unlike her brother, he earned his own way. Just another reason it was becoming increasingly more difficult to maintain her hate. She wanted to. It would have made things infinitely easier. But when she looked at him, she no longer felt the red-hot jolt that used to seethe through her veins. The heat was still there, but it had less and less to do with anger.

"In case you've forgotten, our friends are nesting. Two by two, and all that crap. As the last single guy, I now handle late night calls."

When Drew had first returned to Harper Falls, Tyler had already been back for over six months. Awkward hadn't even started to cover their first few meetings. Tyler had been silently belligerent, Drew quiet, almost stoic. But lately that had started to change, at least on his part.

A few months ago, Jack was stabbed by a drunken ex-employee. They all rushed to the hospital and circumstances had left Tyler and Drew alone for the first time in over ten years. She saw it as the perfect chance to address the elephant in the room. They weren't in love, but they were still attracted. She suggested they have a marathon shagging session and get it out of their systems, then move on.

Drew hadn't taken her up on what she thought a perfectly logical idea. Instead, he got angry — angrier than she had ever seen him. And he had stayed that way. Maybe that was part of the reason Tyler was losing her mad. Let him carry it around for a while. Ten years had been long enough for her.

"Then hand it off to one of your employees. There seems to be an unending supply of them. Hell, you could have sent Boyd."

"Again, romance is in the air."

Drew ran a hand through his dark, expertly cut hair, scrubbing at the scalp underneath. Tyler recognized it as a sign of frustration. When he was younger, mussed hair was always an indication that Drew was nearing the end of his rope. Apparently, that hadn't changed.

Tyler realized this was a fruitless exchange. She was tired and just wanted to get Drew and her brother out as quickly as possible.

"You know what? Never mind. Thank you for coming to check out the alarm, even though it didn't turn out to be anything serious."

"I'm not so sure about that." Drew looked M.J. up and down, his low opinion obvious.

"Yeah? Well, fuck you, Harper." M.J. turned to Tyler, a sneer on his lips. "You taking up with this over-privileged asshole again? You never did have the sense God gave a gnat."

"Watch your mouth." Drew practically growled the words, his body coiled for a fight.

No, Tyler thought. The last thing she needed was Drew beating the pulp out of her brother. The blood would be murder to remove from the concrete floor. Then there was trying to explain to her mother how she'd let *poor M.J.* end up in the hospital. Not tonight, thank you very much.

"As I was saying. Thank you, but as you can see, it's just my brother. You can leave secure in the knowledge you did your duty and I'm fine."

"I'm not comfortable leaving you alone with him."

Tyler wasn't afraid of M.J. Even on his best days he was unpredictable. He rarely attacked face-to-face — too much chance of physical damage. He liked to sneak up on his foes. Better yet, get his younger brother to fight his battles for him. Kyle had a sweeter disposition, but he was too easily swayed by M.J. Left alone, he might have been a good man; he certainly had the potential. Unfortunately, M.J. was determined to have his brother end up as far in the gutter as he was.

"He's my brother."

"Ty—"

"Don't call me that." No one had ever called her Ty — only Drew.

Drew's dark eyes clouded over briefly before he closed them, taking a deep breath. When they opened again, all emotion was gone. The brown was neither warm nor cold. Only flat — neutral. For some reason, that hurt more than any sharp words or angry looks.

"My advice, not that you'll take it. Get rid of him as soon as possible, lock your doors. And for the love of Christ, up the volume on your damn alarm."

He turned and left. Not slamming out; instead, closing the door with a gentle click. The sound made little bumps rise on Tyler's arms. Sometimes loud was just better.

"Over-bred jerk. That's what happens when you're born to money. You think you have the right to boss the world."

M.J. picked up a delicate crystal figurine that had been a gift to Tyler from Dani on her last birthday. The Phoenix rising from the ashes. It had always been one of Tyler's favorite images. Rebirth, the ability to start over and overcome mistakes, adversity.

She knew her brother well enough to know he wasn't admiring the skilled craftsmanship. He was calculating how much it would bring at his favorite pawnshop. Tyler reached over and carefully removed it from his hands, his chipped, dirt-caked fingernails scraping along the edges as he reluctantly let go.

"You aren't welcome here, M.J. Especially when you're in that condition."

Tyler could practically see the wheels turning in her brother's brain. *How to play this?* Intimidating? Contrite? Sniveling? He'd tried them all before and none had worked. He knew she had no soft spot for a man who had bullied her when she was too little to fight back, insulted her when she could no longer be pushed around. There were no more weak spots he could exploit.

Therefore, he stole from her when he could. As far as M.J. was concerned, it was the only thing she was good for. She looked down at him, treated him worse than the dirt beneath her feet. In his twisted mind, she owed him whatever he could take. She was a lousy sister, lifting a few valuables now and then was payback. The least that he deserved.

"You should be careful, Tyler." There was an unattractive whine to his voice. "You and your friends are starting to piss off some of the residents of Harper Falls."

"Is that so?"

This wasn't a new conversation. M.J. loved to jab at her and he saw Rose and Dani as his best option for getting a reaction. There was a time when it would have worked — no longer. She had nothing to defend. Not that her friends were perfect, thank God. What her brother could never — would never — understand was that her bond with the other two women was so strong nothing could begin to chip away at it. She had no need to justify them to M.J. or anyone else. They had earned everything they had, everything they were. That was a concept he would never understand.

"It's late, M.J. I'm tired and you stink. Go home, wherever that is these days, and take a shower."

She walked over to the door and opened it again. She waited silently for him to leave.

"Dad was right."

"Dad was never right, M.J. About anything."

That stopped him for a moment. If there was one person in the world who M.J. had admired, it had been their father. He saw him as the pinnacle of manhood. He had come and gone as he pleased. Treated his wife as an annoying necessity, and turned a blind eye to every nasty deed his oldest son perpetrated. Few had grieved the day Martin Harper's speeding car had missed the curve on a rain-slicked road in Colorado. But M.J. had.

"You're useless." He hissed the words. "You were never anything but a blight to our father and you're nothing but the same to me."

She waited until he was out the door before responding. She should have let it go. Nothing she said would change a damn thing. Still, every now and then it just had to be said.

"I'm going to tell you something, M.J. You, undoubtedly, will take it as a compliment. Believe me, it isn't. You are your father's son. Mean to the bone and so self-centered, a dog could pee on a car tire three counties over and you'd take it as a personal insult."

"Huh?"

"Go away, M.J. And don't come back. If you steal from me again, I'll press charges. Mom won't be able to talk me out of it next time."

"Bitch." M.J. spat as she closed the door.

Tyler smiled at her brother's parting words.

"Damn, right," she said to the empty room. "And proud of it."

DREW SAT IN his car and waited.

He wasn't going anywhere until M.J. had gotten his sorry ass out of Tyler's place and was well on his way back to whatever hole he had crawled out of. If he had to, he would sit there all night.

Absently, he ran his hand over the steering wheel of his car. It was his weakness, that and a certain leggy, gray-eyed hellion. But unlike Tyler, cars didn't talk back. And unlike cars, Tyler couldn't be bought. Not that he would want her that way. If and when they were together, it would be free and clear of anything but giving in to the overwhelming desire that seemed to fill up a room whenever they were in it.

Drew thought about turning on the heat. The October days were still warm, but the nights grew chilly fast. His classic Mustang wasn't made for stakeouts. Back in the day, when he and Jack scrambled for money, living on boxed mac and cheese, they would stand around for hours, sometimes in the pouring rain — even the occasional snowstorm. They became experts at stand and wait.

He could count on two fingers the number of times either they or their clients had ever been in danger. One had involved an irate ex-girlfriend and a hockey player. Drew had come away with a nasty scratch on his neck caused by the ex's three-inch fingernails. The ex had spent the night in jail. And the hockey player had been so impressed by her tenacity, he'd married her. They still sent Drew a Christmas card every year. Five years hitched, two kids and another on the way. Go figure.

The other time had made them. When Jack had saved an up-and-coming actress from a crazed stalker, H&W became the go-to bodyguard service in California. They were a media sensation. They could pick and choose their clients, and charge exorbitant rates. The athletes and movie stars didn't even blink at their fees. In the meantime, Drew and Jack were able to move out of the craphole they had been sharing and each had bought their own place.

It said a lot about how fast circumstances could change. Drew Harper was born to wealth and privilege. If you could buy it, he could have it. When he left all that behind, he wondered how he would cope.

Not only had he survived — he thrived.

And now, years later, he was in the position to buy anything his heart desired. And like then, he only wanted one thing, the one thing that would never be for sale. Tyler Jones.

He sat up a little straighter as the door to the converted warehouse opened. M.J. shuffled out, turning to say something, or to listen. Drew wasn't certain which. The exchange only lasted a few moments. Tyler shut the door, and according to the app on his phone, engaged all the built-in security. Smart lady.

Drew watched to see what M.J. was going to do. He'd always been a mean sucker, and now by the looks of him, he was a drug-addicted one. A dangerous combination, no matter what Tyler thought.

An old, beat-up tan Nova pulled up and M.J. crawled inside. The street light illuminated the driver's side well enough for Drew to get a good look. Kyle Jones. The other brother. If he remembered right, Kyle took his cues from M.J.

He waited a minute after the car pulled away from the curb then followed. He was going to make sure they were down for the night and didn't decide to circle back in an hour or so.

Harper Falls, for all its affluence, had a section of town that was a bit rundown. He hated the word, but Drew supposed it could be called trashy. The rents were low and the inhabitants more on their way down than scrambling to get out. That was where he expected M.J. and Kyle to go. Instead, they turned down a neat little street lined with pretty trees and well-maintained yards.

Jasmine Avenue. Well, now. It seemed the Jones boys still ran home to Mommy. Why the woman put up with them was a mystery for the ages, one Drew would never be able to solve.

It was a safe bet that they were in for the night. Drew could have gone home, spent the night in his big, comfortable bed — and not slept a wink. The driver's seat of his car suited him much better. Putting his head back, he watched as the last light in the Jones house went out. And he let his mind drift back to when Tyler lived there. When they were feeling their way towards love.

ELEVEN YEARS EARLIER

DREW TRIED TO concentrate on what Miranda Lloyd was saying. Something about a boat and her parents. She seemed to think her bright pink lipstick and pushed-up cleavage were all that was needed to keep his attention. A week ago, she would have been right.

Now, after a brief meeting with a tall, lanky brunette, nothing Miranda had to say held the least bit of interest for him. It didn't help any that Tyler Jones and her friends were sitting a mere two tables away. How was he supposed to think of anything else? She had been on his mind constantly.

Not that he hadn't noticed her before. Tyler was the kind of girl that generated second looks. He admitted part of her appeal was that she was so unlike the girls he had known all of his life. Harper Falls was not a big town, but it had very distinct economic and social factions. He and Tyler Jones did not reside in the same ones.

Drew was a Harper. He never understood why a last name should raise him above anyone else. His mother seemed to think the answer was obvious. His family founded Harper Falls. Built it from the ground up. Russell Harper had been a great man, so Regina Harper said. A visionary.

Drew couldn't argue. The town library was filled with books on the subject, all touting his ancestor as either the greatest mind of the twentieth century or a man nearing sainthood. Of course, all those books had been written by relatives or people paid to paint a favorable picture.

From the time he could recognize letters as words, those books were required reading. At first, he took them as gospel. Why wouldn't he? His mother would quote passages as though they were scripture. His father never disputed a single fact. Until he was eight, he thought Russell Harper walked on water. He attended a private school named after the man. His family and friends would never speak a word that didn't adhere to the well-trodden myth. Keeping the darker side of the Harper legacy tucked away was easy when he was little, before the rest of the world, and the internet, intervened.

Drew wouldn't say he had any startling, eye-opening revelation. It was much more gradual than that. He came to the realization that Russell Harper was not a God walking amongst us; he was just a man. To be honest, as the heir to the empire, it was a relief. No one could live up to the image his mother promoted. His great-grandfather had been a brilliant but flawed human being.

It was the beginning of his own personal awakening. The start of him moving away from a Harper-centric universe to where he could see the possibilities outside of the small, sheltered box of Harper Falls. It was also the beginning of a rift with his mother that had grown wider with each passing year.

Drew shook off the creeping thoughts before the melancholia he was becoming increasingly familiar with settled over him. At ten, he saw his future as a single, rigid path. There was no left or right, only straight ahead. Harper all the way.

Now at sixteen, he knew he had choices. When he thought of getting out, seeing new things, meeting new people, any depression over his future would lift. Discovering he had the ability to be his own man was like a fresh breeze after a summer rain.

He took another glance at Tyler Jones. That was what she was. A refreshing breath of air. Nothing stagnant or cloying about her. If he had been intrigued before, their meeting on the bridge had amped his interest a hundred times over. Her face — made up of fascinating angles. Her lips, full and tempting. Then there were those eyes. They were a wild, exciting mixture of colors. Stormy and flashing like silver lightning. Then they changed to the palest violet imaginable. She told a story with those eyes, drawing him in.

"Drew."

"Hmm?"

"What is wrong with you lately?"

Miranda was used to being the center of attention. Boys fell over themselves to impress her. She had to admit that part of Drew Harper's appeal, besides the obvious good looks and money, was his aloofness. No piece of ripe fruit falling at her feet, he provided her with a challenge. Letting him slip through her fingers was not going to happen. It wouldn't be good for her ego or her reputation.

"Let's get out of here and go back to my place. My parents are out of town until Friday. We'll be alone." She purred the word. It was a sound she had often practiced. As far as she was concerned, she had perfected the tone and intent. She'd had boys melting since she was thirteen. With Drew, she might as well had been coming on to a brick wall.

"Drew!"

"What, Miranda?"

His voice had been harsher than he'd intended but, Christ, the girl could get on his nerves. He regretted it even more when he saw he'd attracted the attention of several other customers. Including Tyler Jones and her friends. Their eyes met for only a second, but he felt that same jolt. He would have sworn she felt it too. Until she turned and whispered something to her companions that had them all laughing uproariously.

Drew felt his stomach clench. Maybe she wasn't as different as he'd thought. Laughing at him, whatever the reason, was not cool. Then, just as he was about to give her a huge push off her pedestal, she turned her head towards him, ever so slightly, and winked. No one else saw it. Not her friends, not Miranda. But he did.

"Ready to go?"

Miranda gave him an exasperated look. *Honestly.*

"*Yes.*" She huffed out the word. "I've been ready for ages."

"After you."

Drew pulled out his wallet, tossing enough money on the table to cover their drinks and a healthy tip.

He paused at Tyler's table, not focused on her, but on Rose.

"Long time, no see." Not the most brilliant of lines, Drew admitted to himself. "How have you been, Rose? We miss you at the Academy."

Rose looked over his shoulder at a toe-tapping Miranda and smiled.

"I'm sure they're crying in the halls. How are you, Drew?"

"Good, all's good."

"Do you know my friends? Dani, Tyler, this is Drew Harper."

"Hi." Dani gave him a little wave. *She was a looker,* Drew thought. All that white, blond hair and deep, emerald eyes. Any guy would be drawn to her.

"Drew." Tyler said his name with a straight face but a twinkle in her eyes. Today, they were silvery, sharp, and laughing.

"I think I've seen you around."

His eyes held Tyler's for just a second longer. He would have stayed, used the opportunity to be near her. Unfortunately, Miranda had no desire to exchange chitchat. Not with three girls she considered so far beneath her lofty social status.

"Drew."

Had Miranda always had that whiny quality to her voice? Or was he just starting to really listen? He did know that he was ending whatever it was they had going on. Today was the last day. Bye-bye, Miranda.

"It was nice seeing you again, Rose. And it was a pleasure to meet you, Dani. And you, Tyler."

"We are late."

For what? Drew wanted to ask. They didn't have any fixed plans, or any plans at all, for that matter.

"Just a second. I have to tie my shoe."

Drew knelt to retie his perfectly fine laces. He fiddled for a moment, not looking up, instead enjoying his view of Tyler's long, tanned legs. Under his breath, he whispered, "Ode to Billy Joe." Then stood and continued out of the restaurant.

He wanted to look back. It took all of his willpower not to. Had she heard him? Understood what he said?

If he had given in, glanced Tyler's way, he would have seen a sight that would have taken his breath away.

"What are you grinning at?" Rose asked, exchanging puzzled looks with Dani.

Tyler just shrugged and picked up the conversation about what movie they were going to see next week on their trip to Spokane. She peeked out at the street, keeping another grin to herself. Drew Harper. Who would have guessed?

Chapter Four

DREW JOLTED AWAKE.
Unsure of where he was or why he was there, it took him a moment to shake the cobwebs from his brain and focus.

Tyler. Right. He was outside the Jones house and it was — he looked at his watch — six in the morning. He had fallen asleep sometime after, maybe three o'clock? That was the last time he remembered.

Drew shivered slightly. He wore a heavy leather coat but damn, it was six in the morning. And October. It was still dark. That was something. At least he could get away before the neighborhood started stirring for the day.

Shaking his head and taking a deep breath, he reached to start the car when his phone signaled a text from Jack.

Where the hell are you?

Drew sighed. What a worrier.

I'm fine, he typed. *Go back to your bed and your woman.*

In bed, with woman. Jealous?

Hell, yes. What sane straight man wouldn't be? Warm bed, loving woman. Not Jack's, his own. But these days, his bed was not welcoming and he was miles and a good decade away from the woman he wanted.

Nine o'clock conference call, see you then.

Drew shut off his phone before Jack could respond. He knew his partner worried. They were also best friends — double whammy in the worry department.

He pulled the Mustang onto the street and headed towards H&W headquarters. He wasn't going home. Any empty house, no matter how new or luxurious, wasn't the most welcoming place, especially in his state of mind. Drew figured he would be better off getting an early start at the office.

Returning to Harper Falls after a ten-year absence had not been an easy decision. His life was right on track, right where he had imagined all those years ago. He and Jack took their company to the top, billionaires before the age of thirty.

They were an interesting pair, he and Jack Winston. College had been their meeting ground, computer geeks with a similar vision. Jack had arrived there on a football scholarship. Fast, agile. He was born with the ability to outrun almost anyone else on the field. Throw the ball in his vicinity, his sure hands would haul it in. Jack could have gone pro. More than one sports analyst shook their head in amazement when he chose to follow his real passion, designing software.

They met in class, clicked immediately, became best friends and partners. Long hours tinkering with the first program that had to be perfect. Starts and stops, never enough time or money. A bond had been forged that could never be broken.

Hitting it big changed nothing. Their first million, the ones that followed. The billion-dollar mark they had hit in September. They progressed here together. The arguments were inevitable. Two strong personalities didn't get here by rolling over to anybody.

Knocking heads with Jack, if Drew were honest, was part of the fun. His partner knew when to push and when to pull back. Growing up in a large, boisterous, family gave Jack the ability to fight without getting nasty or holding a grudge. The Winstons did everything in a big way. Big family full of love. The exact opposite of Drew's childhood.

He pulled his car into the large, climate-controlled garage he insisted be included in the H&W compound. He considered his cars his babies. They needed a warm home without harsh lights or fluctuating temperatures. Most of his collection was in a three-story garage near his home. Some were over one hundred years old. Those never moved. Others, like the Mustang, were for driving. He rotated ten or twelve cars between the compound and home, depending on his mood.

Drew waited for the garage door to close before getting out of the car. One of Alex's recruits would give it a wash tomorrow morning. There were perks to having big, anxious-to-please security guards in training around. They could always be counted on to buff the boss' car.

Through the door, he had to pass by the barracks. At any given time, anywhere from five or six to over a hundred men stayed at the compound. When he and Jack hit it big, they had discussed dropping the personal security side of the business. It was more of a pain in the ass than an asset. Jack thought it was good luck, a way of not forgetting their humble beginnings. In the end, they had kept a nominal staff catering to an exclusive clientele. The man they hired to run that end of things had turned out to be a mean drunk, putting Jack in the emergency room with a stab wound.

The current head of H&W Private Security division was an ex-Army badass and Jack's old high school buddy. Instead of cutting back, Alex expanded the business — and did a damn good job. Business was booming all around.

At the moment, though, Drew was the only living soul around. Alex stayed here when he first came to town. Now that he and Dani were engaged, he had moved into her loft. Security cameras and sensor devices eliminated the need for a night watchman. They were a high-tech company. If they couldn't keep their own compound secure from a distance, they weren't very good at their jobs.

Drew used the retinal scan before typing in his personal corresponding code to disengage the alarm system. His office was east facing, the bank of windows gave him a view of Crossfire Hill. Most people would have chosen a westward view. Jack and Alex's offices both looked over Harper Falls and the Columbia River. They also had a straight-across look at Harper House.

Drew had spent the first eighteen years of his life living in that cold mountain of brick and mortar. Looking at it every day was not his idea of a good time. Which brought him back to his earlier musings. Why move back to Harper Falls?

Convincing Jack hadn't been a problem. He was tired of Los Angeles. A small town boy at heart, he embraced Harper Falls and its little quirks wholeheartedly. Buy the better part of a mountain? His partner was all in. Build their homes from the ground up, each only miles apart and minutes from work. Jack hopped right on board.

Then again, Jack was an easygoing soul. Drew had all the edges.

Coffee. That was the first order of business. Like everything else at H&W, the coffee machines were state of the art. Did spending an arm and a leg on a machine with more bells and whistles than he would ever use make a better brew than a good old reliable Mr. Coffee? Damn straight. He didn't care if he never used the milk steamer or the cream frother. One perfect cup of espresso, that was what he asked for; this machine gave it to him.

Christ, his mind was all over the place this morning. Drew settled down at his desk, putting his feet up and staring sightlessly out the window.

When it came right down to it, he moved back to Harper Falls for only one reason. Tyler Jones. Now that he was here? It surprised him how much he had missed his hometown.

Getting away had been his goal. How many times had he and Tyler laid in each other's arms and talked about their dreams? Any place but here. Together. At seventeen, it had all seemed possible. He had barely turned eighteen when it all turned into a mess of epic proportions.

It did no good to replay the past in his mind. Eleven years, countless memories. So many of them were good. No, not good. Amazing. He savored those, the ones that brought him back to Harper Falls and the woman who had stolen his heart when he was a teenager.

It was still hers.

Sometimes, when he was in one of his more optimistic moments, Drew could believe that Tyler still cared. That she would be happy to know he never stopped loving her. This morning he chose to embrace that thought. If he closed his eyes, he could imagine her right now sharing his thoughts. Picturing the two of them, so damn young. So sure that nothing and no one could ever tear them apart.

TYLER TOSSED IN her bed, angry that sleep had eluded her for most of the night. It was all Drew Harper's fault. He entered her thoughts with an increasingly alarming frequency. Grown up Drew. The memories she could deal with — often welcomed. She didn't know what to do with the man he was now.

She rolled over, closing her eyes and drifting. Back. Back to the girl she was and the woman she became in the arms of Drew Harper.

ELEVEN YEARS EARLIER

TYLER HOPPED OFF her bike. The trail down to the river was steep and rocky, with a drop-off that would have made the most intrepid rider hesitate. She was a risk-taker, but she wasn't stupid.

It had become an interesting summer. Usually joined at the hip, she, Rose, and Dani were apart more than at any time since Rose had come to Harper Falls. Dani's aunt was sick, so she and her mother spent more time in Tacoma than they had first anticipated. They came home every other weekend to visit and make sure all was well at home, then back they went.

Rose had a musical to produce. The Harper Falls High Fall Musical Extravaganza turned into a one-woman show. It seemed that either every bit of help she had lined up dropped out because of scheduling conflicts or they just couldn't keep up with the musically gifted Rose.

Even Mr. Niles, the faculty advisor, found it hard to be around a young woman a third of his age who outmatched him in both talent and ambition. Imagine giving up on your dreams, becoming a teacher. Then along comes Rose, bursting with drive and enthusiasm. Not to mention more talent in the tip of her little finger than you could even dream about.

Must have been tough, Tyler thought as she leaned her bike against an outcropping of rocks. The result, in Rose's case, was a bigger workload and a less than cooperative in-charge adult. Luckily, Rose had Principal Mona Harriman on her side. Tough as nails and as fair as the day was long, Principal Harriman was one of the few authority figures Tyler truly respected. Rose was no pushover. If she was working hard, it was because she wanted to. The principal would make sure the others pulled their weight.

Tyler, because of her friends' unexpected absences, spent the summer working when she wanted, which was often — she still needed the money. The rest of the time, she ran free.

She spied the path down to the river the other day, her destination when she ran into Drew Harper. Not, it turned out, an unwelcome occurrence. Her mild interest amped up, she finally admitted to herself she was in the throes of a full-fledged, heart-palpitating crush.

That was the reason she wasn't seeking him out. The thought of Drew was exciting. The chance of making it a reality? Less than zero. A little light flirting in a public place was the closest they would ever come to each other. He was Harper Academy; she was Harper High. The two didn't mix. Never had, never would.

Tyler sighed. You couldn't miss what you never had. She reminded herself of that little bit of clichéd wisdom when she saw it.

The cove was hidden from view. If she hadn't been right on it, she never would have known it was there. Rocks acted like a wall, a narrow passage opening just enough for her to squeeze through. What she found made her grin.

A beach oasis. Smooth sand, as though no one had ever walked there. The June sun touched half of the area, the rest shaded by the sheer cliffs. She could sunbathe in the nude if she wanted to and no one would ever know.

Tyler almost giggled at the thought. Naked just below Harper House. Not that she would ever do it. Just knowing she could was enough. Heady. Exciting. She already thought of this place as hers. She would come whenever she needed to get away, be by herself. Eventually, she would share it with Rose and Dani. For now, though, it was all hers.

"This is private property, you know."

Tyler almost jumped out of her skin. At least she hadn't screamed. Whirling around, she came face-to-face with Drew Harper.

Faced with their crush, some girls might have simpered. Tyler did what she did best; she went on the attack.

"Do you always sneak up on unsuspecting women? What are you, a creepy stalker?"

"You found me out." Drew leaned a shoulder against the cliff wall. "I waited on the off-chance you would come across the river, go down a dangerous trail, and find this hidden spot that no one else knows about. I should be put away as a threat to nosy trespassers everywhere."

Tyler felt her lips twitch. He was quick; she liked that. Guys tended to be intimidated by her. Either that or she just pissed them off. Drew gave back as good as he got. One more plus in his column. She needed to find some minuses and fast before she was a complete goner.

"I don't see any signs. As far as I knew, I was on a public beach."

"I watched you sneak across the bridge, down the path, and in here. You know where you are and who owns it."

He watched her? Was interested enough to follow? She didn't believe for a moment he was worried about her intruding where she didn't belong. If that were true, he could have stopped her before she came down to the beach. He was interested; he had to be.

Tyler felt that fluttering in her stomach increase. So much for shooting down her growing crush.

"No cute comeback?"

Drew straightened, his long, athletic body moving with ease. He came closer, close enough for Tyler to smell a hint of tantalizing cologne. Twice before, she had caught that fragrance. On the bridge and in the café. Breathing deeply. Combined with the fresh, river air, she knew without a doubt it was a scent she would never forget.

"I could report you to the police."

Like that was going to happen, Tyler thought with a little smile.

"You think that's funny? The Harper Falls police department takes trespassing very seriously."

"If you were going to rat me out, you would have done it *before* you followed me."

Tyler widened her smile. She wasn't very experienced at flirting; she wasn't very experienced at all. No boy had ever interested her enough to bother with more than a few experimental, fumbling kisses.

She once read that women were born knowing how to attract the opposite sex. They called it an innate instinct. It seemed like a ridiculous idea. She and her friends laughed aloud while reading the article. How could you just know what to do? And what if you were gay? Did it work the same way?

Suddenly, as Drew came closer, Tyler understood what the writer was talking about. Her body naturally swayed towards his. Her eyelids lowered, her chin dipped until she was glancing under her lashes. She licked her lips, noticing how the movement centered his attention on her mouth. Instinctual? Maybe. Or maybe it just took the right boy and girl. The right combination.

"Are you going to turn me in?" *Where had that voice come from,* Tyler wondered. Lower, almost raspy. She knew it had never come from her before now.

"Maybe." Drew let the words linger, as though he was actually considering the idea.

Tyler was at a loss. Batting her eyes was one thing, now what? She had no moves, no practiced banter. If this went any farther, it would be up to Drew. He was only a year older, yet something told her he was miles ahead of her when it came to this kind of thing.

Maybe he sensed her predicament, maybe he was working on instinct too. The teasing light dropped from Drew's eyes. He lifted a hand, his fingers coming within a whisper of brushing her cheek before he pulled them back. Bad idea. This had already gone too far. They both knew it. Stop now and no one would get in trouble, no one would get hurt.

"I should go."

Tyler went to move past him but found his body blocking her way. She raised her eyes to his, a question in them.

"You can go. I won't stop you if…"

"If?"

Tyler swallowed. Did he want what she thought? Was he going to ask? She wanted him to, wanted to be right. She sighed with relief when she was.

"If you kiss me."

HARPER FALLS HAD been founded as a playground for the rich. It was a getaway destination long before that term became chic.

Russell Harper founded the town with the idea of attracting his wealthy friends and building a place of which America's elite would clamor to be a part. It had worked. Mansions sprung up to the north of town. Houses too big to be practical. Only millionaires need apply.

The town of Harper Falls became an offshoot of that. If you had big, expensive houses, you needed people to care for them and their residents. Maids, housekeepers, butlers. Some lived in. The others, those who took care of maintaining the grounds and the upkeep of the homes, they needed places to live.

Inexpensive housing was built, families moved in. The little blip on the map of Eastern Washington grew. North of Spokane, it would never be a city. That was never the goal. In a perfect world, Harper Falls would have stayed filled with workers who served. One hundred years later, through wars, economic ups and downs, deaths, births, the town survived, even flourished. But it was no longer the town the founding father had conceived.

More than any event, the end of World War II gave Harper Falls a new, and some would say, welcome influx of business people who were not there to cater to the rich. They had bigger dreams. Grocery stores, dry goods, restaurants. These were places that served all, not just those with overstuffed bank accounts.

Many of those original mansions were gone. The Depression had weeded out at least half. Others had moved away, some died with no direct heirs. The luxurious houses on the north side still existed. Now, what they lacked in number, they made up for in size. Per capita, Harper Falls could boast more than its share of multi-millionaires.

Harper Academy, exclusive and pricey, gave their children an excellent education. They supported the local merchants, allowing for highly diverse cross-section choices when it came to your dining and buying pleasure.

If you couldn't find what you were looking for in Harper Falls, just wait. New stores went up all the time.

Tyler wasn't in the mood to enjoy what her hometown had to offer. A restless night with a trip down memory lane meant she had crawled out of bed unrested and needing caffeine — lots of it. Rummaging through her cupboards, she was horrified when her search for the high-octane stuff proved fruitless. Her brain was a foggy mess. If she was going to get anything done, it needed to be razor sharp.

After piling her hair into a messy bun, she grabbed her keys and jumped into her car. She never ran out of coffee; it was her life's blood. She certainly wasn't going to settle for the decaf stuff Dani always tried to push on her.

She drove into the heart of town past the spot where her sculpture would be permanently on display. Usually, she thought about that. In less than two months, her creation would be there for the whole town to see. This morning it didn't register. Coffee and sleep. She needed them both. The sleep would have to wait.

For a split second, Tyler considered stopping by to see her mother. Anita Jones always had fresh coffee ready. There was a time when few people visited the Jones home. It was too volatile, unpredictable. In the six years since her husband's death, Anita had come out of her shell. Neighbors dropped by, women from the various clubs she had joined were always around. Though she would never be a world-beater, she now had a circle of close friends who valued her opinions and company.

The problem was that no matter how much progress her mother had made, she still allowed her sons to take advantage whenever they needed money or a place to stay. Tyler knew at the moment, M.J. and Kyle needed both. Anita would never turn them away. If she didn't give them money, they stole it from her purse. Tyler visited her mother often but only when she knew her brothers were far away.

Pulling to a stop in front of *Toro,* the newest coffee shop in town, Tyler grabbed her purse and got out of the car. She waved when she saw a familiar face but kept her head down, her eyes focused. No time for small talk until she had something hot, strong, and black.

The smell of coffee and cinnamon filled her nose, making Tyler want to float across the room like a cartoon character. Nothing like the smell of fresh roasted beans and ooey-gooey pastry.

Toro followed a long tradition in Harper Falls of naming businesses clever, sometimes nonsensical names. No one knew where it started or why it had caught on. Residents liked to see what name each new entrepreneur would come up with. With few exceptions, they tried not to disappoint. This was one of Tyler's personal favorites.

The story went that the owner struggled mightily to find something that wasn't too cutesy. *Hot Stuff?* No. *A Hill of Beans?* Hardly. *Toro* had been his contribution to the community. Distinctive, a little obscure. It was a conversation starter. Even if the coffee and pastries hadn't been top notch, which they were, wanting to hear the story behind the name would have brought people in.

Toro, bull. Bullfight. What do they call out during those fights? Olé. What do people drink? Café au lait. Hence, *Toro.* Okay, maybe it was more than a little obscure. It was fun; that was what mattered.

The morning rush was just waning, meaning Tyler didn't have long to wait. Her friends joked that eventually she would just chew on the grounds, eliminating the need for a machine or water. It wasn't quite that bad. Well, sometimes, on mornings like this one.

"Nice hairdo, Tyler. Did you use an eggbeater or get caught in a cyclone?"

Jilly. Just what she needed. With a grateful smile, she took the steaming cup from the barista and took a tentative sip. Not even Jilly Underwood in the morning would make her stupid enough to scald her mouth.

"Picked up any lumberjacks lately, Jilly?"

"What are you talking about? I do not date lumberjacks."

Tyler thought about letting it go. Jilly was an easy target, too full of herself and always initiating contact. *Walk away*, a little voice urged. *Be the bigger woman.* Unfortunately, the coffee was too hot to gulp and Tyler felt more than a little bitchy.

"Wood." She said it loudly, taking another sip from her to-go cup.

"Wood?"

"I heard you were looking for men who were carrying wood. I just assumed you meant lumberjacks. Was I wrong?"

"I—" Jilly looked around, her cheeks blooming red at the chuckles directed her way. "That wasn't what I meant. I, oh, never mind." She turned on her heel, heading out. Then turned and hissed. "Bitch."

"That seems to be the general consensus lately." She said to the woman's retreating back.

Tyler took a deeper drink of the slightly cooled coffee and sighed. First her brother and now Jilly. Generally, she didn't care about either's opinion. Called that twice in less than a day did make one stop and think. Maybe it was time to consult with the two people she knew would pull no punches. If Tyler were becoming a permanent bitch on wheels, Rose and Dani would tell her. What were best friends for?

"NO. ABSOLUTELY NOT."

"I agree. You've been a bit edgy. But permanent bitch? Not even close."

The three friends were at Dani's loft, sharing some wine and Chinese takeout. After her run-in with Jilly, Tyler had called Rose, then

Dani. Girls night in had been the proclamation. No men allowed. No doubt about it. There were no truer friends.

"I'd be worried if you weren't bitchy." Dani handed Tyler a glass of icy golden chardonnay. "You have a deadline to meet for the centennial celebration, not to mention other commissions to finish. Then there's Drew. He seems to be copping an attitude lately."

"You noticed that?" Tyler had started to wonder if she imagined Drew's change in demeanor.

"Who wouldn't?" Rose asked with a shake of her head. "All that anger. It can't all be pent up sexual frustration."

"It's a big part of my problem."

"Just off the top of my head, I can think of a dozen guys who would help you with that. Unless…"

"Unless there's only one I want?" Tyler finished for Rose. "I asked, he said no."

She appreciated her friends' restraint. Both could have pointed out that the way she asked hadn't been terribly flattering to Drew or herself for that matter. Fucking, screwing. Call it what you wanted. She propositioned him; he turned her down.

"I can't seem to stop thinking about the past. That summer Drew and I—"

"Fell in love?" Dani finished for her.

"It's become a movie on a loop that I can't shut off. Last night, I rewound to the beginning, the day we met on the bridge."

"A big moment in your life." Rose reached over and squeezed her hand. Connection. Her friends grounded her.

"It was like yesterday. I could feel the summer heat, the first stirring of attraction. Not like now. It was tentative, innocent. I didn't know what it felt like to touch a boy; I just knew I wanted to find out. I knew I wanted that boy to be Drew."

"I'm sorry those memories make you sad." Dani added her touch, clasping Tyler's free hand.

"Not sad." Tyler searched for a word. "Okay, maybe a little. Mostly I wonder at how open I was. When did I put up all these barriers? Why can't I let another man in the way I let in Drew? Damn it, ten years is long enough."

"I'll talk to Jack."

"And how exactly will that help?"

"He can kick Drew in the ass, get him to finally tell you why he did what he did."

"He didn't love me?"

"Tyler…"

"Doesn't that make the most sense? We were kids playing grown up. All the plans we made, stupid promises."

"They weren't stupid." Dani protested.

"Weren't they? I practically had us out of college, married, happily ever after, the ten seconds after our first kiss."

"And he was right there with you."

"I thought so at the time. Maybe he just wanted to get in my pants and was really good at saying the right things."

"For almost a year?"

She nodded at Dani. "Can't argue there. I wasn't that good."

Rose and Dani looked at her. She knew what they were saying without any words. Really? *Really?*

"You're right. What Drew and I had was genuine. He loved me. That doesn't mean he didn't change his mind. I think that's why I've been going over it again and again. When did that change? Why?"

"If it didn't? What if he loved you then? What if he still does?"

"Spoken by a woman who had her first love ride up on his trusty motorcycle and sweep her off her feet."

"This isn't about me," Dani assured her. "Alex and I, our situation was completely different."

"Yes." Tyler conceded. "My problem is simple. Drew Harper. I can't make him talk. His secrets are his own and if he decides to keep them, I'm going to have to live with it."

"Or you could just grind his balls to dust."

"I used that threat not that long ago. He wasn't exactly quaking in his boots."

"I—"

"Enough." Tyler gave her friends a reassuring smile. "I've paused the story of Drew and Tyler."

"Paused?"

"Didn't I mention that I've acquired a new super power? The movie runs through my head, frame for frame. If I get interrupted or need a break, I stop. Hours later, I can magically pick up right where I left off. My brain has become a Blu-ray DVD machine."

"Sounds interesting," Dani said.

"Sounds like a pain in the rump." Rose clarified.

"You said it, smut mouth. I just want to put it all aside and talk about something else. Anything else. Can we move on? I'm sick of the subject."

"I got an interesting offer this morning."

"Do tell." Tyler smiled at Rose. She asked they change the subject, subject changed.

"A television producer called my agent. It seems Jack and I would make fascinating reality show stars."

Dani snorted, her mouthful of wine spewing across the room.

"You don't agree?" Rose asked as the other woman wiped her chin.

"A camera following you and Jack? Pure gold. I just wondered if it was possible to telekinetically rip that producer a new one."

The three friends laughed. Rose was notorious in the music business for loving her privacy. From the beginning of her songwriting career, the offers to make her a singing star poured in. She was the whole package. Looks the camera loved and she wrote songs other artists clamored over. Her voice wasn't the strongest, but it was true and had an edgy quality that amped up the appeal.

They tried to lure her in front of the camera, onto the stage, into the recording studio. Every time, she told them no. She didn't hesitate; she wasn't tempted. Rose O'Brian wrote songs — period.

"I'm not mad at the producer. She has a job to do and she saw an opportunity. I understand ambition. As long as she takes no for an answer, I won't provide her with another poo hole."

This time Tyler lost it— almost. She just managed to keep all her wine in her mouth.

"*Poo hole?*"

"You know I'm trying to watch the swear words when I'm around Jack's many, many nieces. It's just easier if I refrain all the time."

Jack had six older sisters, all of whom produced nothing but daughters. He and his father provided the only testosterone in an estrogen-based family. He should have been a spoiled-rotten, self-centered jerk. All those women telling him from birth how wonderful, handsome, and perfect he was.

Instead, he was the easiest-going man Tyler had ever met. Tall and gorgeous, Jack Winston possessed a smooth, unpracticed charm that melted more than one woman's resolve. Add to that killer blue eyes and sexy smile? Rose hadn't stood a chance.

"What did Jack have to say? Maybe his dream is to be a TV star."

"You tease." Rose laughed. "The look on his face when I mentioned the offer? I wish you and your camera were there, Dani. He was even more horrified at the idea than I was."

"That is one of the many reasons why you and Jack are so well-suited. Seeking publicity does not appeal."

They spent the rest of the evening consuming egg rolls and laughing, drinking good wine. After two glasses, Tyler switched to water. Her walk down memory lane needed a clear head. Alcohol had a tendency to make her dreams go all psychedelic. Fun on occasion — not when trying to sort out an already complicated situation.

Was Drew tied up in knots? Was the past making it hard to live in the present? It would be nice to know that she wasn't alone. If she knew that his nights were restless, maybe she could find a little peace. In this case, misery didn't just love company; it craved it.

"I ASKED HER for a kiss."

Drew was drunk. He could stand — with a little help. He could remember his own name — couldn't say it clearly — but remembered it.

They had started out with a couple of beers. *Tom Tom's*, the legendary bar just to the south of town was their usual hangout. Jack and Drew had a rare woman-free night on their hands so the three of them had decided to grab a few long necks and shoot some pool.

How he had gotten to the point where Jack was pouring him into the passenger side of his SUV, Drew had no idea.

"Are you going to be sick between here and your house?"

"Probably."

He said with such matter-of-factness that Jack had to laugh.

"Then hang your head out the window like Edgar," Jack said, referencing his beloved dog. "The air will do you good."

"I haven't known him long." Alex helped Jack leverage Drew's long body into the cab, making sure his legs were tucked in before shutting the door.

"You're wondering if this is a regular thing?"

"No, just the opposite. Drew doesn't strike me as the lose control kind of guy. Watching him throw back those tequila shots made *my* head hurt. He's going to feel it in the morning."

"Hopefully he'll chuck most of it up before I get him home. Out the window."

Jack added that last bit for Drew's benefit. His friend gave him a wave of acknowledgment.

"I'll get some liquid and a couple of aspirin into him. His head will be pounding; maybe I can help lessen the severity."

"She said no."

"What was that, buddy?"

"The kiss." Drew raised his head to glare at Jack and Alex. Why weren't they paying attention? This was important.

"I asked Tyler for a *kish*, she said no."

"Sure, no woman wants to kiss a man who slurs the word."

"Still wanted it," Drew mumbled.

Jack sighed "This thing with Tyler better come to a head soon. I don't want to make a habit of pouring him into his bed."

"One night doesn't make it a habit," Alex reassured him. He glanced over at the man slumped in his seat. "Just in case, we'll keep an eye on him."

Drew tuned out the conversation. He wasn't turning into a drunk. Tonight had been an anomaly. He was tired, forgot lunch, and drank too much, too fast. And his brain was full of Tyler.

He shut his eyes and drifted. Back, back to that day he followed her down the cliff to the little cove no one else knew about. Just him. And now Tyler. He never intended to call the police. He liked finding her there. Asking for a kiss was pure impulse. He knew she wouldn't agree. But oh, how he wanted her to.

ELEVEN YEARS EARLIER

"INBREEDING."

"I beg your pardon."

"It's the only explanation. You seem normal, then you come up with that ridiculous kiss idea. You should check your family tree. Go back a generation or so. First cousins marrying can really jam up the old gene pool."

"Ah."

Now he understood. It took him a minute to figure out her train of thought. Interesting. He liked it. There was something to be said for having a conversation with a girl who could keep you on your toes.

"You think my family practices incest?"

"Harsh word, Pretty Boy. First cousins, not brother and sister." She shook her head. "Isn't that what rich families do to keep the bloodline pure?"

"What kind of stuff do you read?"

"Anything I can get my hands on."

"Maybe you should consider scaling it back a bit if inbreeding is the first place your brain goes."

"It wasn't the first place. It was just the most interesting."

"Right."

Drew looked at her again. Not just a stunning face but a brain to boot.

"It's a theory, I'll give you that. Cousins marrying cousins was a royalty thing, not a rich thing. Just to clarify."

"Got me there. I was giving you an out, an excuse."

Drew watched as she gathered up her backpack and slung it over one shoulder. He couldn't make her stay. Well, he could, he was bigger and stronger. Imprisoning girls was not his thing. He would have to come up with an intellectual reason to keep her with him a little longer.

The trouble was his mind was blank. As a rule, finding ways to manipulate a situation to his liking was a breeze. He didn't think it was egotistical to know his strengths, or to use them whenever necessary.

First, he was a Harper. The name had clout, especially in this part of the world. It was also his very last resort, one he never used. Never. He couldn't get away from who he was; it was in his DNA. He loved his father. But when it came to getting what he wanted, Drew refused to fall back on family reputation and money.

Second, he was a good-looking guy. Nature had been kind. He had a strong, healthy body and a face women liked. A lot.

Third, and probably the most important, he liked people. His charm wasn't manufactured or practiced. It was as natural as breathing. When he met someone for the first time, he looked them in the eye. His smile was warm and he listened.

Sounded simple, but it amazed him how many people didn't. Oh, they shook their heads, mouthed the right words. But they didn't always hear what was being said. Because he was interested, Drew did.

Tyler Jones interested him. So he started simply. He started by looking her in those amazing gray eyes, and he smiled. The best part of all? The thing that made his day? She smiled back.

Chapter Five

"MOM. ANYBODY HOME?"

Tyler let herself into her mother's kitchen. The back door was unlocked. Nothing new there. It was a small town. Safe for the most part. Anita Jones had never gotten into the habit of keeping people out. It had always been the ones already in the house that caused her pain.

Things happened though. The last few months had seen Jack stabbed, Dani almost killed, and the rest of them on edge to the point of brand new security systems all around. If she could have talked her mother into locking her doors during the day, she would have. Tyler knew she would have been wasting her breath.

"Tyler? Honey, is that you?"

"Yes."

"I'm in the laundry room folding clothes. There are warm muffins by the stove and the coffee is fresh. I'll be out in a minute."

She took a plate from the cupboard along with a mug. Pale blue with delicate white roses painted on the border, the dishes originally belonged to Great-Grandmother Snyder. Depending on who told the story, they either came from the old country, packed on her husband's back as they trekked across snow-covered mountains to freedom. Or they were purchased in Macy's housewares department just after she married a nice country lawyer and settled down to raise five children.

Great-Grandmother enjoyed her sherry. After a few, her stories grew more and more elaborate. Tyler never met the woman, but she wished she had. The lady had style.

Blueberry muffins, her favorite. Tyler took in the scent, enjoying the aroma of cinnamon streusel. After pouring herself some coffee, she took a seat at the kitchen table.

Little had changed in this room. When she was a little girl, the walls were stark white. Her father dictated those things just as he did everything else. Martin Jones didn't like color, so Anita kept things as plain and simple as possible.

She could still remember the blowup after her mother had dared to let Tyler paint her room cherry red. You would have thought the world was coming to an end. Her father never entered that room, never looked inside. The only reason he found out was the same way he found out everything — M.J. Her oldest brother was the family snitch. Martin couldn't be bothered to pay attention to his family yet he wanted things done his way. He paid M.J. a few bucks a week to keep him informed. It was the perfect arrangement for both men. Martin made sure things ran to his liking, M.J. got away with murder because he never reported his own misdeeds.

After her husband's death, Anita maintained the same level of rigid perfectionism. Until recently. Tyler didn't know why her mother suddenly painted the kitchen walls a cheery buttercup yellow. Or what prompted the change of drapes in the window from starched white to a pale blue that perfectly complimented the new walls.

Not big changes, not for most people. For Anita Jones, they were monumental.

"I'm sorry, baby. That took longer than I expected."

Her mother entered the kitchen toting a basket filled with freshly laundered clothes. Men's clothes. Unless she had taken a lover, something Tyler would thoroughly approve of, she was back to waiting hand and foot on M.J. and Kyle. Of that, Tyler had major objections.

She stood and took the basket from her mother, kissing the woman on her cheek. She smelled of vanilla. Tyler breathed in the scent. It comforted, felt like home. Lord, how she loved her mother. That was why it broke her heart when the woman let every man in her life treat her like dirt. She never stood up to her husband. With her sons, she carried on the warped tradition. They dictated, she served.

"M.J. and Kyle have moved back in?"

"It's only until they start their new jobs over at Myles Wilburn's new feed store. Right now, they're between paychecks."

You couldn't be between something you never had. Her brothers worked only when absolutely necessary. Neither held down a steady job. They sponged off friends and their mother. No one made them accountable.

The worst was when their father died. The insurance payout had been modest by some measures. For Anita Jones, it was more money than she had ever seen. With smart planning, it was enough to give her a good life with no financial worries. Or would have been if she hadn't let M.J. steal most of it. Too late, Tyler found out that her mother granted him access to her bank accounts. He convinced her it made sense, in case of emergency.

The only thing that stopped him from draining every penny was his greed. He grew tired of taking a bit here and a bit more there. When he tried to take out the remaining balance in one lump sum, the bank called Anita. Anita called Tyler. M.J. was lucky he got away with being shouted down in front of the bank. If Anita and a security guard hadn't been there, he wouldn't have walked away. He would have crawled, bloody and bruised.

M.J. never liked her. After she nixed his "windfall" and humiliated him in front of a fair amount of Harper Falls, his dislike had morphed into barely disguised hatred. Not that it stopped him from hitting her up for money now and then. Tyler imagined he enjoyed stealing from her. It didn't add up to much. Yet as far as she was concerned, anything was too much.

After all that, their mother forgave him, welcomed him back into her home. Tyler wondered how she could do it. Surely even a mother's love had its limits. Anita's seemed to be limitless.

Tyler kept waiting for the day M.J and Kyle ran out of options. That seemed unlikely, though. As long as their mother took them in, fed them, did their laundry, neither brother was forced to grow up.

It drove Tyler crazy. How many times had she pleaded with her mother to cut them loose? It always ended the same way. Her mother close to tears and Tyler with a huge knot of guilt in her stomach. This time she kept her mouth shut. The boys would move on eventually. Tyler just hoped it was sooner than later.

"You are such a good girl," Anita said when Tyler pushed her into a chair and poured her cup of coffee.

"I'll bet you've been on your feet all morning. Take a minute. Visit with me."

"I could use a minute. The Halloween party at the senior center is coming up and I have so much baking to do. Then November will be here. Where has the year gone?"

"They say the older you get, the faster time passes. I can attest to that."

"Oh, yes. My ancient daughter."

Anita laughed. It was a lovely sound, light and carefree. Tyler hadn't heard it enough when she was growing up. It made her mother look younger. She no longer looked older than her years. Today there was a sparkle about her that Tyler had never seen. Something was different.

"You colored your hair."

Anita lifted a hand to the newly lightened strands.

"Is it too much? Your brothers didn't notice until Marcy Dodd stopped by and commented. They think I look ridiculous. Should I change it back?"

Tyler felt her blood simmer. Damn her brothers for undermining Anita's self-confidence. She looked amazing and she needed to know it.

"The color suits you perfectly, Mom. It is exactly what I would have picked for you. Did you have it done here in town or did you go to Spokane?"

Anita's smile returned, bigger than before.

"I went to that new place next to the hardware store."

"*Permanently Awesome?*"

"That's the one. Carol Anne Wiggert recommended it. She had all that long hair cut off. I swear, Tyler, you wouldn't recognize her. I thought I needed a change and walked in one day, just to make an appointment. Well, they had a sudden cancellation and fit me right in."

Good, Tyler thought. Given time to think about it, Anita might have chickened out.

"You should see the place, Tyler. So pretty. Not at all like most beauty parlors. I felt like I was in one of those fancy salons you see on TV. I was sure it would be too expensive. But you know what? They were having a Grand Opening special. Half off. How could I walk away from that?"

"No one in their right mind would."

"And there's something else." Anita hesitated. "They need a manicurist. Just part-time to start. You know I do nails at the senior center. And my friends sometimes come over when they want something special done. I thought, well, maybe I could… It's a stupid idea. Never mind."

"You should apply, Mom. You love doing nails. Why shouldn't you get paid for it?"

"I've never worked outside the home. Having somebody relying on me to be there on time and do a good job. No, I'm not capable."

"You listen to me." Tyler took her mother's hand and looked her straight in the eye. Gray eyes, so like her own. But they had a timidity Tyler's never had. Sadness that broke a daughter's heart.

"You have taken care of this family for most of your life. Seventeen when you married. You deserve something for yourself. As for not being capable? You'd be doing the owner of that salon a favor if you chose to work there. I don't know a more loyal, hardworking, conscientious person. Only a fool would let you get away."

"Oh, Tyler." Tears filled Anita's eyes. "I love you, baby."

Tyler laid her cheek against her mother's and breathed in vanilla.

"I love you too."

"HOW'S THAT HEAD feeling?"

Drew winced. It was the third time Jack had asked him that particular question. Correction. Yelled it. And then laughed like a demented hyena at Drew's inevitable reaction. He was better than he had been at seven o'clock. He woke up with a splitting headache and tongue with more fuzz than the lint trap in a communal clothes dryer.

An hourly dose of aspirin and gallons of water took his pounding head down to a dull roar. He was about to hit the underground swimming pool to knock out the rest of the cobwebs. Seeing where he was headed and figuring it was his last shot at tormenting his friend, Jack gave him one last jab.

"That stopped being funny two hours ago."

Jack sauntered in through the open office door. They rarely closed themselves off, wandering in and out during the day. Alex was out running obstacle course drills with twenty bodyguards who had arrived early for weeklong training. Before Jack's old high school buddy arrived, the job was split between the two partners. Not his favorite thing to do; this morning his head would have exploded just thinking about it. He liked Alex, he was now a good friend. At the moment, he loved the guy.

"It's still a knee-slapper." Jack took the seat opposite Drew, his big body filling out the chair.

"Not," Drew mumbled.

"If the circumstances were reversed, you would be all over me."

"You don't get hangovers."

"Don't hate me because I have an awesome metabolism."

"Need I remind you what happens when you drink too much?"

Jack had the grace to wince. Overindulging in alcohol made the normally sensible man highly susceptible to suggestion. Nothing dangerous or illegal. In college, it resulted in a tattoo on his shoulder. The last time, and he swore it *was* the last time, he made a bet that he could stay celibate for a month. It had been stupid and juvenile. The upside? Rose. Any amount of booze and stupid bets was worth that.

"I'm a happy and contented man. I see it as my duty to remind you why you aren't."

"How is yelling until my ears ring reminding me?"

"Why did you get drunk?"

"I had my reasons."

"Fine, we won't mention any names. By the way, did I mention Rose, Dani, and *Tyler* are planning a big Thanksgiving celebration?"

"Thanks for not saying her name."

Jack smiled, this time with a big dose of sympathy.

"Rose asked me to knock some sense into your head. Remind me to do that after it's back to normal."

"Why?"

He had been on Rose's, and Dani's, shit list for a long time. Understandable. He broke the heart of their best friend. Why wouldn't they hate him? Lately, he thought he saw a bit of a thawing. They didn't glare or shoot imaginary daggers into his genitalia. Apparently, something he had done had pissed off Jack's fiancée. He had no idea what it was.

"The ladies have decided it's time for you to spill your guts."

"Spill my…?"

"You know what I'm talking about. Ten years, asshole. Tyler deserves some answers. Stop stewing; stop drinking. Stop trying to kill yourself in those idiotic races."

"I don't race because of Tyler."

"Right."

"I like it," Drew said.

He hated the defensive tone in his voice. This wasn't the first time Jack brought up the subject and it led to a fierce argument. Which was why the last time he left town for a race, he hadn't told Jack until he was in the air. And then it was by text. He returned no worse for wear. End of story. He was a big boy. If he wanted to participate in unsanctioned races, no one could stop him. Or make him feel guilty.

Still… Surreptitiously, Drew hit the screensaver on his computer.

Jack didn't need to know about the race in Australia he was checking out.

Jack noticed but kept it to himself. He wasn't going to raise a fuss before the fact. Next time, he would find a way to stop Drew from what he considered life-threatening behavior. Even if it meant knocking him over the head and tying him to his desk for a couple of days.

"What if she doesn't care?"

Jack frowned, trying to decipher Drew's sentence.

"Tyler. What if, after all this time, she doesn't care why I left her?"

"She cares, that's the point."

"No. She wants to know. Like a jigsaw puzzle that's missing a piece. It drives you crazy. You want to finish."

"Like an itch you can't reach?"

"Exactly. It's an annoyance. Once you find that piece or scratch that itch, you forget about it — move on."

"Are you saying you would rather be an unscratchable itch?"

"Yes. Maybe." Drew ran a hand through his hair. "At least I would be in her life."

"That is—"

"Sick? Twisted?"

"Sad. Really, really sad."

"Jesus." Drew grabbed a bottle of water and gulped down half. "I'd rather be twisted."

"You are," Jack assured him. "Not about this. That thing you did to that girl back in Los Angeles? Twisted."

Drew shrugged. "It was her idea."

"You didn't have to comply."

"I was… intrigued. Besides, she already had the equipment. All I had to do was show up."

The two old friends shared a laugh at the memory. Those had been wild times. They had both been open to experimenting sexually. They were young; women were plentiful. As long as they stayed safe, nothing was considered out of bounds.

This was a different world, a different time. Jack had his Rose. His days as a carefree bachelor were a thing of the past. No regrets. Sixty or seventy years with the woman he loved sounded like heaven.

Drew was past the point where getting out of a strange woman's bed every morning held any appeal. He wanted something long-term — something forever. The trouble was, in all his travels and adventures, the only woman he wanted was the one he left behind. He was twenty-eight years old. For almost half his life, his heart belonged to one woman.

"It's time."

"I'd say past time."

"No matter what, I won't stop loving her. How will I be able to stay in Harper Falls, Jack?"

Jack had thought of that. If Drew left, the partnership would survive. Their friendship would too. He just hoped for everyone's sake, it never came to that.

TYLER WONDERED IF she had hidden masochistic tendencies. Why else would she be at the gate leading to Drew's house? He hadn't invited her. He might not be home; if he was, he might be with another woman.

Now wasn't that a pleasant thought that just occurred to her? She was about to back her car up and forget the whole thing when his voice unexpectedly came out of the small box right outside her window.

"Tyler. I wasn't expecting to see you tonight."

Damn security cameras. And motion detectors. And who knew what other gizmos he had to trumpet of an approaching vehicle. She could have gone home, no one the wiser. Now she was stuck.

"I wasn't expecting to be here."

There was an awkward pause.

"Would you like to come in?"

"Sure."

Tyler rolled her eyes. Scintillating conversation. Then again, how witty could you be over an intercom?

She inched her car forward through the opening gate. Her previous trips to this part of Crossfire Hill were to meet Rose. That meant she turned left, not right, taking the road to the house Jack had built when the partners bought the property. Taking a right towards Drew's house was never an option. Not for her.

She was invited, through Jack or Rose. Last month there was an informal get- together to celebrate Alex's birthday. Tyler went to Dani's for cake the next day and skipped coming here. Over the past few months, she found herself in his company more and more. Until now, she wasn't able to bring herself to visit his home; it was too personal — intimate.

Tonight was all about intimacy. Being at Drew's seemed to make sense. Or it had when she talked herself into coming that afternoon. Showering, taking more time than usual with her hair and makeup. Picking out just the right thing to wear.

All that kept her too busy to think about what she planned. She kept busy on the drive up, going over and over what she would say, how she would say it. Now that she was only a few yards away, she was almost positive she'd made a terrible mistake. She would make some excuse and leave. She rounded the last turn and saw the house for the first time. Pulling the car to a stop, she knew she couldn't leave. She couldn't even move.

It was their house. The one they planned, the one they dreamed of building when he became a software king and she conquered the art world. They lay together, her sketching, him making suggestions until it was perfect.

She burned all the drawings. Except for the one she crumpled and threw at his feet right after he broke her heart. She wanted no reminders of what would never be. Yet here it was. Exactly as she remembered.

Clean lines. Both she and Drew spent their childhoods in traditional houses. His on a much grander scale, but it amounted to the same thing. They wanted different.

It was a modern design. At the time, they laughed calling it Frank Lloyd Wright meets the Jetsons. Looking at it now with an older, more experienced eye, Tyler was amazed at how much they got right. The front was nothing but windows. Perfect for the location. The view from the inside would be of the trees. Pines, tall enough to shield but not block out the morning light. They would be a bitch to clean but who thought of that when you were a teenager designing your dream house? Tyler doubted Drew took out a bucket and rag when all those windows needed spiffing up. He could afford to have it done professionally.

An unbroken balcony circled the house's second story. Tyler wondered if Harper Falls was visible from up there. If she could manage to get out of her car and approach the house, she might find out.

Her heart pounded in her chest like a jackhammer, and her stomach was in a million knots. Not a great combination. She didn't know if she was about to have a heart attack or throw up. Wouldn't it be just perfect if she did both?

I could still leave, Tyler thought, warming to the idea. It would be embarrassing, running like a scared rabbit. Drew wasn't likely to chase her down the road or block the gate.

Was that what she wanted? To run?

When the front door opened and Drew came out, walking towards her car, Tyler sighed with relief. The choice had been taken out of her hands. Now that she saw him, she knew she wasn't going anywhere.

Drew walked toward Tyler on shaky legs. She was the only person who ever made him nervous. At fifteen, she laughed at his quasi-sophistication, knocking him down to earth, making him feel real for the first time in his life. All these years later, having her here at the house he built with her in mind, he felt sixteen again. A little unsure and a lot scared.

ELEVEN YEARS EARLIER

DREW DIDN'T KNOW how or when it happened, but he and Tyler were firmly in the friend zone. A short two weeks after he teased her about giving him a kiss, he was no closer to getting one. If anything, he was miles farther away.

It became a daily occurrence to meet down by the river, in their cove. That was how he thought of it now. *Theirs*. By some unspoken agreement, Tyler would be waiting. Afternoon was best. They both worked in the mornings, saving money to make their big breaks from Harper Falls.

It was something he hadn't shared with another living soul. His plans for the future, one away from here and his family's expectations. Telling Tyler had been as natural as breathing — it just happened. They would sit, drinking the lemonade she brought, or eating the apples he provided. And they would talk.

Tyler opened up about her family. Her absentee father. The mother she adored but whose timidity was so frustrating, she wanted to shake the woman at times. Beg her to stand up for herself against her bully of a husband. M.J. and Kyle took so much pleasure in making their mother's life miserable. Just once Tyler wished the woman would give as good as she got.

Tyler loved her mother — she didn't have very much respect for her.

Drew let Tyler in on his family secrets. His mother, the great and powerful Regina Harper, was a cold, unforgiving person. No one could live up to her exacting standards. Not the husband she never loved nor the son whom she looked upon as an asset — her link to the future.

He figured out early in life that Regina didn't have the time or patience to be a mother. Not by any standard measurement. There had been a different nanny every year. He wasn't allowed to form any long-term attachments. She might not want the job of raising him, but she wouldn't allow another woman to take on that role. As a result, Drew grew up with no mother figure.

And his father, Tyler asked. That was a hard one. Drew's first instinct was to say Russell Harper was just like her mother. He stopped himself. His father was not a weak man easily cowered by a stronger personality. He didn't love his wife; she didn't love him. It wasn't something either of his parents could hide.

Drew was still naive enough to think things like that were fixable when he asked his father why they didn't get a divorce. The answer was simple. Harpers married for life. It seemed extreme. It certainly made them both unhappy. The family had an image to maintain, Russell told him. Someday he would understand.

"That is really screwed up. I thought my parents were the top of the weird list; they could take lessons from yours."

Tyler sat on a big, smooth rock, her long legs swinging to her own beat. *They were great legs,* Drew thought. Shapely, tan and went on forever. He thoroughly approved of the shorts she always wore. They were paired with different-colored tank tops. Plenty of skin was on display for him to enjoy.

"Hey, are you listening?"

"Sorry."

Drew pulled his eyes away from her legs. The look she gave told him she knew where his gaze had been. Her smile made him wonder if she liked him looking.

"What did I miss?"

"I asked if you had a good relationship with your dad. The way you talk about him, my guess would be yes."

"He's a good man," Drew said. "When it's just the two of us, things are great. We go fishing out on our boat. Regina doesn't do water. I think he uses it as a way to leave her behind."

"You always call her Regina, never Mom."

Drew shrugged. "I don't think of her that way. I've been assured that she gave birth to me though it's hard to imagine her doing anything that would ruin her figure. If we didn't have the same eyes, I would have my doubts."

"Maybe they used a surrogate. Regina's egg, your dad's sperm. Petri dish, artificial insemination. Nine months later, an heir is born and Reggie keeps her trim bod. No chance of stretch marks, either."

Tyler was kidding, he knew that. Funny thing, it was an idea he toyed with from time to time. There were no pictures of a pregnant Regina. All he had was her word for it. And his father? It might be an uncomfortable conversation; Drew was sure his father would tell him the truth.

"I wasn't serious." She playfully punched him in the arm. "About the whole surrogate thing. I'm sure you came into this world the way most of us did."

"I don't think it would bother me." Drew realized he felt comfortable talking about anything with Tyler. His old circle of friends would have crucified him over this, spreading the details all over the school before the first bell. Now that he thought about it, calling them his friends was a bit of a stretch. Their parents threw them in the same group since infancy. Birthday parties, dances, dating. This was the first time in his life that he stepped out of that crowd. He wasn't even sure why. Habit? Complacency? The knowledge that it was all temporary?

The day after graduation, he was out of here. Everything up to that point was just treading water. Or it was, until Tyler. Now he saw his final year of school as more than just a jail sentence. Where, if he was a good boy and played by the rules, his life sentence would be commuted and he would be let out early for good behavior.

"Do you ever feel like you're in prison?"

Drew looked at her in surprise. When had she started reading his mind?

"Yeah. You?"

"Only every day. It didn't always feel this way, you know? Rose and Dani understand. We all want out. We *will* get out." She turned to Drew, facing him fully, her eyes steely gray with determination. "You're the only person who knows. Dani's parents love her so much, they'll be fine with her leaving cause they know she'll be back, at least to visit. Rose doesn't have anyone but us, so there isn't anyone to stop her."

"Will your family stop you?" From what she said, it didn't sound like they cared enough to bother.

"Mom would be okay if I told her. She would miss me, but I think she'd give me her blessing. My father and brothers, though, I'm afraid they would do anything to keep me here."

"Why?"

She broke eye contact, suddenly fascinated by the water lapping at the shore. When she turned back, the gray had turned from steel to cloudy and pale.

"Because they *can't* leave. My father should have taken off years ago, we all would have been better off. Now he's painted himself as a martyr, doing his duty to the bitter end."

Drew picked up her hand, covering it with both of his. She squeezed, a silent thank you for his show of comfort.

"My brothers talk like they would leave. If they had the money, if the economy was better. The truth is they don't want to go. Life is good for the Jones boys. A free place to live, hot meals, and someone to clean up after them. Why would they trade that for a place where they would be expected to fend for themselves?"

"They resent that you can, and do, take care of yourself."

"And my father is scared to death that I will be a success, be happy. Misery loves company after all. Even if that company comes in the form of a daughter you never wanted or loved."

After a few minutes, Tyler shook her head, throwing off the bad feelings. She smiled and damned if it didn't almost reach her eyes. At least the clouds were gone.

"How about you? Is anyone going to stop your migration?"

"No, because they don't know the trip is permanent. I'm allowed four years of college at the school of my choice. Dad just assumes I'll be back."

"And Regina?"

"No assumptions. As far as she's concerned, it's written in stone and traced over with permanent ink. I'm a Harper. Nothing else needs to be said."

"Nothing?"

"Just constant reminders of duty, legacy. How nothing has tarnished the family name for six generations."

"Why not seven? What did the generation before the sixth do that was so terrible?"

"Hell if I know. Maybe some enterprising immigrant changed their name. Could be Harper was originally Harpinski. Can't have that on the family tree." Drew gave an exaggerated shudder.

"That would be wild." Tyler chuckled.

"Regina would roll over in her soon-to-be premature grave. The only thing that's stopped me from suggesting it is my need to keep on her good side for one more year. I'm respectful, both in words and in deeds. I've become a master at toeing the proverbial line."

This time when Tyler glanced his way, there was a definite twinkle in her eyes.

"What would she do if she found out how you've been spending your afternoons?"

"She wouldn't be happy."

"Yeah, my father would throw a hissy too. Reaching above myself is how he would put it."

"I'm not above you, Tyler."

Drew was horrified at the thought. She couldn't believe he thought that way.

"Damn straight you aren't. I wouldn't be here if I imagined for a moment that you believed that crap."

"Good. I like our time together."

"Still," she cocked her head, a slight smile on her lips, "we'd both be in for it if anyone found out. We're taking chances with our futures. I say we make it count."

Leaning over, she glued her lips to his. And just like that, they moved out of the friend zone.

DREW'S VISION CLEARED, the past fading away. The years slipped away bringing him face-to-face with a very different Tyler, tougher, more reserved, and even more beautiful. No longer a girl, he hoped she would give him the chance to get to know the woman she was now.

Taking a deep breath, he reached out and opened her car door.

"Hi."

"Hi."

Once upon a time, they never ran out of things to say. Now "Hi" was the best they could do.

"Is there a problem? I mean, I wasn't expecting you, or anyone, tonight."

Drew held out a hand to help her from the car, snatching it back when she got out on her own.

"There is a problem."

"What?" He tensed. "Did M.J. come back? Is he giving you trouble?"

"I can handle my brother."

Tyler moved closer. Drew stepped back, his eyes suddenly wary. Sighing, she grabbed the front of his t-shirt, the fingers of her other hand threading through his thick, dark hair. Soft. She remembered the feel like it was yesterday. Her hope had been that he would be as eager as she was. The attraction was still there, it was time to do something about it. Apparently, he wasn't going to make this easy. So she did what she had all those years ago when he wouldn't make the first move — she kissed him first.

Prime rib to a starving man. Ten years without even a taste, Drew couldn't help but devour her.

The kiss was primal, out of control. Mouths seeking angle after angle, tongues dueling. And the way Tyler tasted. Sweet and spicy and utterly delicious.

In his dreams, he imagined this differently. Slower. He would show her how a man kissed as opposed to the boy he had been. One touch of her lips on his and all those grand plans flew out the window along with any common sense he ever possessed. Tyler was in his arms. Familiar yet new. He needed her and he was never letting go.

Drew's hands went under the hem of her shirt slowly sliding up her smooth, hot skin. He could feel the erotic combination of vulnerability and strength in the subtle muscles of her back. She had filled out, they both had. He wanted to spend days discovering all the differences then start all over again, just in case he missed something the first time.

The kiss was neverending though the desperation; instead of lessening, scaled higher. He could lift her into his arms, carry her into the house, rip every scrap of clothing from her delicious body, and fuck for hours.

Fuck. Well, fuck.

The word wasn't exactly a bucket of cold water, the desperate heat running through his veins needed more than that. But it did lift the haze. If he didn't stop this right now, there would be no turning back.

"Tyler."

The word sounded foreign, all guttural. His voice was hoarse with passion and his body screamed every swear word known to man. *Why are you stopping? Beautiful woman. Willing. Her hands are all over you.* Right now, she was reaching between his legs. The first caress was almost his undoing. It felt so good, so right. No one could touch him like Tyler.

The sexual haze enveloped him again. *Don't fight it,* his body urged. *Feel her lips on your jaw, your neck. God. Her teeth biting your earlobe.* That alone brought him close to going over the top. Damn his good intentions. Talking was way overrated. Pulling her in until their bodies were flush and he could feel every long, luscious inch of her — plastered against him. Drew was going in for another kiss when her words did what his own reasoning couldn't. It wasn't a bucket of cold water; it was a fire hose — turned on full blast.

"Fuck me, Drew. Right here, up against my car. Let's get this thing done, once and for all."

"Holy Christ."

He wrenched himself away from her, turning so he couldn't see her passion-filled face. She wanted to get him out of her system with one colossal fuck fest. Tyler had suggested it before. The perfect solution. What had she called it? One and done?

Resting his hands on the hood of her car, Drew let his head droop forward trying to regulate his breathing. Was that all she thought was left? Sex. She would take her fill and walk away. No looking back. No regrets. Well, he wasn't going to make it that easy — not on either of them.

"This isn't going to happen, Tyler."

There was a long pause prompting Drew to venture a peek in her direction. She looked wonderfully disheveled. Her glossy near-black hair mussed, her lips puffy and slightly open.

Do not think about how they got that way.

But mostly, she looked royally pissed off.

"Are you saying no? Honestly?"

Tyler let off a stream of foul language that had Drew raising his eyebrows. Imaginative and lengthy. If it hadn't been directed at him, he would have been impressed.

"You've expanded your vocabulary in the past ten years."

"I knew those words back then. I just never had a reason to use them."

Rearranging her clothes, she glared. Molten steel. Her eyes burned with fury and frustration.

"I would say fuck you, Drew Harper, but what would be the point?"

When she tried to open the car door, Drew put a hand over hers.

"Don't go, Tyler. Come inside, talk to me. Let me talk to you."

She turned her head slowly, surprise replacing anger on her face.

"Now? After all this time, you want to talk?"

"I need you to hear me out."

"I can't fault you for your nerve. I needed to *hear you out* ten years ago. Or five years ago. Even three. Hell, you could have come to me as soon as you moved back to Harper Falls. Why now? What's suddenly changed?"

When he didn't answer right away, Tyler rounded on him. A mixture of anger and frustration making her reckless.

"Did you enjoy watching me date other men?"

"What?" Realizing where this was going, he held up a hand as though it could stem her words.

"Don't do this, Tyler."

"Don't do what? Remind you of all the men I've been with since you've been in town. How about all the ones I've had in the last ten years. My memory is excellent. You might want to take a seat, though. This could take a while."

"Stop it, now."

He reached for her, wanting to shake some sense into her stubborn head. She easily sidestepped him, putting the car between them as a barrier.

"You might be bigger, but I'm fast. Fast." She savored the word. "Isn't that what they call a woman who gives it up easily? I certainly was fast with you. How long did it take you to get into my pants? I was an eager little virgin, ripe for the picking. Well, you might have been the first but there have been plenty since."

"Is this what you need? Will it make you feel better to throw the names of your lovers in my face?" He yelled the words hoping sheer volume would relieve some of the pressure building in him. Not even close.

"Lovers? Who said anything about love? I liked some of them, a lot of them. Others were just convenient. For instance, Niall. The Scots do have a way about them. And then there was Forrest. Do you know he was an actual lumberjack? How funny is that?"

"That's it."

It would have been fruitless to chase her around the car so instead he went over. It happened so quickly Tyler didn't have time to do more than gasp. One second, there was almost three tons of steel between them; next, she had over two hundred pounds of angry male in her face. He might have been intimidating. Even though she topped off at five-nine in her bare feet, Drew took her by another five inches. That wasn't going to make her back down. She had just made him angry; she'd been nursing her bad mood for ten years.

"What are you going to do? Hit me? Shake me until my teeth rattle? You outweigh me by almost a hundred pounds. Go on and show me what a big man you are. I dare you."

He would never physically hurt her. She knew it. There really was no intimidation factor when the threat of violence was off the table. There was something he could do.

Tyler was prepared for more words, not being flung over his shoulder. Before she could protest, Drew threw open her car door and dumped her inside.

"Go home. I'm not going to fuck you so there's nothing for you here."

He slammed the door before heading back towards the house.

The hell if she was going to let him have the last word. Tyler fumbled with her keys, finally getting them into the ignition giving her power to lower her window.

"I didn't even make a dent in that list."

Tyler felt a sick kind of satisfaction when Drew stopped. From where she sat, she could see the muscles in his back bunch. He didn't turn, she wanted him to turn, so she gave another dig.

"I could start ranking them for you. Aren't you curious if you made the top ten?"

This time it was his fist that clenched. Still, he stayed facing the house.

"You know—"

"Goddamn it. Go. Now. And don't come back. I mean it, Ty."

Stunned, she silently watched him enter the house, closing the door with a click, not a slam.

She tried once, twice to start the car. It took a third try before she realized her hand was shaking. His words hadn't upset her. She welcomed his fury. It was what he called her that had her barely able to get the car moving in the direction of town.

Ty. No one ever called her that, not if he wanted to live. Her name was Tyler, no nicknames. She let Drew get away with it because when he said, Ty, it always sounded like a caress. Or that was what she used to tell herself. Silly, teenage fancy.

How dare he use it now? He had no right, not anymore. It took her back to the first time. Tyler hated remembering and yet the memories came. It wasn't after their first kiss. The one she initiated. No, he first called her Ty after their second kiss. Dazzling, breathtaking. The moment Tyler Jones fell in love the Drew Harper.

Chapter Six

ELEVEN YEARS EARLIER

TYLER FOUND BIRTHDAYS to be odd occasions. At least hers were. Mom always made a fuss. Cake, presents. When Tyler was younger, neighborhood kids would be invited.

It was the only day out of the year she could count on her father to make an effort. Pleasant and friendly, somehow he pulled both things off without it seeming fake or forced. This was the father she longed for. When she was six or ten or even thirteen, she looked forward to the man he became every twenty-third of July.

Now, at the ripe old age of sixteen, she hated it. It was cruel. In her darker moments, she wondered if he did it deliberately. Like he was taunting, giving her a brief glimpse of what she would never have.

This morning she didn't have to worry about that. Her father was out of town on business. Even better, M.J. and Kyle had bummed a ride with friends to The Gorge.

Considered one of the most scenic concert destinations in the world, it was located almost halfway between Spokane and Seattle. Boasting views of the Columbia River on one side and the Cascades on the other, people flocked there every summer, drawn by a variety of musical acts, both current and classic. Tyler couldn't imagine how her brothers could afford tickets to see Steely Dan, but she didn't complain. Any time she had a few days sibling-free, she was happy.

She spent the morning with her mother. Birthday pancakes were a tradition. She opened her presents. A lavender-colored blouse and art supplies. High-end art supplies.

"Mom."

Tyler was giddy with excitement. A sketchbook, oil paints. The charcoal alone must have cost a pretty penny. She looked at her mother. The love and pride shining from her eyes made Tyler bite back the protest she had planned on making.

Anita Jones enjoyed giving her daughter the tools that would help her live out her dreams. She only wished it were possible to do more. As it was, it had taken almost a year to save up for these few items. She started saving right after Tyler's last birthday.

Sweet sixteen. How was it possible her baby was almost a woman? She looked again. No, she *was* a woman. In the blink of an eye, the little girl had grown into someone any mother would be proud of. Beautiful inside and out.

Anita choked back the tears knowing Tyler wouldn't appreciate an emotional scene. How could she explain to her daughter the combination of feelings she had swirling inside. Happiness warred with sorrow knowing Tyler would soon be gone.

They never spoke of the future after high school, but Tyler's yearning for something outside of Harper Falls was almost palpable. When the time came, she would see her girl off with blessings and no regrets. For now, she would savor the time they had left.

"Thanks."

Tyler hugged her mother. They were both slender, all the women on her maternal side ran towards thin. Anita was borderline gaunt. In the long run, she knew it wouldn't make a difference, but for one morning, Tyler was determined to try and fatten her mother up.

"Sit and eat with me."

"Oh, honey, I have so much to do. The church bazaar is in a few weeks and I have a whole basket of mending to catch up on."

"It's my birthday. I get one wish, remember? Mine is to have you share my special breakfast."

"When you put it that way."

Tyler smiled. It turned out to be the best birthday morning ever.

She spent the next six hours weeding Mrs. Bradshaw's garden, mowing Mr. Eastman's yard, and washing the Cyprus twins' windows. Tomorrow morning, Dani and Rose would be with her for a bigger job down on Swan Lane; today she was on her own. Her get-out-of-town fund was growing bit by bit. If one of the scholarships she planned on applying for came through, in two years she would be out of Harper Falls, no looking back.

"Tyler Jones."

Lottie Cyprus waved at her from the porch. Sweaty, her once clean fuchsia colored t-shirt streaked with dirt, Tyler waved back. She was just finishing the last window. Twenty in all, they sparkled like diamonds giving her pride for a job well done. Be on time, do it right the first time, and stick by the motto the customer is always right meant return business. And big tips.

"Morning, Ms. Lottie." Tyler glanced at her old Timex. "Afternoon. Wow, the day is really flying by."

Only two hours until Drew. Today it would have to be an abbreviated visit. That evening, Dani and Rose were taking her out for dinner followed by a sleepover at Dani's house. Mrs. Wilde always made some outrageously delicious cake, then the three friends would hunker down for a marathon of Indiana Jones. They almost never made it to the fourth one. Just as well, it sucked.

Then, groggy from too much sugar and too little sleep, they would stagger to Dani's room where they had spent so many nights together. It was silly to get choked up over bunk beds, yet Tyler felt a little teary. Two more years, she reminded herself. Not tomorrow.

She couldn't deny things were changing. Soon, she would tell her friends about Drew. Almost a month since that first meeting on the bridge. Was it wrong to want to keep it to herself a bit longer? The secrecy made it all the more exciting.

"Tyler? I've called out three times, dear. Is the heat getting to you?"

"Sorry, Ms. Lottie."

She put down the bucket of dirty water and sprinted over to the porch.

"How are you today? I hope you've stayed off your ankle like Dr. Romoray told you."

Lottie Cyprus was all of five-foot-nothing though Tyler suspected when push came to shove, she fudged and added a few inches. Tiny but tough, that's what she called herself.

She and her identical twin sister, Dottie had lived in the same house in Harper Falls their entire lives. It was a huge, rambling two-story building. No particular style, it was located in what was called no man's land. Not north with the mansions, not in Harper Falls proper. The Cyprus family had money with a small m, not a capital one.

With no boys to inherit and carry on the family name, the twins made a pact. They would only marry if the man agreed to change his name to theirs and live in the ancestral home. Born there, married there, gave birth in one of the downstairs bedrooms. Each had buried two husbands. Now in their nineties and blessed with vitality and good health, they enjoyed visits from a combined seven children and nineteen grandchildren. Great-grandchild number seven was due next month. Great-great-grandchild number three a few months after that.

"You are so sweet, always asking after my and Dottie's health. Your mother raised you right."

"She sure tried."

Lottie laughed, showing a set of strong, white teeth. They weren't the ones God gave her, but they were hers, bought, and paid for.

"You have a fire in you, Tyler Jones. That's a good thing; don't you dare let anyone tell you different."

"They tell me all the time. I just don't listen."

"That a girl. Here, take this glass of lemonade. Made fresh this morning."

Tyler drank every drop, the cold, tart liquid sweetened to perfection. There was nothing better on a hot day. At the moment, Tyler felt like she could have guzzled a gallon of it. But like Ms. Lottie said, her mother raised her right. One glass was polite; she didn't ask for more.

"Thank you."

Instead of handing back the glass, Tyler escorted the old lady through the front door, waving at Ms. Dottie, who was knitting and watching *The Price Is Right*, and into the kitchen. It was like stepping through time. Original everything kept in pristine condition. Not her style. Tyler liked things more modern. She admired it though. As an artist, she found beauty in the past as well as the present.

"Now you be on your way."

Ms. Lottie settled herself at the kitchen table and started shucking peas picked right out of her own garden. Her slightly gnarled hands fast and sure.

"I imagine you have a young man waiting for you."

"What makes you say that?" Was Ms. Lottie hinting at something? No. She couldn't know anything. Could she?

"A pretty young woman like you? It would be a crime if you didn't have a string of boys clamoring for your attention."

"No time. You take care. I'll be back next week to deadhead your rose garden."

Sighing with relief, Tyler waved goodbye, exiting out the back door. She put the bucket and cleaning supplies away before grabbing her bike and heading home for a quick shower and something to eat. Fifteen minutes later, her clothes were in a heap by her bed and cool water was running in a blissful stream over her body.

So far her birthday had been pitch perfect. Great breakfast, productive and lucrative morning. Talking with Ms. Lottie was always a kick. And now a refreshing shower followed by the turkey sandwich her mother left in the fridge.

So why wasn't she smiling? Because of that one moment of panic she felt when she thought someone knew about her and Drew. One innocent comment from a friendly old lady had cast a tiny little shadow over her bright sunny day.

If she were a girl from Harper Academy, there would be no need to hide their friendship. If he were just a boy from Harper High, no one would blink an eye. Just last fall, she went on a date with a boy whose parents had money. They hadn't seemed to mind. Why were she and Drew such a bad combination?

She didn't have to think very long or hard about the answer. She was a nobody and Drew wasn't just rich. He was the crown prince. Heir to the Harper empire, he would carry on the family line. Someone like that did not dally with someone like her. What if, God forbid, the unthinkable happened? The mixing of their bloodlines would irrevocably sully the Harper name.

Tyler reached for a towel, fashioning it into a twisted turban for her wet hair. She grabbed another towel and dried off. When she caught a glimpse of herself in the foggy mirror, she stopped. *This is the freaking twenty-first century,* she wanted to scream. Hadn't the lines between the haves and have-nots blurred enough to let a couple of teenagers be friends? Maybe more? Hell, Prince William had dated a commoner. Why couldn't a Harper date a Jones?

Because, Regina Harper would spontaneously combust and burn down the whole town with her.

The whole thing was ridiculous and a bit exhausting. Tyler didn't care if they needed to keep their meetings a secret. As long as Drew wasn't ashamed of their friendship, she didn't care about anything else. She was ninety-nine percent certain he would agree with her assessment.

She pulled on a pair of clean shorts and a t-shirt tie-dyed in orange and blue. For her peace of mind, she needed to be one hundred percent positive. But how?

The answer was a simple one. She would ask him.

"HAPPY BIRTHDAY, TYLER"

Tyler gasped, spinning to find Drew sitting on the group of rocks just inside their little cove. He never got there before her. Today he was waiting, so handsome in his khaki board shorts and clean white t-shirt.

His skin sported a golden summer tan making his brown eyes appear even richer than usual. Tousled, as always, his dark hair was streaked with bits of blond, naturally achieved by the hours he worked in the blazing July sun.

Drew found a summer job just outside of town at a local farm. He called himself an odds and ends guy. Any little thing that needed doing, from moving irrigation pipe to washing the dog, he did it. Because of the heat, his boss rarely required him to work past one or two in the afternoon.

"You're early."

And he knew it was her birthday. For some reason, the two events combined to make her a little nervous. Then there was that third thing. The question she needed to ask.

"Busted water line and a broken finger."

"You're hurt?"

Tyler's gaze quickly searched out his hand, looking for any injury.

"Not me." He held up his hands, wiggling ten digits, all in perfect working order. "Dave Stern, owner of the farm. He managed to pretty much crush the index finger on his left hand while trying to fix the broken pipe. His wife rushed him to the hospital and gave me the rest of the day off."

He hopped from his seat to take her into his arms. It was still so new. There was an intimacy between them now. One kiss and everything had changed. Tyler liked it — a lot. She'd never known a boy before who could make her feel this way, all tingly; so aware of her body. The closest she came was reading a steamy romance novel. Hot sex scenes stirred up her body and fueled her imagination. This was the first time she had experienced those feelings because of another person.

She felt hot and cold at the same time. Her heart raced; her mouth suddenly dry.

Tyler was sixteen years old. She was growing up during the computer age where curiosity was easily satisfied. With a website for everything under the sun, teens no longer had to wait for their parents to fill them in or rely on sketchy information from their peers. Any kid with a laptop knew what was what. Sex was no mystery to Tyler, at least not the mechanics of it. She knew how things worked, what went where. The biology of why her body reacted the way it did; she knew that too.

She quickly discovered that there was a world of difference between knowing and feeling. She had the body of a young woman. Her experience lagged way behind.

Tyler gazed up into Drew's eyes and like always, her nerves melted away. Sweet. He had the sweetest expression. How could she have any doubts when he looked at her that way?

"I repeat. Happy Birthday, Tyler."

"How did you know?"

"I told you. I'm good with computers. Your school records contain your date of birth."

Tyler's gray eyes widened. "You hacked into Harper High's computer system?"

"Hacked is such an ugly word." Drew shrugged, a half-smile on his lips. "It shouldn't apply when the interested party means no harm. I wasn't changing grades or messing with anything important. I just needed a teeny bit of information."

"You could have asked me."

"Then I would have missed that look on your face."

"What look?" Tyler demanded, teasing right back. "I have a look?"

"Mmm." Drew traced a finger along her hairline, trailing across her cheek. "Wide-eyed surprise. Then a touch of embarrassment, followed by cautious delight."

"Wow, I had no idea I was such an open book."

"Not open, never that. I've made a point of studying you. Don't worry." Drew chuckled. "I'm not even close to knowing all your secrets. I know how ladies like to be mysterious."

"Why?"

"Why what?"

"Why would anyone want to be mysterious?" She asked the question, genuinely puzzled. "If I liked a boy, I wouldn't hold anything back. My secrets would be his; his secrets would be mine. Shouldn't that be the point? Sharing the good and the bad? I would want someone I could tell everything. They would know I could be trusted to keep it safe."

Drew pulled her into a hug, his chin resting on the top of her head. He knew just how to hold her. Not too tight, his arms strong yet gentle. Tyler relaxed and sighed. She wanted to stay like this forever.

"Do you think, someday, you could like me that much?"

I think I already do. Tyler didn't say the words aloud. She couldn't, not yet. She turned, reluctantly stepping out of his arms. It was time for a change of subject.

"Would you be ashamed to be seen with me?"

"What? That's a ridiculous thing to ask. Why would it even occur to you?"

"If we met in town, passed on the street, would we stop and talk? Would you take my hand, take me for a pizza, or go to the movies?"

"No."

"Then you are ashamed."

"Yes." Drew grabbed her arm, afraid she would rush out before he could explain. "Not of you, never that. I'm ashamed of Regina."

"I don't get it."

"Sit with me? Please. Let me explain."

She desperately wanted to understand, so she let him lead her to the blanket he had spread out before her arrival. Sitting cross-legged, she faced him and waited.

"I've told you how she is. Cold doesn't even begin to describe her. Nothing means more than appearances. She and my father haven't been together in any way for years. Yet she insists they share a bedroom because servants talk. She isn't fooling anyone, not really. But it *appears* they're still close, so she's satisfied."

"Yikes."

"I know my father has a mistress. Funny word. Old-fashioned though accurate, I guess."

"Does it bother you?"

"Not a bit," Drew said. "I'm glad he has someone."

"My father cheats."

Tyler said it straight out. No mistress, instead one-night stands with women he met on the road. It wasn't old-fashioned or loving. He did it because he could. It was as simple as that.

"How do you know?"

"I know because he told me."

"Are you kidding me?"

She almost smiled at the outrage she heard in Drew's voice. Except when it came to her father, there was nothing to smile about.

Wouldn't it be wonderful? If only it could be a terrible joke. Tyler didn't want to know that her father screwed around. Of course, he blamed her. She had to get on his case. She had to give him hell for how he neglected his wife, how he treated her worse than a servant. Tyler could never leave well enough alone — she deserved to hear the ugly truth.

"I was disrespectful. Martin Jones insists on blind obedience and gets it. I broke an unspoken rule when I dared question his behavior."

"So he punished you by sharing the dirty little details of his sordid love life."

"For most of my life, I wanted his love. I tried so hard to love him."

"You feel guilty."

Of course, Drew would understand. His relationship with his mother was messed up too.

"Children are supposed to love their fathers. I can't. I don't love him or respect him. Sometimes I think I..."

"Hate him?"

"You too?"

She reached for his hand, needing the connection. Drew laced their fingers together, staring at the bond. Like he was willing it to be permanent.

"Indifference is impossible when it comes to Regina Harper. Though you would be hard-pressed to find anyone who admitted to loving her. She's an ice queen, Tyler, even when she gets angry —

especially when she gets angry. That controlled fury is so much scarier than a fiery rage. I know what she's capable of. She could hurt you, Tyler."

"You mean hire some thugs to take out my kneecaps?"

Tyler tried to make a joke, lighten the mood. Drew wasn't laughing, not about Regina.

"As far as I know, she's never resorted to anything violent — she's never had to. Money and influence are her weapons."

"Well, she can't bankrupt me; I don't have enough to make it worth her time. I'm already a social pariah. The only people whose opinions matter love me unconditionally. The number is small, but they're fierce."

"Dani and Rose."

"And my mother. Add in Dani's parents."

"Good group."

Squeezing his hand, Tyler asked, "Who do you have?"

"My dad."

"No friends? No one at Harper Academy?"

He looked into her eyes and Tyler's breath caught in her throat.

"I have you." A vulnerability crossed his face. "I do, don't I?"

Tyler leaned close until her forehead rested against his, her free hand moving over his heart.

"Always."

Drew kissed her. The first brush of his lips a mere whisper. The second, firmer but tender.

"Have you… I mean do you French?"

"Kiss?"

"Mmm." Drew ran his thumb over her lips until there was just enough room for him to graze the pad over her bottom teeth. She watched him watch her mouth. Parts of her body began to throb. She knew what it meant, she'd felt it before. This was the first time it was caused by a boy, not the words in a book.

"I have." Twice. "I didn't like it."

"Wanna try it with me?"

"Yes. But... I don't think I'm very good at it. I don't want you to be disappointed."

"Boys are dumb."

"Hmm?"

She expected him to start kissing her. His remark threw her off.

"Boys. We can be such idiots." Drew shook his head as though amazed. All the while, he continued to explore the edges of her teeth, the softness of her lips.

"We try to act like we know everything, that we have all this experience. Most of the time, we bluff our way through and when the kiss is bad, we blame the girl. The girl blames herself. If we would just admit upfront that we were new to all this too, everyone could take it easy; learn together."

"I can tell you're no novice. You've done this before."

Drew gave a lopsided grin.

"Maybe once or twice."

Tyler stared him down. Once or twice? *Really?*

"My point," he said, lightly pinching her bottom lip, "is you shouldn't judge something by a couple of less than stellar experiences. And since I've had a bit of practice—"

This time Tyler snorted in disbelief.

"Watch it."

Instead of a pinch, Drew leaned in and bit her lip, not hard enough to hurt, just enough to make his point.

Tyler didn't snort — she gasped. Her breathing became a little ragged and her eyes widened. She didn't know people did that in real life.

"Sorry." Drew pulled back, dropping his hand. "Did I frighten you?"

Was he kidding? Fright was the last thing she felt. She licked her bottom lip, testing, hoping it tasted different. Nope. Maybe she needed more than just his teeth for that.

"Do it again?"

"You liked that?"

Drew looked deep into her eyes, as though trying to gauge the truth of her response. Girls lied, Tyler knew that. Sometimes it was to get what they wanted; sometimes they just said what they thought the other person wanted to hear.

"I try to always tell the truth, especially when it really matters."

She heard him release his breath, apparently relieved by her answer.

"This matters."

"More than anything."

"Good."

Drew kissed her cheek, then her jaw, then just below her ear. It all felt wonderful. She wanted more. She wanted… she wasn't sure. She just knew she wanted it with Drew.

"We still need to take it slow." He shifted, his eyes meeting hers again. "Believe me, when it's good, it's even better when you take your time."

Oh boy, she thought. It was the only thing she had time to think before his lips touched hers and her world tipped just slightly off its axis. Forever.

"The secret is to shut off your brain. Don't think, feel."

"I…What?" Her brain was halfway to mush; thinking was not an option.

"That's right." He took her mouth with his, long, deep. "Sometimes you breathe through your nose, sometimes we share. Try it; take it from me, Ty."

Ty? Was that her? No one called her that. Drew kissed her again and she stopped questioning, stopped doing anything but being in the moment.

Drew threaded his fingers through her hair, his long fingers massaging her scalp. His touch burned, then soothed, then enticed. He could have gone farther; Tyler would have let him. Instead, his hands stayed in her hair, not pushing beyond her limits. Slowly easing her along at her own pace.

This was how kissing should be. Not sloppy or awkward. It wasn't like the books described; they got it wrong. Of course, none of those authors had ever kissed Drew Harper.

Instead of ramming his tongue into her mouth, he coaxed, waiting for her lips to soften of their own accord, parting willingly to invite him in. No poking or jabbing. Drew caressed, glided. When the angle of his head shifted, it happened naturally, Tyler moving with him in perfect synchronization. Was experience the difference, or was it just that this time, she had the right kisser?

"I could do this for hours, days."

"Okay." To Tyler that sounded like heaven.

"Tempting," he whispered. "You have no idea. I have to stop now or I won't be able to."

"Then don't."

Tyler was in such a haze, she missed what he was saying, missed his meaning.

"Ty, I want you — all of you. Do you understand?"

"Sure you want—" Her eyes became wide, silver pools. "Oh. You want sex."

"Technically, yes. I hope when, if, it happens, that it will be more than just sex. You've never done it, have you?"

"No," she admitted. "Have you?"

That was a stupid question. Girls must throw themselves at him every hour on the hour. He wouldn't be human if he turned that down.

"Does it bother you that I'm not a virgin?"

"Does it bother you that I am?"

"In case you haven't noticed, guys are kind of weird."

"No, kidding."

"Then you *have* noticed?" He smoothed back her hair, wrapping one lock around his index finger. "Silky."

"Boys are silky? I don't think so."

"Your hair, wiseass."

Tyler playfully stuck out her tongue. Drew's eyes latched onto to it, the brown of his irises turning a molten chocolate. That was her first hint at the sexual power she possessed. It was a heady realization. She would need practice. She would have to learn how to use her feminine wiles. Drew would be the perfect guinea pig. Both willing and patient, he would let her know what worked and what didn't.

"I think you were trying to make a point?"

Drew frowned. "Was I? Remind me. And stop licking your lip; it drives me crazy."

Lip licking — good. Tyler filed that tidbit away for future use.

"You said guys are weird."

"I know that." He still seemed wonderfully fixated on her mouth. Tyler didn't mind; she just wanted to finish their conversation.

"No, you were telling me about it."

"Was I? Oh, right." Clearing his throat, he continued. "We like women who can teach us what's what; we also like the idea of being the teacher. It makes us feel all manly. There isn't much left to conquer in the world. Mountains have been climbed; rivers have been forged. Only one man got to be the first to step on the moon."

"Honestly? You're comparing my virginity to landing on the moon?"

"Walking, not landing. Three guys were on Apollo 11. Who do we remember? Neil Armstrong."

"I'm speechless."

"I get that. What woman wouldn't want this kind of insight into the male brain."

Was he serious? Tyler wasn't sure. Then she saw his lips twitch, the little twinkle in his eyes.

"Funny." She gave him a playful punch in the arm. "I hear the comedy club in town has an open mic night. You should sign up. If you were trying to lighten the mood, mission accomplished."

"I never want you to feel pressured. That's the most important thing. I don't want you to do anything you're not ready for."

"Understood. But just so you know? When I do something, it's always my choice. I can't be harassed, wheedled, or intimidated. So *when*, we do it? It will be my choice. I'll be ready."

"*When* we do it?"

"When," Tyler said with firm conviction. She now knew that Drew would be her first. There was no question for either of them.

"This was not how I expected this afternoon to go."

"Hadn't planned on the sex talk, eh?"

"Sex does have a way of sidetracking a guy."

"And a gal. We think about it too, a lot."

Drew smiled. "Good to know. *Really* good."

Chuckling, Tyler fell back on the blanket. The sun had moved quite a bit farther west. Their day was almost over.

"Now, where was I?" He reached behind a rock and brought out a small box wrapped in bright blue paper. "Happy birthday, Ty."

Tyler sat up and took the package. *Please, don't let it be something expensive.* It was just the right size for jewelry. Plastering a smile on her face, she was determined not to let him see anything but joy and gratitude. And then she would find a discreet way to make him take it back.

"I knew you wouldn't want me to spend a lot of money."

Drew shifted, his eyes finding hers. He was nervous, Tyler realized. This time when she smiled, it was completely genuine. Knowing he cared so much about her reaction to his gift made all the butterflies that had hatched in her stomach fly away.

Tyler removed the paper, gasping when she saw the beautiful hand-painted wooden box. The colors were muted shades of green and gold done in a swirling pattern that seemed to have no beginning or end. It wasn't expensive; it was priceless.

"It's beautiful, Drew. Where did you find it?"

"Last week when I was in Spokane, I walked downtown. There's this little shop. I almost didn't notice it. That was in the window."

"Thank you."

Tyler kissed his cheek, then went back to admiring her gift.

"Open the lid."

Intrigued, she did as he instructed. Inside was a long silver chain with a key dangling from the end.

"It's the spare to my Thunderbird."

His classic, bright red, nineteen-fifty-five baby? Tyler had seen it around town. It had been a gift from his father for his sixteenth birthday. Drew was car crazy, always had been. He explained that he saw this car as the first of many. He planned on restoring them whenever possible. Finding diamonds in the rough and bringing them back to their former glory.

The Thunderbird was pristine. Rarely driven, practically showroom new. As much as he loved the car, he thought the former owner was crazy. Cars were meant to be driven. If you didn't take them out on the open road now and then, what was the point?

"I hope you'll consider that my version of giving you my class ring."

Tyler swallowed. Holy cow.

"You want to go steady? Do people even do that anymore?"

"I don't care what other people do." He took the chain and put it around her neck. "Will you be my girl?"

She was in love. The realization hit her like a bolt from the sky. Tyler Jones loved Drew Harper. Now, didn't that sound like a recipe for disaster? Ignoring that cheery thought, Tyler threw her arms around him and shouted her answer.

"Yes."

Chapter Seven

FOR ONCE, TYLER drank orange juice for breakfast, not coffee. And for once, she didn't mind.

Dani and Rose pulled her from her studio where she had spent the night attaching the last large piece of the sculpture, finishing in the early hours of the morning. It was such a major accomplishment Tyler forgot the time and called her best friends to share the news.

Dani was already up. Alex had an early training session to lead, so she went out with her camera to capture the guys being put through their paces on the H&W obstacle course. She considered putting together a promotional brochure to advertise the expanding personal security business. Every one of their bodyguards was already in high demand, but it never hurt to spread the word in different directions.

Rose didn't answer her phone. It seemed engaged couples liked to use the early hours before dawn to catch up on more than their sleep. Not that they had fallen behind. Jack had no problem keeping her satisfied morning, noon, and night. That morning, while Dani snapped pictures and Tyler performed a happy dance over her nearly completed statue, Jack was being particularly inventive.

Rose had a glow about her that said she had been well loved. Tyler was happy for her friend. It was hard, though, not to think about her own empty bed and the loving she wasn't getting. It had been too long and that little tussle with Drew yesterday had done nothing to tamp down her libido.

"When do we get to see the finished masterpiece?"

"In exactly one month, three weeks, four days, and," she glanced at her watch, "seven hours. Just like everyone else."

"As your oldest and dearest friends, you'd think we could have an advance viewing."

"As my oldest and dearest friends, that can probably be arranged. Now pass the salsa; my eggs are naked."

None of them cooked. Rose tried, her successes finally starting to outweigh her failures. Since she and Jack had become homebodies, preferring to eat in, the couple alternated playing chef. Rose admitted they were both happier with the outcome on Jack's nights in the kitchen.

Dani and Alex had dinner with her parents when they wanted a home cooked meal; they enjoyed the food and the company. Otherwise, they were systematically making their way through the menus of their favorite Harper Falls restaurants.

Tyler didn't even own a traditional oven. Her microwave was there to heat things up — mostly bagels and yesterday's coffee. She liked to eat; she just had no desire to be the one who prepared what went into her mouth. Why cook when so many tasty alternatives were available?

Rose passed around a bowl of scrambled eggs. The toast was lightly buttered and browned. No burned spots in sight. Crispy bacon and a bowl of fresh strawberries rounded out the meal.

"These are really good, Rose. Fluffy and not an eggshell to be found. I'm impressed."

"Me too," Rose said. "I'm impressed that Jack fixed all this before he left this morning and put it in the oven to keep warm."

"Gorgeous, rich, a God in bed, and he cooks breakfast for you and your friends? You hit the motherlode." Tyler reached for more bacon. She had yet to exceed her daily allowance of pig fat.

"And he loves you." Dani smothered her toast with blackberry jam. The label read *From The Kitchen of Bobbie Wilde*. Since she had several jars in her cupboard at home, she already knew how good it was.

"He does love me." Rose still couldn't quite believe her luck. Who could have guessed that when she hit him up for a one-night stand, she propositioned the love of her life?

"Dani scored a winner too. Alex looks at you like you hung the moon. And his butt looks amazing in a pair of jeans."

"It looks even better out of them." Dani gave Tyler a speculative look. "I think I can speak for Rose when I ask you, what the hell is going on?"

Tyler shook her head. "Rose has given up using that kind of language, so if you spoke for her, you'd have to wash your mouth out with soap."

"Something is up," Rose said to Dani.

"I agree. What do you think is going on?"

"Drew?"

"Oh, definitely, Drew."

"Aren't you two clever. Yes, it has to do with Drew."

"Well, don't keep us waiting. What happened?"

"I don't think I hate him anymore."

"Oh, honey," Rose reached for her hand. "I'm so glad. It's exhausting, hating someone. Especially when you have to see them so often. What brought it about?"

Tyler told her friends everything. She started with her trip to Drew's house.

"Did you really mention ex-lovers?" Dani wanted to know. "And by name?"

"Not my finest hour." Tyler pushed her plate back, no longer very hungry.

"Hey, he deserved a kick in the ass, pardon my French. He's waited this long to talk and he decides to do it after he just had his tongue down your throat? Not cool."

"How was the kiss?" Dani wiggled her eyebrows.

"Even better than I remembered." Way better.

"Well, sure. He wasn't playing monk. I'll bet he could have slung around a few names of his own."

"More than a few," Rose chimed in. "To hear Jack tell it — and you know what, I'm just going to shut up now."

"I'm fine," Tyler assured her. "How strange would it be if he'd given up on sex for ten years?"

"I've heard that if a woman abstains long enough, she sometimes re-virginizes."

Rose laughed. "Dani, you need to stop reading those rags when you're in the checkout line at the grocery store. More eggs anyone?"

Both Tyler and Dani shook their heads.

"I'll admit it's been awhile," Tyler said. "Not long enough for anything to grow over down there. Besides, Drew did the deed when I was sixteen. How horrifying would it be if he found out it didn't take?"

"Does that mean you still plan on getting naked with him?"

"Yes, please. That kiss almost blew the top off my head."

"Are you going to let him explain? Before the sex? Or even after?" Rose asked.

"I want to know. He's hinted that there's more to it than simply the end of our teenage romance. It's time he spilled the whole story."

"We all know you had more than a teen fling," Rose said with a firm conviction. Dani nodded vigorously in agreement.

"I'd forgotten," Tyler said, shrugging. "Or more accurately, I didn't let myself remember. Lately, I've had these vivid flashbacks."

"Like dreams?"

"Sort of. Sometimes it happens when I'm asleep. Most of the time I just remember. I've been hurt and angry for so long, I thought those feelings were lost forever." Tyler looked at Rose, then Dani. "He was so sweet, so careful. It couldn't have been an act."

"He loved you, Tyler," Dani assured her.

"Dani's right. It doesn't matter how old you were. Where is it written that love isn't real when you're sixteen? Or seventeen? Where's the cut-off point?"

"It was so intense." Tyler's eyes turned almost black with emotion. "I want that back — the good memories. I lived it. I deserve not to have my gut cramp up when I think back on them."

"It sounds like you're well on your way."

"I'm going to see Drew again. This time I'll listen before I jump his bones. I hope I still want to after I hear what he has to say."

"Either way, at least you'll finally know," Rose said with an encouraging smile. "Then you can — sorry, that's Jack's ringtone."

Rose walked to the coffee table and picked up her phone.

"Hey, miss me already?"

"Does Alex call you every hour?" Tyler teased.

"No. He texts between playing drill sergeant. Yesterday he—"

"Are you kidding? What the hell, Jack?"

Tyler and Dani exchanged concerned looks. Whatever was going on, Rose wasn't happy about it.

"Do you know where he is? Last night? Well, his timing really sucks. Can you get the details? Right. No, this time I have to tell her. I love you too. Bye."

"Damn idiot man," Rose muttered as she turned back to her friends. Her eyes briefly met Dani's before she turned to Tyler.

"There's something we didn't tell you." She hesitated, looking at Dani again.

"Oh, come on." Dani groaned in disgust. "I thought he was over that crap."

"It would seem he was just taking a break."

"Who, what, and where, ladies?" Tyler felt like she was listening to some kind of secret code. "If you have something to tell me, spit it out."

"Go on," Dani urged.

Taking a deep breath, Rose let it all out, not pausing, or breathing until she said it all.

"A few months ago, we found out that Drew participates in underground races that are really, really dangerous and we didn't tell you because we didn't want you to have one more thing to worry about and Jack thought he was done with it, but now he's taken off again and one of these times his luck might not hold and he could get seriously injured or worse."

Tyler sat, unmoving.

"Did you hear me?"

"Of course she heard you," Dani said, frowning. "It's a lot to take in all at once. We're sorry we didn't tell you last time, Tyler. We thought we were doing the right thing."

"We'll talk about that later." The fact that her two best friends broke their honesty pact was the least of Tyler's worries. She would get pissed at them later.

"Does Jack know where Drew is?"

"Yes. He said somewhere in Mexico."

Tyler stood, grabbing her purse and heading towards the door.

"Call him back. It's a big country. I need to know Drew's exact location."

"What are you going to do?"

"Apparently, I'm not over my mad."

"What does that mean?"

"It means when I find him, I'm going to kick some Harper ass."

"I REALLY APPRECIATE you doing this, Jack."

"What good is having an international pilot's license and half a dozen planes if I can't use one of them in an emergency?"

"Is this an emergency?"

It felt like one. She planned on getting to Spokane, finding the first flight to Mexico, and worrying about connections once she was on the ground. Jack took that worry away in an instant. Almost before she could blink, they were on a private jet and in the air.

"Semi-emergency. Drew has raced off and on for ten years. One time, he came back with a black eye and that wasn't from the race. Some guy blindsided him at a bar the night before."

"Are you saying it isn't as dangerous as Dani and Rose led me to believe?"

Jack hesitated.

"The truth, Jack. I need to go into this knowing everything I can."

"It's dangerous," he finally admitted. "People die, Tyler. As good as Drew is, and he's the best driver I've ever personally seen, things happen. Other drivers happen."

"How many races has he participated in?"

"Rose told me you'd ask. Around seventy, seventy-five." Jack shook his head in amazement. "You really know each other, don't you?"

"You know her, Jack."

"I don't want you to misunderstand. I'm not jealous of what you three have; I'm damn grateful she had you. Rose told me she never would have gotten through what happened with her aunt if it hadn't been for you and Dani."

It wasn't something Tyler liked to think about. She could still see Rose, in that hospital bed, wasted away to almost nothing.

"She's tough. She would have made it back without us. I'm just glad she didn't have to."

"Play it down if you want. I know Rose wouldn't be the woman I love if it weren't for her friends. For that reason alone, I would fly you to hell and make damn sure you got back safely. It helps that I like you. Rose, or no Rose."

"Dani and I wouldn't have let just any man marry our best friend." She patted his leg. "You're good for her. And we like you too."

"Wow, we fell into a real Kumbaya moment, didn't we?"

"The plane is practically the *Good Ship Lollypop*."

Tyler picked up her iPad and continued her research. The races were considered underground because they had no sanctioning organization to make sure things ran by a set of rules. The no-holds-barred atmosphere was the appeal.

Anyone could enter — first you had to know how. The events were embedded. If you knew the code, it meant you were either a former participant or you'd befriended someone who was. Organizers found the venue, posted the location and date. There was an entrance fee that could be paid right up to the start of the race. As far as rules went, there were none. You had to start with the other racers; if you finished first, you won. What you were willing to do to get from point A to point B was between you and your conscience. Nobody else cared.

Some of the pictures that were posted online made Tyler shudder. Mangled pieces of metal that no longer resembled automobiles. Broken bodies — lucky to be alive. Then there were the *not* so lucky ones.

She kept scrolling, unable to help herself.

"Stop."

Jack plucked the tablet from her hands, closing the case, shutting out the brutal images.

"That isn't helping."

"I know but—"

"Those are extreme cases, Tyler. No one has died in any race Drew has run."

"Yet."

"Rose told me you planned on kicking his ass."

"Amongst other things."

"Keep that thought. If anyone can stop him from racing, you can."

Tyler wasn't so sure.

"I did this, didn't I?"

"What do you mean?"

"We fought. Last night. Now he's in Mexico? I don't see that as a coincidence."

"He was looking into this race last week, Tyler. He already planned on going."

"Maybe."

"The demons that push him latched on long before he got involved with you. The way I see it, Regina Harper sent her husband to an early grave. Officially, it was a heart attack. Drew believes his father simply gave up. Death was the only way out of that sham of a marriage. How messed up is that?"

So messed up. Tyler was hardly one to judge. Her family reeked of its own kind of dysfunction.

"Maybe Drew and I should stay as far away from each other as possible."

"Why would you say that?"

"Come on, Jack. Drew and me, Regina and my father? It's beyond twisted."

"You and Drew were two kids who fell in love. What's more natural than that?"

"And our parents?"

"Unnatural, both of them." He gave her a sympathetic smile. "Honey, you don't know what went on between Regina and your dad. The picture Rose and Dani found showed two people, clothes on, embracing. It might have been perfectly innocent."

"Then why did Regina freak out? That picture getting in with the others sent to Dani for the commemorative book she's doing was obviously an accident. But why keep it in the first place unless it meant something?"

"If I could tell you the answer to that, I would have to start thinking like Regina Harper. Can you imagine the warped kind of logic she lives with every day? No thanks."

Jack checked the controls, making sure all was running smoothly. He turned slightly until he faced Tyler.

"I was one of the lucky ones, growing up the way I did. The Winstons are sickeningly textbook perfect. You know what that means?"

"What does that mean?"

"I am immensely underqualified to give the kind of advice you need. Doesn't stop me though, ask Drew. So here goes, and pardon my language ahead of time. I say, fuck Regina. Fuck your dad. Grab on to your chance, Tyler. Work your ass off for it, don't let go. No matter what."

"And if Drew isn't interested?" The thought made Tyler's stomach sink.

"Oh, he's interested. I'm not sure he thinks he deserves you."

"I'm no catch."

"Eye of the beholder." Jack gave her a crooked grin, his blue eyes warm and caring. "He's been my best friend since the first day we met.

He's stubborn, opinionated, and yes, a bit screwed up. He's also loyal. He's always had my back. And one more thing."

"Yes?"

"He loves you."

"How can you tell?"

"Let's just say between myself, Alex, and Drew, I recognize the signs."

"Can I have my iPad back?"

"Tyler…"

"Not for that. There's something else I want to look at."

Taking her word for it, Jack handed her back the tablet.

Tyler pulled up a page she'd been looking at earlier and studied it before turning to Jack.

"Can we make a stop this side of the border? Preferably in a town with a good-sized mall."

"What do you need?" Jack asked, clearly puzzled.

"That."

Tyler handed showed him the picture she'd pulled up. Jack looked for a moment before letting out a long whistle.

"Seriously?"

Tyler shrugged. "If I'm going to do this, I might as well go all the way."

Chapter Eight

THERE WAS DUST everywhere.

Tyler stepped out of the truck. Her feet hit a surface made hard by the relentless heat of the sun and hundreds of cars that over time had worn deep grooves into the ground. From what she could see, they had stepped into a loud, chaotic mess populated by grease-covered drivers of cars that had seen better days. And though she was no expert, it was a good guess those days occurred several decades ago.

Tyler adopted her best tough girl sneer, cocking her hip and studying the nails on one hand as though the whole thing was a terrific bore. Inside, she shook like a leaf. Thank God Jack insisted on escorting her to the race site. If it had been up to Tyler, he would have dropped her at the airport, convinced all she needed was a rental car and MapQuest.

"Do you think all the races are like this?"

"Some might be a bit more upscale, but I doubt it. These things don't have sponsors to impress or spectators paying through the nose for luxury boxes. This is bare bones."

Tyler looked at him, amazed at the tone of his voice. "You sound impressed."

"Not exactly, but now that I'm here, I get the appeal.

"You mean the smell of unwashed bodies and," she sniffed the air, "outhouses?"

Jack laughed. "There's something primal. We live in a very manicured world, Tyler. Don't get me wrong, I enjoy a hot shower and flush toilets. But a man likes to beat his chest now and then."

"Drew gave me a variation on that speech back when we were teenagers. Something about no new worlds to conquer, no mountains to climb. Only back then, he compared walking on the moon to my virginity."

"Did you slap his face?"

"He was joking — mostly."

"I have to say you nailed the outfit, including the platform shoes."

"Candies." Tyler put her foot out to display the wooden-heeled slides. Their quick stop in San Diego had been well worth it. "They were big in the eighties. Apparently women here are stuck in a fashion time warp."

"Now, don't be a snob."

Jack looked around. It was a colorful crowd. Moving closer to Tyler, he gave a warning frown to a couple of men who gave her the eye. Her long legs and short shorts made her stand out even in a sea of similarly dressed women.

"We need to find Drew."

Unaware of the attention she garnered, Tyler craned her neck, searching.

"How do we do that?"

"Magic."

Jack pulled out his phone and hit speed dial.

"Oh, right." She felt a little foolish that she hadn't thought of it. Now she was doubly glad Jack was with her.

"Not to worry." It took several rings but Drew finally answered.

"What is it, Jack?"

"No need to bite my head off."

"I'm a little busy and I don't need you checking up on me. Unless H&W is burning to the ground, I have to go."

"Wait." Jack stopped him before he could hang up. "Can you see the parking area from where you are?"

"I guess. Why?"

"Look for a red truck, it's the only one. Near the south end."

The phone went silent but not for long.

"Goddamn, mother fucking son of a bitch."

Jack smiled at Tyler. "I think he sees us."

"Is he mad?" Not that it would matter; Tyler was prepared for a fight. She just wanted to know the degree of mad she would be dealing with.

Jack refrained from wincing as Drew let off another string of colorful swear words.

"Mad? Not really. He's just a little surprised, that's all. He's on his way over as we speak."

"What the hell were you thinking, Jack?" Drew continued to yell at Jack over the phone. "Bringing Tyler to a place like this? And who the hell dressed her? These animals are going to be on her like white on rice."

"That's a whole lot of questions, my friend. Why don't you ask her yourself?" Jack waved when he saw a very pissed off Drew barreling down on them. He turned slightly and whispered, "Tone it down a little. If you go off on Tyler, I'll be the one kicking *your* ass, understood?"

"Shut the fuck up."

Tyler continued to search until she finally saw Drew. He dodged his way through the crowd, still talking on the phone, his eyes pinned on her. She wasn't sure what she'd been expecting to feel when she saw him, but the burst of raw sexual attraction knocked her for a loop.

Over the years when she would close her eyes and think of Drew, and that happened more often than she liked to admit, Tyler pictured him several different ways. Happy — his smile always sent a zing through her. Tender — that moment just after sex when his eyes filled with wonder and a bit of concern — he always wanted to be sure she enjoyed it as much as he did.

Sometimes, when she was in the mood for a little emotional torture, she thought of how he would say I love you. Never a hesitation, never a doubt. It was enough to make a girl's heart sing — and a woman's heart break all over again.

This Drew, obviously pissed off and ready for a fight, was a new animal altogether.

He was an overheated, dirty mess. He was the sexiest thing Tyler had ever laid eyes on.

The ends of his hair curled slightly, his face damp, one cheek smudged with grease. The black t-shirt he wore hugged his muscled torso like a second skin outlining a body filled out to perfection.

Then there were his arms. When he was eighteen, they were lean. He had been in good shape and strong for his age. Now, his biceps bulged with power, barely contained in the sleeves of his sweat-dampened shirt.

Tyler wanted to unbutton those worn jeans from his trim waist, lowering them until she had an unobstructed view of the bulge between his legs. First, though, she prayed he would turn around. That ass had to be as amazing as the rest of him. She could go down on her knees, kiss the firm, round cheeks, and fondle his hard cock all at the same time.

"Are you okay?" Hearing her slight moan, Jack glanced Tyler's way. He thought the combination of heat and worry might have gotten to her.

"Hmm? Did you say something?"

Jack looked closer. Flushed face, lips slightly parted. Her gray eyes the darkest he'd ever seen them. He grinned. It wasn't the heat that had gotten to Tyler. Unless he was completely off base, Drew's sexual dry spell was going to come to an end — soon.

"Tyler, get your ass back in that truck. And Jack." Drew reined himself in before he punched his best friend.

"Now, Drew…"

"I don't want to hear it. Get her back to Harper Falls before this crowd of rutting boars stops drooling and rushes her all at once."

"Our girl is drawing a fair bit of attention."

"This *woman* doesn't appreciate being talked about like she isn't standing three feet away."

"You want me to talk to you?" Drew rounded on her, making Tyler gasp. Standing this close, she could smell the musk, feel the heat. Saliva pooled in her mouth and she swayed towards him, her body drawn into his erotic orbit.

"Steady." Drew reached out, afraid Tyler might faint. "The heat can creep up on you. You should be wearing a hat."

"Honestly?" Jack shook his head. Clueless idiot. "She doesn't need a hat, she needs a good... Ah, hell. Look at her eyes, asshole."

Frowning, Drew did what Jack suggested. Her pupils were dilated, the gray so dark her eyes appeared to be almost black. If it were any other woman, Drew would have thought she was on drugs. Tyler didn't do that crap. Taking a deep breath, he realized her problem and he felt his body tighten in response.

"There you go," Jack chuckled. "Not so stupid after all."

"Kiss me."

"What?"

"Kiss me, now." Tyler licked her lips. She hadn't meant it to be provocative; they were just dry. It was just a happy bonus that Drew's eyes followed the path of her tongue like a starving man.

"I'm not going to kiss you, Tyler. Not with this audience."

"That's the point. I read that guys at these races respect a man's old lady. Kiss me, let them know I'm with you, and I'll be safe. It's the perfect solution."

Drew looked at her mouth again. He was tempted. Leaning closer, breathing in her unique scent. He could almost forget where they were. Almost, but not quite.

"You getting out of here is a better solution."

"You were slow at seventeen, Drew Harper. I guess some things never change."

Tyler didn't give Drew a chance to stop her. She threw her arms around his neck and glued her lips to his.

He could have pulled away. He could have let the catcalls and wolf whistles penetrate the sexual fog that enveloped his brain the second her mouth met his. He could have done a million things to stop her.

Instead, he did what came naturally — he kissed her back.

Jack only watched for a second before he got in the rented truck and drove away. Tyler would be safe with Drew. Hopefully, this would be their start back to each other. He'd done his part; getting Tyler safely delivered. The rest was up to them.

DREW PULLED TYLER close until nothing but two thin layers of clothing separated them. The heels on her ridiculous shoes brought their mouths to the same level, making it easy to devour her warm, sweetness. She had a taste he craved, his drug of choice. He'd been too long without a fix.

Tyler drowned. The air around them was brutally dry, but she sunk into a glorious pool of hot, sexy man. She didn't need water. She didn't need to breathe. She only needed Drew.

Their tongues explored, rediscovering. Tyler had almost forgotten how much better this was with Drew. Now that she remembered, she never wanted it to end.

Drew angled his mouth across Tyler's, licking at her full, bottom lip before his teeth bit, harder than he had intended. Her moan of approval was almost his undoing. He bit again, a little softer, then soothed with his tongue before taking her mouth again.

His hands began to stray. He slipped under her shirt, reveling in the feel of her soft skin against the rough pads of his fingertips. He wasn't so far gone that he didn't remember where they were, though it was a close thing. A few more minutes and he would have had her naked and up against the nearest car, their audience be damned.

"I think we've proven our point."

Reluctantly, Drew stood back. He didn't drop his arms; Tyler felt too good and he wasn't crazy.

"Point?"

Tyler felt wonderfully dazed. It had been too long since she had been in a Drew haze. She wanted to savor every moment.

"We wanted to establish that you're with me. We did that, and then some."

"Right."

Tyler stumbled back, batting his hand away when he would have steadied her. What had she been thinking? For a few heady moments, she'd let the past blur the present. She wasn't Drew's woman. He had no problem remembering that even when she let her lust-glazed brain forget.

It seemed so real. Hadn't he felt it? Even a little bit. Maybe she was a masochist but she had to ask.

"Was that just an act for the crowd, Drew?"

Hell, no. Drew looked around at the eager, interested spectators. He wasn't playing this out in front of a bunch of strangers. Leaning close, he whispered so only she could hear.

"I want you more than my next breath. What I don't want is a bunch of bubbas and bubbettes getting their vicarious thrills off us."

Tyler didn't answer. Drew had said everything that was necessary. She held out her hand, smiling when he took it. Eyes locked on hers, he raised the back to his mouth.

"I'm still angry that you're here."

"But kind of glad, too?"

"Maybe. A little."

"Maybe tomorrow you'll be a lot glad."

If that kiss was a prelude to getting naked, Drew had no doubt he'd be ecstatic. He was just mad enough not to share that with her.

"Come on." Drew pulled her towards his improvised pit area. "I left my crew battling valve problems."

"With all this dust, I imagine they get clogged easily."

Blocking her body with his, Drew guided Tyler through a sea of potential gropers. In this bunch, it wasn't just the men who could get handsy. In the past, he'd gotten more than a few pinches and butt slaps. Mostly from women, though he never paused to find out.

"Since when do you know about engines?"

"You'd be surprised what I've learned in the past ten years." She leaned closer. "About a lot of things."

Drew suppressed a groan. If she were trying to get a rise out of him, she could stop, immediately. His erection sprang to life the second he saw her. Being sexy came naturally to Tyler. Dressed in those Daisy Dukes? She was off the charts.

"I plan on asking about that — later."

When Drew had called these guys a crew, she'd pictured the kind of professional pit crews that she saw on TV. His "crew" consisted of two men and an old mangy dog. Tripper and Al nodded when Drew introduced her. No one introduced the dog. She hoped they fit the cliché *don't judge a book by its cover*. Otherwise, she was even more worried about Drew's safety than before.

"I don't know about this, Boss. We've tried blowing out the valves. The engine is coughing like crazy."

"Have you tried reprogramming the EGR valve judgment criteria?"

The three men looked at Tyler as if she had grown a second head. She just shrugged.

"Hey, I'm not just another Pit Lizard."

Tyler enjoyed seeing Drew wince. The flight to Mexico had given her plenty of time to research this world Drew occasionally inhabited. It was scary, dangerous and like Jack said, exciting. Finding the term for a racing groupie had been pure coincidence. As it turned out, a happy one. His reaction was priceless.

"Jesus, Ty, you aren't a Pit Lizard, and where the hell did you even hear that term?"

"Around," she said, shrugging with a wide-eyed, innocent look.

"And the valve reprogramming?"

"I read a lot of stuff. Some of it sticks, some of it doesn't. I guess that stuck."

She could tell Drew wasn't buying it. He was right though; she wasn't going to admit anything.

Back when they dated, Tyler became an encyclopedia of car knowledge. She wanted to talk to him about his favorite subject. Why she remembered some obscure valve procedure was a complete mystery. The brain sometimes popped out useful information at the strangest times.

"Since you weren't invited, I have no intention of entertaining you. Sit over there in the shade and behave. There is water and juice in the red cooler, the blue has sandwiches." Drew pinned her with a serious look. "Don't go wandering off. It isn't safe for a woman on her own. Hell, it's fifty/fifty for a man."

"What about that woman over there?"

Drew glanced to where Tyler pointed. A woman, dressed similarly to Tyler, made her way through the crowd. She paused every now and then to flirt and flaunt her cleavage.

"She wants to find trouble."

"Oh, so she *is* a Pit Lizard." Tyler looked closer, fascinated. If she could have five minutes with that woman, imagine the tales she could tell. Never mind the internet, *there* was her fountain of information.

"No. Absolutely not."

"What?" Tyler innocently batted her eyes.

Drew grabbed Tyler's hand and pulled her over to the makeshift tent. It wasn't much, but it did provide some welcome shade when they were on a break.

"Sit." He pushed her into a canvas director's chair. "Drink." He handed her an icy cold bottle of water. "And do not move."

"Drew."

"Yes?"

"I know you're pissed. I just needed—"

"We'll talk later, Ty."

She watched him go back to his crew and sighed. He couldn't be too angry if he called her Ty. It had always been a term of affection between them.

Tyler rummaged through her bag until she found her phone. It didn't seem likely that there would be service out here in the middle of Hell's neighbor. Still, it never hurt to try. She scrolled to Rose's number and hit dial. When it started ringing, Tyler grinned. Well, what do you know?

"Tyler. We weren't expecting to hear from you so soon. Let me put you on speaker so Dani can get in on this."

"Hey," Dani chimed in a few seconds later. "How goes it in purgatory."

"You've spoken with Jack."

"He called right after he left you. Is it as bad as he described?"

"Nah. It's a vacation getaway. I can see the brochures now. Tired of cool mountain breezes and pristine beach resorts? Come to Sepsis City, we're a disease waiting to happen."

"Take pictures," Dani said. "They are worth a thousand words. From the sound of it, you'll need them all."

"I don't plan on being here long enough to write a book. Or even a short story. Now if I could only talk to Miss Pit Lizard 2015, I might consider it."

"What is a Pit Lizard?"

"Google it." Tyler ran the bottle of water over her neck in a futile attempt to cool down. "I don't know how he stands this. The heat alone would send me over the edge."

"Some people thrive on it. In Afghanistan, I would see natives out working away during the hottest part of the day. Others would stay inside three or four hours until it cooled down. Everybody is different."

"Mmm. I don't know about different, but Drew's ass looks amazing in those jeans."

Bending over to check something under the hood, the material stretched over the curve of two very nicely formed cheeks. And Tyler thought the heat was bad before. Add sexual frustration and she felt like her skin was going to burn off.

Thinking quickly, she opened the water and poured the contents over her head and down her body. Her sigh of relief was loud and long.

"Did you just orgasm looking at a butt?"

Tyler laughed with her friends.

"Cold water; hot body. And now *wet* jokes. I'd like to think we're above such things."

"True." Tyler could almost see Dani nodding with a twinkle in her green eyes. "We're much too sophisticated for low-brow humor. Maybe Drew is thirsty. Your cup is overflowing; give him a drink."

"Ha, ha. Not bad for off the cuff. Rose? You want to chime in before I say goodbye."

"I wish. I've got nothing. Be safe and keep your powder dry."

"What does that mean?"

"No idea. I was trying to link dry with wet vagina. Instead, I got an obscure World War II reference. The be safe part goes, though. Any idea when you'll be back?"

"Drew is having engine trouble. If I'm lucky, he'll have to pull out and I won't need to use my feminine wiles to talk him out of it."

"Keep us informed. Love you."

"Love you back."

Tyler put her phone away, her eyes still on Drew. The more she watched, the less she thought this race thing was about his screwed up state of mind. He was having a great time. Maybe he did need something to conquer. If that was the case, she wasn't going to be able to sex him out of racing tomorrow. She would keep her fingers crossed that the car would be her unexpected ally.

She took a book out of her bag and a bottle of juice from the cooler. She didn't know how long Drew would be. Luckily, she came prepared. Settling back, she relaxed with some welcome old friends. It didn't take long for her to tune out the noise around her and immerse herself in the lives of the March family.

Every time she read *Little Women*, she talked herself into believing Beth would survive. This time it would be different. Of course, that never happened. The outcome was a foregone conclusion. Beth's tragic end couldn't be changed no matter how hard she wished.

She glanced up from her book. Drew still worked in the blazing sun, sweat covering his face. Were they like a book, she wondered? Had the chapters already been put down in permanent ink? Or could they rip out the pages and start again?

Drew looked up as though sensing her interest. He waved, a half-smile on his face. Tyler felt a surge of hope. They still had time. Nothing had been etched in stone.

She went back to her book. The author chose the direction of her characters' lives. She and she alone manipulated who died and who had a happy ending.

Ten years ago, Tyler stood by and watched as others dictated a very important part of her life. She was determined never to let anyone write her ending, not this time.

Chapter Nine

TYLER DIDN'T KNOW how it was possible, but somewhere between Jo meeting her Professor Bhaer and Laurie marrying Amy, she dozed off.

Between the noise and the heat, she wouldn't have thought sleep possible. Now here she floated in a dream.

"Relax."

Drew played leading man. Nothing new there. She could almost feel his arms around her. The problem was she always woke up alone. Her dreams were a big, fat tease, always ending in frustration.

Tyler twisted, determined to get away from a fantasy that broke her heart over and over again.

"Ty, baby. Stop or I'll drop you."

"Drew?"

"You were conked out. I'm taking you to my RV where you can stretch out."

"Not a dream."

Drew laughed. "The way I look and smell, more like a nightmare."

"You look fine." Edible. "And you smell, well, not great. But better than those other unwashed souls out there."

"That's because I shower more than once a month."

"Lovely. You've just managed to do the impossible. Make them even less appealing."

The tension from her body drained. This felt good, being in his arms. It felt right.

"Drew — wait a minute. You have an RV?"

"Two. Tripper and Al share. I have my own. They're a must out here in the middle of nowhere. That and a generator. Practically all the comforts of home."

"You mean all this time I could have been in the cool—" she thought for a second. "It is cool in there?"

"That's one of the reasons I have a generator."

"Right. Why was I suffering when I didn't have to? Unless it was your way of punishing me for coming here."

"No. I'll punish you in a way that will give me a lot more pleasure than making you sweat. I didn't want you alone, Ty. When I said it isn't safe, I meant it."

"Even with the door locked and your gun nearby?"

"Not even then." He turned his head, his eyes meeting hers. "Why would you think I had a gun?"

"You used to be a bodyguard. You run a hugely successful security firm. Of course, you would bring a gun to a place like this."

"Smart girl."

"Smart boy."

Drew put Tyler down in front of the RV. There was a keypad next to the door. He punched in the numbers before fitting a key into the lock.

"I could have walked." And she could have said something sooner.

"I could have let you. I think we both preferred my method."

"Now don't start getting cocky, boyo. We're in early stages here. I'm still on board for some hot sex. And I agree that we should talk. Getting smug is reserved for further down the road."

"Give me a timeframe. A week, month? Next year?"

Tyler held back a smile. "Let's just play it by ear."

"No problem. After you."

From the outside, the RV looked like a vehicle on its last legs. Rust, dents, a crack in the back window that ran from side to side. The interior looked like something out of *Recreational Vehicles Beautiful*.

"Drew, this is not what I expected."

"The exterior is just for show. I'm not looking to advertise my financial situation."

"Outside, it's *King of the Road*; inside you live like a king. Impressive."

"Roger Miller."

"Very impressive." Tyler gave him a slow smile. "How did you know that?"

"You and your friends don't hold the monopoly on song and movie references."

"True. It doesn't hurt to have a smartphone at your fingertips."

"How did you know?"

Tyler tipped her head towards the wall behind him.

"Never stand with your back to a mirror if you want to hide what's in your hand."

Drew glanced back and groaned. "Busted."

"Really impressive keyboard skills, though. Fast *and* blind. You always did have mad computer skills but with that typing ability, you'll make someone a terrific secretary."

"Personal assistant. Get on the P.C. train, Tyler."

"Sorry," she laughed. "How about a tour."

"There's not a lot to see. Sitting area, kitchen. Bathroom and bedroom in the back."

Not big but luxurious. Even though Tyler wasn't up on the latest in RV chic, she imagined this was as good as it got. Granite countertops, Sub-Zero fridge. The upholstery on the chairs wasn't that wash and wear stuff you found in most RVs; it was soft. She wanted to sink in and stay for days.

"You said there's a bedroom?"

Tyler turned toward him. She didn't mean to lick her lip; nerves — a reflex. Drew's eyes widened slightly, his breathing deepened. Honestly, she wasn't trying to be deliberately provocative. But they were as close to a bed as they'd ever been. As teenagers, they hadn't needed one. They jumped each other every chance they had, any place they could find. That had never included a bed.

"I need a shower, a cold one. Make yourself at home. Snoop through drawers. I won't be long."

"Men snoop too."

"Did I say otherwise?"

Tyler trailed behind him, her eyes never leaving his butt — until he pulled off his grimy t-shirt. Holy mother of God. Every part of that man was perfection. His back rippled with muscles no desk jockey should possess. Long and well-defined, she wanted to start from the top and lick every inch. Including that lovely little dip just shadowed by the waistband of his jeans.

"I would *love* a shower."

"I won't be long."

"Just think of the water we could save if you let me wash your back."

Drew stopped in the middle of unsnapping his jeans. Tyler's finger was running up and down her chest, drawing attention. The ends of her sleeveless blouse were tied into a knot just below her breasts, leaving plenty of smooth skin bare.

She had been a distraction all afternoon, now she was driving him and his control crazy.

"Go green, Drew. Conserving water is a good thing."

"Stop," he shouted when she began to loosen the knot. "If you get in that shower with me, I would clean you top to bottom — twice. Before I was done, we'd run out of water. Nothing green about that."

"You don't know what you're missing," Tyler called the words to a closed door. He could move fast, especially when motivated.

Sitting on the edge of the surprisingly spacious double bed, Tyler considered sliding out of her clothes and greeting him wearing nothing but a smile. The idea had a lot of appeal but in the end, she decided to wait. She really needed a shower. After which they could get all sweaty again — together.

She heard the bathroom door open.

"When you say you won't be long, you aren't kid—"

"Something wrong?"

He had to know how good he looked. Long, muscled body, still slightly damp. And the ridiculous excuse for a towel riding low on his hips. He was enough to make women beg and gay men weep.

"Nope." Tyler stood, popping the button on her short shorts. Mr. Drew Harper wanted to parade around barely hiding his privates? It was time for her to get in the game.

"I'm *excited*," she pulled the knot on her shirt loose, her eyes glued to his, "to get in the shower, that's all."

The blouse hit the floor followed quickly by the shorts. She stood in front of him in nothing but two scraps of crimson lace.

"Evil," Drew whispered under his breath.

"Did you say something?"

He just shook his head, watching as she released her hair from its high knot. She shook it loose, the long dark strands settling over her shoulders, the ends swaying against the tops of her breasts.

"Like what you see?"

"You'll do."

"Now that's an understatement if ever I heard one."

Her gaze drifted down the front of his towel. It was highly satisfying to know she caused the tenting that was threatening to knock the cloth from his hips.

"You used to like me naked. Since false modesty would be silly at this point, I'll point out that I look a damn sight better than I did at sixteen."

She advanced. Close, but not too close. This time the first move had to be his.

"I can see the pulse in your throat. Your heart is beating like a humming bird's wings. Is that for me, Drew? The ragged little breaths. That lovely erection. Why are you waiting?"

"Ty…"

"Yes?"

"Take your shower."

"Unbelievable! You are just… Unbelievable!"

Tyler stomped past him, slamming the bathroom door. The little gesture felt good — briefly. Turning the water on, she piled her hair back up. Stepping under the cool, refreshing spray, she just stood there, her brain zipping around.

Why? This was the third time she had offered herself to him. He might be able to control his impulses; his body was another matter.

Well, she was through. If he wanted her, he would have to do something about it. If he didn't? He better take another shower and wank himself off. She sure as hell didn't want to look at a hard cock all evening when she knew she wasn't going to get to enjoy it.

The shower felt wonderful. Unfortunately, it didn't do much to cool her down. She dried off then remembered she'd left her bag in the lounge area. It had her brush, lotion, and lip-gloss. Essentials, especially in this dry heat.

Holding up a towel she found out it wasn't long enough to cover everything. Two would work, one for the top, one for the bottom. Perfect solution. If she had two towels. Drew hadn't been expecting company so it wasn't a surprise to find the bathroom lacking in extra linen. It presented an interesting quandary. Call out and ask him to get her bag. Or parade half-naked through the bedroom to get it herself.

She still hadn't decided when Drew knocked on the door.

"I have your bag, Tyler."

Without a word, she opened the door just enough to reach through and pull the oversized purse inside. The only naked part of her he saw was her arm.

She could have brooded. As good as it might have felt to punish him by lingering over her post-shower activities, Tyler decided the only one to suffer would be her.

The room was small and steamy. The ventilation did little to clear the air and the effects of her cool shower would soon be obliterated if she didn't get out soon. Moving quickly, she slathered lotion on her body. Brushing her teeth and hair completed the transformation.

Wiping at the fogged-over mirror, she peered at herself and decided she would do.

The loose summer dress she tucked in the bag was all she needed in the way of clothing. When she threw it in earlier that morning, she wasn't thinking beyond having something along that traveled well. No fuss, no muss. Worrying if Drew would find the pale yellow sheath seductive was the last thing on her mind. After the last half hour, she couldn't have cared less.

Prepared to ignore him and march into the other room, Tyler opened the bathroom door and stepped into the wonderfully cool bedroom. Her plans to glide past him, calm and collected, ended when she saw the prone form on the bed. Drew was stretched out, the sheet around his waist — sound asleep.

Every drop of self-righteous indignation drained from her body. It was hard to stay angry with an exhausted man who hadn't really done anything wrong.

Tyler stayed still, not wanting to disturb him. More than anything, she wanted to join him, crawl in bed, and wrap herself around his body. The idea of just sleeping with Drew, waking with him close. Something couples did every day and took for granted.

The ache she felt deep inside had nothing to do with sex. She wanted something even more basic. A connection. A closeness. The thing that would give her the right to join him without an invitation. The feeling that she belonged in his arms and he belonged in hers.

He needed his sleep. Ready to spend the night alone, Tyler turned only to be stopped by a hand on hers. Drew's fingers locked with hers as though willing that connection she was just thinking about.

"I didn't want to wake you."

"I only nodded off for a second. We got an early start and I didn't realize how much that sun had drained me."

"I'll let you get some rest. Trapper told me your race starts at eight."

"Mmm." Drew ran his thumb along hers, amazed that such strong hands could be so soft.

"You need to let go."

"That's always been my problem, Ty. I can't let you go."

"You did once. Quite easily and without a backward glance."

Drew swallowed hard past the lump in his throat.

"Let me hold you?"

Tyler hesitated. It was what she had longed for just moments before. Now she found it hard to take the two steps that would put her in his arms.

"Please." Drew moved to the other side of the bed, tugging her hand.

Nodding, she slid in beside him. She didn't remove her dress or get under the sheet. She laid her head next to his, their faces a mere whisper's breath apart. Drew took her hand, resting it on his hip while he trailed his hand up her arm until he cupped her neck. He didn't pull her any closer. His touch was gentle, a soft, easy caress. Unconsciously, she started making the same movement. Her hand lightly massaging. The thin sheet was the only thing separating her hand from his skin.

"We've never shared a bed."

"Funny, a little earlier I was thinking the same thing."

Time ticked away unnoticed. They were contented just to be, their eyes half closed yet intent on the other.

"I keep thinking about us. How it was."

"You too?" she asked. Her hand tightened, squeezing his hip, then relaxing again.

"For the first time in a long time. I used to try not to remember. Then for a while, my memories became all muddled. I could see you clearly; it was everything else that became distorted."

"Like a photograph that over time had become faded and a bit blurry? I know what you mean."

Drew sighed, relieved that she understood, that it was the same for her.

"I was scared, Ty. I didn't want it all to slip away. Lately, though, I've seen it all so clearly. The first time we met. Every trip down to the cove."

"Our first kiss." Tyler shifted closer. She started to feel that elusive connection again.

"Especially our first kiss. You tasted like green apples."

She smiled. "My favorite Jolly Rancher flavor."

He knew that. There was a package in the drawer of his desk. He was never without them. For ten years, they were his touchstone to Tyler. That little bit of information he kept to himself for now. Someday. Maybe.

"Our first time." Tyler looked down, feeling strangely shy.

"God, I was scared."

"It didn't show."

"I knew you were nervous." He smoothed back her hair, curling the end around his finger. "I wanted to be your rock, calm your fears."

"Fears? I don't remember having any. I knew what I wanted. I knew I wanted it with you. I was a little nervous, though."

"It was all I could do to keep from shaking. What if I messed up and you ended up hating sex for life? I chanted in my head, *Make sure she has an orgasm, make sure she has an orgasm.*"

"I didn't have an orgasm." She reminded him.

"No, you did not."

Tyler brought his hand to her lips, her kiss warm and sweet.

"It was lovely, Drew."

"Is that what they call damning with faint praise?"

"No." This time instead of kissing his hand, she punched him on the arm — hard.

"Hey."

"I can't believe you didn't know."

"Know what?"

"Lovely was perfect. What I dreamed of."

"Really?"

"Yes."

Looking into his eyes, Tyler willed him back. Asked him to go with her to that day. She asked him to see it, not as an eighteen-year-old with orgasms on the brain. She wanted him to see, to feel, what it was like for a sixteen-year-old virgin who thought she knew what to expect and ended up getting so much more.

ELEVEN YEARS EARLIER

"I GOT YOU something."

Tyler caught the bag Rose threw to her. Curious, she looked inside.

"Holy... How did you get these?"

"From a very sympathetic drug store owner in Spokane."

She looked at Dani.

"Did you know about this?"

"I paid half." She grinned. "Hey, no glove, no love."

Tyler picked up the box of condoms. It didn't burn her hands. Apparently, Father Steven was wrong. Birth control did not come directly from hell to tempt young people into sin. It seemed unlikely that rhetoric changed in the three years she had stopped going to church with her mother. Not that it mattered. She was going to have sex — soon. When she did, she wasn't taking any chances.

"Weren't you embarrassed?"

Two weeks ago, when Tyler finally confessed all, Rose and Dani did exactly what she expected — supported her unconditionally. The questions had flown, of course. When had it started? How far had they gone? When were they going all the way?

That last question had led to the subject of protection. Tyler wasn't able to get on the pill in time for the big event. She would need a doctor in Spokane for that; she couldn't risk going local. Then, even if she started taking them tomorrow, their effectiveness would be iffy. According to their research, the best time to start taking them would be within six days of her next period.

Tyler had no timeframe for when she and Drew would have sex. She didn't have a doctor though Planned Parenthood was an option. After long and involved discussions, they finally decided to skip the middleman and go right to condoms. There was always more than pregnancy to consider. As Dani pointed out, no matter how much you love him or trust him, any woman who takes a guy's word for where he's dipped his wick, is just asking for an STD.

Hardly the most romantic sentiment, Tyler thought. Then again, friends weren't supposed to encourage stupid behavior. Rose and Dani had her best interests at heart. That was why she was currently holding a box of Trojans.

"It wasn't the easiest conversation I've ever had. I don't know what I would have done if the owner hadn't been a woman."

"Did she grill you?"

Rose shook her head.

"Like I said, she was sympathetic. The only uncomfortable part was when she went into detail about the proper way to use them. Not at all creepy; she was great. Still, I'm glad we were the only ones in the store at the time."

"You hit the jackpot with her."

Tyler opened the box and took out a packet, handing it to Rose.

"Teach on, Wise One. We who haven't a clue bow down to your infinite wisdom."

Three days later, Tyler parked her bike in the usual spot by the river. She hadn't seen Drew in almost a week because of his yearly camping trip with his father. He had been reluctant to leave her, but he couldn't blow off his dad. Tyler wouldn't have wanted him to. Rituals were important.

Once he left for college, Drew wasn't planning on coming back. That meant this would be his last chance to spend time alone with the man he loved and respected. His inability to curb Regina aside, Russell Harper was a good person. He had gifted his son with compassion and kindness.

Though it was still a year until Drew would be gone, this was his time to start saying goodbye. Tyler would never begrudge him that.

She unpacked her bag. Thermos of lemonade, blanket. Book to read in case Drew was delayed. The condoms tucked away, within reach but not sitting out like a glaring beacon declaring she was ready and willing. She was, she just didn't want to be that obvious.

"Ty."

Before she could even turn around, Drew swooped her into his arms. His kiss was long and intense, as though they had been apart months instead of days.

Tyler kissed him back with the same desperation. Lord, how she'd missed him. In a short time, she had gotten used to their daily visits. Her Drew fix, as Dani put it. Maybe she was addicted.

The feel of his lips on hers sent a rush through her body. Tyler had no frame of reference, but she wondered if this was how it felt to shoot drugs into your veins. The fire, the instant euphoria. Floating and grounded all at once. Knowing you never wanted it to end. Wondering, even before you were off your high when you could do it again.

"I missed you."

Drew breathed the words against her mouth, not wanting to break contact. He and his father had arrived back that morning. After a week away, the extra hours, knowing she was just across the bridge yet completely out of reach, had seemed interminable.

Of course, Regina had decided it was time for one of her State of the Family Addresses. Drew had practically been bouncing off the walls by the time she finished criticizing his and his father's lack of Harper pride. It was the same old schtick. Drew tuned her out. How many times could she remind him of his duties? Didn't she ever get tired of it? Finally, realizing she might as well have been talking to herself, she set him free.

He kissed her again, not able to get enough.

"Mmm, green apple. I've grown very fond of that flavor."

Tyler laughed, delighted by his words, delighted by him.

"Good thing. I'm not sure I could give up my Jolly Ranchers."

"Not even for me?"

"Maybe," she conceded. "But if you loved me, you'd never ask."

Tyler froze. Damn it. Why had the word love slipped out? She felt it — desperately. Drew hadn't even hinted he felt that same.

"Then I promise, I'll never ask."

Tyler felt her heart kick up a beat.

"No?"

Drew took a deep breath. This was big. He wanted to get it right.

"I love you, Tyler Jones."

"Drew." She gasped his name, her mouth suddenly dry.

"Say it, Ty. Don't make me beg."

"No, I wouldn't." She was mortified that he'd even think such a thing. "I love you. So much. It's so big the words got stuck in my throat for a second."

Drew picked her up and swung her around until they were both breathless. Finally, he put her down but kept her wrapped in his arms, his mouth close to her ear. This was their place, no one to see or hear. Still, he suddenly felt the need to whisper.

"I've never said it before. Not to anyone."

"Not even your father?" Tyler whispered back. She tightened her arms around him, wanting to comfort. She had people to love. Her mom. Rose and Dani. It was hard to imagine not having anyone.

"I love him," Drew said. "I do. And I know he loves me. We just don't say it. I guess it's a guy thing."

Tyler thought it was a family thing. Dani's father told his son he loved him. All the time. She guessed it was easier to say when you'd been around it all your life. From everything Drew told her, Russell Harper hadn't known much love in his life. Not as a child, certainly not as a married man. At least he knew how to show his son how he felt.

Actions were great, yet Tyler knew words mattered; she didn't have a problem saying them. She promised herself now that she was free to do so, she would tell Drew every day. Over and over. Starting now.

"I love you." She kissed the side of his neck. "I love you." Another kiss, this on his jaw. "I love you."

Tyler pulled back a little until her eyes met his. It was all there for him to see. The crystal clear gray so bright and true. Never doubt, they said. I love you.

"Ty." He breathed in; a faint hint of green apple filled his senses. It was a scent that would always mean Tyler. "You have no idea what you do to me."

"Maybe not. Not yet. But I want to learn."

Taking his hand, she led him to the blanket.

"Show me, Drew. Now."

"Tyler." Drew felt a touch of panic.

She knelt, pulling him down with her. They had done things. Touched, explored. All with their clothes on. She knew the feel of his skin, but she never watched her hands running over the hot, smooth surface. She wanted that, dreamt of it.

"Kiss me. Make love to me." She laughed. "In books, the woman always says make love *with* me. Someday I'll say that. When I know what I'm doing. Teach me, Drew. Teach me how."

"I didn't tell you I loved you so you would have sex with me." He wanted her to be sure. It was a big step. A line she couldn't hop back over.

"I'm glad you said it first, before we did this." Slipping her hands under the hem of his t-shirt, Tyler silently urged him to raise his arms. She felt powerful, emboldened. Pulling the material over his head, she tossed it to the side.

So lean. Slim but way better developed than any of the boys who ran around her neighborhood shirt-free. None of them made her breath catch or her palms itch to touch. Drew did both. The best part. She already had permission to touch to her heart's content. That day seemed unlikely to come. How could she ever get her fill? She would want him forever — longer.

"You aren't pressuring me or manipulating me."

Tyler smiled at his gasp. She barely grazed his stomach. What other responses could she get? She was going to enjoy finding out.

"Maybe you should take my shirt off."

Drew closed his eyes, giving himself a quick talking to. He was the one with experience. Time to stop letting Tyler drive this train. His nerves be damned. If he wanted to make it good for her, he needed to take control.

"Don't be so impatient. We have all the time in the world."

Which was true. No one would come looking for him. Even if they did, they wouldn't look down here. Tyler ran wild. Her friends would worry if she didn't come home on time, not her family.

"Do Rose and Dani know where you are?"

"Yes."

Tyler was too busy tracing the ridges of his abs to give him more than a vague answer.

"Will they miss you?"

"Hmm."

Drew chuckled. "Will they miss you if you don't come home tonight?"

"Why wouldn't I go home?" Tyler frowned. Her bedroom was just across the river. There was no reason she shouldn't be in it by dark.

"I want you to stay here. With me."

"All night?"

"All night." Drew cupped her face with his hands, giving her a gentle kiss. "In my arms."

"I'll call them. Later."

This time his kiss was firmer. He let the passion grow slowly, letting Tyler understand how her body was reacting. He went through each step, shortcuts were not allowed.

He spoke in low, intimate tones. Telling her how beautiful she was, how much he wanted her, needed her. The pace of their lovemaking was measured and controlled. And because of it, that much more exquisite. He didn't hurry or rush. They had all night. As far as Drew was concerned, they had forever.

TEARS RAN DOWN Tyler's cheeks unchecked. She didn't know when they started. She lay in his arms as a woman remembering what it was like to lie there for the first time.

It made her heart ache. This time not with grief or regret. This was the ache that you felt when something finally began to heal. Ten years of an open wound, raw and painful. Tyler could actually feel it begin to stitch itself together. It wasn't going to happen overnight. The scar would be visible. But it would happen. For the first time, she not only let herself have hope, she believed.

"I didn't want to make you cry. I promised myself that would never happen again."

"That was a stupid promise. And futile." Tyler leaned over him, brushing at his cheek when one of her tears fell there.

"We're passionate people, Drew. The longer we spend together, the likelier one of us will cry."

"You think I'm going to cry?"

"It can happen to even the manliest of men. Someday, Drew. You never know."

He wasn't going to argue. Not when she was relaxed, her warm body close. They were in a place he had despaired of ever being again. He didn't want anything to ruin this moment.

"I don't know what the future holds for us, Drew."

Tyler put her head on his chest just above the beating of his heart. She loved that sound. When they were younger, she would stay like this after they had made love, lulled to sleep by the rhythm.

She still found it comforting. But she didn't want to sleep. She had more vigorous activities on her mind.

"Ty, I still need to tell you why—"

"Not now."

She interrupted him with a slow, hot kiss.

"I need you, Drew."

"Ty, sweetheart. I need you, too. You have no idea."

He didn't think she knew? Ten years. Maybe it wasn't fair that she saw every other man she had known as a placeholder — a pale imitation. She had the real thing now. Time to enjoy all of him. Top to bottom. Inch by mouth-watering inch

Smiling, she straddled his hips, the sheet the only thing between her and his growing erection. Tyler rested her hands on his chest, leaning down to lick him starting at his belly button. Up, up. Her mouth found his and the passion flared faster than a match touching tinder.

"Tell me you've missed this. Tell me I'm the only woman who has ever made you feel this way. Lie. I don't care; just say it."

With a growl, Drew flipped her around until she was under him, her arms pinned above her head. He took her mouth, desperate, needy.

"Look at me," he said, his breath ragged. "Open your eyes, Ty. Look at me."

The gray of her irises was smoky, her gaze slightly blurred. It took a moment until he was certain she could see him — really see him.

"I've only lied to you once. Ten years ago when I told you I didn't love you, that I never had. Every word was like a knife twisting in my gut. Never again. Do you understand? No more lies."

Tyler stopped breathing. It wasn't an explanation, but it was exactly what she needed to hear. He had loved her.

She felt it. Her heart mending a little bit more.

"Air, sweetheart. Breathe. Tyler, breathe."

She did, pulling in the much-needed oxygen. Breathing easy for the first time in years.

"I've never wanted a woman as much as I want you."

"No?"

He smoothed back her hair, his warm brown eyes taking in every inch of her beautiful, precious face.

"Only you know how to touch me, Ty. Here." He took her hand, bringing it to his face. She cupped his cheek, her thumb running over the day's growth of beard.

"And here."

This time he brought her hand to rest just over his heart.

"Drew…"

"Shh."

He kissed her again, a bit of the desperation replaced by something deeper. It was too soon to tell her how he felt. He still had so much to make up for, so much more to repair. Someday, though. Soon he would tell her. She was his first. The first to touch his heart. The first and only.

Tyler pushed up, deepening the kiss. Her tongue found his, sliding, tasting.

The mood switched again. Heat rose. Needing his flesh against hers, Tyler pushed at the sheet that still separated them. When her hands finally found the bare cheeks of his ass, she gave a shout of triumph. Removing one inconvenient piece of bedding wasn't the biggest accomplishment, but at the moment it felt damn close.

"I'm naked," Drew said, his voice heavy with passion. "You aren't."

"Pull the stupid dress off. Rip it. I don't care. I'm not wearing anything underneath."

"Music to my ears."

Drew would have done just as she suggested. He was about to turn the dress into a shredded rag when someone pounded on the RV door.

"Ignore it. They'll go away."

Instead, the noise got louder. The person had moved from the door to the small window just over their heads. The knocking was so hard it rattled the bed.

"Goddamn it." Drew leaned over and pounded back. "Unless you want to be spitting blood and teeth, you better get the hell away from here."

"Boss?"

"Tripper?" He looked down at Tyler. Her expression was somewhere between frustrated and amused. Drew had a hard time finding any humor in the situation."

"Go to bed. Whatever it is can wait until morning."

"It's Al, Boss. He got into a fight over some whiskey and a woman. A couple of guys beat the shit out of him."

"Son of a bitch."

Drew rolled off the bed. Within seconds, he had on jeans and a t-shirt. He pulled on his boots before opening a hidden panel behind the dresser. Expertly slipping a full clip of bullets into a gun, he tucked it into the waistband of his pants.

"Tyler—"

"Give me a second to put on my shoes."

"I want you to stay here. Keep the door locked and whatever you do, don't let anyone in."

"Are you crazy?" She exclaimed. "You have the muscles and the gun. I'm sticking with you."

Drew didn't have time to argue.

"Fine. But put on some underwear first."

Chapter Ten

THE BLAST OF heat that hit her as they left the RV wasn't a surprise. However, it was unwelcome. The sun was down; had been for several hours. Yet it felt like the temperature had risen, not decreased. How was that possible?

"Tell me what happened?"

"Al hooked up with some old buddies he used to hang with in the Navy."

"What are a bunch of water jockeys doing in the desert?"

"That's what Al kept asking. The more he drank, the more he complained about the heat and the sand. He hated the Navy, Boss. Half a bottle of tequila, and he's missing every last thing about it."

Drew had taken her hand the instant they left the RV, keeping her close. His eyes were constantly moving, anticipating any threat.

Earlier, there had been one big crowd, now the groups were smaller, more specific. It made it harder to guard against an unexpected attack. There was a lot of drinking and drugs. Mini-fights broke out without any notice. Drew didn't want to inadvertently be dragged into one. A gun might beat a knife ninety-nine percent of the time. Right now, dealing with a bunch of unruly drunks in a dark, isolated area made the odds a hell of a lot less in his favor.

"If I tell you to run, run. If I say hit the ground, do it. Understand?"

Tyler realized now was not the time for smartass quips.

"I understand."

They made their way through the shadows, trying to avoid any kind of confrontation, friendly or otherwise. To Tyler, it seemed to take forever. In fact, five minutes probably passed from the time they left Drew's RV to when they got to the one Tripper and Al shared.

"Why did you move? You know it's safer to keep close to each other."

Tripper shrugged. Tyler could see the worry on his face.

"Al—"

"Jesus, Tripper. You told me when you recommended Al that he wasn't a drinker and you could handle him. Did you lie?"

Not waiting for an answer, Drew pulled open the door to an RV that looked identical to the one they had just left.

Still holding her hand, Drew went in first, gave a quick look around, then pulled her inside. The similarities between the RVs ended at the door.

Not that this one was a dump. It just looked more like your standard issue recreational vehicle. The real differences came in the upkeep. Or lack of it.

Empty beer cans and bottles littered the floor. Dirty clothes in piles, takeout containers, flies. The smell of sweat, dirty feet, and rotting food was enough to make anyone gag. Add a top note of cheap aftershave. It had Tyler looking for the nearest window. Unfortunately, those had been covered with black construction paper to block out any light.

Either Drew was used to the pigsty or he didn't care. It certainly wasn't his first priority.

"I'm sorry, Boss. I didn't realize he'd been drinking until one of his buddies showed up. They brought a couple bottles of the cheap stuff. The women they brought were even cheaper."

"Really?" Tyler hated that kind of attitude. She might not admire the women that followed these guys around. As a career choice, it seemed a bit limited. Calling them cheap just pissed her off. Men loved taking what was offered. Then they loved acting like the woman was the problem.

"Sorry, Miss Tyler."

"Don't apologize to me. Go find one of the *cheap* women and tell her you're sorry."

"Tyler." Drew sighed. "Can we save the feminist rhetoric for later? Once I have all this taken care of, I'll be happy to help kick the ass of every disrespectful jerk within a five-mile radius."

Not the right time. Tyler got that. Sometimes she couldn't seem to help herself.

"Sorry. Is there anything I can do?"

Drew opened the bedroom door. He looked in, cursed, then turned back.

"Clean towels, if you can find any. And hot water."

"I'm on it."

"Tripper? Get the first aid kit from under the sink. Chances are you're going to have to get this idiot to a doctor."

"He won't go. That's why I came after you. Says nothing is broken. Most of the blood is from a cut on his scalp where Sandrine hit him with a bottle."

"I imagine Sandrine had her reasons."

"Well, they was—"

"I couldn't care less, Tripper."

They worked on Al for the next hour. Cleaning his cuts and bruises. Cleaning him up in general. He had sobered up enough to protest when Drew tried to get him to go for professional help. It didn't appear anything was broken. The main concern was internal bleeding and a possible concussion.

"You can't make him go, Drew."

Tripper fixed a pot of coffee. He used the end of his grease-stained shirt to wipe the rim of a mug before pouring in the acrid-smelling black liquid. He offered it to Tyler.

"No, thank you."

Even a coffee addict like herself drew the line somewhere.

"Boss?"

Drew shook his head. Al was sleeping. Or passed out. Probably a combination of the two.

"I'm counting on you to watch him, Tripper. Wake him every hour. I'm still worried about a head injury. Those can jump up and bite you in the ass even when you think you're fine."

Taking a big swig of coffee, Tripper wiped the back of his mouth on his shirtsleeve.

"I know I let you down. I swear I've never seen him drink like that." Tripper shook his head. He had a worn face, the kind that made it hard to tell if he was thirty or sixty.

"What's done is done. Don't worry about it."

"It was a woman."

Tripper whispered the words, glancing furtively at Tyler.

"You can speak up, Tripper," Tyler assured him. "I'm not going to give you grief again. Who am I to talk? I showed up dressed like a stereotypical groupie. What does that say about me?"

"That you have the longest legs I've ever seen?"

Realizing that he spoke aloud, Tripper's eyes almost bugged out of his head.

"Sorry, Boss. Sorry, Miss Tyler."

"Nothing to be sorry about," Drew assured him. "She does have pretty spectacular legs."

"Yes, sir."

Tripper said it almost reverently. How could she have a problem with being admired? And in such a non-creepy way.

"I'm going to check on the car."

They were on their way out of the RV.

"If the people who did that to Al know who he works for, they might decide to take their remaining frustration out on my ride. It would be a nice bonus to knock me out of the race."

"Well, shit. Sorry, Miss Tyler. I never thought of that. Want me to go?"

"No." Drew took Tyler's hand. "You stay with Al. Most likely the car is fine."

Tyler didn't speak as they made their way back to Drew's RV. There were still a few pockets of loud partying. For the most part, though, the campground had settled down for the night. The drivers might be a rag-tag bunch; they still had to respect the need for some sleep.

Right behind the RV was a tent that Drew and his crew used to put the car in at night. It wasn't big enough for anything else, leaving about a foot of walking space around the vehicle.

Tyler sat on the hood while Drew made a quick inspection.

"Everything looks okay." He turned to her with a sigh, his eyes looking tired and slightly bloodshot. Even worn down from a long day, he was still the best-looking man she had ever known.

"You're awfully quiet."

Drew joined her, pulling himself up until his back rested on the windshield.

"Shit." He shifted, pulling the gun from behind his back and sitting in on the car's roof. "It's been so long since I've carried one of those, I forgot it was there."

"Why?"

His head tipped back on the roof, eyes closed, Drew raised a brow.

"Why did I stop carrying a gun?"

"No. Why do you do this? Jack says part of it is the thrill. He also thinks you have a semi-death wish. Some complicated crap about your mommy issues and me. Rose says this is your version of running away to join the circus."

Drew snorted but didn't speak.

"Dani just thinks you're an idiot asshole."

"Is that hyphenated?"

Tyler wrapped her arms around her legs, hiding her smile behind her knees.

"It can go either way."

They sat in silence for a few minutes listening to the blissful silence. It had gotten quiet enough to hear the noises of a desert at night. Owls, nighthawks, some kind of cat that made Tyler glad she was in here, not out there. The sounds blended in an almost hypnotic tone that could easily lull someone with less on their mind into a deep sleep. She wasn't that lucky.

"What's your theory?"

She waited for him to ask, wondering if he would.

"A bit of all the above."

She turned, resting her cheek on her knee. Her eyes met his, now open, alert.

"But that's too easy."

"How so?"

"If I thought you wanted to go out in a blaze of glory because Regina didn't show you any love, I would kick your ass from here back to Harper Falls."

"I'd let you."

"Exactly."

She chuckled slightly, Drew joining her.

"My ego likes the idea that I might be at the heart of it."

"Is that so? I'm surprised you'd admit that."

"That I have an ego? It's quite healthy. It also lives in the real world. You wouldn't still be doing this ten years later if I were the only reason."

"You always were the smartest one in the room. Any room."

"Smart enough." She gave his leg a playful nudge with the toe of her sneaker."

"That leaves runaway or idiot."

"Idiot asshole."

"How could I forget?"

She scooted back until she was stretched out next to him, their arms touching. Taking his hand, she laced her fingers with his. It was a surprisingly comfortable position, considering they had nothing but hard steel and glass underneath them.

"You like it. Part of it's the danger. Jack got that. Dani should have. She's a bit a thrill-seeker herself. You, on the other hand, like the competition."

"Damn."

She turned her head. The look on Drew's face was part consternation, part admiration.

"You don't deny it?"

"What would be the point?"

Drew tugged her body until she was laid out on top of him.

"Nobody's ever understood me like you, Ty."

He cupped her butt, softly grinding her against his already rock-hard cock.

Moaning, Tyler took his head in her hands, kissing him like the world was ending. She pulled back, out of breath and grinning.

"You could enter legitimate races." She trailed kisses across his face as she spoke. "Indy, NASCAR, Formula One. Money certainly isn't an issue. Though I imagine plenty of sponsors would jump at having you as the face of their racing team."

And what a face it was, Tyler thought. Drew would be the perfect poster boy. Sexy, gorgeous. He would have a huge following in no time.

"Ty."

Drew's fingers flexed, tightening on her ass. Was he supposed to think when she kissed him like that? She asked him questions. She must be expecting cognizant answers.

"Hmm?"

"You know what you're doing to me, don't you?"

She shifted again until his legs opened, cradling her hips even deeper. He was hard and ready. Just the way she wanted him.

"I have a pretty good idea." Batting her sparkling gray eyes, Tyler smiled. "Now, tell me about why you like to race in the wind instead of going legit."

"You really want to do this now?"

She nodded, bending for another kiss.

"No."

He gently pushed her off, giving himself room to think clearly. He wanted her too much. Right now, the blood in his body could either flow to his cock or his brain — not both.

"Five minutes. Ask me anything. After that, your body is mine. Nothing but moans and dirty talk. Got it?"

Tyler's gaze drifted to the lovely bulge between Drew's legs.

"It can wait." She wasn't sure she could.

"You started this, Ty."

"Fine." Tyler sighed. "Tell me why you race in the wind."

"You did do your research. Do you know why they call it that?"

"I couldn't find the etymology. Is it because you feel free when you don't have rules to follow?"

"I love your brain, Ty." And I love you. Too soon. Don't blow this by pushing her too far, too fast. Drew cleared his throat.

"The no rules is part of it. A big part. But the origin comes from actually running from the law. Racing out here, away from civilization, was too tame back in the day. They wanted the police to show up. The longer someone could elude the cops, or be in the wind, the more of a legend they became. There were no trophies, no money. It was all about reputation."

Fascinated, Tyler leaned closer.

"That's changed, hasn't it?"

"There are still street racers. I was never interested in killing pedestrians so I've always avoided urban areas."

"Tell me what you love about all this. Jack told me you'd pretty much stopped until a few months ago."

Jack had a big mouth. Though Drew had to admit, he was glad Tyler was here. For the first time, he felt her moving towards him instead of away. That might not have happened as quickly, or at all, if they weren't together now.

"I started racing back in college. I was so angry, Ty. After leaving Harper Falls, I did three things. Worked, went to class, and got into fights."

"Drew." Tyler picked up his right hand. She ran her thumb over the knuckles, searching for some long-ago injury.

"I didn't lose very often."

Or at all. He had been a scary son of a bitch. Taking his rage out on any jerk he came across. If he caught a guy pushing his girlfriend around, Drew took him down. Pick on someone who couldn't defend himself? He stepped in. He would think of Regina, her cold cruelty, and he would beat the shit out of any poor sucker who got in his way.

"Jack never mentioned any of that."

"Jack never knew. I had it pretty well out of my system before classes started. I met Jack that first week. There was only one fight after that; my last."

"What happened?" Tyler held her breath.

"I didn't kill anybody, so you can relax. I did knock out an innocent guy, though. I was at a dive bar, as usual. I was already sick of fighting. Sick of my self-pity. I was calling it a night when I saw what looked like a big guy beating on a much smaller one."

Naturally, Drew couldn't walk away from that. He clocked the big guy. Knocked him on his ass. Then, when the police arrived thirty seconds later, he found out the "little guy" had attacked a woman. The "big guy" had stopped a rape and Drew had rewarded him with a fist in the face.

"Were you arrested?"

"Nope. I deserved to be. Instead, I made a lifelong friend."

The man hadn't pressed charges. He told the police Drew had been helping him. That it was the rapist who knocked him down.

"He saw something in me, Ty. Recognized the rage. He's the one who introduced me to racing. I don't know if it saved my life. It probably kept me out of jail."

"I'd like to meet him someday."

"You already have."

Tyler thought for a moment.

"You mean Tripper?"

"The one and only. He helped me get my first car dirt-cheap. Showed me the ropes; watched my back. I stopped fighting and took my aggressions out on the race course."

"And you loved it."

"I did."

Drew had taken to the world of unsanctioned racing like a duck to water. Early on, he couldn't afford to travel very far. Tripper would let him know when there was a race close enough to college to get there and back in a weekend.

"And after you graduated?"

"There wasn't much time for that. Jack and I spent every waking moment on our computers or being bodyguards. Tripper and that world became a thing of the past."

"What made you start again?"

"Tripper showed up in Los Angeles. He looked like hell, Ty. If you think he's gaunt now, you should have seen him then. Six feet tall and I doubt he weighed one-forty. He'd been sick, needed money. I would have given him every spare dime I had. I just didn't have any. We poured everything we earned back into H&W. Jack and I were so close, Ty. Closer than we knew. Three months later, we sold our first program. We were rich."

"But Tripper needed the money right away," Tyler said. "Even if you had known what was about to happen, he couldn't wait three months."

"He'd borrowed from loan sharks to pay his medical bills. The money was due and some mean ass dudes were on his trail."

"Jesus, Drew." Unconsciously, Tyler squeezed his hand — hard. "This is like something out of the movies."

Drew peeled her hand off his. Tyler gave him a sheepish grin, leaning over to lightly kiss the fingers she had almost crushed.

"Sorry, you develop a pretty strong grip as a sculptor."

"If you ever get your hands on my dick, I'll keep that in mind."

"*When* that happens, I'll be just the right kind of rough. Trust me, you'll love it."

Drew swallowed, then swallowed again. The blood he needed for thinking was quickly traveling south again. Okay, time to move this story along to its conclusion.

"Tripper needed money. He knew about a race just across the Mexican border with a big purse."

"You're a good friend. An idiot, but a good friend."

"Hey, I kind of resent that."

"The fact that you only *kind of* resent it speaks volumes."

"Fine," Drew grumbled. "The point is, I entered the race, won, paid off Tripper's debt. End of story."

Drew reached for her, his intent clear. Time for sex. Tyler swatted his hands away.

"Oh, no you don't. You can't leave it there. Why are you still racing? If you still feel the need to take care of Tripper, money is no longer a problem."

"Can't you let it go? I've already decided this is my last race. I'm hanging it up, heading for the stables."

"Save the clichés, Drew. I'm thrilled, ecstatic, over the moon."

"Good, then come here."

Tyler put a hand on his chest, keeping solid foot between them.

"Finish the story, Drew."

"Jesus, Ty." Drew ran a frustrated hand through his hair. "Fine. You want to hear it all? I thought it would keep me young."

"Vanity?" Tyler thought for a moment she had to have misheard. "You risked serious injury or worse. Because you were what? Staring your twenty-fifth birthday in the eye?"

"H&W was taking off. It was grown-up time, Ty. Racing was my way of putting my responsibilities behind me for a few days."

"And Jack? What would he do if you broke your neck?"

"Jack is the most stable, together person I've ever known. He was going to be fine before he met me; he'd be fine if I disappeared tomorrow."

This time she knew she heard him, she just couldn't believe what was coming out of his mouth. Unable to stay still, she hopped off the car and began to pace. She didn't have much room, only taking a few steps before she had to turn and walk the other way.

"Tyler. Why are you so angry? You didn't know what was happening."

"So if you had died, I wouldn't have cared? Is that what you're saying?"

"I don't know. Would it have mattered?"

Tyler went from hot to cold in an instant.

"Of all the horrible things you've said to me, that is the worst. By far."

And he knew it. Drew quickly slid off the car gathering her close. Tyler didn't fight, he wished she would. Her body was stiff, her face turned away.

"I'm sorry, Ty." Drew tightened his arms around her. "I said it without thinking. I didn't mean it."

"I've never wanted you dead. Not at my lowest point." She softened — just a little.

"You did want to punch me."

"I dreamt about it." She smiled. Then frowned. "Never anything serious, Drew. I'm glad I didn't know about all this. I would have worried."

"And that would have pissed you off."

"Yes, because I wouldn't have wanted to care. I told myself often enough that I didn't. Finding out in such a dramatic way that I was just kidding myself? It might have sent me after you just so I could kick you in the ass."

"Now I wish you had found out." He took a deep breath. Might as well get everything out on the table.

"The race before this one? That was the first time I thought of you."

"I don't understand."

Drew turned, lifting her so she sat on the trunk. He stood between her legs, hands on her waist. His eyes were dark, a little sad.

"Regina pulled that crap ass move."

Tyler nodded. "I still can't figure out how she knew which were my designs. I thought I was getting around her by submitting entries under four different names.

"She has eyes and ears everywhere," Drew said with disgust. "If you really want to know, I'll find out."

Tyler thought about it for a moment, then nodded.

"Isn't knowledge the ultimate power? If we ferret out Regina's moles, we become better prepared for whatever crap she'll pull next."

They both knew that was bound to happen. Regina couldn't leave well enough alone. And if Drew and Tyler took this home? If they were seen together around town? Who knew what might happen in that twisted mind. This time the top of her head might finally blow completely off.

"I'll start asking around — discreetly. Now," Drew looked at his watch, "I said five minutes. It's been more like half an hour. Prepare to start moaning."

Laughing, Tyler held him back. There was one more thing she had to know.

"How did you get her to back down?"

"You deserved a fair shot. I reminded her of that — from a distance."

"Drew." Tyler sighed with exasperation.

"I was livid, Ty. That sculpture is supposed to represent the best of Harper Falls. I read the contest manifesto. Open to anyone? Come on. How many people in that town are qualified to do a sculpture of any kind? And on the scale they wanted?"

"It was almost like they had me in mind from the start."

"You don't think they did? Or at least Regina did. She had a plan in mind from the very beginning."

"She was never going to let me or anyone else in Harper Falls do that sculpture."

"Like I said," Drew lightly tapped the side of her head, "smart. Still, you submitted your designs."

"I had to try."

"And she shot you down."

"I didn't take the news well. I told myself I was prepared. That it didn't matter."

"In other words, you lied to yourself."

"Big time." Grinning, Tyler thought about the day she got not one, but four rejection letters.

"I threw a bit of a fit. Happily, there were no witnesses. Dani and Rose let me vent."

"What are friends for?"

"Exactly. And I have two of the best. It was bitter, Drew. Knowing my design was perfect. I know that sounds egotistical."

Drew smiled. "Maybe. Just a little."

"A whole lot. But if I don't believe in myself, who will? That design was good."

"I know."

"You saw it?" That was a surprise.

"It wasn't hard to find a sympathetic member of the selection committee." A couple hundred bucks slipped under the table hadn't hurt either.

"Regina didn't just back down. She completely removed herself. Tell me what you did."

He pulled out the big gun.

"I threatened to throw her out of Harper House."

Tyler was speechless. She, Rose, and Dani had spent a lot of time speculating. What was there that would make the Ice Queen blink? What leverage did Drew have? Eviction had never occurred to any of them.

"You can do that?"

Drew nodded.

"My father left Harper House to me. I own every brick, every piece of furniture. She can't sell a piece of silver without my consent."

"Oh, that has to sting."

Tyler didn't feel an ounce of sympathy. She didn't feel satisfaction, either. That surprised her. Years of resentment, even hatred. Knowing Regina Harper's wealth was now a paper lion should have had her doing a jig.

"It's an empty feeling, isn't it?"

Drew recognized that look on Tyler's face. It mirrored how he felt when the lawyers told him the contents of his father's will. He should have rejoiced in Regina's downfall. After all her machinations. Her scheming to marry a man she didn't love or even respect just so she could have the money and power of the Harper name. To discover you've been left with nothing but your stacks of designer clothes and a few pieces of jewelry. The Harper Diamonds, the ruby necklace, emerald earrings. They were Drew's to give to his wife if he ever married. They were his to throw into the Columbia if the whim hit him.

"My father got the last laugh, so to speak. Too bad he had to die to get it."

Tyler could tell Drew didn't feel as glib as his words would indicate. Hoping to give some comfort, she put her hands on his shoulders, lightly massaging the tight muscles.

"Mmm, don't stop."

Enough. Question and answer time was over for now. Later. Not now.

Tyler increased the pressure of her fingers. Drew's neck was one big knot.

"You need to relax. How are you going to drive tomorrow when you can't even bend your neck?"

"It isn't quite that bad."

Drew demonstrated by making a circular motion with his head. He winced at the popping sounds. That couldn't be good.

"Bad enough. Turn around."

He complied without argument, sighing with pleasure. What Tyler lacked in skill she made up for with enthusiasm and strong fingers.

"I thought you were going to use sex to stop me from racing." Drew shifted his head to the left. "Oh, yes, baby. Right there."

Smiling, Tyler hit the spot again. This time she laughed aloud at Drew's almost orgasmic reaction.

"I was going to get you all revved up and then withhold sex until you agreed not to race."

"Well, that's honest." Drew moaned again. If Tyler kept this up, he might not need sex. Check that. No massage was *that* good.

"But I changed my mind."

"Good," he sighed. "Wait. You changed you mind about what? Sex?

No, sex? Do I have a vote?"

"I already know how you feel about the subject."

"Sex. Yes, please."

Tyler leaned forward. Just above where her fingers were trying to work some magic, she licked at Drew's neck. She made a long, slow journey up. His skin was salty and hot. Delicious. Savoring the flavor, she went in for another taste.

"I changed my mind about trying to convince you not to race. I don't like it, but I won't ask you not to."

"Between your hand and that tongue, right now I might agree to anything."

"Which is why I'm not asking." Tyler sank her teeth into the side of his neck, then kissed. Finally, she licked.

"Ask. Just don't stop."

"Does it matter that Al is out of commission?"

"A bit."

Drew turned his head once more, hoping she would move to that side. Tyler happily complied, kissing, nipping gently.

"Don't forget the tongue."

"Someone's getting greedy. I like it." She found out this side of his neck was equally delicious. "I'll take his place."

"Ty, honey, you have to stop jumping around with your subject matter. My dick is about to burst out of my jeans. Following *one* conversation is almost more than I can handle."

Tyler's lips curved. She rubbed her smile onto his skin.

"Al. Whatever he does, I'll do it."

"No."

"Is it highly technical?"

"Al is my spotter. He rides along and watches for potential shitstorms."

"I can do that."

"No. Tripper can do it."

She reached around and cupped him between his legs.

"I'm riding with you. End of discussion. And then you're hanging it up. From then on, I'm all the excitement you'll need." She squeezed. "I promise. I'll keep you young."

Drew spun around.

"End of discussion? Bullshit. I'm hanging it up because it's time." He ground himself into her, pushing her dress up to her waist. "Because I want to be there for you."

"Drew." Tyler's head fell back. Her breathing erratic.

"As for excitement? You're all I've ever needed. Come on. Let's take this back to the RV."

"Here. Now."

Tyler wound her legs around Drew's hips, pulling him tight. Her mouth found his, desperate, needy.

"I can't wait another second. Please, please, please tell me that's a condom I feel in your pocket."

Part laugh, part groan, Drew pulled out the foil packet.

"Mmm, always prepared."

"When you're around, I'd better be."

"Enough talk. Drop the pants, glove up, and get inside me."

"Has anyone ever smacked your ass? Cause if you keep bossing me around, I'm sure as hell going to."

"You can try. It'll just get you a pair of bruised balls."

With a growl, Drew ripped open the packet using only his teeth. His hands were busy tearing off Tyler's underwear and making sure she was ready for him. He almost wept when he felt her wet, slick heat surround his probing fingers.

"I could stop. Right now." He breathed the words into her ear, his teeth latching onto the lobe and giving a firm tug.

"I could grab hold of your dick and twist. Where would be the fun in that? I'd rather have you pounding me until I swear I see God."

"You'll be calling his name, don't you worry."

Taking her mouth, he ran his tongue along the seam until she was open and panting. He added another finger between her legs, stretching. Their moans mingled. She felt like heaven.

"Beg me. Tell me how much you want this."

Drew adjusted his stance until he was lined up, his cock aching to trade places with his fingers.

Tyler reached for him circling his rock hard length. She stroked. Once. Twice. She could feel the beat of his heart next to hers. Fast and wild.

"Beg me," she demanded. "I know you want it. Say you can't go on unless you're balls-deep inside of me."

Their eyes met. It was a battle of iron wills. The pleading was there, unspoken. Neither was willing to bend. Not with words.

Tyler nodded. Drew grinned.

"Now."

They shouted it together and surged forward.

One fluid movement joined them. It wasn't slow or easy. It was hard and animalistic. Sweat poured off them. They grunted and strained. This was going to be fast — they had no patience for anything else.

"Tell me you're close."

Drew threw his head back, the sound from his throat more bark than laugh.

"Jesus, Ty. It was all I could do not to come the second I was in you. I'm just waiting for you, honey."

"I don't need any more time. I've had ten fucking years."

Rearing up, she bit him on the neck. Hard.

It was the catalyst for a massive chain reaction. Drew's hips pulled back, pushed again, and hit Tyler's sweet spot. She saw stars. She saw a burst of lightning. She saw God. And Drew called His name.

The only sound in the tent was their breathing. Not quite as harsh as a few seconds before, it still filled the quiet, a reminder of the maelstrom that had just occurred.

Drew held Tyler close, afraid that if he moved, she would slide off the car and he would crumple to the ground. The only thing preventing both was his locked knees and they were none too steady.

"I need air and water."

"Sounds good."

"I can't move."

"Good sex can paralyze. It's a medical fact."

Tyler found the energy to smile, just barely.

"Great sex."

"Yes," Drew agreed.

"But that's not why I can't move. I think my ass is glued to the roof of the car."

"Impossible. There hasn't been enough time for all that lubricant to dry."

To prove his point, Drew gathered his last reserve of energy and stood. He brought Tyler with him, smoothing her dress back down so it covered her butt.

"Thank you. I was afraid we'd have to explain to the other drivers why there was a layer of skin decorating your car."

"Just hold on and let me get us back to the RV. I'll check your ass out when we get there."

Drew grabbed the gun, tucking it back into his rebuttoned jeans.

"Wait. How did I miss you getting rid of the condom?"

"Next time I promise to let you watch."

"Smartass."

Tyler wondered how she had gotten so comfortable with Drew carrying her around. This was twice in less than a day and she was content to relax in his arms. She squeezed one. His fabulously strong arms.

She was no lightweight. Even with a slender build, at five-nine, Tyler's body was strong. Strong meant muscle mass — she needed it to move around bulky pieces of sculpture. And muscle weighed more than fat.

"Why are you pinching me?"

Drew shifted her enough so he could unlock the RV. He didn't put her down until the door was locked up tight again.

"I wasn't pinching." Tyler ran her hand over his bicep and sighed. "I was admiring your ability to lug me around with such ease."

"Lug you around? Is that what I do? Kind of makes you sound like a sack of potatoes."

Instead of lifting, Drew backed her into the bedroom. He pulled off his t-shirt. Before Tyler could admire the view, he grabbed the hem of her dress.

"Lift your arms."

She did and the garment was whisked away leaving her in just her bra.

"I need another shower."

"Me too."

Drew traced her lips with one finger. He moved it down, over her chin, to her throat. His touch was light yet to Tyler, it was as though he caressed her entire body.

"I love bras with front closures."

He flicked it open with ease, pushing the straps down her arms. Tyler let it fall to the floor. She stood before him, naked. Ten years ago, she had felt shy, insecure. She worried that her breasts were too small, her legs too skinny. Instead of slim hips, she wanted curves. She longed to trade her pale skin for a more golden hue. Nothing had seemed good enough. She knew Drew wanted her. She just wished she had more to give.

She had been such a girl, Tyler thought. Now she was a woman. She was proud of her body. Every scar, every imperfection. They made her unique. They made her feel how every woman should feel. Beautiful.

Pulling her shoulders back, Tyler stood straight, letting Drew see the woman she was now.

Drew reached out, cupping her breast. His eyes were glued to the rosy-hued nipple that tightened when he ran his calloused thumb over the tip.

"You used to take my breath away. Did you know that?"

"I know I wanted to."

"You didn't even have to try. I was yours from that moment on the bridge when you hit me with those ever-changing gray eyes."

"You were the most beautiful boy I had ever seen." Tyler whispered the words almost reverently. "He wouldn't even be able to compete with the man you've become."

"Ty."

Drew kissed her. *I love you.* He felt deep down it was too soon. Things still needed to be said. Past actions explained. It couldn't stop him from feeling it, though. His heart didn't understand the passage of time. He loved her then. He loved her just as fiercely now. He would love her always.

"Jeans off, mister."

With a shake of his head, Drew ditched his pants and followed Tyler into the bathroom. Not wanting it to be far away in case of emergency, he put the gun next to the sink.

"When we get back to Harper Falls, you and I are going to have a talk about this bossy attitude of yours."

"Why is it okay in Mexico but not in Harper Falls?"

Tyler gave him a flirty look as she clipped her hair up and out of the way and stepped into the shower stall.

"It isn't okay in Mexico. Doing something about it right now is just… problematic."

"Problematic. Good word. Like this?" The stall was barely big enough for two, giving Tyler happy access to Drew's growing erection. She wrapped her hand around him and gave a gentle yet firm tug.

"That can be problematic." He hissed the words. Tyler added a bit of soap to her hand. The hiss turned into a moan.

"What shall we do about it?"

When Tyler would have increased the pressure and upped the rhythm, Drew pulled her hand away.

"No, you don't. I'm not doing anything in this tiny shower when we have a roomy, comfortable bed waiting in the next room. Wash up, dry off, and do it fast."

"Now who's getting pushy? And if you say *I'm the man,* you'll be taking care of that," she nodded towards his fully distended penis, "by yourself."

"If I added a please, would that help?"

"Always."

Tyler shut off the water. She stepped out of the stall, grabbing two towels. Drew took one, dried himself with just a couple of swipes. Tyler was more thorough. Watching her was a treat by itself.

She lifted one leg, resting her foot on the small counter. Careful to get in between each toe, she then reached for the bottle of lotion she must have left after her earlier shower. She was careful not to miss an inch, smoothing the cream over skin that Drew had found out was already wonderfully soft.

"Need some help?"

Tyler looked back at him with a small, provocative smile.

"Yes," she purred.

Grinning back, Drew reached for the bottle.

"You can help by getting out of here. I need more room to finish what I'm doing."

Already dismissing him, Tyler turned back, switching legs.

Drew narrowed his eyes, his gaze dropping to her rounded ass. An enticing few inches separated them. With a shrug, he thought, *why not?*

Tyler yelped. The sound of the slap he gave her on the way by was more startling than the actual contact. Still...

"That," she said with a frown, "was uncalled for."

"Depends on your point of view."

His view had been great. How was he supposed to resist an opportunity like that?

"You know I bruise easily."

"Honey, if that little tap caused a bruise, you need to see a doctor. Fast."

"Hmm. You have a point. I guess it wasn't that hard. Let's not start making a habit of it. Okay?"

Tyler joined him in bed. She was warm and fragrant. Running a hand up the side of her long leg, Drew had to admit he liked the results of her post-shower activity.

"You might like it." Drew gently squeezed her butt. "Some women like being spanked."

"I follow the live and let live philosophy."

Tyler straddled him, using both hands to press his shoulders into the mattress. She leaned close until her mouth just brushed his.

"Let me guess. You'll let me live as long as I don't slap your ass."

"Bright boy."

Tyler kissed him hard. It was fun being the aggressor. She liked being in charge. Her fun lasted about ten seconds.

Drew easily flipped Tyler around until she was under him.

"Party pooper."

"Play time's over."

He slid into her, one fluid movement that had them both gasping with pleasure. Tyler arched her neck. She reached for him, her hands finding his strong arms.

"Look at me, Ty. Keep your eyes on mine."

That was a request Tyler found she was happy to comply with. The intensity of the deep chocolate color had her sinking faster than the movement of his body over hers. He told her things in those few moments that she wasn't ready to hear with words. They made her breath catch. Her heart melt.

"Drew."

"Shh." He kissed her long and deep. "I know, Ty. I know."

Unlike earlier, this was a slow ride. There was no need to hurry. No feeling of desperation. They could take their time. Touch. Explore.

Drew held Tyler's hips, maintaining their connection, as he slid to the side until they were on their sides. Lifting her leg, he draped it over his hip, beginning a gentle, almost lulling rhythm. She liked this position. Face-to-face.

It was surprisingly satisfying. Every time he moved, he seemed to touch someplace new, someplace no one else had ever come close to.

"You like that?" Drew asked after she gasped with pleasure.

"You know I do."

"How about that?"

Tyler moaned. Just a gentle thrust, a slight change of angle. It sent a shiver through her. It vibrated down, enveloping Drew's cock.

"Holy shit, Tyler. What did you just do?"

"I was about to ask you the same question. Don't stop. Never let it end."

That was like asking the earth to stop turning. The end was inevitable. But they made it last as long as they could. Long, easy strokes became a bit faster. Warm, gentle kisses grew harder, almost fierce.

Tyler's hand dug into Drew's arm pulling him, urging him on.

Drew's fingers cupped Tyler's ass, bringing her closer with each thrust of his hips.

At the last moment, they froze, just for a second; crystal gray eyes locked on molten brown. They cried out together. They fell into bliss as one.

"HOW MANY TIMES do I have to say it?"

"Since you love the word, you might as well give it another go. Maybe this time will be the charm."

It was five o'clock. In the morning.

An ungodly hour as far as Tyler was concerned. She might stay up to see the sunrise. *Getting* up an hour before was just plain foolish.

"Tell me again why I'm tying my shoes in the dark?"

"Because you're too stubborn to turn on a light?"

Drew flipped the switch next to her head, the bedside lamp illuminating her hands and foot.

"Well, sure. Thank you, Thomas Edison."

She moved to the other foot, securing the laces with a quick bow.

"I told you to stay in bed. The race won't start for another three hours. And since you'll be here, locked inside, you could have slept through the whole thing."

"Now he's a comedian," she said to no one in particular.

"Be reasonable."

"Not a specialty of mine. Sorry."

Tyler buttoned up her jeans. She had traded the groupie girlfriend clothes for sneakers, jeans, and a t-shirt. She felt a slight twinge of regret over her choice. In her defense, yesterday when she had packed *I'm With Asshole* seemed appropriate.

"Lovely."

"Hey, I was going to wear it inside out. If you reconsider, so will I."

"Enough."

Drew took her by the shoulders. He was frustrated so he refrained from shaking her. He *did* give a look that had made men bigger than himself think twice about taking him on. Naturally, Tyler was not impressed.

"Give me three good reasons why I can't go with you."

"I'll give you ten."

"Jesus, Drew. Stop being such an overachiever."

"Make me laugh. I haven't done nearly enough of it in the past ten years." Drew kissed her nose. "I won't cave, Ty. Not over this one."

"Then don't race. You don't need to prove anything. If Tripper needs the money, write him a check. Hell, I'll write him a check. If it's too dangerous to take me along, don't do it."

She had a point, Drew thought. It wasn't as if he hadn't considered packing it in and heading home. Whatever thrill these races once provided had waned long ago. The time before the last one was supposed to *be* the last one. All the crap with Regina, his mixed up feelings for Tyler, sent him back.

He won the race but couldn't have cared less. If Jack hadn't given him a shitload of grief, that would have been that. How screwed up was it for him to enter this race just to throw a symbolic middle finger at his best friend? There wasn't even any satisfaction since Jack didn't know. Screwed up? More like morbidly twisted.

"You know what? Never mind." Tyler turned away, gathering up her things. She threw the few items into her bag then went to the bathroom and cleared it out.

"Tyler."

"Drew."

"If I don't do this, it will feel like I quit because you made me."

"Oh, my God. The male ego. Infinitely big and just as indecipherable."

"It is what it is."

"Idiot!" Tyler threw her bag into a corner. "Fine. Go. But if you get killed, don't come crying to me."

Drew was flabbergasted. Was this really going to be their first fight after ten years? It appeared so. He wasn't backing down. Tyler had her back to him, stiff as an iron rod. Sometimes there was no figuring life out.

"I'm not going to die."

Drew waited. Nothing. It seemed she'd had her say.

He grabbed his gun and keys. He threw one last look her way.

"Keep the door locked."

"Fuck you."

"Promise me, Tyler."

"If I don't, will you have to stay?"

"Are trying to piss me off?"

"Yes."

"Mission accomplished."

Drew wrenched open the front door, ready to storm out. Clenching his fist, he turned back.

"I know you aren't stupid, Tyler. I'm going to rely on that and assume you will stay in here, door locked."

"It was pretty stupid of me to come after you."

"Stubborn."

Tyler just pointed at her t-shirt then at him.

Instead of slamming the door, Drew shut it with an almost imperceptible snick. He wasn't ten steps away when the door flew back open.

"Damn it, Tyler."

Drew whirled around ready to have it out. Those three words were as far as he got.

Tyler threw herself into his arms with a jump, her legs wrapping around his waist. She peppered his face with kisses then hugged him close.

"Don't die. Promise me you won't die."

Drew held on, his face buried in the side of her neck. He inhaled her warm, citrus scent with long, deep breaths.

"I promise to stay put, door locked. Promise you won't die."

"Tyler. You are enough to drive a man to drink."

"Promise." She tugged on his hair, pulling his head back for a long, passionate kiss.

Drew was in no hurry. He let the kiss go on and on until she was ready for it to end.

After a while, when his lips were free, he said, "I promise not to die, Tyler."

"Tell Tripper I'll track him down if he lets anything happen to you."

"He's already half-afraid of you. That threat ought to push him over to downright terrified."

"You joke, but I'm dead serious."

"I know it."

He smoothed back her hair, letting her feet drop to the ground but not quite ready to let her go.

"One hundred miles. Fifty there, fifty back."

"Okay."

Drew gave her a light kiss on the end of her nose before watching until she was inside and the door firmly shut. He didn't try the knob. She promised to lock the door; it was locked. And it would stay that way.

TYLER REFUSED TO pace.

Instead, she sat, fidgeted, and tapped her toe. She rearranged Drew's cupboards, cleaned the bathroom, and dusted everything within an inch of its life. Unfortunately, it wasn't a very big area. When she was done and looked at the clock, an hour had passed. One lousy hour.

How long did these races usually take? She should have asked. Grabbing her phone. Looking it up would kill a couple of minutes.

Thinking for a moment, Tyler remembered her iPad was one of the things she had so unceremoniously jammed into her bag. The bag she had then thrown across the room in anger. Great. Poor tablet. There was a good chance it had been taken down by friendly fire. Just an innocent bystander. A casualty in a senseless war of wills.

Okay. She was officially going around the bend. At least there was no one around to witness her descent into silliness.

Now, where was she?

That's right. IPad. Bag.

She turned towards the bedroom only to freeze in her tracks. Someone was trying to get into the RV. The rattling of the doorknob made the hair on the back of Tyler's neck stand up.

Looking around for something she could use as a weapon, her eyes skipped over the broom, a dustpan, and a long metal rod that seemed to have no particular purpose. It would do in a pinch but was unlikely to stop an assailant for long. Especially one who was bigger and stronger.

Furniture polish. That had to hurt if sprayed in the eyes, right? There was bleach, but she would have to toss that. Too iffy. Pledge it was.

Standing to the side of the door, Tyler held up the can, ready to do battle.

Thank goodness she hesitated. Just for a second.

"Drew?"

He stepped into the RV looking exactly as he had when he left. No blood, no broken bones. Relief flooded her body.

"If you plan on polishing my knob, I'd prefer you used your mouth. That stuff stings."

"Precisely the point.

Tossing the can away, Tyler walked into Drew's waiting arms.

"You didn't race."

"Nope."

"For me?"

Drew held her tighter.

"For us."

Chapter Eleven

"**H**E JUST WALKED away?"

"That's it. No more racing. No more taking stupid chances."

"Because he loves you."

Tyler hesitated. Love. After all they had been through, why was that the thing that made her nervous? Dani and Rose wanted their friend to have what they had. Men who loved them beyond all else.

If there was one thing Tyler had learned, it was that nothing was guaranteed. There was a time she would have sworn Drew was her present and her future all rolled into one. Ten years and a broken heart later, Tyler no longer believed in a sure thing. She wasn't getting ahead of herself this time. Day to day. It was her new mantra.

"We aren't quite there yet."

Rose patted her hand. No one understood better how difficult it was to commit fully to another person. Luckily, Jack had been unwilling to take no for an answer or she might still be alone, convinced that love was not for her.

"Give it time. You'll get there."

Rose had invited them all to dinner. She was trying out a recipe Jack's mother had assured her was failsafe. She loved her future mother-in-law, trusted her. Still, when it came to the guest list, only friends were present for what she hoped would be her first successful, grownup sit-down meal prepared entirely by herself.

If it turned out to be inedible, they could share a good laugh and order pizza.

"I think you're worried for nothing. It smells amazing."

"Maybe." Rose bent down to peer through the glass door of the oven. "Jack's mom was very encouraging over the phone. Of course, this is a woman who doesn't understand the concept of not being able to cook. She's a master. Her daughters and granddaughters came out of the womb knowing the difference between a whisk and spatula."

"There's a difference?" Tyler asked. She poured herself some more wine before steering Rose away from the kitchen and back to the living room.

"My question exactly. She seemed to think I was making a joke so I went along with it."

"Sit."

Dani patted the cushion next to her.

"I know I'm being silly. Dinner will be fine. No. It's going to be great. I just wish Jack could have been here a little earlier, for moral support. He always makes cooking fun. If something gets burned or dropped, he laughs it off. I'm the one who gets tied up in knots."

"Where *are* the guys?" Lila Fleming, Alex's sister, sat in a plush chair next to the fire. Jack's dog Edgar, a favorite of them all, lay with his head resting on her feet. He'd had a busy day protecting the yard from squirrels and was content to sleep while his Rose entertained her friends.

"I think Jack is kicking Drew's ass down in the gym at H&W."

Tyler snorted. "In his dreams. You may think he's a superhero. I say Drew can take him, any day, anytime, anywhere."

Lila was new to the group so it took her a moment to decide if Rose and Tyler were actually arguing. In her experience, women could get fierce about their men. Especially with other women.

She shouldn't have worried. There was a definite twinkle in the eyes of the two friends. Make that three friends. Dani wasn't going to let her man's fighting skills go unremarked.

"Alex is an ex-Army badass. He has the scars to prove it."

"Two votes for Alex," Lila chimed in. Though come to think of it, she had no idea what they were voting for. "Why am I voting for Alex?"

"Because you're a good sister and we have hot men who we like to brag up," Dani laughed.

"They aren't really fighting?"

"I doubt it, Lila."

"I don't," Rose said with a shudder. "Ninety-nine point nine percent of the time, Jack is this easygoing, unflappable sweetheart. Piss him off? Scary. One time I walked in on the aftermath. Jack took down guys that had him by over fifty pounds. Blood, crying. It was pitiful."

"You thought it was hot."

"Okay," Rose conceded. "We had wild shower sex while those poor guys were still trying to get back on their feet."

"They are friends, right?" Lila found it all a bit confusing.

"And partners," Tyler nodded.

"Tell her what happened," Dani urged. "Tell us all. You've been pretty vague about your trip to Mexico. Time to spill."

"We just got back yesterday. When have I had time to do more than give you a rough outline?"

"You have plenty of time now. Wait a sec." Rose jumped up and grabbed the open bottle of wine, giving everyone a refill. She plopped back down next to Dani, a look of anticipation on her face. "Go."

Laughing, Tyler started at the beginning, as much for her own benefit as Lila's. It had been such a whirlwind; she still tried to wrap her head around some of it.

Almost an hour later, she sat back. It was an amazing story. Full of action, adventure, intrigue, laughter, sex. Her friends were particularly interested in the sex. Then the ending where the man sacrifices his last race to be with the woman he… cared about. Pure gold. Better than a Hollywood rom-com any day.

"I give it four and a half *wows*."

"Why not five?"

"Because," Dani said. "He still hasn't told you why he did what he did."

"That's as much my fault as his."

"Why?" Rose asked. "He's ready to talk… finally. Suddenly you aren't ready to listen?"

"I know. I wish I had a simple answer."

"Give us the complicated one."

"I've been letting myself remember what it was like when Drew and I were together. I told you that."

"Yes. Those memories helped you lose all the anger you have carried around."

"For the first time in a long time, I could look at Drew without seething. I like how that feels."

"We like how it looks on you."

Surprised, Tyler turned to Rose. "How it looks on me?"

"Is that the right way of putting it?" Rose asked Dani.

"Sometimes, not always, you seemed sad," Dani explained. "More so in the past few months when you've been pushed into Drew's company."

Rose nodded. "Before I got involved with Jack, it was easier for you to avoid any contact. Suddenly, he was everywhere. I know you acted like it pissed you off."

"It did," Tyler insisted.

"Yes. It also made you sad. The pissed off suited you. That was healthy. It even brought a nice rosy glow to your cheeks."

"Well, crap."

"Like the one you have now."

"Go on, I'm fascinated."

"Uh oh." Dani turned to Lila. "Tyler likes to think she's tough as nails. Let me tell you a secret. She's a marshmallow. Cries during greeting card commercials, coos over pictures of puppies."

Tyler sighed. Her friends could be royal pains in the butt. Good thing she loved them.

"I think you're straying from the original point."

"No, just setting the scene. As hard as you try, my friend, it's impossible to always hide the sad. Seeing Drew brought you down. Rose and I are ecstatic to see you happy again."

"I am happy," Tyler nodded. "If I hear what Drew has to say, I might lose it. I don't know if I can stand another broken heart — the same broken heart that is finally starting to heal."

"Oh, Tyler." Rose felt her own heart tighten in sympathy. "I understand the need to keep the past in the past. I can speak from experience. Once the air is cleared, you will knock this two-ton weight off your chest that you hadn't realized was there."

"Tonight. We'll go to his place. Finally, everything can be brought out into the open. Let the chips fall where they may."

"It will be fine, I know it." Dani patted her knee. "And, you can tell us what Drew's house looks like."

Tyler looked at the other women. Well, that was a surprise.

"None of you have been there?"

"No."

Dani and Lila shook their heads.

"Any particular reason?"

"I guess there hasn't been any reason to go. We always seem to end up here or we go out."

"He's just down the road. Drew never invited you and Jack over?"

"I get the feeling he likes his fortress of solitude. But as I said, you can describe it to us in detail. Jack says he just finished putting in a pool. On the roof."

Tyler didn't have to close her eyes to picture it. A pool on the roof. It was such a silly thing. Or so it seemed when she was sixteen and planning her dream house. She and Drew got a little silly at times. Then again, why not? The basic design was grounded in reality. After that, they threw in pure fantasy.

That's what the pool had been. Something Tyler had seen in a magazine. She never really imagined she would know someone who had one. She couldn't wait to see it.

"What is that little smile about?"

"Just thinking about stuff."

Dani and Rose exchanged glances.

"You're thinking about having sex in that pool."

"Pool sex? Really?"

They all turned to Lila, laughing at her wide-eyed amazement.

"I mean, obviously I've read about that kind of stuff."

"Ah, do you remember when you were that young and innocent?"

"Yes," Dani said, her green eyes twinkling. "I was twenty-two and just out of college. Then I spent two sex-filled weeks with little Lila's big brother. Talk about an eye opener. *Innocent* went out the window after the first day."

"Hey, there are some things a sister doesn't need to hear."

"I agree." Rose winked at Lila. "All you need to know is that Alex keeps Dani happy — in *every* room of the house."

"Enough," Rose said, taking pity on Lila. "Look at her cheeks. We have a blusher, ladies. That's a first for this group."

"That's because, according to Father Malloy, we are shameless hussies."

"And proud of it."

Tyler, Dani, and Rose clinked their glasses together.

Lila laughed with them. She took a sip of wine. It wasn't easy to make new friends. She had come to Harper Falls on blind faith. Her business was booming, her brother was safe, in love and only a few minutes away. Lila could honestly say the women in this room were three of the best she had ever known. The day she decided to move across the country was a very good day indeed.

"You still haven't told me why Drew and Jack are fighting. Or not fighting. Was that point ever settled?"

"It seems unlikely. Though Jack has a good reason to be pissed. You see, Drew had been lying to him for almost ten years."

"I DID NOT lie."

Drew didn't know how many times he said that in the last ten hours. He did know Jack wasn't buying it.

"Did you let me believe you were borderline suicidal?"

"Maybe, but—"

"Then you lied."

As soon as he arrived at work that morning, Drew called Jack and Alex into his office. As his best friend for the past ten years, Jack had dealt with the racing issue much longer than Alex. Still, he didn't think anyone would mind if he explained it all at once. It seemed silly to tell the same story twice.

Jack didn't mind Alex being present. His problem was with Drew. He listened in silence until the story was completely told. Then he let loose with a string of expletives. Drew gave him points for some creative combinations. *Horse ass sucking ball licker?* Really?

"Somebody should be writing these down. I could have used some of them yesterday when I went off on you," he said to Alex during a brief pause.

"You think this is funny?"

"No."

Drew tried to sound contrite — he failed. The fact was he did think it was a little funny. If not the situation, then Jack's reaction to it. His normally laid-back partner was blowing a gasket. How could he not find that amusing?

"Yes, you do. I know that smirk."

"I do not smirk."

Jack rounded on Alex. Up until now, he had kept wisely silent.

"I ask you as an impartial observer. Is that or is that not a smirk?"

"I'm Switzerland," Drew said, holding up his hands "In fact, I don't know why I'm here. This is between the two of you."

"You're here because this twisted, shit-eating jerk pulled you into his lies."

"Wow. I hope you use some industrial strength antiseptic before you kiss Rose with that mouth."

"And that's another thing. Do you have any idea how hard it was for Rose and Dani to keep your activities from Tyler?"

"When did I ask them to do that?"

"When you put them in the position of not wanting to cause her any more pain."

Jack held up his hands to mimic a scale.

"Lie to her or hurt her?"

The hand representing the lie sank.

"Surprise, surprise. You picked the lie."

"All I can do is say I'm sorry, Jack. You took a few unrelated incidents and came up with a false conclusion. Maybe I should have set you straight. I didn't. Water under the bridge."

"I don't think so."

"Are you honestly telling me that after everything we've been through, this is going to break our friendship?"

"What?" Jack gave him an *are you crazy* look. "I'm pissed, Drew. Seriously, bone-deep, pissed. I'll get over it, eventually."

Drew sighed with relief. Pissed he could handle. Losing Jack? He didn't ever want to go there.

"What can I do? Name it."

Jack shook his head. "This is one I'm going to have to stew over, Drew. No quick fixes."

Drew sighed. He didn't feel like laughing anymore. In essence, he had lied to his best friend. Letting him think the worst. Leaving him to worry without explanation. What Drew thought to be a minor omission was a much bigger deal to Jack. He would respect that and deal with the fallout. However long it took.

"There might be a way."

Drew turned to Alex.

"A way to what?"

"To get Jack over his mad. Or at least speed up the process."

Hell yes, Drew wanted to shout. Whatever it took, he was on board. He looked at Jack. Ultimately, this was up to him.

"What did you have in mind?"

"In the Army, if a couple of my guys had a dispute, I would have them fight it out. In this case, since you're the injured party, I'd say one shot. Hard as you want. Pick your spot."

"You want me to hit Drew? You think that will clear the air?" Jack sounded unconvinced, but he looked intrigued.

"Not clear, exactly. More like lessen the toxic smoke he's been blowing out of his ass."

"I thought you were Switzerland?"

"Jack is right," Drew said with a bit of twinkle in his eye.

"When you pulled Dani into this, you pulled me in," Alex told him. "Fine."

Drew didn't have any room to grumble. Jack was as angry as he'd ever seen him. Alex needed to stand up for his woman. He wondered what Rose and Dani would have to say when he saw them? Not something he was looking forward to. Maybe if he showed up with a bruised face, they would cut him a little slack.

"What do you think?"

He could almost see the wheels turning in Jack's brain. Drew knew from experience that his partner would weigh the pros and cons carefully before coming to a decision. It might take hours, even days before—"

"Count me in."

Okay. So much for mulling things over.

"Let's do this."

Drew moved his jaw from side to side, making a memory of how it felt pre-punch. It might be hard to chew for a few days.

"Not now. We have a video conference at eleven-thirty. I'd rather not have to explain why one of us has a messed up face."

"One punch," Drew called after the exiting Jack. "That was the agreement. Jack? Damn it, Jack. Answer me, you bastard. What are you laughing at?"

Alex shook his head. He followed Jack out of Drew's office without a word.

"Brilliant," he said when he was sure Drew was out of earshot.

"Brilliant and evil. He's going to spend the day thinking about that punch. When are you going to do it? What part of his body will you hit? Did you see him rotating his jaw?"

"I did. He deserves to suffer a bit."

"Mission accomplished."

Alex slapped Jack on the back then left to take care of some paperwork. A necessary evil that could only be put off so long.

Jack sat in his chair, swiveling until he faced the bank of windows that covered the west-facing wall. He was not a man easily angered. When he got mad, it didn't last long. The rage he had vented at Drew was already gone. By the end of the day, he doubted he would be able to raise enough steam to make punching his friend at all satisfactory.

With a weary sigh, Jack lifted his gaze. Harper House. One look at the imposing structure and he felt all his remaining anger fade away. Drew had grown up in that place. Not a home. A cold edifice dominated by an ice queen who wasn't capable of even the smallest gesture of kindness or affection.

Yet in spite of that, Drew had a big heart. He was loyal to a fault and when he loved, he did so with everything he had to give.

Jack couldn't imagine what it was like to give your heart to a woman and then live without her. Ten years. An eternity.

It was a relief to find out Drew's racing was never motivated by a death wish. Jack would have appreciated discovering that little bit of information sooner. Still, if it helped get him through, Jack wasn't going to quibble.

Thank God it was over. Drew and Tyler were on the road back to each other. The racing was a thing of the past. Hopefully, any bumps ahead would be mild ones.

He didn't need to hit Drew to get over his anger. Smiling, Jack formed his hand into a fist. His mad had fizzled. When he punched his buddy, it wasn't going to be a chore. It was going to be pure, unadulterated pleasure.

"FINALLY! I THOUGHT they would never get here."

Rose had spoken with Jack an hour earlier. Not to check up, she assured him. She needed to know when they would arrive for dinner. As ruses went, it wasn't a very good one. Jack knew the real reason she called. He didn't satisfy her curiosity. Instead of giving her an update, he told her they would be along soon.

"They certainly took their sweet time."

Rose came to stand on Tyler's left. Dani joined her on the right. Lila trailed behind, happy to observe from the doorway.

"I'm not rushing down there. It isn't like they're returning from battle."

"Right," Rose nodded. "Why do men think fighting is the only solution?"

The three women exchanged grins.

"Fine," Rose conceded. "We've kicked some ass in our day. It isn't our choice, is it? If one of you pissed me off, I wouldn't challenge you to fist-a-cuffs at twenty paces."

"How would that work? Don't you have to be next to someone to punch them out?"

Rose snorted, bumping Tyler with her hip.

"You know what I meant, smarty pants."

Jack's SUV pulled to a stop. Alex followed right behind on his motorcycle. Drew was next, driving his car-of-the-day — an ice gray Porsche.

A 1967... something. Nice. Tyler couldn't remember the model. Not that it mattered. It was a car Drew used to covet. He would show her pictures, dreaming of the day that he would have one of his own. Looking at the sleek lines, she had to admit it was even better looking in person.

"Do you realize we have six cars here? That isn't counting the one in the garage that I drove earlier to do some errands. As environmentalists, we suck."

Tyler was only listening with half an ear. She waited for Drew to step out of his car. She swore that if Jack had messed up that gorgeous face, she would never talk to him again. Then she would give Drew the silent treatment. He deserved what Jack gave him.

Wait. Did that make sense? The second she saw Drew she stopped worrying about it. As far as she could tell, he looked... perfect.

It was after six, which meant the sun was down. Floodlights illuminated the driveway. The three men walked towards the house, each crouching in turn to pet Edgar. The dog knew his job. Fawn over Jack; he *adored* Jack. Then greet anyone lucky enough to be with Jack. You had to love a dog who had his priorities straight.

"Are we late?"

"Yes," Rose answered. She stood with arms crossed over her chest. "Are you hurt?"

"Not a scratch."

Jack waited where he was. Drew and Alex flanking him.

"He looks like he did when he left this morning," Rose whispered to her friends.

"I don't see a mark on Drew."

"I see three mouth-watering men waiting for us." Dani looked at her friends. "Why are we up here when they are down there?"

Not waiting for them to answer, Dani ran down the steps and into Alex's waiting arms.

"Looks good to me."

Rose skipped the steps, jumping to the ground.

Jack didn't wait for her to come the rest of the way.

"There's my girl," he said before taking her mouth with his.

Drew walked past the two couples, his eyes on Tyler. He jogged up the steps stopping a few inches from her.

"You came to me."

"Someday, when I've earned the right, I'll stand and wait for you. I figure that day is still a ways in the future. I have a lot to make up for, Ty." He picked up her hand, lacing his fingers with hers.

Neither of them noticed when their friends went in the house or heard the closing of the door. They were in their own world.

"Someday," Tyler agreed. *Soon*, she thought to herself.

"After dinner." He kissed the back of her hand. "Will you come home with me?"

"Yes."

"I have a story to tell you. It won't be easy to hear."

"I know. It won't be easy to tell."

Drew gathered her close, swaying slightly to music that played only for them.

Tyler pulled back just enough to examine his face.

"How are you?"

"Jack let me off easy. I'll tell you about it later."

"Another story?"

"This one has a happy ending."

Tyler took a deep breath. Her eyes were a hazy gray. A little worried, a little unsure. She lay her head on his shoulder.

"I want one of those."

"Me too, Ty." He wrapped his arms tight around her waist. "Me too."

Their own happy ending. What had seemed impossible only a few days ago was now right there for the taking. Drew was determined to finally have the woman of his dreams. Nothing, and especially no one would stop him. Not this time.

Chapter Twelve

TYLER FOLLOWED DREW in her car.

Dinner had been relaxed, free of any lingering anger or tension. The story Drew promised to tell her entertained them through most of the meal. He and Jack trading off on the narration. Every now and then Alex would throw in a piece of colorful commentary. By the time dessert was served, they were laughing; hard feelings put behind them.

Rose passed the bowl of fluffy, perfectly prepared mashed potatoes. The meal that she had agonized over was a hit. Roast chicken was crispy on the outside, juicy and succulent inside. Warm buttermilk biscuits disappeared in record time. The braised carrots and onions had just the right amount of bite left to them. Jack's mother warned about the horrors of mushy vegetables. Rose followed her instructions like a pro. She beamed like a proud parent as her food was eaten with obvious enjoyment.

"You had to wait all day?" Tyler asked between bites. "That couldn't have been much fun."

"Not just wait. This guy," Drew tipped his head toward Jack, "kept popping his head into my office. *Tick, tock*, he would say doing a fair Vincent Price. *I am the voice of vengeance.*"

"Really, Jack? Melodramatic much?"

"I thought it was effective," he said, winking at Rose.

She just shook her head. She loved the man, every sexy, goofy inch of him.

"Effective? Hell, by the end of the day, I didn't know what to expect. Was he going to hit me? Dip me in wax?"

"Wax?" Lila looked around. Everyone was laughing except her.

"Movie reference," Alex explained.

"Oh, right."

"We didn't watch much TV when we were growing up," Alex told their friends. "I had to do a lot of catching up when I started seeing Dani. I'm still clueless about half of the time."

"You're getting better," Dani assured him. "Though you would get a lot more out of our movie marathons if you would pay attention and keep your hands to yourself."

"I always took girls to the movies to neck. Old habits die hard. Besides, I don't remember any complaints the other night when we missed the end of *From Here to Eternity*."

"True," Dani smiled. "That beach scene gets me every time."

Preferring not to hear any more about her brother's love life, Lila spoke up.

"So what happened? Obviously, Jack didn't clean your clock. How did you get out of it?"

"Jack is so understanding and compassionate he decided to forgive and forget, right?"

"I hate to disillusion you, my love. When I met Drew down in the gym, I had every intention of punching him out. My degree of mad diminished by the end of the day but not *that* much."

"Yet here he sits, unbruised and unbowed."

"Oh, he's bowed," Jack assured Dani. "I got my apology, a very sincere one. Then when I went to hit him, the bastard made me laugh."

"What did you say?" Tyler asked.

Drew shrugged. "I just pointed out that since I'm such an idiot, it must be my good looks that attracted you. If Jack broke my nose or knocked out a tooth, you'd dump me in a heartbeat."

"Because right now you're barely hanging on in the looks department," Lila scoffed. "A broken nose would make you hideous."

"Exactly. I would end up alone the rest of my miserable days."

"Drawing a lipstick-covered face on the back of your hand to represent your simulated girlfriend. He even has a name for her. Jackoff Judy."

"Alex!"

"I'm just repeating what Drew said," Alex told Dani.

"I planned on leaving that part out."

"Oops," Alex grinned. "My mistake."

"The point is I was laughing so hard I couldn't work up the ire or the strength to do more than give him a shove."

"It was a pretty hard shove," Drew assured Jack, rubbing the side of his shoulder.

"You do realize that I don't come off very well in this story."

"I was thinking the same thing," Rose nodded. "According to you, Tyler is so shallow, one little imperfection and she's out the door. Not very flattering, Drew."

"Lord, don't tell me I have something else to apologize for?"

"Cut the dramatics, Meryl Streep," Tyler laughed. "We're good."

The group soon moved on to another subject, then another. The talk was light and entertaining. Overall, a normal evening spent with friends. One Tyler hoped would be repeated many times in the years to come.

As she eased her car to a stop, Tyler slammed the brakes on her thoughts. It was too soon to picture Drew and her together years from now. *Baby steps*, she reminded herself. Get tonight out of the way. See what tomorrow brings.

Before they left Jack and Rose's, Drew told her about his underground garage. He said to follow him so her car would be secure for the night. Tyler hadn't known what to expect. Some version of the Batcave? A silly thought. As it turned out, she wasn't that far off.

The entrance was off to the side of the house, hidden by a grove of trees. The ground seemed to open up right before her eyes. Two large doors slowly lifted up revealing a gently sloping ramp. As instructed, Tyler drove her car in behind Drew's.

Tyler had no idea how technically difficult it was to set up a place like this. She didn't care. She would let Drew worry about stress joints and retaining walls, or whatever was involved. Tyler just let herself marvel.

This was like no underground parking garage she had ever seen. Naturally, cement and beams were the dominant materials. After that, all bets were off.

Tyler parked next to Drew's Porsche, her Camry looking a little sad in a sea of Rolls Royces and Alpha Romeos. All tucked away in their luxurious, state-of-the-art hidey-hole.

"What do you think?"

"The only word that comes to mind is *wow*. *My* bedroom isn't this nice." Tyler did a full circle turn. "How many cars do you have?"

"As of yesterday? Two hundred and thirty-four." He thought a moment. "Make that thirty-three. I sold one to a guy we were trying to do a deal with. The Maserati sealed it."

"Naturally."

"Too much?"

"Yes." Tyler spun around, trying to take them all in. She stopped when she was face-to-face with Drew. "I want to drive every one of them."

Tyler understood. Of course, she did. Why had he been worried? Someone else would have been surprised by the number of cars in his collection. Maybe even appalled. Tyler didn't even blink. No one understood him like Tyler did.

"It will take a while. Some are in New York, Los Angeles, and London. I like to have my own car to drive when I travel."

"Why don't we start with the ones here in Harper Falls? By the time I've worked my way through them, we might be ready for New York, Los Angeles, and London."

"Sounds like a plan."

"You could kiss me. That's also a plan."

"An even better one."

His lips were soft against hers. Gentle. They held a promise of more to come. Tyler sank into him, her arms banding around his waist.

Lovely, she thought. Passion was wonderful. She was all for it. This, though, this was something else. Exciting in a different way. A kiss that spoke from the heart.

"Ready to see the rest?"

Drew took her hand, leading her to the back of the garage. As they approached what looked like an elevator, Tyler's stomach did a sudden flip-flop.

"I don't know, Drew."

"What's wrong?"

How to explain? Stepping into the garage was one thing. Once she entered the house, there was no going back. Secrets were about to be revealed, the ugly part of their past dredged up. Five minutes ago, she would have said she was ready. Now she wasn't so sure.

"I'm scared too."

"Do you remember the last time you said that to me?"

Drew nodded. "When we were talking about the first time we made love."

Smiling, Tyler tightened her fingers around his. They survived that just fine; they would get through this.

"Together?" he asked.

Tyler took a deep breath.

"Together."

The elevator doors opened. Tyler peered around before following Drew inside.

"What?"

"I thought there might be some outerspacey gizmo that could teleport us from room to room."

"Not yet." Drew laughed.

Just a plain old elevator. Tyler had to admit she was a bit disappointed.

"Not yet? Does that mean you're working on one?"

"I have to admit that kind of thing is beyond my capabilities. As soon as one is available, though, I'm on it."

Tyler had a million questions running through her head. Nonsensical, outrageous questions about toilet seats and biodegradable trash bags. The moment the elevator doors opened, she couldn't remember even one.

Drew stood back, waiting for Tyler's reaction. He wanted her to love the house as much as he did. He wanted her to see the details, the little touches. This was her house as much as his. Dreamed of as teenagers. Laughing over silly details, pounding out minor disagreements.

What if her tastes had changed? What if she didn't want a bank of windows in the front of the house to catch the morning sunlight? What if—

"I can't believe you remembered the oversized kitchen island." Tyler ran a hand over the smooth, black granite shot with lines of sparkling bronze.

"What do you think of the cupboards?"

"The color is perfect."

A warm oak, they went all the way to the ceiling. Tyler hated that open space that would get dirty and greasy. She cleaned the area often enough in her mother's kitchen to know she didn't want that in her own.

Perfect. How else could she describe everything from the hardwood floors to the non-window treatments?

"Hidden blinds? Just like at my place."

"I wondered if you still had an aversion to curtains."

"They get dirty," Tyler shrugged.

Tyler loved every inch of the place. It wasn't exactly as she had pictured her dream house. For some reason when she was seventeen, she thought a purple couch and matching accent wall would be the height of chic. Thank goodness Drew hadn't agreed. Then or now.

Drew had the time of his life watching Tyler explore. This was how he pictured it when he was alone in this big house. It always felt a little lonely, a little empty. He would buy new things to fill the spaces. He knew what was missing. The one thing his money couldn't get him. Tyler.

"I can't believe you did this, Drew."

Tyler sat down on a big, overstuffed chair that was the perfect shade of sea foam. Actually, she sank in more that sat. Again, perfect.

"Is it too much? Too weird?"

Scooting over, Tyler patted the cushion, inviting him to join her. She snuggled close, breathing in his scent.

"This is how I would picture us. I never dreamed..."

"What?"

"You remembered it all."

He thought about the framed drawing in his office. He hated to move. The perfect place, the perfect moment. The perfect woman.

"I want to show you something."

Taking her hand, he led Tyler out of the room and down a wide, well-lit hallway.

"Pale lavender," Tyler whispered when she saw the walls. "I thought you said the color wasn't manly enough."

"I guess my definition of manly has changed."

Of all the things he could have said, for some reason *that* made her heart go zing.

Drew opened the double doors at the end of the hall, a dim light turning on when they entered.

"Motion sensitive?"

"Mmm, I hate walking into a dark room."

"Still have that zombie phobia?"

"They eat a person's brains, Ty. That is nothing to laugh at."

Tyler was about to disagree when her eyes fell on the wall behind his desk.

"Oh, Drew. You saved it."

Her hand lifted then fell back to her side. It was the drawing she made of the outside of this very house. Meticulous in detail, and done on a thirty-six inch square of the finest quality paper Tyler could afford at the time. She spent hours with her colored pencils, getting every line just right. Even the landscaping was there. She researched how each plant would look and then she did her own interpretation. It was to be her gift to him on the day he graduated from high school.

Instead, it ended up a crumpled ball thrown at his feet. He broke her heart; she destroyed their dream house. At the time, it seemed so symbolic. She looked closer. Creases, small but definite could still be seen. It *was* the original.

"How?"

"A lady who worked for my mother ironed it out as well as she could. Then I rolled it up and kept it until I…" Drew sighed. "I didn't look at it again until I was planning this place. Too painful, I guess."

Tyler held out her hand, needing the connection.

"You got it just right, Drew."

They stood for a few moments, in silence looking at a piece of their past.

"Pretty clever for a couple of kids."

Tyler laughed, putting her head on his shoulder.

"We were always a little ahead of the curve. I sometimes wonder if I wouldn't have been better off staying a kid a little longer."

"I know what you mean. I always wanted out; you were the same. You can't plan your escape and stay a child. Not if you really want out."

"We never would have met."

"Do you…" Drew swallowed. It hurt to even think the words he needed to ask.

"No regrets, Drew."

"Come on."

Tyler understood the doubt she heard in his voice.

"Don't get me wrong. I have cursed you so many times. I'm surprised you still have your balls or your dick."

"Pictured chopping them off?" Drew winced at the thought.

"Mostly they shriveled up, leaving nothing but tiny little, dried nubbins. Useless and pretty hilarious."

"Normally I'm a big fan of that inventive mind of yours. This time I'll take a pass."

"My point is. I wouldn't change a moment of the time we had. The way it ended? Yes, of course. But not anything before."

"Thank you, Ty. That means the world to hear you say that."

"Show me the pool."

"Ty." Drew shook his head, a little smile on his lips.

"I know. I pushed you to tell me. I gave you grief because you wouldn't. Now I'm stopping you." She sighed. "This feels so good, Drew. I don't want it to end, not yet."

Drew understood. If he could, he would wrap them up in cotton, preserving this moment, insulating them from the rest of the world. A lovely thought, one that was utterly unrealistic.

"Ty," Drew sat on the edge of his desk drawing her between his legs. He touched her cheek tenderly. "Right now, we are standing on silt. Our foundation is shaky. Once everything is out in the open, we can move to bedrock. Like this house — built to last."

"Or we can watch it all crumble. The break has been healing, Drew. This could shatter it irrevocably."

"Only if we let it." Drew's eyes met hers. "I've been living in limbo, Ty. If I tell you why I left, that's it. End of story. Either you forgive me or you don't. For too long I've been afraid of the answer."

"Not anymore?"

"A little. The difference is, now I know there's still something there to fight for. The past few days have shown me that. And I will fight, Ty."

"No walking away this time?"

Drew shook his head. "Neither of us knows how you'll react to what I'm going to tell you. You might get up and leave. You might tell me you never want to see me again."

He stopped her before she could protest.

"You don't know, Ty."

Tyler opened her mouth then closed it without speaking. He was right. She couldn't anticipate her reaction.

"Hey, don't be sad."

"Aren't you?"

"Look where we are, Ty. A month ago, even a week, could you imagine standing here? I dreamed of this a million times, never believing I could have it. Now that I do, I'm not letting go ever again. Be prepared to have me in your life, Tyler Jones. This right here?" He pulled her close, kissing her with everything he had. "*This* is the new norm."

A little breathless, Tyler laughed. It was such a happy sound, filling the room. *No*, Drew swore to himself, he was never going back to a Tyler-less world.

"Tonight, we put the past behind us."

"Agreed," Tyler nodded. "One thing first."

"Ty…"

"I'm not stalling, I promise."

"Okay, one thing."

"Take me to your bedroom. Make love with me. Slowly. Like we have all the time in the world."

Without a word, Drew took Tyler by the hand. He led her out of the office, back down the hall, and up the long curving staircase. She didn't take the time to notice the details. She already knew them all by heart. Right now, she was focused on the man in front of her. Her world had narrowed to him. Anything else could wait a little while longer.

Drew guided her into the large open room. More glass, another amazing view. The morning sun would wake the occupants. That had been a minor bone of contention. He liked the early morning. Tyler wasn't a fan. As she recalled, they never settled that dispute.

Hearing Tyler's chuckle, Drew turned. "What?"

She pointed towards the windows.

Realizing what she meant, Drew laughed. "There are other bedrooms."

Walking around, Tyler took in the clean lines of the furniture. Not matchy-matchy. Pieces that complimented, not parts of a set. The walls painted the color of rich cream. Neutral yet warm. He had chosen a bed that in a pinch could probably sleep six average adults. You could get lost in a bed like that. Or with the right person, be very, very comfortable.

"How many other bedrooms?"

"You know."

Four. Room for company. Room to grow.

Tyler ran her hand over the soft hunter green quilt. Dark colors on the bed in the fall and winter. She wondered if he had bedding in spring colors for when the weather turned warm again.

"I like this." She said. "Maybe I'm a morning person after all."

"Over the years, I've found late nights to have a certain appeal."

Compromise. A little of this, a little of that. Like designing a house. Or building a future.

"You're wearing too many clothes."

"Funny." Drew pulled his shirt over his head then started to unbutton his jeans. "I was thinking the same thing about you."

Keeping her eyes on the show, Tyler toed off her shoes. That was as far as she got. Before she could blink, Drew was naked. Tall, muscular. Hard. She couldn't think, or move.

"You've fallen behind."

Behind? Yes, he had a beautiful one.

"Lift your arms, honey."

Automatically, she did as he asked.

"There you go. Now step out of your pants. Very nice." He whistled. "Very nice indeed. I wholeheartedly approve. The color of that lace matches your eyes."

Tyler sucked in her breath as Drew ran a finger down her chest to the edge of her bra.

"I really like that you don't go for any of that stupid padding. When I do this," he cupped her breast, "all I feel is you. A perfect fit."

Tyler's head rolled to the side, her mouth parted on a silent moan. No one could touch like Drew. A few brief caresses and heat ran through her veins.

"I need a taste."

Happy to oblige, she lifted her mouth in anticipation. This time her moan filled her ears. Not her mouth. Drew feasted on the tip of her breast. He pulled on her nipple, biting. It sent a shot of pleasure to her center that had her knees buckling.

"Got ya."

Drew caught her before she collapsed, easing her back onto the bed. His big, strong body hovered over her for just a moment while he admired how she looked. Finally, he had her in his bed. The long nights fantasizing, convinced this would never become a reality. She wanted it slow? Good. After so long, he was in no mood to rush.

"They are too nice to rip." Drew lightly caressed the skin above her panties. "Lift your hips, honey. That's right. Damn. And I thought all that lace was pretty."

He slid down to the floor spreading her legs. Starting at her ankle, Drew kissed a serpentine trail up her leg. Every inch of skin needed to be explored. His mouth worshiped, his tongue tasted.

"Sweet."

"Hmm?" Tyler's question was vague. Somewhere between his journey from her foot to her knee, her brain had turned a lovely, sex-hazed mush.

"You." His tongue bathed the tender skin behind her knee. "Sweet. I don't know how but you taste even better than I remember."

Tyler almost came off the bed when his teeth nibbled the spot. When had that become an erogenous zone?

"I don't recall you ever doing that before."

"I've had a few years to study."

"Not the best time to bring up other women."

"Books," he reassured her, his mouth continuing its journey. "Long, lonely hours at the library."

Tyler's laugh turned into another moan, this one longer, louder.

"If you learned that from a book, I'm calling Lila to have her send the author flowers."

Drew lifted his head just long enough to look into her eyes. What she saw took her breath away.

"Get ready to buy out the store."

What he did next could not have come from a book. This he had to practice because he did it to perfection.

Drew slowly kissed his way up her thigh. Firm yet so soft under his lips. The scent of her arousal was a heady perfume filling his senses, making his head spin.

He reveled in taking his time. He didn't have to keep an eye on the clock or worry about someone finding out. They were free to spend all night together. All week if they chose. The knowledge was a heady aphrodisiac adding to his already raging libido.

"I loved doing this to you." He went in for his first taste. His tongue taking a long, slow swipe between her open legs.

"I loved when you did it."

Drew smiled at the catch in her whispered words. He did that to her. He caused that catch in her breath, that moan, that sigh. Knowing he could do that to her made him feel ten feet tall.

"I had no idea what I was doing. You were the first. I never wanted to do it until you."

How could she want to laugh, cry, and scream out in pleasure all at once? Drew was making her crazy — in a very good way.

"You didn't come the first time." He tasted again. "Or the second." And again.

Tyler's fingers slipped through Drew's hair until she gripped his head, pulling him closer. She needed him to stop teasing. She was so close.

"Third time was the charm."

He covered her with his mouth, his lips and tongue taking her higher and higher. Closer. Closer.

"Drew."

Tyler called out his name as she spiraled out of control. Her hands massaged his scalp to the rhythm of her pulsing orgasm. On and on. Starting at her center, radiating out to the tips of her toes, the ends of her fingers.

Did he feel that? That final jolt? Some of that energy had to go from her back to him. She refused to believe something that strong wasn't shared.

Drew kissed the inside of Tyler's thigh before joining her on the bed. He gently rearranged her pliant body, settling next to her. He smoothed her hair from her face.

Such a lovely face, he thought. At the moment relaxed, a small, satisfied smile lifting the corners of her mouth. He bent and gave her a light kiss.

"Feeling good?"

"You might say that. You might also say the sun is a little warm in July. Both would be accurate. Both would also be huge under-exaggerations."

"Really good?"

Tyler chuckled. "Close enough."

She slowly opened her eyes. Clear gray, Drew observed. The color of relaxation. Contentment. Happiness. He had done that.

"You look mighty pleased with yourself."

"I have good reason to be."

"That you do."

Tyler turned on her side to face him. She leaned close, kissing his chest, his chin, his lips. She lingered on his lips.

"Thank you."

"Believe me, it was my pleasure."

He made a big production licking his lips, causing Tyler to laugh again. Her eyes drifted from his smiling face down. His chest, broad and lightly dusted with dark hair. Her hand touched, so hot and powerful, his muscles jumping slightly as her touch became a caress.

"You had such a beautiful body. You were long and lean."

"You seemed fascinated. You would touch me, explore. I was more than happy to let you."

"This." Tyler wrapped her cool fingers around the heat of his erection. "I never got tired of seeing how different you were here, before and after."

"Mmm."

"Oh, that is a sound I remember very well."

She bent to take him in her mouth, letting her tongue become reacquainted with the feel of him; his taste.

"I should have been nervous, the first time I did this."

"Weren't you?" Drew's voice was slightly hoarse. "I was so busy watching my dick sliding in and out of that gorgeous mouth, I didn't notice anything as mundane as nerves."

Tyler snorted, the vibrations eliciting another groan from Drew.

"Do that again."

"Only if you make me laugh."

"Knock knock."

"Stop." Tyler laughed so hard she had to sit back to breathe. "Keep in mind, if I'm laughing while I'm down there, I might start biting. Not on purpose, mind you. You never know."

Drew didn't respond; he just looked at her, eyebrows raised.

"No. You like that? When did you acquire a taste for pain? And should I be worried."

"Not pain, per se. More like an edge. Bite me, a little. Not too hard."

Drew noticed she didn't look the least bit worried. Tyler looked intrigued.

"You'll tell me if I go too far?"

"Believe me, honey. You'll know."

Drew held back Tyler's hair so he had an unobstructed view. She kept her eyes on his as her mouth enveloped his cock. Slowly, she lowered. He was a mouthful, yet Tyler had no problem taking all of him. Up. Down. Up. Her tongue lapping at the fluid gathered at the tip.

She didn't bite. Instead, she bared her teeth, running them down his length. The pain was slight — noticeable. It added that edge he mentioned.

"You like that?"

"Heaven, Ty. You have no idea what you do to me."

If it was half of what he did to her, she had a good idea.

Tyler went back to pleasuring him. She could tell he was close. She

192

wanted to feel him come undone; to know she was the cause. Putting her hand at the base of his cock, she squeezed, harder than she would have before his little pain admission. She was rewarded when his breath hissed out, followed by a groan of pleasure.

Drew wondered how much more he could take. He wanted this to go on and on. He tried his damnedest not to blow too soon, but Tyler made it impossible. He raced towards the finish. When she reached for his balls and gave a forceful tug, that was it. With a shout, Drew came in a glorious rush.

He held Tyler's head as she took all he had to give, before falling back, drained and sated.

Tyler lay sprawled over Drew, a goofy grin plastered on her face. Never a big fan of the swallowing portion of a blowjob, she hadn't hesitated. It was natural with him, everything was.

"I like that we can have fun. Who says sex has to be serious all the time?"

Drew ran his hand along her back. Soothing and affectionate.

"The last time I laughed in bed was…" He thought hard but couldn't think of another woman what hadn't been a quick fuck, a tension easer. It wasn't a fact he wanted to brag about. It just was.

"Yes?"

"The last time was with you."

Tyler turned her head to look at him. She gave a small nod.

"Same for me." She sighed. "Does that make us sad and pathetic?"

"No. Maybe. Hell, I don't know, Ty. I've always enjoyed sex. I never considered giving it up."

"Me neither."

"I don't want to worry about what was." He rolled off the bed, taking her into his arms as he went. "I have you now. You make me laugh. You make me come. You make me feel like the top of my head is going to blow off. I don't need anyone else, ever again."

That sounded good to her. It sounded perfect.

"Hey. Where are we going?"

Drew gave her a quick kiss.

"I want to show you my new pool."

Tyler wrapped her arms around his neck. She really liked being carried. Especially when they were both naked.

"You want to take a swim?"

"Eventually."

SEX IN THE water was not as easy as the books and the movies would have you think.

If you didn't know what you were doing, it could be awkward at best, dangerous at its worst.

"We could use one of those nice lounge chairs. They look sturdy."

"Trust me."

"I do."

Tyler looked at the pool. She imagined it was an engineering masterpiece. Great for swimming winter, spring, summer or fall. She didn't think sex in the deep end was a good idea.

"I read about these people who hit their heads and drowned."

"They both hit their heads?"

Drew put her down on a white wrought iron chair. Tyler wiggled a bit. The cushion was nice and thick. Good thing, because Drew took one off another chair and tossed it on the textured cement, saving wear and tear on his knees when he knelt in front of her.

"No. He hit his head; she drowned trying to save him."

"Sounds like a pair of amateurs."

He gently spread her legs, putting one over each of his shoulders.

"I'm an amateur."

Smiling, Drew moved closer. "That's okay, Ty. I turned pro years ago."

The secret, it seemed, was to get slicked up before hitting the water. Claiming he was all out of the bottled variety, Drew went about making sure she had plenty of nature's lube. Using his hands, his mouth, a little dirty talk. In no time, she was more than ready.

"Shouldn't I return the favor?

"Honey, keep thinking like that and you'll lose that amateur status in no time."

Tyler didn't worry about where the condom had been hiding. She watched as Drew expertly rolled it on. She then used her mouth to make the latex nice and wet.

"Thanks, Ty."

Drew kissed her, keeping contact while he sat.

"Straddle me," he whispered against her lips. "You know what to do."

"You do know the water is over there?" Tyler asked, eyes twinkling.

The teasing light left her eyes, the color going from bright to hazy gray as she rested a knee on each side of him. Lifting slightly, Tyler began a slow decent, taking him into her a little at a time.

Drew put his hands on her hips, not to rush, just to hold her steady. He let her set the pace though it killed him. He shifted slightly, a subtle hint to take him, all of him. *Now.*

"Patience, fella. I'm riding you this time."

Taking one of his hands, she brought it to her breast. She didn't have to tell him what to do. Her head fell back, her mouth slightly open as he gently squeezed her sensitive flesh. She finished, joining with him at the same moment he took her nipple into his mouth.

"Yes, that's right," she moaned.

"Don't move."

"I have to."

Tyler tried to rise up only to be stopped by a combination of his hand on her hip and his teeth on her nipple. Drew scraped the distended bud, smiling as she cried out again, not in pain but pleasure. His tongue soothed before he reluctantly moved away.

"Hold on, Ty."

Drew rose to his feet, his arms under Tyler's butt making sure she didn't slip away. In seconds, he lowered them both into the shallow end of the pool.

"So you do know where the water is."

"Smartass."

To emphasize the remark, Drew gave her a slap, not too hard but enough to sting.

"Hey," Tyler exclaimed, more startled than hurt. It was awkward because of her position, but she managed to reach around and slap him, returning the favor.

"There, how do you like it?"

"Honestly? Not a fan."

"Me neither."

Drew kissed her, his mouth gentle.

"No more of that, I promise."

The water was lovely, lapping around them like a warm caress. Drew turned, his knee going down on one of the steps. He settled Tyler, leaning her back, his hand cushioning her head against the rim of the pool. Their bodies were only half submerged, almost as if they were in the world's biggest bathtub.

"Ready?"

Tyler answered by threading her hands through his hair, pulling him down for a deep, carnal kiss. Tongue against tongue, her sighs mingling with his. She lifted her hips, seeking movement from him. Drew happily complied.

The water lent itself to slow and easy movements. It was hard to rush, which was fine with them both. The build took time, bonding them, moving them closer. Not to where they had been. There was no going back. They weren't those young people anymore. This was different, richer. Hopefully, with time, stronger.

Their eyes met as he gave one final thrust tumbling them over. They rode the wave high and long, coming down slowly. Breath ragged, Drew rested his forehead against Tyler's. He didn't have to look to know she was smiling. That little, contented curve to her lips that she got after he pleased her. He considered it his reward for a job well done.

"I'm not going to ask how you got so good at pool sex."

"Probably wise decision."

"I thought maybe there was someone I should send a thank you note to."

Hiding his grin, Drew lifted her into his arms, leaving the pool. "No."

"No, I shouldn't send a note? Or no, one note wouldn't be enough."

"Just no."

Happy enough with his answer, Tyler let him dry her. Getting back into the elevator, she watched as the doors closed, shutting off her light mood. They couldn't put it off any longer. Drew took her hand, linking their fingers. He was going to answer the question that plagued her these past ten years.

Tyler sighed. She hoped it didn't turn out to be a case of be careful what you ask for.

Chapter Thirteen

TYLER WATCHED DREW turn off the bathroom light.
After a quick shower, Tyler went through her nightly routine. Skin lotioned, teeth brushed, face cleansed. Her hair was dry and shiny. Drew had given her a Spokane Chiefs t-shirt to wear.

"Comfortable?"

"Yes. Great bed."

"Can I get you anything? Water? A shot of whiskey?"

They were both nervous. It helped, being in this together.

"Come to bed, Drew."

Nodding, he dropped the towel from around his waist and crawled in beside her.

"Not a big jammie guy?"

He settled in, drawing her close.

"I dropped the jammies when I was twelve."

"You've been sleeping in the nude since you were twelve?"

"It's been a progression. T-shirt and underwear. Just the underwear."

Tyler snuggled into his side. She approved heartily. All this long, muscular male in nothing but his birthday suit. He smelled good too. Big and citrusy. Yum.

"I wouldn't object if you wanted to lose the shirt."

"Later," Tyler said, kissing the side of his neck. "After."

"Right."

Drew took a deep breath. Tyler rubbed his arm. It was meant to comfort, to encourage. *I'm here,* she was saying. *I'm not going anywhere.* It was what he needed. The nerves dropped away, the butterflies calmed.

"It was Monday morning. I had an extra spring in my step. One more month and I would be free. I could taste the end of high school. Harper Falls was practically a distant memory.

"I was almost out the door when Regina called me into her office. I didn't think anything of it. I assumed it would be her usual reminder of my duties as a Harper. In a way, I guess I was right."

TEN YEARS EARLIER

"CLOSE THE DOOR, Andrew."

Drew refrained from correcting her. She was the only person who insisted on using his full name. She would simply tell him it was a mother's prerogative. It was a ridiculous statement. Regina Harper was not a mother. Not by any definition Drew was familiar with.

The fact that she threw the word around whenever it suited had long ago stopped pissing him off. He didn't care because it didn't matter. What hurt when he was eight, now was a minor annoyance. Regina didn't understand that. She never would.

"I don't want to be late. Last week. I would hate to miss anything." Another thing she never understood — sarcasm.

"I know your schedule, Andrew. Your first class isn't for another hour. Have a seat."

Of all the rooms in Harper House, Drew hated this one the most. The heavy smell of French perfume. The dark furniture. The dark carpet, the dark walls. No light, no air. Someday, when he was head of his own company, his office would be nothing but windows. No shadowy corners or walls of books that nobody was allowed to read.

In *his* office, he would be able to breathe.

"Stop fidgeting, Andrew. You are eighteen. Mature young men sit politely and pay attention."

"I guess I'm not that mature."

Oh, boy. He knew that look. The tightening around her mouth, the narrowing of her eyes.

She was only a few years past forty. Attractive, trim. Regina Harper was as rigid with herself as she was with others. Regular exercise, sensible meals. She had the body of a woman half her age. It was her discontent with life that would be her downfall. Plastic surgery and chemicals could smooth the wrinkles; nothing could wipe the icy disdain permanently etched between her brows.

Had she ever been happy, Drew wondered. *Had there ever been a twinkle of joy in those dark brown eyes?* He had inherited her eyes. The same color, same shape. That was where the similarities ended. Drew looked at the world with wonder. Saw the endless possibilities right there for the taking.

Regina's world was Harper Falls. She had power, influence. People looked to her to make decisions. She ruled. The rest of the world held no interest beyond the occasional shopping expedition to New York or Paris.

That lack of curiosity for the outside world was not something Drew could understand. He would have been sympathetic if Regina showed any signs of being happy. In a world of her own making and not a content bone in her body. What a miserable way to live your life.

"Who are you escorting to the Lilac Ball?"

Regina's annual charity function to raise money for the town's hospital. Drew knew it was a worthy cause. No one was turned away who needed medical attention. Lack of insurance, no money. It didn't matter. He was proud that his family founded and supported Harper Memorial.

The ball was another matter. It was a vanity project, pure and simple. He hated being forced to attend. Every year, he was expected to escort the vapid daughter of a socially acceptable family. Money and connections were the only qualifications. Wit and intelligence seemed to have been bred out, not a desirable trait in the Harper Falls elite.

"I'm not."

"Full sentences, Andrew." Regina sat up even straighter. Drew wondered how she managed to function with a stick constantly shoved up her ass.

"I will not be attending the Lilac Ball. With or without a date."

"I see."

Drew wasn't expecting an explosion. Regina never raised her voice. However, her lack of surprise at his announcement did throw him a bit.

"Am I to assume you will be spending the evening with Tyler Jones?"

If this were a movie, Drew would have admired the way Regina played him. The slow build, never giving a hint to her end game. As an observer, he would have applauded her tactics. As a participant, he felt her cold stare chill him to the bone. His mind scrambled. With no warning, he wasn't sure how to proceed.

"What do you think you know?" Answer a question with a question. It bought him time to think.

"I know everything. I know about your little meeting place down by the river. I know this has been going on for almost a year. Please tell me you've been using protection. The last thing we need is a mongrel Harper in the family tree."

"You go too far, Regina."

Drew was too angry to notice Regina's reaction to his use of her name.

"It is Mother, do you understand? What would people say if they heard you call me by my given name?"

"I don't give a damn what people think, *Regina*. I stopped thinking of you as my mother long ago. I'm not going to play the hypocrite just so you can save face."

If anything, her eyes became colder, her back straighter.

"You will stop seeing that Jones girl. Immediately."

"Are you out of your ever-loving mind?" Drew was flabbergasted.

"I love Tyler. I plan on spending the rest of my life with her."

"That is impossible."

"Don't worry. We won't be here in Harper Falls. No uncomfortable holidays to get through. Dad can come and visit his grandchildren. You won't be a part of our lives."

Drew wasn't certain, but he thought Regina actually choked at the mention of grandchildren.

"Is she pregnant?"

"No."

"Good. That would have been...unfortunate."

"Because she isn't worthy?" Drew scoffed.

"Because she's your sister."

"What?"

"WHAT?"

Tyler shot straight up in bed, her eyes a stormy gray.

"Calm down, Ty."

"Are you kidding? Was she kidding? Please, tell me she was kidding."

Drew took her shoulders, easing her back down onto the bed. He leaned over her, smoothing back her hair.

"She wasn't kidding. She doesn't know how."

"Drew—"

"We wouldn't be here, like this, if we were brother and sister, Ty."

"Then what was she up to?"

"Let me finish."

TEN YEARS AGO

"YOU HEARD ME, Andrew."

Drew was reeling. *Tyler was his sister?* Impossible. Please, let it be impossible. He started running scenarios through his head. None of them made sense.

"Is Martin Jones my father? Or are you telling me Dad is Tyler's? Unless there is some other twisted combination that hasn't occurred to me yet."

"The specifics don't matter, Andrew."

"They are all that matters. You want me to believe that I've been—" God, he couldn't even say it. "If I'm to accept this, you need to give me some facts."

"If you insist."

Regina tapped her manicured nails on the surface of her desk. *Nerves*, Drew thought. She didn't show them often. That she did so now gave him a spark of hope.

"Well? Spill it, Regina."

"Watch yourself, Andrew. You will show me respect while in my home."

"If I'm to believe you, that moral high ground you're so fond of standing on is about to crumble into a million little pieces. You can't have it both ways. Are you a cheat who gave birth to another man's child or not?"

"Nineteen years ago, I was briefly… involved with Martin Jones."

"Am I his son? Yes or no?"

Again, Regina hesitated.

"You can't even say it. Why start a lie then refuse to follow through?"

"I don't want to embarrass your father."

"Which one?"

Regina raised her eyebrows, the look she gave him saying what she wouldn't. It was a lie. Drew was certain.

"He loves you. This would devastate him."

Drew doubted it. Any illusions Russell Harper might have harbored about his wife were lost long ago. This sham would only add to the knowledge that she was beyond contempt.

"And then there's his heart. You know what the doctor said about avoiding stress. Leave Russell out of this, Andrew. It will be best for all of us."

Drew swallowed. His father's condition wasn't life threatening. Not yet. Adding any worry wouldn't help though. He would try not to involve him, unfortunately at this point, Drew wasn't sure that was possible.

"Two days, Regina." Drew stood indicating he was done. "Show me some proof or back down. If you still want to play the cryptic messenger of doom, I'll be forced to go to my father."

"And say what?"

"Simple. I'll tell him your story. Then I'll ask him to join me for a little test. You can lie. DNA won't."

He thought she would stop him before he got to the door. Her bluff had been called. Game over. Turning back wasn't a good idea. Lot's wife came to mind. For the first time, Drew understood the temptation. Sometimes it was impossible not to take one more peek at the disaster.

"Two days, Regina."

No pillar of salt. She wasn't that powerful. Her cold eyes, though. The eerie emotional calm. He knew that image would stay with him the rest of his life.

TO SAY IT was the longest forty-eight hours of his life would have been a gross understatement.

Drew was in a hell of his and Regina's making. After little sleep and a stomach that considered food the enemy, by the time the deadline finally arrived, he kicked himself for not sticking to his gun and forcing her hand right away. Maybe it hadn't been such a good idea to watch all those old movies so he could keep up with Tyler's many references. Now he kept asking himself *what would Humphrey Bogart do?*

Relying on the advice of a dead actor's fictional exploits probably wasn't the smartest way to go.

He wished he could share that bit of lunatic thinking with Tyler. No one would appreciate it more. Except he couldn't tell her — not any of it. Until he knew the truth, he had to avoid her at all costs. He couldn't trust himself not to blurt out everything. Well, he wasn't going to burden her with information that he hoped was false.

Leaving a note seemed the safest thing to do. *School was catching up with him. He needed to study.* Lame, maybe. Tyler would understand when he was able to explain.

It was relief, not dread, that Drew felt when he went to confront Regina. Time was up. The end of her crazy scheme was finally here.

"Andrew."

"Regina."

"Have a seat. There's no reason not to be civilized about this."

Drew remained standing. It wasn't a power play. He just wanted to be as near to the door as possible. When he had the truth, he wanted a quick and easy exit.

"I'm here for a simple yes or no. Dragging it out won't help."

"You're right." Regina nodded. "Russell is your father. There is no doubt."

Evil bitch. Drew wanted to spit the words at her. He also wanted to jump across the desk and strangle the life out of her. To avoid the later, he refrained from speaking at all.

"Before you run off to see your little girlfriend, there is one more thing."

Of course there is. With Regina, the crap was neverending.

Leaving would have been useless. Eventually, she would track him down. Instead, he decided to face the worst now. He would rip off the bandage in one fast pull and hope the wound underneath wouldn't start bleeding again.

"I'll admit my ploy about your paternity was not well thought out."

"No kidding."

"In my defense, I had only just found out about you and that Jones girl. It was a bit of a shock, to say the least."

"Suggesting incest was the first place your mind went? How sick is that?"

"The *point* is," Regina went on, "I've had more time to think."

Drew felt dread replace anger. Too much time. He gave it to her and now he had the feeling he was going to pay the price.

"Spit it out. Do your worst."

For the first time, Regina smiled. The curve of her mouth was slight. Not happy, certainly not joyous. Satisfied, Drew thought. She knew she was going to win.

"I will destroy every member of the Jones family. Top to bottom. Financially, socially. The hole will be deep, Andrew. It will take generations to crawl out; even then the taint will never completely go away."

"Tyler doesn't care about money or social standing."

"Why am I not surprised." Regina's contempt was palpable. "I understand your little friend is quite fond of her mother. Anita Jones is a timid, inconsequential woman who will never survive my wrath. Will Tyler be able to look at you every day knowing the Harpers destroyed her family?"

"*One* Harper."

"The name will be bitter on her lips, Andrew. How long before she hates you? Can't stand to look at you, to have you touch her? A year? Two? By then, it will be too late. You'll be married, maybe a child, or two. Picture it. It isn't pretty, is it?"

Drew felt cold and hot all at once. He couldn't deny any of Regina's words. She wasn't bluffing. In fact, he thought part of her hoped he would defy her so she could have the pleasure of devastating the lives of an entire family. It made him crazy to know he shared the blood of such a sick, ruthless individual.

He knew he was stuck. His father would be unable to stop her. No one had that power. *No*, Drew thought. That wasn't true. She gave him a choice. She gave him the power.

"What do you want me to do?"

"Break it off. Immediately. You will have nothing to do with her ever again, Andrew. Not in a month, not in a year. If word gets to me that you're sneaking around, meeting in secret, I will follow through on my threat. There is no statute of limitations."

"Fine."

Drew turned to leave. There was nothing else to say. Game, set, match. The evil bitch had won.

"Andrew?"

"What."

He rounded on her, teeth bared, murder in his eyes. There was little satisfaction in seeing a brief hint of fear in her eyes. Unfortunately, it was too little, too late.

Regina recovered her composure quickly, her gaze as cool as ever.

"You will be the villain. Tyler is to believe this breakup is entirely your doing, your own idea. My part in it can never come out. Is that clear?"

"Crystal."

Drew didn't slam the office door. He didn't scream to the heavens about injustice. Instead, he got in his car and drove. He had one thing on his mind and one thing only. What to say when he broke the heart of the woman he loved.

Chapter Fourteen

DREW WAITED, HOPING Tyler would say something, anything, to fill the silence.

He spent ten years imagining this moment. Practicing what he would say. He tried to anticipate her reaction. Anger, disbelief? Disdain? Sometimes she would say a simple *fuck you* before walking out of his life for good.

On a good day, he would let himself fantasize a happy ending. Those were rare — vague. She still loved him; nothing else mattered. That was his favorite. It was also the rarest. He wasn't very good at letting himself off the hook.

"Speak to me, Ty. Yell, curse. Hit me. Do something. Please."

Her face was turned away from him. That happened towards the end of his story. Instead of turning back, Tyler shook her head.

"You can't even look at me?"

"I—" she started. Then she shook her head again.

Tears, he groaned silently. He heard tears in her voice. He never imagined her crying; it was too painful. He preferred her anger.

"Can you forgive me, Ty?" Drew reached out a hand, pulling it back before he touched her slightly shaking back.

"I was eighteen and powerless. I wanted to throw her threats in her face, tell her to go to hell. Instead, I caved. Telling you I didn't love you was the hardest thing I've ever done. Part of me died that day, Ty."

"Now I understand."

Her voice was muffled. Drew closed his eyes. He didn't hear anger; he heard contempt.

"Ty—"

"You were the best man I ever knew."

Tyler sat up, turning towards him. Her face was streaked with tears, her gray eyes sad. Sadder than he ever remembered.

"You know as well as anyone about my father and brothers. Other than Dani's dad, I thought all men were like the ones in my family. Then I met you."

Drew thought he might be sick. This was worse than he imagined. And that was pretty bad.

"Maybe it was unfair of me to turn you into my hero. Teenage girls can be silly sometimes. I got over the broken heart, mostly. I never got over the loss of my hero."

I wanted to be your hero, Drew thought. *I hated taking that from you.*

"I can't believe what you did."

"I didn't think I had a choice."

Tyler took his hand lifting it to her cheek. Her eyes were swimming with tears.

"There's always a choice, Drew. You picked me. You let me paint you as a villain. You let me hate you so my mother wouldn't suffer."

"I should have told you sooner. Years ago."

"I wouldn't have heard you," Tyler said. "I mean *really* heard you. I wasn't ready."

"Are ready now?"

This time when she looked at him, her eyes were dry and clear.

"Do you know what I see when I look at you? I see a man. A strong man. Kind. Someone I can count on — trust." She went into his arms. "I see my hero."

TYLER STRETCHED HER arms above her head. She didn't need to open her eyes to know it was morning. Some crazy person let the sun in.

Drew.

She grinned.

This time when she stretched, she used her entire body. Her muscles felt loose. Amazing what a night of lovemaking will do for a woman.

Sitting, Tyler pulled her legs up until she rested her cheek on her knees, her arms wrapped around her legs. Last night. So much happened. So much said.

The end result? Tyler felt free for the first time in ten years. Free to let go of the past. She was ready to open her heart. Not to a new man — to the only man.

"Drew Harper."

She whispered the words. No more of that. Tyler sat up straight. This time they didn't have to hide. She could shout his name and there wasn't a damn thing anyone could do about it.

"DREW HARPER."

"I hope that was a happy yell. I don't think I've had time since your last orgasm to piss you off."

Drew leaned against the doorframe. Tall and gorgeous, dressed in faded jeans and dark blue sweater, he was nothing short of mouthwatering. She was sorry to have missed the shower that left his hair slightly damp. *Next time*, she thought. They would have plenty of next times.

"I was testing a theory."

He stood, sauntering over. When he reached her, he sat, taking Tyler into his arms. His kiss was slow, letting her know he was glad to find her in his bed. Tyler responded by wrapping herself around him. There was no place she would rather be.

"What theory?"

"Hmm?"

Drew smiled against the side of her neck. He loved that he could

210

turn her brain to mush with a single kiss. It was only fair; she could do the same for him.

"My name? Yelled? Theory?"

"Right." She pushed at Drew. "If you want an intelligible answer, you better stop that."

"You taste like…"

"Like?"

"Give me a minute. I need another sample."

Laughing at his silliness, she turned her head to give him better access. A few more seconds of that and her brain wouldn't be mush; it would be goo.

"You taste like Tyler. My favorite flavor in the world."

He didn't just have control of her brain, Tyler realized. With only a few sweet words, he had her heart in the palm of his hand. She trusted him to keep it safe this time.

"We can tell the world."

Tyler didn't have to explain. Drew understood.

"I'll take care of that right after breakfast. You want a shower first?"

"Yes. Give me ten minutes."

Tyler didn't tarry. She was washed, dressed, and headed down the stairs in under ten minutes. The smell of freshly brewed coffee and frying bacon greeting her like old, welcome friends.

She had assumed they would go out to eat. Seeing Drew expertly cracking eggs into a bowl was a definite surprise.

"You can cook."

"I can't tell. Was that a compliment or an accusation?"

"That depends. Are you any good at it?"

"Sit and decide for yourself."

It turned out he knew his way around the kitchen. Perfectly browned toast, crispy bacon, fluffy scrambled eggs. The coffee tasted like it was sent down from the Gods. It might not have been the most complicated of meals, but it was better than Tyler could have done.

"Good?" Drew asked after her first few bites.

"If you can make meatloaf, you'll never get rid of me."

"Meatloaf is one of my specialties."

"Well, then."

Realizing the implication of their teasing words, Tyler applied herself to her eggs, not looking at Drew. *Too soon,* her brain screamed. *Stop listening to your libido. Forget what your heart is saying. Slow down.*

"Any big plans for the day?"

Tyler's eyes met Drew's. Smiling, she sent him a silent thank you. He understood. Which made it even harder not to jump ahead five or six steps. *Soon,* his gaze replied. *When we're both ready.*

As it happened, Tyler did have big plans. A truck was coming to her studio to pick up the Harper Falls statue.

One month from tomorrow would be the unveiling. The town would finally see the results of her sweat and sleepless nights. Before then, the statue would be housed in a building near its final resting place. She was happy to free up space in her studio. After months of living with her creation, she was ready to let go. Tyler would still have access to finish the last tweaks, the final polish.

"Feeling any separation anxiety?"

Drew insisted on following her home. Tyler knew it was silly. It was broad daylight. Nothing was going to happen in the fifteen minutes it took her to drive from his place to hers. She could have stopped him, but didn't. She knew it made him feel good to make sure she arrived safely. It made her feel good too.

"It's time," she said, answering his question. "It's only when I'm unhappy with what I've done that turning it loose is a problem. When it's right, like now, I want to send my art out to hopefully be enjoyed."

"Can I have a peek?"

"Soon," she promised. "I planned on showing it to Dani and Rose next week. You can come if you want."

"I want."

Drew took her in his arms, giving her a thorough goodbye kiss. He waited until she disengaged the alarm system and unlocked her front door before he drove away in his vintage Mercedes-Benz roadster. Weather on this early November morning was crisp but sunny.

According to Drew, perfect for tooling around with your top down.

Chuckling at her boy and his toy, Tyler walked into her studio. Before she could get the door shut, a hand reached out, blocking her movement.

"So, M.J. was right. You've taken back up with Drew Harper."

TYLER ALMOST JUMPED out of her skin.

"Goddamn it, Kyle. It isn't any of your or M.J.'s business. What do you think you're doing lurking around here?"

She stood in the doorway, not letting her brother in. When he was on his own, Kyle was easy to handle. Even though it was usually M.J.'s influence that always got him into trouble, she still didn't want him here.

"I need your help."

Tyler knew she couldn't have heard him correctly. It would take some colossal nerve for her brother to ask her for anything. He was either high or desperate.

She looked closely. Kyle didn't look like he was on anything. In fact, he looked good. Healthy. His clothes were neat and clean. His hair combed, freshly washed. He was even shaved instead of sporting the irregular stubble normally favored by both her brothers. When he cleaned up, Kyle was a good-looking man. It wasn't his fault that he resembled their father to such a startling degree.

Hoping she didn't regret it, Tyler moved back, letting him in.

"Would you like some coffee?"

"Sure, if you're having some."

Tyler moved to the kitchen, keeping one eye on Kyle. He seemed interested in her sculpture of two angels embracing. Tomorrow it would ship to New York, the hefty commission giving her bank balance a nice boost.

"Do you still take cream and sugar?"

"Just cream. I'm off sweets."

Okay, Tyler thought, handing him a mug. Since when did Kyle worry about what he put in his body? Something was up.

"Stop fidgeting and have a seat, Kyle."

"Sorry." He sat opposite her, his hands wrapped around the mug of steaming coffee. She thought he looked nervous. Not squirrelly. A case of plain, old nerves.

"I like what you've done with this old place. M.J. always said—"

"I can imagine what M.J. said. If you want my help, that should be the last time you start to quote our brother."

"Right. Sorry."

"That's two sorrys, Kyle. What's up?"

"I thought I knew what to say. I practiced, rehearsed. Now that I'm here, I don't know if I can go through with it."

"Say what you have to say."

"I've met a woman," he began in a rush.

"Nothing new there." The bars he hung out in always had a dubious crop of women willing to give up the goods for a couple of drinks — or a couple of bucks.

"No. Tammy is different. She's nice, sweet."

"That *is* different," Tyler agreed. "Where did you meet her? I don't remember a *nice* Tammy here in Harper Falls."

"Wenatchee. I took a job driving some furniture from Spokane to Tacoma. I stopped for something to eat. Tammy is a waitress. We got to talking. I stopped again on my way back." Kyle shrugged. "I love her, Tyler."

"I'm happy for you."

Tyler meant it. The more she looked at Kyle, the more she could see the changes in him. If this Tammy was the reason, Tyler wanted to shake her hand. Anyone who could get her brother away from M.J.'s influence was a person worth knowing.

"The thing is…"

Tyler sighed. Why was there always a *thing*?

"You might as well spit it out, Kyle. Sitting there squeezing that mug won't make it any easier."

Kyle set the mug on the table then started wringing his hands instead.

"There's a job in Mill Creek. Just north of Seattle? I'd be managing the feed store."

"A job is good."

"It is. A good job, I mean." Kyle swallowed. "I haven't told anyone."

Anyone meaning M.J. He wouldn't be too happy at the thought of losing his minion. Kyle would be wise to be packed and gone before telling their brother his plans. He was like a lobster in a box. If he saw Kyle trying to get out, M.J. would grab on with his fat old claws, pulling him back in.

"Tammy's coming with me, Tyler. It will be a fresh start for both of us."

"If you want my opinion, I say go. Now. Get in your car and don't look back. You can call Mom when you're settled."

"I would." Kyle sat up straight, looking Tyler in the eye. "I need money."

Tyler felt all her newfound hope pop like an overinflated balloon. She should have known it was too good to be true.

"Congratulations, Kyle. You really had me going. Tammy was a nice touch. Did M.J. tell you to tug at my heartstrings before you asked me to loosen the old purse strings?"

"No." Kyle reached out, pulling his hand back when he saw the warning in Tyler's eyes.

"You should go, Kyle."

"I swear I'm telling you the truth, Tyler. I've been a lousy brother. Worse than lousy," he conceded when Tyler snorted.

"Here."

Kyle took out his phone, quickly punching a few buttons before handing it to Tyler.

There were pictures. Lots of them. Kyle and a pretty redhead hugging, laughing. Another with him holding a little boy. Tyler looked at her brother.

"Tammy has a child?"

Kyle nodded, beaming.

"The spitting image of his momma."

Tyler looked at the pictures again, then at Kyle. Well, damn. He *was* in love. With mother *and* son.

"Mom's met her."

"Really? When? She hasn't mentioned anything to me."

"I asked her not to. I brought Tammy to Spokane a few weeks ago. We all had dinner. They seemed to hit it off."

Tyler thought for a moment, coming to a quick decision.

"How much do you need?"

She could see the relief seep into Kyle's body.

"Moving costs, first and last month's rent. A security deposit."

Tyler left the sofa, walking to her desk in the corner of the room. She took out her checkbook.

"Groceries, incidentals."

She tore off the check, handing it to her brother.

His eyes widened when he saw the amount.

"Tyler, I don't know how to thank you. I promise to pay you back as soon as possible."

Tyler shook her head. "Here's what I'm going to do, Kyle. Every month for the next six months, I'm going to send Tammy a check. Consider it my contribution to the cause. The first hint I get that any of that money is making its way back to M.J., not only do I cut you off? I track you down and kick the shit out of you."

Kyle nodded. "Sounds fair."

Tyler chuckled. Who would have thought? She was having a laugh with her brother.

"You have a real chance here, Kyle. Don't blow it."

She walked him to the door.

"And don't worry about paying me back. Consider it a wedding present. You are going to marry the girl?"

"As soon as we get settled."

Before she knew his intentions, Kyle gave her a hug. Another first. A little awkward and kind of sweet, Tyler hugged him back.

Kyle was halfway down the steps when he turned back. He hesitated.

"Watch out for M.J."

"I always do."

"No. This is different. We went out for a drink last night. I figured it would be my way of saying goodbye without actually saying it, you know?"

"Okay."

"He talked about you. A lot. That's how I knew about you seeing Drew Harper again. He," Kyle frowned. "He hates you, Tyler."

Tyler blinked in surprise. She knew M.J. disliked her, but hate?

"Why?"

"He could never intimidate you. That was fine when you were little. He would lock you in a closet or knock you down. There came a time when he couldn't do that anymore. You started to fight back. Being a bully only works when your victim is afraid. You never were."

That wasn't entirely true. She used to be afraid of M.J. He was bigger and stronger. Then she realized he was a coward. He hid behind crude language delivered in a loud voice. If actually confronted, he ran. Her fear evaporated fast when she realized he never met anyone head on. That was when she learned to watch her back.

Tyler had a sudden thought.

"M.J. was the one who told Regina Harper about Drew and me."

Kyle nodded.

"He got a pretty good chunk of cash for that information. Even after Drew left town, Mrs. Harper paid M.J. to keep an eye on you."

"And since I've been back."

"I wondered. M.J. hasn't said."

"What do you think?"

"I would say yes. Every now and then, he shows up with some money to wave around. I don't know where else he would get it."

"Right."

"Take care, okay?"

"You too."

Tyler waved as Kyle pulled away. Feeling a shiver that had nothing to do with the sudden November breeze, she closed the door. Making sure to engage the locks and set the alarm, Tyler went to her little kitchen for another cup of coffee.

She stood with her back against the counter, sipping the hot liquid. It was unsettling to find she was being spied on. Knowing it was done by her own brother added another layer of creepy.

Shaking off thoughts that threatened her happy buzz, she put her cup in the sink. She had a statue to move. Or supervise moving.

Tyler walked around the figure, trying to be objective. *It was good*, she thought, picking up a section of protective wrapping.

Regina Harper and M.J. could go to hell.

This was what mattered. This was what she cared about. Her work. Her friends. Her Drew.

Smiling, Tyler put the last piece of tape on the last piece of bubble wrap just as the truck pulled up outside. Perfect timing. In fact, at the moment everything was perfect.

"GOOD FOR KYLE."

"Good thing he has such a generous sister."

"Mom will be happy," Tyler said to Rose and Dani. "All that praying has finally paid off. At least one of her sons is trying to get his life together."

They were having drinks at *Tom Tom's*. The Friday night crowd was just getting started. Loud but not rowdy — not yet. You could be yourself at *Tom Tom's* as long as you respected the women and tipped your server. All other rules were out the window.

Tyler thought back to the first time she came here. Jack and Rose were just starting their relationship. Dani hadn't a clue that shortly, Alex would be back in her life. And she threatened to grind Drew's balls into dust. At the time, she meant it. In retrospect, she was glad their animosity never escalated to that extent.

"What are you grinning about?"

Drew took the seat next to Tyler, giving her a warm hello kiss.

"Just thinking about your balls."

"Drew's balls are funny?"

Alex joined Dani, taking her hand as he sat down.

"I've seen him naked. I don't remember them being particularly hysterical," Jack said.

"How close a study did you make?" Rose asked him.

Jack winked at Rose, his blue eyes filled with their usual good-natured twinkle.

"You got me there, sweetheart. I claim no more than a glancing acquaintance."

Drew groaned. He wanted to slap his best friend across his grinning face.

"You have no acquaintance with my balls, glancing or otherwise. Why are we even talking about them?"

"Tyler said you have funny balls," Jack shrugged, thoroughly enjoying his friend's frustration.

"A little help here," Drew said to Tyler. "Clarify your earlier statement so we can leave my balls in peace."

Tyler took pity on Drew. She reminded everyone of the night back in May, going into detail since Alex wasn't familiar with the story.

"I was pissed at Drew."

"Nothing new there," Dani chimed in.

"True. I'd just found out about that celibacy bet you idiots made. I was afraid it was going to backfire onto Rose. Being a good friend, I warned Drew. If Jack made her cry, I would rip off his balls and grind them into the dirt." She winked at the other women. "No big deal."

"So you say," Drew countered. "My balls were scared. They jumped up inside my body; I couldn't find them for days."

"They were in no danger. Jack got in a fight with a bunch of bikers distracting us all. He was a hero, Rose didn't cry. End of story."

They all laughed, rehashing the finer points Tyler either left out or missed when Jack and Rose were out in the parking lot.

"Balls aside," Alex quipped, turning to Jack. "Did you really take on those bikers by yourself?"

"I was more of a placeholder until Rose came to my rescue. She jumped on the back of the biggest guy there." He lifted Rose's hand to his lips. "My hero."

"Ah," Tyler and Dani sighed.

"Now we're an old engaged couple," Rose sighed. "Soon to be married."

"You finally set the date?" Tyler exclaimed.

"When?" Dani demanded.

"May 20th. The one-year anniversary of the night I propositioned Jack."

Rose beamed at the memory. Jack looked pleased himself.

"It was the best one-night stand I never had."

Chapter Fifteen

"**I** LOVE ROSE, but if I have to look at one more bridal magazine, I might go stark raving mad."

"She hasn't gone Bridezilla on you?"

Tyler smiled at her mother, a bit surprised she knew the term. Anita Jones was moving into the twenty-first century. A new hair color, new job, reality television. Tyler couldn't wait to find out what was next.

"Not my Rose. It isn't her attitude I object to. It's the number of mind-numbing periodicals we've poured over in the past week. I didn't know there were so many."

"It's a huge industry. Why last week alone, I did the nails for three brides and seven bridesmaids. I'm booked solid in December. Holiday weddings are very big."

"You sound like you're enjoying your new job."

Anita nodded, her eyes bright. For that reason alone, Tyler wanted to offer the owner of *Permanently Awesome* a big hug.

"The other women who work there are so nice. Right off, they made me feel like one of the girls. The customers are nice too. You wouldn't believe the gossip I hear."

"Blush-worthy?" Tyler asked. "Spill, Mom. I haven't heard anything juicy in weeks."

"Oh, I could never tell. Some of those things are, well, I'm sure they must be made up."

A blush spread across Anita's cheeks, making Tyler chuckle. Sweet and old-fashioned in so many ways. A bit of a prude. She wondered what her mother would say if she knew about some of the things her little girl did with Drew Harper. Luckily, there was no reason for her to ever find out.

But she did need to know about Drew. He was Tyler's main reason for visiting her mother.

"Mom—"

"I did hear one piece of gossip that might interest you."

Tyler swallowed. Oh, boy.

"You've heard."

"About you and Drew Harper? The salon was buzzing all afternoon yesterday. It was all anyone could talk about."

"Honestly?"

Tyler understood about small towns. They lived on gossip. It was their life's blood. The fact that she and Drew were seeing each other was juicy. But all afternoon? Good Lord. Get a life, people.

"I wanted to be the first to tell you. I mean, last night was the first time we've gone out in public. How could they have known so soon?"

"It only takes a whiff of a hint, Tyler. You know that."

"This town fed on me and Drew so long the first time, they should still be full. After Drew left town, and everything came out, it was hard for me to show my face."

"Last time was about forbidden love. That kind of gossip, especially when it involves a Harper, never completely dies."

"I suppose," Tyler conceded. "This time we're adults. We won't hide or pretend. If it works or fails, it will be because of us — period."

"Good."

"That's it? Good? You had a lot more to say ten years ago."

Anita looked into her daughter's stormy eyes and sighed.

"I wish I could take my words back, Tyler. You were hurting. Drew was gone. I should have held my tongue. I was afraid for you. I saw

Drew Harper as a man much like your father."

"Drew is nothing like Martin Jones. He wasn't then and he certainly isn't now."

"No." Anita gave Tyler's hand a comforting pat. "You wouldn't be with him if he were. Back then, though, I was glad he broke your heart before he could destroy your life. I made the mistake of putting you in my shoes."

Tyler took a deep breath. She didn't want to be angry. Not with her mother. The anger she felt for her father, that was another thing.

"You were mild in comparison to Dad. He said some things I will never forget. Slut. Whore. Trash. God, his face got red. For the first time, I thought he might hit me. Or have a stroke."

"He was overreacting to his own... disappointment."

Tyler frowned. "What disappointment?"

"About nineteen years earlier, Martin had an affair with Regina Harper."

"You knew about that?" Tyler asked in surprise.

"*You* knew?"

Tyler shrugged. It seemed they were both surprised.

"I knew it was a possibility. When did you find out?"

"While it was happening."

Anita got up from the table. She needed to be moving, to do something. Emptying the almost full pot of coffee, she proceeded to make a new one. The familiar task soothed her enough so she could continue.

"I knew almost from the start that you father cheated on me — often. I also knew none of those women meant any more to him than I did."

"Oh, Mom."

"I had no illusions that my marriage was a love match. M.J. came along six months after we said I do. Martin always felt I forced him to settle down."

"Asshole."

"Yes. He was an asshole, wasn't he?"

223

"Mom!" Tyler exclaimed.

"That felt good," Anita said with a smile. "It's taken me thirty-five years to say that out loud."

"Do you want to say it again? You've earned the right."

"Once is enough, dear. Now, about Regina Harper and your father."

"It isn't necessary, Mom."

"Now that we've started, it should be finished; once and for all."

Tyler nodded. Her mother was right. It was time to finish it.

"I knew something was different. Martin had a bit of a bounce in his step. Instead of coming home smelling like stale beer, he sort of glowed."

"You think they were in love?" It was hard for Tyler to picture.

"Your father was. I started to worry that he would leave me. What would I do? How would I survive with two small children and no work experience?"

"You would have been fine."

"Yes," Anita agreed. "But I didn't know that then. I was scared, Tyler. So I followed Martin."

"Good for you."

"Of course you would say that, my fearless daughter. I was shaking the entire time. I had no idea what I would do if I found him with another woman. Maybe I could reason with her, explain why I needed him more that she did."

"Does that ever work?"

"Probably not."

"Especially with Regina Harper," Tyler said.

"Can you imagine my surprise when Martin turned his car onto the bridge? I followed, still not making the connection."

"Why would you? She would be the last woman anyone would suspect."

"Exactly. I thought your father must have some business with Russell Harper. Then when he drove past the turn off to Harper House, I was really confused. A few minutes later, he turned. There was a cottage. Small but nicely maintained. He went in, didn't knock or hesitate."

"Their love nest?"

Tyler winced at the term. Stupid and thoughtless.

"I'm sure that was how he saw it. I sat frozen. I don't know how I got the courage to move. I knew my husband was in there so I sneaked up to the window and looked in." Anita sighed. "You can imagine the rest."

"I'd rather not."

"It wasn't pretty. Then I did something I'm not very proud of."

"What," Tyler asked. "Tossed a rock through the window?"

"I took a picture."

"A picture." *The* picture?

"Grabbed the camera before I left the house, never thinking I would have the nerve to use it. I don't remember actually taking the picture. I knew it was in there though. I went to Spokane, had the film developed. Before I could talk myself out of it, I sent the picture to Regina Harper. Anonymously."

Fascinated, Tyler asked, "What happened?"

"She broke off the affair. Your father stopped going out. He became more attentive. Not that his new attitude lasted long."

"And that was it?"

"About seven months later, I saw Regina in town. She was very pregnant. I was in agony worrying that Martin was the father."

"How do you know he wasn't?"

Tyler held her breath waiting for the answer.

"Simple math. Another five months passed before she gave birth to Drew. The affair was over well before she conceived."

Tyler let her mother's story sink in. It went to show you never knew people. Their pasts were mysteries often best left that way. In this case, she was glad to have it all out in the open. The fewer secrets she and Drew had to deal with the better.

"Did you ever think about leaving him?"

"I did." Anita closed her eyes as if trying to block out the painful memory. "It was soon after that. I was tired. My husband didn't love or respect me. My sons were well on the way to being the same. I prayed for the strength to go on."

"How'd that work for you?"

"I know you have a problem with the church."

"I'm fine with the church. It's the hypocritical men who run it that make me question your devotion."

Anita chose not to respond. This was not a new argument, nor was it one either of them would ever win.

"I always found comfort in my faith. Suddenly, I couldn't feel God with me anymore."

"You stayed so you must have found peace again."

"I'm happy to say I did."

"And now you finally have your reward."

Anita gave her daughter a puzzled look.

"Reward?"

"All those prayers. Kyle has a job, a good woman. Isn't that what you always hoped for? I doubt there's any hope for M.J." Tyler shrugged. "At least one of your sons is moving in the right direction."

"Tyler, I don't pray because I expect God to reward me. That comes in the next life. Don't roll your eyes, young lady. You might not believe He's watching, but I do."

"Sorry, Mom. I try to respect your beliefs. It just seems so random, futile."

"It can appear that way."

Anita looked around.

"I'm going to share my deepest secret. I've never told anyone, not even during confession."

Tyler nodded. She couldn't imagine what it could be. She thought Anita told her priest everything.

"I *did* get my reward."

"What was it?" Tyler found herself whispering, enthralled.

"A baby girl."

Tyler had no words — none.

"Your father was so angry when he found out I was pregnant. We weren't exactly intimate on a regular basis. I said all the things I knew he wanted to hear. I was sorry. It was an accident."

It was the only time Anita openly defied her husband. She deliberately got pregnant then refused to have an abortion. Her belief in God was enough of a reason; her wish for a daughter sealed the deal.

"I know he wanted you to get rid of me."

"Martin never should have told you that. He was a mean, spiteful man."

"Obviously, I'm glad you didn't do it. You know how I feel about a woman's right to choose. What I can't forgive is him asking you to do something knowing you considered it a mortal sin."

"He couldn't force me, so he stopped talking to me. He pretended I didn't exist."

"Lucky you." Tyler couldn't remember the number of times she wished her father would completely forget about her existence. He didn't pay attention to her often. When he did, it was rarely a happy occasion.

"I spent nine months praying that God would finally give me a little girl to love. Doing the laundry, fixing breakfast, vacuuming the floor. I prayed on the way to the hospital, all through labor. When the doctor held you up, my sweet baby girl, I knew God was with me, Tyler. He had finally answered me."

"I'm sorry I wasn't what you wanted."

"Why would you think that?"

"Come on, Mom. I was willful, argumentative. I got into fights, at home and at school. How many times were you called into Principal Harriman's office?"

"Only six."

"*Only*? Since they were all before my senior year, I'd say that was a lot."

"We had some good talks, Principal Harriman and I." Anita smiled. "Do you know how those visits always ended?"

"I can imagine," Tyler said, shaking her head.

"I don't think you can. She would tell me, off the record, that she wished there were more students like you. Your methods were sometimes a little… violent. I mean punching Randy Kincade in the nose."

"He wouldn't stop picking on the smaller students. He was warned, suspended. Nothing worked until I showed him what would keep happening unless he stopped."

"Which is why she admired you. It's also one of the many reasons I'm glad you're mine."

"You must have wanted a sweeter, nicer little girl. One you could dress in pretty clothes and teach to cook."

"That was the girl my mother got. I wanted something different for my baby."

"You did?"

"Yes. I wanted a girl who was independent, fierce, loyal. I wanted her to be strong, compassionate. With a strong body and a soft heart. She wouldn't suffer fools. She would stand up for those who couldn't stand up for themselves. I didn't pray to be given just any little girl, Tyler. I prayed for you."

Tyler didn't wipe away the tears; she let them fall on her mother's hand as it cupped her cheek.

"Do you see now why I will always get on my knees for God?"

Nodding, Tyler slid to *her* knees, her arms encircling her mother.

"I love you."

"I love you too, baby girl. Always."

TYLER COULDN'T BELIEVE it was only one-thirty.

Such an emotional morning left her feeling drained; like days, not hours had passed. All she wanted to do was crawl into bed. Not because she needed comfort or to hide. She wanted to savor the conversation she'd shared with her mother, let the wave of peace settle a little deeper.

All those years. The questions, the guilt, the anger. Cleared up in one morning. It was easy to wish it would have happened sooner. The question was, like with Drew, would she have been ready to listen. So many things over the past few months had configured to make all this possible.

Maybe she needed to watch her best friends fall in love with good men. Men who were open about their feelings — their love. Forgiving Drew, understanding her mother. Tyler wondered if it all had to happen, one after the other, for her to understand how rare a chance she was being given.

Open your heart, Tyler.

She wanted to. She would. Tyler twirled around, laughing, arms spread. Hell, what choice did she have? Love and good feelings bombarded her from every direction. Only someone made of stone could resist. Tyler Jones was not stone. Right now, she was a grinning mass of happy — with a marshmallow core.

Hearing the mail drop through the slot in the door, Tyler practically skipped over. She scooped up the periodicals, catalogs, and letters. Nothing would bring her down, not today.

Not looking at the stamped return address, Tyler ripped open the manila envelope at the top of the pile. The first line of the letter made her stomach sink. She read it again. The stomach hit the floor.

Whirling, she grabbed her keys, heading out the front door.

When she arrived home, she was on the top of the world. Now, less that thirty minutes later, her home was being pulled out from under her.

"I DON'T UNDERSTAND how this could happen, Mrs. Lawrence."

"I know it's upsetting, Ms. Jones. Unfortunately, there isn't anything I can do. Your loan was purchased by a third party. According to the terms, they have the right to call that loan in."

"They aren't calling in the loan," Tyler pointed out through clenched teeth. "This is a foreclosure notice. I'm not being given the option to do anything but get my things together and move out."

Tyler took a deep breath. She spent the excruciatingly long trip to Spokane going over the letter in her head. She was going to lose her home, her studio. Every penny she put into it would be gone. All the steps forward wiped out in an instant.

Only it wasn't an instant. This took place months ago. Why hadn't she been notified? How could it all be taken away with the arrival of a tersely worded letter?

"The original loan was fairly straightforward. Make your payments on time, no problems. Then last winter the wording was restructured."

"I applied for a home improvement loan."

"Right." Mrs. Lawrence thumbed through the file, pulling out the paper. "Solar panels. Pricey."

"Practice. I use a lot of electricity in my work. Since those panels were installed, my Avista bill has been nil. If fact, I have a surplus. I'm going to start selling it back."

"That's very admirable, Ms. Jones. I'm very Green myself. I've started bringing coffee from home in my little thermal cup. No more styrofoam for me."

Tyler gave the woman a blank stare. She had the grace to blush.

"Right. Sorry. Not exactly on the same level." She cleared her throat. "The point is, when you increased your loan, the terms of the first loan changed."

"I'm aware of that. I had my lawyer look over the new agreement."

"Smart," Mrs. Lawrence nodded with approval. "Did he point out the new clause stating the bank had the right to sell your loan at its discretion?"

"Yes, of course. Mr. Teegue, the man who handled all of that, assured me that never happens. On the off-chance it did, I was supposed to be informed."

"Which you were. According to our records, the letter was sent at the time the loan changed hands."

"I received no such letter. Believe me, I would remember."

"I'm truly sorry. It's out of our hands. You have my sympathy."

Great, Tyler thought bitterly. That and a five dollar bill would be enough to fill up Mrs. Lawrence's thermal cup at her favorite coffee kiosk. It wouldn't save Tyler's home.

"I suggest you contact your local post office. If you can prove the letter wasn't delivered, that might buy you some time."

As solutions went, it was pretty lame. But it was all she had. Tyler stood, shaking the woman's hand.

"Can you at least tell me who bought the loan?"

"Of course. A holding company by the name of RRAH Limited. Based in Seattle. I have a phone number."

After leaving the bank, Tyler got in her car. She took out her phone and dialed the number Mrs. Lawrence supplied her with. Taking a deep breath, she waited while it rang.

"RRAH Limited. How may I help you?"

"I need to speak to someone about a loan that was purchased from my bank."

"Your name?"

"Tyler Jones."

"One moment, please."

Tyler sighed, preparing herself to be on hold for some time. To her surprise, the woman came back in less than minute.

"I'm sorry, Ms. Jones. The gentleman in charge of that account is on vacation. If you can call back in two weeks, he will be back in the office."

"I don't have two weeks," Tyler said through gritted teeth. "There must be someone covering for him while he's away."

"Yes, but he is out on business. I don't know when he'll be back."

"Can I leave my name and number? It's extremely important that I speak with him. Immediately, if not sooner."

Tyler left the information with little hope she would get a return call. How could this be happening? It felt like a bad dream that she would wake up from. Give it time. Except time was the one thing she didn't have. In less than a month, she would literally be out on the street.

Her hand shook as she put the key in the ignition. Damn it. She couldn't drive back to Harper Falls until she got her nerves under control.

Tyler looked at her phone. Should she call Dani or Rose? They would lend sympathetic ears. Hell, they would try to lend her money. Even if it helped, which at this point it didn't, she wouldn't take it. They knew that. They could make the offer. She could turn it down. No one would feel better.

Drew. Tyler reached for the phone then snatched back her hand. Again, there was no point. She didn't want Drew throwing his weight around to save her. She had to do this on her own. Fail or succeed, she was responsible. Crying on Drew's shoulder might feel good for a little while. Then what? She would tell him and her friends when and only when, all possible avenues were exhausted.

Taking a deep, calming breath, Tyler tried again to start her car. This time she was stopped by the ringing of her phone.

Drew. What, was he psychic? She briefly considered letting it go to voicemail. Nope, she could use the sound of a friendly voice.

"Hi."

"Hi, yourself. I wanted to check in to make sure we were still on for tonight."

Tonight? Tyler searched her brain. *Was there something special going on?*

"I'm sorry. It's been a crazy day. Did we have plans?"

"Pizza, hanging out. Off the charts sex. Nothing special."

"Sounds pretty special to me."

Right now, it sounded like heaven.

"Then it's a date." There was a pause. "Hey, is everything okay?"

"Sure. Why do you ask?"

"Your voice sounds a little funny. Tense."

"I had a long visit with my mother this morning. I guess I'm still a little wound up."

Boy, talk about the understatement of all understatements. She was wound tighter than a Kansas tornado.

"Uh oh."

Tyler smiled. *Wow*, she *actually* smiled. Talking with Drew was always a good decision.

"Wrong. Uh oh is your mother, not mine. We cleared up some things. Old business that had festered way too long. I'll tell you about it tonight."

"Okay. Until then, take it easy. Breathe. Think of me going down on you. I know I will be."

Tyler's eyes widened. That was by far the most original way to end a phone call she'd ever experienced. It almost made her forget her problems. *Almost.*

This time, when she turned the key, her hands were steady. Time to go home. First thing on her agenda? Stop at the post office.

Chapter Sixteen

"THE LETTER WAS delivered, Tyler."

"I didn't get it, Walt."

Tyler went to school with Walter Frome. She liked him. She knew his wife, gave out candy to his kids on Halloween. Right now, she wanted to reach over the counter and pull his heart out of his chest. Probably a good thing that he didn't know what was going on in her head.

"Carla is the mail carrier in your part of town. She's good. Reliable."

"I'm not accusing anyone of anything, Walt. I know I didn't get the letter, that's all."

"You got that big, fancy security system put in last month. Any chance someone could have broken in before that?"

"And stolen one piece of mail?"

"It was a thought."

Tyler made her lawyer her next stop. After looking over the document from this morning, he said it came down to two choices. Fight, which would stop any foreclosure. It would also be expensive and, in the end, futile. Or she could find whoever was behind RRAH Limited.

Then what? Beg them not to take her home? Tyler was fine with a little groveling. There was only one big problem. Finding someone who didn't want to be found.

Drew. She kept coming back to him. He was co-owner of a billion dollar security firm. In all likelihood, he would have a name for her in a matter of hours.

Don't be stubborn, Tyler told herself. *Call. Now.*

With a resigned sigh, she got out her phone and dialed.

Voicemail. This was not her day. She didn't bother to leave a message; she would see him later. She tried Jack. Again, not picking up. Then Alex. Oh, come on. How could they all be unavailable?

Needing to vent on someone, she hit speed dial. Rose was out. Dani too. Was there some mass orgy that she wasn't invited to?

Frustrated beyond words, she did the only thing that came to mind. She went home and worked. Nothing cleared her mind like losing herself in her art. Today, as she ran her hands over the beginnings a whimsical sprite hiding in a bed of wild poppies, it took almost an hour for her brain to hit neutral. When it did, when she let go of everything else, her sculpture began to sing.

Time had no meaning when she was focused on releasing her subject for the lump of clay or block of marble. She knew it was in there, begging to see the light of day. To be given the chance to inspire or delight.

This particular project was for a backyard garden. A woman in San Diego saw a piece of Tyler's in a gallery while visiting relatives in Chicago. Her only instructions for the commission? Make it light and fun.

Standing back, looking critically at the winking figure, Tyler thought, *mission accomplished.*

She was a sweaty, tired mess. And she felt better. If she were forced to live in an alley, making a cardboard box her home, she would be fine as long as she could create.

Now that was ridiculous. Even without her home, she would never be homeless. There was money in the bank. Generous friends. In a pinch, her mother would take her, though with M.J. in and out, that was not going to happen.

Then there was Drew. Why did she always think of him last?

Tyler smiled a little sadly. That was easy. She thought of him last because she wanted him. First, last. Always.

The doorbell made her jump. Glancing at her watch, she was amazed to see how late it was. The bell rang again. It had to be Drew.

Tyler gave a quick look to be sure before disengaging the locks. Damn, there were a lot of the suckers. She fumbled with the last one before throwing open the door.

"I'm a dirty, sweaty mess so if you don't want me in your arms, you'd better speak up. Now."

Drew wordlessly stepped into the studio, shut the door, and pulled Tyler into his arms. He didn't know what was wrong. Something told him this was going to take more than a hug to fix. But it was a start.

Tyler sank in and held on. Closing her eyes, she let the feel of his arms around her begin to chase away all the crap of the day.

"Let me help."

"You are," Tyler assured him. She burrowed deep, taking in his smell, his warmth.

Drew could feel her distress. She practically vibrated with it. He was fine with holding her as long as she needed. Scooping her off her feet, he headed for the big overstuffed chair in the lounge area. He settled them both, his right hand running along her back — soothing. His left hand cupping her cheek, his thumb lightly caressing the soft skin.

Tyler felt like she had held her breath all day. Drew's touch gave her the ability to exhale. The process was slow. She wasn't sure how long they sat there. She did know his patience was infinite. He didn't ask. He didn't push. He waited.

"It's a long story."

Drew kissed the top of her head before tipping her chin so he could look into her eyes.

"I'm not going anywhere." He looked deep. "For you, I have all the time in the world."

"Don't be sweet — not yet. I'll cry. Once I start blubbering, I'll never get everything out."

Now he was worried. Tyler blubbering? This was bad.

"Want me to be mean?" he asked, trying to inject a little humor. "What did Cher say to Nicholas Cage in *Moonstruck*? Oh, that's right. *Snap out of it.*"

"She slapped him first. Twice."

"If you don't mind, I vote we skip that part."

Tyler nodded, a little smile on her lips. *There we go*, Drew thought, *now we can get started.*

"Tell me your troubles, Ty. Let me make it better."

"I don't think anyone can do that," Tyler said with a sigh.

"We'll see. Now, spill. You'll feel better, I promise."

She started from the beginning. Her emotional visit with her mother. The letter. The trip to Spokane. It all came tumbling out. Not incoherently. Tyler was surprised at how calmly she was able to convey the turbulent events of the day.

Drew let her talk. There was no need to interrupt or ask questions. Once Tyler got started, she told him everything in detail. He felt his emotions run the same gamut as hers. Happiness for the deeper connection she found with her mother. Worry and despair that she might lose her studio.

Guilt. That one was his own. The idea that she needed him — needed her friends — and no one could be found, burned like acid in his stomach.

"I'm sorry, Ty." Drew pulled her closer. "I had a meeting that lasted all afternoon. Jack and Alex spent the afternoon with their ladies. If none of them answered their phones, they were probably having a little afternoon delight."

That made Tyler smile again.

"I wasn't that far off."

"What do you mean?"

"When I couldn't get in touch with any of you, I thought there was an orgy and I wasn't invited."

Drew laughed.

"We are all strictly the one-on-one types."

"Good to know."

"Can I see the letter? The one that came today?"

Tyler disengaged from him long enough to retrieve the piece of paper. Handing it to Drew, she sat next to him while he read.

"You lawyer is right. We need to find the owners of RRAH Limited. Money speaks. I can—"

"No."

"No, what?"

"No, you won't fix this with your money."

"Tyler, be reasonable."

Tyler felt the rise of a familiar heat. Anger. Good. She spent the day feeling helpless, crushed. She hated being a victim. It was time to stop. Getting mad felt better.

"Reasonable? That's an interesting word to toss around. You have money. Lots of it. I don't. Since when does rich equal the ability to reason? My observations say just the opposite."

"I want to help. Why is that wrong?"

"Because your first impulse is to throw money — your money — at the problem. I need help. I need you to find me a name, not flaunt your big bucks."

"Flaunt? Did you say flaunt?"

"You heard me right."

"Tyler."

Drew stopped. He knew what she was doing. She needed to swat at somebody. He was handy. Safe.

Drew let that sink in. Tyler knew she was safe with him. She could kick and punch at him trusting he would take it. Give a little back.

Tyler was a fighter. She needed a man who could hold his own. Drew felt a wave of satisfaction. He grinned. He was that man. And Tyler knew it.

"Are you smiling? Seriously?"

"Here's what I'm going to do for you, Tyler Jones." He held up three fingers. "First, I'm going to call Jack. He can find out the name behind RRAH Limited."

Drew took down one finger.

"Second, I'm going to order some soup from *Pansy's Diner*. I know the plan was pizza," Drew said when Tyler would have protested. "I'm guessing you haven't eaten all day. You need something comforting."

"Pizza is comforting."

Ignoring her remark, Drew wiggled the last finger.

"Finally, I'm going to strip you down to your lovely birthday suit, get you in the shower. Wash you. Kiss you. Pamper you. We'll eat. We'll make love." Drew gathered her close. "We'll figure out what to do."

Tyler didn't want to argue. It all sounded too good.

"Isn't Jack busy?"

"Jack had been *getting busy* with Rose all day," Drew laughed. "He won't mind, Ty."

After Drew had given him the Reader's Digest, Jack not only didn't mind, he rushed Drew off the phone so he could get started.

Tyler listened with one ear while placing their dinner order. She was lucky to have amazing friends. She could get by on her own; it was good to know she didn't have to.

"Now, I believe I said something about washing you."

Tyler eluded his grasp. She laughed, slapping his hands away when he made another grab.

"One of us has to be out here when the food arrives."

"Call back. Tell them to delay delivery for another half hour."

Tyler sidestepped him, shaking her head. She pulled off her t-shirt, uncovering a mint-colored bra trimmed in matching lace.

"Now that's just not fair," Drew said with a frown. "I want to find out if your panties match."

"No problem."

Tyler unbuttoned her jeans, shimmying them down her hips. She stepped out, showing Drew her underwear was indeed color-coordinated.

"Need help unhooking that?" he asked hopefully.

Tyler shook her head. "Front closure."

She teased the bra open, showing more skin while keeping her breasts fully covered.

"Don't poke the bear, honey."

"More like a big, sleek cat. Jaguar? Panther?"

"Go take your shower before I pounce." He pretended to lunge after her, enjoying the view of her butt as she scampered out of the room.

Alone, Drew picked up the letter again. He took out his phone, aimed, sending the picture to Jack with a few notes. It shouldn't take long. Digging was a specialty of his partner. If the information turned out to be what Drew thought, the owner of RRAH Limited was going to be sorry *she* ever started this. He planned on finishing it — once and for all.

MARTIN JONES JUNIOR sat in his beat-up Chevy Nova, smoking cigarettes, throwing back cheap whiskey. He stared, his hatred growing, at the sleek black Ferrari parked in front of his bitch sister's studio.

That should be his car. He deserved better than this piece of crap he won in a poker game ten years ago. Even then, it was a rust bucket that refused to start every other time. The smell of cat piss still lingered from the visible stain in the backseat. How was that possible?

He checked his watch. That fucker Drew Harper probably wasn't leaving until morning. What he saw in Tyler, M.J. would never know. A skinny ballbuster. He liked his women quiet, respectful, in bed and out. His sister never knew when to shut up. M.J. imagined she was the same during sex. He shuddered at the thought.

He lifted the almost empty bottle to his lips. Damn. Should have brought a spare. There was still time to stop by the liquor store. Old Lady Harper was paying him to watch Tyler and her fancy-ass son, not the outside of a building. She'd never know if he cut out early.

M.J. turned the ignition. The car coughed, reluctantly starting on the first try. Tomorrow, he would give Mrs. High and Mighty his weekly report. Boring as hell. Maybe he'd make up a fight. A big one. That would make her happy and might earn him a bonus.

M.J. flicked his half-smoked cigarette out the window. Tyler had always been a pain in his ass. He hated her from the moment his parents announced her imminent arrival. Then she turned out to be a girl. Ugh. Worthless.

It seemed only fair that she turned out to finally be good for something.

THE HOT SHOWER made Tyler feel like a new woman. Telling everything to Drew, having someone who listened, sympathized, eased the feeling of doom she'd been burdened with most of the day. The warm soup and crusty bread from *Pansy's Diner* would help too. Drew was right. She needed something in her stomach.

Instead of getting dressed, she put on a slinky little nightie the color of ripe plums. She loved how the silk felt against her skin. Tyler couldn't wait to see Drew's reaction. Deciding they might not get to dinner if he saw it too soon, she covered up in a thick terry cloth robe. A present from her mother, it was about as sexy as gym socks. She bundled her hair into a messy bun on top of her head, adding a touch of lip-gloss.

"Perfect timing. The food arrived a couple minutes ago." Drew turned, his smile widening when he saw her.

"What?"

"I'm more tempted to eat you than the soup."

Tyler smoothed a hand down the soft robe. "Really? I was going for sexless."

"Not possible, honey. A big head to toe paper bag — maybe. I look at you and zing — instant want."

Tyler wondered how any woman could resist a man who looked at her like that? Drew's eyes told her he found her beautiful, sexy. As she stood there in a frumpy robe and no makeup, she felt like she was.

Now, the meal eaten, the dishes done, they were in her bed. Her in the nightie that garnered just the reaction she hoped. Him, big, gorgeous

Drew Harper, sprawled at her feet — painting her toenails.

"You're awfully good at that."

"Natural ability. I swear you're my first."

"Steady hand," Tyler observed; the toes on her right foot clenching as he worked on the left. Soooo sexy.

"Mmm." He leaned close to his work, carefully avoiding going outside the lines. Looking up, he gently blew on the wet polish. "We were smart to go with the *Scarlet Pimpernel*. Much better than *That Touch of Pink*."

Holy crap, Tyler thought. If he kissed her instep, she might explode on the spot.

"You know, I've seen *Bull Durham* five, maybe six times."

"Me too." Tyler breathed the words. Drew's thumb rubbed a spot on the bottom of her foot that should have been illegal.

"As I recall, when Kevin Costner did this for Susan Sarandon, she was tied up."

Tyler's eyes popped back open. Was he serious? She looked closely. Maybe, a little. Mostly teasing.

She was warm, relaxed. Though Drew's attention soothed her worries, he couldn't eliminate them completely. There was still an underlying tension. No amount of gentle sweetness could take care of it all. It made her feel slightly restless, yet just reckless enough to try something she might not otherwise consider.

Tyler looked Drew in the eye, her smile a wicked challenge. *You toss out an idea*, she was saying, *you better be prepared to follow through.*

"There are some scarves on a hook behind the closet door."

Chapter Seventeen

DREW BLINKED. WAS Tyler saying what he thought she was saying?

"Unless you're not up to it. Or maybe you don't like the idea?"

Tyler? Tied to the bed? At his mercy? Even a dead man would rise to that occasion.

Drew hopped off the bed, retrieving two long silk scarves. Turning back, he tested the strength and softness. Once he had her tied, he didn't want her pulling loose or scraping up her wrists.

For a moment, Drew considered asking Tyler if she really wanted to do this. One look at her gave him the answer he sought — no words needed.

"Feeling a little wild tonight, are we?"

Not expecting a response, Drew put one knee on the mattress. He took her left hand, gently kissing her wrist before slipping on the scarf. He secured it to the headboard, tugging once to make sure it wouldn't come loose.

"Aren't I supposed to have a safe word?"

Drew quickly tied her other wrist before meeting her twinkling eyes with his own.

"How about, *Untie these fucking scarves, Drew. Now.*"

"Kind of a mouth full, but it works for me."

After arranging the pillows behind her head, Drew gave Tyler a long, thorough kiss that primed them both for what was to come.

"Comfortable?"

"Mmm."

"How are your wrists? Are the scarves too tight?"

"All's good."

Standing back, he surveyed his handy work.

Tyler was laid out on a background of cream-colored sheets like a pagan feast. Crimson-tipped toes curled into the material, her arched feet transitioning into a pair of long, shapely mouthwateringly bare legs. He knew the skin was smooth, soft. He could spend hours on them alone.

That tiny scrap of silk he'd earlier found to be hiding under her bulky robe cupped the area just above her thighs.

"I'm in charge."

"Yes," she agreed. Then couldn't resist adding, "For tonight. Next time, we switch places."

Drew let that remark slide. *Next time,* depending on the mood, who knew? He was focused on now.

"Spread your legs. Just a little. That's right."

Silk moved, outlining, adorning to perfection. Drew joined her on the bed, his hands on each ankle. He caressed the skin then lifted one foot to nibble lightly. His teeth grazed her instep, biting hard enough to elicit a moan of pleasure, not pain.

"You like that?"

"Oh, yes."

Smiling, Drew bit again, just a little harder followed by a soothing kiss. His mouth continued up, stopping to worship her calf, that little spot behind her knee he knew was particularly sensitive. The inside of her thigh. He couldn't get enough of her. He knew he never would.

Tyler ran her tongue over her suddenly dry lips. She leaned her head back, eyes closed, savoring every second of Drew's slow, erotic journey.

Her hands gripped the scarves, tugging. It was liberating, having him in complete control. A novelty. Nothing she would want every day. Tonight? It was exactly what she needed.

"So pretty."

Tyler slowly opened her eyes. Drew lifted the material from between her legs. He lounged like a pampered Sheik, everything before him his for the taking. Holding her breath, she waited as he hovered, his mouth mere inches from taking his first taste. His gaze met hers. *Watch*, he silently told her. *See how much I love doing this to you. Feel.*

At the first swipe of his tongue, the air rushed from Tyler's lungs.

"Mmm," Drew murmured against the sensitive skin, the vibration sending shots of pleasure through her body.

"Drew."

He tasted again.

"The best dessert ever."

Tyler was in a zone of pure bliss. Every sense was focused on Drew and his magical mouth. He took her up, up, up. Had her straining to tip over the edge, only to scale back, leave hanging.

"I need…"

"I know, honey. I'm driving. Relax, enjoy the ride."

Tyler's arms flexed, her legs tensed. She shifted until her foot ran along Drew's back. She couldn't use her hands to touch him so she used what she could to encourage, urge on.

Drew was happy to tease the pleasure from Tyler a little at a time. Her taste was intoxicating. Hearing her sighs, her moans, gave him satisfaction as he had never known. This was for her. The better he could make it, the happier he would be.

"I can tell you're close." Drew ran a finger across her opening. "Do you want me to end this," his finger entered, "or should we continue to play?"

"Play." She said the word in a breathy burst. It was too good. She wanted more.

Smiling, Drew proceeded to reward her for giving him the right answer.

A second then third finger joined the first. His mouth worshiped her, kissing, tasting, leaving her writhing. She begged for release while hoping it would never end.

When his other hand moved above his mouth, finding the source of the pleasure, applying just the right amount of pressure, it was too much. Tyler's body tensed. Wave after wave engulfed her. At first a massive burst, her skin suffused with heat. Drew held her, encouraging her to hold the feelings, gently petting her as she coasted down from an exhilarating flight. She was left limp, her smile happy, relaxed.

Drew released her from the scarves, checking for any abrasions. Seeing none, he lightly rubbed the skin, kissing the inside of each wrist.

He settled next to her, taking her in his arms. He liked the way Tyler automatically burrowed closer. Lying in each other's arms was becoming natural, for both of them.

"You still have your clothes on."

It was a sleepy observation, one that had him smiling.

"I didn't have time to take them off." He smoothed back the hair from her face. Such a dear, beautiful face. "I was wonderfully distracted."

"Mmm." Definitely a sound of agreement. "Your turn."

Drew didn't answer. Tyler was so close to falling asleep, he didn't want to do anything to interrupt the journey. Waiting until her breathing was steady, he slipped from the bed. He arranged the blanket over her, kissing her forehead, before taking his phone and quietly moving across the room.

Drew disengaged the alarm then went outside into the cold November night. Hitting speed dial, he waited.

"I expected to hear from you sooner."

"I've been busy."

"Me too," Jack countered.

"What did you find?" Drew braced himself. Knowing what was coming didn't stop the dread from settling in.

"You nailed it. It only took me a couple of hours. A dodge and a weave then boom. It was a crappy job, Drew. I'd say you were meant to find out — fast."

"Yeah." Drew no longer felt any dread. He was weary of the game. He should have ended it long ago.

"What are you going to do?"

"Tonight? I'm going back to my warm, sleeping woman."

"That sounds like a winner," Jack said. He paused. "Tomorrow? Cause if you need help hiding the body, I'm with you. Hell, I'll call Alex. He's ex-Army. I'm sure he has all kinds of nifty tricks up his sleeve."

"Thanks. I know you guys have my back." Drew took a deep breath. "No. This is going to be a bloodless coup."

"Long time coming."

"Inevitable."

Neither man spoke. It wasn't an awkward silence. Just two friends lost in their similar thoughts.

"Have you filled Alex in?" Drew asked after a while.

"He was here earlier when you called. Rose and Dani were halfway out the door before we could convince them to wait until morning."

"I appreciate it, Jack. I know Tyler would have welcomed their company but…"

"You needed to be alone with her. I get it. How is she?"

"Better. This news. I don't know what her reaction will be."

"Pissed," Jack said. "Rose says Tyler has a backbone of steel. I haven't seen anything to make me dispute that."

Pissed, Drew thought a few minutes later as he ended the call. That sounded right. It was certainly better than sad and trembling. It killed him to see his strong, brave Tyler that way. She bounced back. She always did. Drew gave a tired sigh. It was time to make sure she stopped having to.

Drew turned to go back inside then stopped, glancing at his watch. Not too late, he decided. Calling up his contacts, he hit the second on his list. The one right below Jack.

"Alex. I hope I didn't get you up. I need a favor."

TYLER SIPPED HER morning coffee. It tasted better than usual. No mystery as to why. It always tasted better when somebody else made it. Drew had a cup waiting before she popped her eyes open. Even the smell was enough to start her motor. A couple of drinks got her running on all cylinders.

"I could get used to having coffee in bed."

"Okay."

"Okay, what?"

"Okay, I'll bring you coffee in bed every morning."

Tyler's motor might be running at full speed, but her brain was still in second gear. What was Drew saying?

"Drew…"

"We'll talk about it later." He gave her a quick kiss on the cheek. "I'm going to jump in the shower. Oh, if you notice my car is gone, don't worry. Alex picked it up last night."

Tyler watched him go. She could care less about the well-being of one of his babies. Tucked safely away for the night in its climate-controlled garage. Or hanging in her driveway. So what?

It was the thing before. Had he asked her to move in with him? They couldn't live here. Soon it would no longer be hers. Tyler shook off the thought. Whatever happened with the studio, she wasn't letting go of Drew. As he said, they would talk later.

She pulled on a pair of jeans, thick socks and a baggy yellow sweater. After a long, warm fall, it finally felt like November. The place was surprisingly warm for so early. Again thanks to Drew. Tyler always forgot to turn on the heat. By the time she thought of it, most of the day had passed. Unless it was below freezing outside, there were days she didn't bother at all.

Taking her cup, she padded to the kitchen. Giving herself a refill, she stood with her back against the counter, looking around.

She would miss this place. Funny how easily she'd become resigned to the idea that she was going to lose it. She was sad — she wasn't devastated. There were other places, better places. This was her first. That made it special.

The doorbell brought her out of her musings. Setting her cup aside, Tyler went to see who it was. Looking through the peephole, her eyes widened. Standing back, she took a deep breath. She must have been mistaken. It couldn't be. Cautiously, as though it might bite her, Tyler looked again.

Well, damn. What a way to ruin a perfectly good morning.

Tyler pulled back her shoulders then took a deep breath. Her wish for a mirror had nothing to do with her wardrobe, her hair, or the lack of makeup on her face. She wished there was time to check her expression. She wanted calm, composed. Hiding the sneer would be difficult. Tyler thought for a moment then shrugged. That might not be such a bad thing after all.

Deciding she was as ready as she was going to get, she opened the door.

"Regina Harper. As I live and breathe."

Tyler barely contained her groan. Where the hell had that come from?

"Miss Jones."

In terms of proximity, this was the closest she'd gotten to Drew's mother. It felt… strange. Uncomfortable. Something she hoped never to repeat.

"Are you going to ask me in?"

Of course, Tyler remembered. Vampires needed to be invited before they could enter someone's home.

Tyler felt her lips twitch, something the eagle eye of the other woman didn't miss. Regina's lips tightened. Humor, in any form, was not appreciated. When aimed at her, it was verboten. *Heil, Regina.*

"Come in."

Tyler stepped back to let Regina Harper enter. A whiff of French perfume filled the air causing Tyler's nose to twitch. Ugh. Expensive didn't mean good.

Regina walked around, examining — careful not to touch. Tyler shouldn't have worried about her sneer. Queen Reggie had hers beat by a mile.

Take her coat. Tyler heard her mother's voice as clear as a bell. *Ask her to sit. Offer her a cup of coffee.* She wondered if etiquette applied when your enemy came to call.

"Nice coat."

Recognizing sarcasm when she heard it, Regina's eyebrows lifted — sort of. Botox, or whatever toxins the woman had injected into her face prevented much range of movement.

"Chinchilla."

No kidding, Tyler thought. *I was going to guess Dalmatian.*

"I can do the stare down as long as you, Regina. Cut to the chase. Why are you here?" *And how can I get you to leave as quickly as possible?*

"You're exactly what I expected," Regina purred. And sneered. An interesting combination.

"Is this where I ask what you mean?" Tyler shook her head in amazement. "I don't play that game, Reggie."

Regina stiffened further. How she didn't break into tiny pieces, Tyler didn't know.

"This is no game, Miss Jones," Regina assured her. "But, if it were, you have lost." She almost smiled. "At last."

"Fine," Tyler sighed. "I give. How have I lost? I'm back in Harper Falls. I'm breathing." *I have Drew.*

Tyler refrained from adding the last part. Yes, he was the source of the contention between them. Yet only one of them loved him. She refused to discuss Drew with a woman who looked on him as a possession she would never have, instead of the son she didn't deserve.

"I have a business proposition for you, Miss Jones."

Business? Tyler frowned. Then the light bulb went on. Well, shit. How stupid could she be? Why hadn't she thought of it sooner?

"You're RRAH Limited."

"Yes." This time Regina did smile. It was full of self-satisfaction. "Would you like to know what the initials stand for?"

Tyler didn't answer — she was still reeling.

"Regina, Russell, Andrew, Harper."

"Together for the first time."

"You think you're very clever, don't you?" Regina hissed. "Perhaps that sharp mind is what attracted Andrew."

"No doubt. That and my big breasts." Tyler watched the other woman's eyes move to her chest. "Yes. *That*, in case you missed it, was also sarcasm."

"Enough! I will pay you twice what this hovel is worth if you leave town. Find some place new. You can start over — debt-free."

"I'm already debt-free. You saw to that." Tyler turned her back on Regina so they both had the same view of the studio. "As soon as you take possession, I owe nothing. Clean slate."

"Don't be a fool. I'm offering you more money than you've ever seen. Considering your... profession, it's more money than you will ever see at one time."

"I wonder." Tyler paused. She knew she shouldn't do this. She could hold her tongue. Throw Regina out. Leave it alone. Common sense said it was what she *should* do. Ah, what the hell. This was probably the only chance she would ever get.

"Do you think it was your money that my father wanted? Or was it you?"

For a second, Tyler thought Regina was going to faint. She turned white as a sheet; she swayed.

Before Tyler could decide whether to try to catch the woman, Regina pulled herself together. Her eyes narrowed; her gaze laser-sharp.

"You have a lot of nerve, young woman."

"Not nearly as much as you, Regina."

Tyler turned towards the bathroom door. Drew. How could she forget he was here?

Drew circled around Regina. If this was about picking sides, without words he firmly established where he stood. Right beside Tyler.

Fresh from the shower, his dark hair still damp. In jeans, a t-shirt, his feet bare. Drew looked cool, calm, controlled. Only his eyes gave away the storm of emotions he felt. Without thinking, Tyler reached for his hand; her only thought was to comfort. Drew laced his fingers with hers, squeezing gently, letting her know it was all right. That *he* was all right.

Ten years. In all honesty, when he left Harper Falls, he never thought to see Regina again. Even after he returned, he avoided any situation that would bring them together. If another ten years passed before it happened again, he would be just fine with that.

"Andrew. I didn't know you were here."

"That's obvious. I'm sure you wanted to catch Tyler alone to share your generous offer. Sorry to crash the party."

"I won't apologize for trying one more time to save you from polluting the Harper bloodline."

"That ship sailed when you gave birth to me."

Regina gasped. It seemed Drew knew her weakness. Tyler was surprised to find out she had one.

"I can trace my family back to Plymouth Rock."

"Give the blue-blood crap a rest, Regina. No matter how long your family's lineage, the fact remains they needed money. I don't know if you convinced my father that you loved him. Maybe he was dazzled by your beauty. I'll admit you were a looker."

"You've said quite enough, Andrew. You have a legacy to maintain. Tyler Jones is not the woman to help you do that. You've played at your little company, had your bout of rebellion. You have a duty to your name and this town. Now it's time to step up."

"You don't get it," Drew said in amazement. He turned to Tyler. "She's delusional. You heard her. *Playing* at my *little* company?"

Tyler could feel the anger vibrating through him. She would have tried to put an end to it if she didn't think he needed to get it out. He'd held it in his entire life. He needed to get this off his chest. All of it.

"I'm here, Drew. It's okay."

"You!" Regina pointed a finger at Tyler. "Before he became involved with you, he was headed down the proper path. He was a Harper, through and through. You ruined him."

"Wow." Tyler looked at Drew. "What do you say about that?"

Drew lifted her hand, kissing the back.

"Thank you."

"You're more than welcome," Tyler smiled. "I wish I could take all the credit. Regina here did most of the work. She pushed you out of town long before you fell under my evil influence."

Drew smiled back, his eyes warm, loving. The storm was clearing.

"Stop this, Regina. The Harper name will be fine. You will continue to reign over the town. Nothing has to change. All I ask is that you leave Tyler alone. This is her home. Let her continue to make her regular payments. Drop the foreclosure."

"No."

"Regina—"

"I will burn this place to the ground before I let her stay here. Nothing you can say or do, Andrew, will make me change my mind." Regina lifted her chin. There was no heat in her words — no passion. Just cool determination.

"I don't believe you will throw me out of Harper House. If you do? Fine." She looked at Tyler. "We will both be without our homes."

Without another word, Regina Harper turned, calmly walking out, her steps even and unrushed.

The door was barely shut when Drew took Tyler into his arms. He buried his face in her hair, swaying.

"I'm sorry, Ty."

"Me, too. I'm sorry you grew up with… that." Tyler hugged him with all her might. "I'm so grateful you're stronger than she is. Somehow you became your own man; a good, fine man."

"I had my father." Drew sighed. "Which is why Regina was right. I won't throw her out of Harper House. Dad asked me to let her stay there. There's nothing in writing; he didn't make me promise."

"He asked. You want to honor that." She rested her head above the beat of his heart. "Like I said — a good man."

Drew tipped up her chin taking her mouth with his. The kiss was a comfort to them both. Sweet, gentle. Loving.

Tyler felt her heart swell. She loved him. Not as a young woman of sixteen. This time the stars were out of her eyes. She didn't expect the perfect love — or man. For the rest of her life, she would fight, laugh, seduce, cry. She would be ferocious, relentless, tireless. Whatever it took to keep him, this time she wasn't letting go.

"We'll fight her, Ty. This is your home; we won't let her take it from you."

"It's just a place."

"What?"

Tyler leaned back to look into his eyes, her smile serene.

"This morning I looked around. I realized something important."

"Tell me." Drew gave her cheek a caress.

"These are only walls, a ceiling. This place is not who I am. What if it burned to the ground? Would I cease to exist? Would I curl up — give up?"

"Hell, no."

"Damn straight, hell no. I have my health, my talent. I have good friends. My mother." She laughed. "I might even have Kyle." Her gray eyes became a little dreamy. "Most important? I have you."

"Never doubt it, Ty."

"You are so pretty."

Startled, as much by the sentiment as the abrupt change of subject, Drew frowned. He looked uncomfortable. Almost embarrassed.

"Jeez, Ty. Really? Why would you say that?"

Tyler smoothed back his hair, her smile teasing and sincere.

"Remember that first time we met on the bridge?"

"Like it was yesterday."

"I meant it when I called you 'Pretty Boy.' Now you're a man. Handsome, sexy."

"I like that." Drew smiled back.

"You'll always be my pretty boy. Seventy years from now, I'll still think of you that way."

"When you put it that way…" Drew nipped playfully at her fingers. "Let's keep it between us, if you don't mind. Kind of our little secret. Of course, if you want to spread around the handsome and sexy part, I can live with that."

"I'll bet." Shaking her head at his silliness, Tyler gave his chin a quick kiss.

"I need more coffee." Drew watched as she poured herself a cup. "Want some?" she asked, holding up the pot.

"Sure."

Drew took the cup, thanking her. He knew what he wanted to say. Weighed the words. Then spoke. "Move in with me."

Tyler didn't hesitate; she simply shook her head.

"No?"

"No."

"Why not?" Drew demanded. "I'm all alone in that big house — our house. You need a place to live."

"Not this second." Tyler set her cup down, crossing her arms over her chest. "Even Regina can't throw me out tomorrow. I have a month, according to my lawyer. It will take some time to find a new studio. That means finishing the projects I can. Putting things in storage."

"All of which you could do living with me," Drew reasoned. "There's more than enough empty garage space for storage. As for a new studio, you already have one."

"I do?"

Drew hitched his shoulders. "I had it built with the house. It needs some final touches. You decide. The room can be finished to your specifications."

"Why didn't you show it to me when I was out there?"

"Because it was …"

"Too soon."

"Fine," Drew said. "You have to admit, Ty. A lot has happened since then. Not just this shit with Regina. Between us."

"I agree."

"Our lives are intertwined. They always have been. Ten years and thousands of miles couldn't change that."

Lord knows she tried, Tyler thought. Thank goodness she was lousy at purging him from her heart.

"I plan on spending every night with you."

"I like that plan."

"Then why delay the inevitable?" Drew gave her his most charming smile. It was almost enough to make her give in. *Almost.*

"Drew." Tyler took a deep breath. How could she explain something to him that *she* barely understood?

"Do you know what I see when I look at you?" he asked, circling back to her earlier comments about him.

"A hard-headed fool?"

"Now you're reading my mind." His smile was teasing. "Though I would never call you a fool."

"I've had my moments."

"Haven't we all?"

Drew tipped his head slightly as if studying her. After a moment, he gave a nod.

"Yup. Beautiful, smart. Fiercely loyal to those you love." He paused, then added. "Eminently lovable."

Don't cry, Tyler told herself. This was not the time for tears. Not when she was so happy.

"If you need a little more time, I can live with that. I'm not going anywhere."

Hadn't she told him that not too long ago? It was good to hear him say it. Some things bear repeating — often.

"Come with me."

Tyler took Drew's hand, leading him back to the bed. Neatly made, a pile of linen on the corner chair.

"When did you have time to change the sheets?"

"I'm a man of many skills. Stealth bed making is just one of them."

Tyler ran a hand over the quilt. "Much nicer than when I do it. Sorry."

She pulled back the covers, disrupting his handiwork. Pulling, she toppled them both onto the bed. They rolled, Tyler ending up on top, her mouth fused with his.

"If this is the end result, you can mess up my freshly made bed anytime you like."

"Good answer."

Tyler kissed Drew again. This time slower; her intent obvious.

Drew's hand gripped her hips, adjusting until the juncture of her slightly spread legs fit perfectly against his erection.

"God, Ty. What you do to me."

"How soon do you have to be at work?" She practically moaned the words against his mouth.

"Work?" he asked, already pulling the sweater over her head. "What's that?"

Chapter Eighteen

"**M**OM WANTS EVERYONE there for Thanksgiving."

"Thanksgiving?" Tyler looked slightly appalled. How did it get to be that time of year again?

"You know," Dani said, face straight. "That day every November we worship cranberry sauce and football."

"I thought it was turkey and giblets."

Dani considered Rose's statement.

"What are giblets, anyway?"

"Usually the gizzard, heart, and liver of a bird."

"Nasty."

All three friends agreed. Luckily, no one they knew used it, for dressing or otherwise.

"Explain again the difference between stuffing and dressing?"

"Enough," Tyler laughed. Once started, this kind of back and forth could go on for hours. "You know the difference."

"Only because Mom made me peel those yummy little pearl onions while she made the dressing. The Wilde family refuses to stick anything up a turkey's ass. Roasting, carving, and devouring the poor thing is fine. Just avoid the anal cavity."

Tyler almost spit her wine across the room.

"Your mother did not use the words ass or anal."

Dani shrugged. "Fine. Cavity. *Tomato, tomahto.*"

"Let's call the whole thing off," Rose added.

"Yes," Tyler begged. "Please."

It was Wednesday at Rose's. The informal get-together served two purposes. Catching up on all the news. There was plenty of that. It took almost an hour for Tyler to repeat in detail everything that happened between yesterday and this evening.

Less than forty-eight hours. There was more to say than if a normal, low drama month had passed.

Dani and Rose called that morning just before Drew left. She was able to assure them she was fine, promising to fill in the blanks later that evening. After two large glasses of wine, just the right amount of sympathy and understanding from her friends, followed by some of their usual nonsensical banter, Tyler felt almost back to her old self.

"It would make more sense to have everyone over here," Rose said. She started to pour herself some more wine, hesitated, then with a shrug went with half a glass.

"You know Mom." Dani shook her head when Rose held up the bottle. "It isn't the holidays for her unless the old house is bursting at the seams with people."

"I guess we all feel that way. My first real memories of a happy Christmas were spent with your family." Rose thought about it, smiling. "This year, with all the added bodies, I'm afraid your folks' house will go beyond bursting to exploding."

"Our numbers have grown quite a bit since last year. Alex, Jack, and Drew take up a lot of room. Add half a dozen bodyguards that always seem to be in town. I don't expect that to change, even for the holidays. I'm afraid you're right, Rose."

"Maybe a smaller, just family get-together that your mother can host."

"Hmm, maybe." Dani turned to Tyler. "You've gotten awfully quiet. What do you think about our holiday housing dilemma? You and Drew could host. Finally, crack open the seal on that big house of his."

"He asked me to move in with him."

Rose nodded. "You weren't ready. Is that bothering you?"

"Shouldn't it be?"

Tyler looked at Dani and Rose. Her best friends. They knew her almost better than she knew herself. Right now, she desperately needed some insight. This morning, before Drew left, she was fine with her choice to wait. It was too soon to move in with him. As the hours passed, she began to wonder if there was more to it.

"Is Drew pressuring you?"

"No."

"Do you wish he was?" Rose asked.

"Yes," Tyler admitted, hating herself for it. "How screwed up is it for me to wish he would swoop me up, take me home. Force me to live there."

Dani and Rose shared a glance before breaking into laughter.

"I know," Tyler sighed. "When has anyone ever forced me to do anything?"

"If Drew tried, he would be singing falsetto for a month."

Her friends were right. Tyler always insisted on making her own decisions. Just this once, why couldn't she forget that?

"I'm going to make a suggestion that won't be very popular."

"Right now," she told Rose, "I'll take anything you've got."

"Okay. Remember you asked for it."

"That sounds ominous. Can I change my mind?"

"No," Rose chuckled. "I promise, it isn't that bad. It's... emotional."

"What's left? In the past few weeks, I've hit every high and low I can think of."

"Except one." Rose set her glass down, taking Tyler's hand. "For the first time since it happened, you've let yourself go back. You've reclaimed your memories. It's made you happy. Dani and I have watched you bloom with the old love that's filled your heart again."

"I know," Tyler nodded. "Taking back those good times helped me let go of the past."

"It could be you stopped too soon."

"I don't understand."

Rose looked at Dani.

"Rose thinks, and I agree, that you need to remember it all. Not just the good."

No. Tyler knew what they meant. Even the thought of that last day, the day Drew broke up with her — crushed her — made her stomach begin to clench.

"I know how hard it is to relive the bad stuff." Rose squeezed her hand. "It helps. Telling Jack about that summer with Louise was the hardest thing I've ever done. It made me feel sick. I was sure he would run, never to return. Instead, it made us stronger."

"Drew already knows what happened," Tyler said. "He was there."

"This isn't for Drew. It's for you. Complete the cycle, Tyler. You've let yourself remember all the good. Go back to the bad. Then let go of it, once and for all."

TYLER LET HERSELF into her studio, automatically flipping on the light switch near the door. She went through the routine of turning the locks and setting the alarm. Once done, she tossed her keys into the little iridescent blue bowl she made herself just for that purpose.

When she left Rose and Dani, her original plan was to drive the short distance to Drew's house. Knowing if she was going to take another trip to the past, she would have to do it alone; she called him to beg off. Work was a lame excuse. But a believable one. He was disappointed, making her promise to call him first thing in the morning.

There was a lot to think about. Correction. There was only one thing to think about. What was the song? *How Do You Mend A Broken Heart?* In this case, it seemed she needed to break it all over again.

Tyler moved to her little kitchen. Her first instinct was to make a big pot of coffee — extra strength. Her own version of comfort food. Reluctantly, she rejected the idea. At the moment, caffeine, that lovely stimulant, was not what her system needed.

Grabbing a bottle of water from the fridge, Tyler took a heavy quilt from the bed. She toed off her boots, leaving them in a heap. Settling down on the sofa, she pulled up her legs, wrapping herself in a comforting cocoon of soft cotton.

Tyler took a deep breath. She tried, somewhat successfully to relax her body. Closing her eyes, she let her mind drift back.

TEN YEARS EARLIER

TYLER FELT LIKE she was about to burst. She made herself slow down before she took the path to the river. The last thing she needed was to end up in a broken heap on the beach. Not today.

She put her bike out of sight before turning toward the water. The surface seemed to sparkle a little brighter than usual today. The May air was fresher, the sun providing the perfect amount of heat.

Instead of walking into the little cove, Tyler danced. Her steps bouncing to the happy tune that played in her head.

She had news. Great, glorious, world-changing news. She wanted to shout it to the skies. Everyone should know; everyone that mattered to Tyler. And they would — after she told Drew. He needed to be the first. She giggled to herself. He was always her first.

Enjoying her own private little joke, Tyler tossed her backpack to the side. She glanced at her watch, willing the minutes to tick by.

Soon.

Never soon enough.

It seemed like hours had passed when she finally heard the sound of Drew coming down the path. Another look at the time told her it was only ten minutes since her arrival. Was that possible?

It didn't matter. Drew was here now. She waited impatiently, her feet restlessly shifting in the sand. There. She grinned, launching herself at him without a bit of hesitation. She knew he would catch her.

She was right. Drew's arms, strong and sure, didn't let her fall. Tyler wrapped her arms around his neck while her legs encircled his waist.

"Hold on," she laughed, raining kisses on his face.

She felt Drew's arms tighten, pulling her close. He buried his face in her neck. Tyler could hear him take a deep breath, then whisper, "You smell like heaven."

If there was a slight edge to his voice, desperation in his embrace, Tyler didn't notice. She was too excited to feel the difference in his rigid stance. She turned away, not seeing the way he reached for her again only to pull back, his fisted hands staying glued to his side.

"I thought you would never get here."

Tyler opened the side flap of her pack, pulling out a piece of paper.

"I have things to do that don't involve you."

Again, she missed signs. The tightness in his voice, his blank, cold expression.

"Look."

Tyler held out the paper, her face beaming. Her smile slipped, just a little when he glanced away.

"I don't have much time today, Tyler."

"That's okay."

Tyler excused his attitude. Naturally, he wasn't excited. She hadn't told him yet.

"I got it, Drew."

"Look, Tyler. I have something to tell you."

"No, no." She hurried over to him waving the paper. "Me first. Do you know what this is?"

Drew sighed, obviously impatient.

"Silly of me. How could you know?"

"Tyler—"

Tyler. Not Ty. She felt her excitement turn to worry. Pushing it aside, she continued.

"Art school. I sent some of my work, not expecting much. Mrs. Trainor, you know, my art teacher? She wrote a letter of recommendation."

She saw Drew look at his watch. He seemed impatient.

Her smile slipped. *What was wrong?* He never acted like this.

"I…"

Maybe she imagined it.

"It doesn't matter, Tyler."

"How can you say that when you don't know what *it* is?"

This time she shoved the letter in Drew's face, willing him to read it. To care.

"The art school I told you about. The one only twenty minutes from Georgia Tech? According to this paper, I'm a shoe-in. They were so impressed they said they will set a scholarship aside for me next year."

"That school isn't your first choice."

"Wrong. It *wasn't* my first choice. After you got your scholarship, I decided to apply here. It's just as good as the one in Chicago."

"You shouldn't give up your dream school because of me." Drew didn't look at her; he looked past her. "Go to Chicago."

Tyler didn't know what to say, or what to do. Why?

"You've been a little distracted lately," Tyler said, trying to find an excuse for his behavior. "Is there something wrong at home? Is it your dad?"

"He's fine. I'm fine."

"Then why—"

"Look, Tyler."

Drew pulled back his shoulders. He met her gaze straight on. They were eyes she didn't recognize. No longer a soft, warm brown. Instead, they chilled her to the bone.

"This was fun. We had a few laughs."

"Don't," she whispered.

"I've decided to leave Harper Falls right after graduation."

"I thought we would have the summer together."

"It will be easier for me to find a job if I go now. I can move into the dorm right away."

"I see."

"Do you?" If possible, his eyes turned harder. "I'm eighteen, Tyler. Too young to tie myself to anyone. You want more than I can give. I want… variety."

"What does that mean?"

"Don't make me say anymore."

"Why not? I want to hear every bit of it."

She saw a flicker in his eyes. Was it regret? It only lasted a second before the cold returned.

"Fine. Just remember. You asked for it."

Tyler felt the stirrings of anger. He acted as if this was her fault. Tyler lifted her chin. She was used to men giving her a verbal kick in the gut. Her father. Her brothers. She never thought she would add Drew to that list.

"Stop stalling. Say it all."

"I want to be able to fuck other women. When I want. Where I want. Having you nearby would cramp my style."

"I'm not enough for you."

Shut up, Tyler, her brain screamed. *He's knocked you to the ground. Use your head. Stay down.* Her mouth wasn't listening.

"How many others have you fucked while I was spreading my legs?"

"There's no need to be crude."

"That's no answer."

"There's only been you," Drew sighed. "It was... fine."

Fine? What happened to the best ever? When did she become *fine?*

"I'm ready to find some women with more experience."

"And lots of them."

"I knew you'd understand. Take care."

Drew gave her an awkward pat on the shoulder before turning to go. If she hadn't been in shock, she would have left him with a bloody stump on the end of his arm.

Tyler didn't know how long she stood there. A minute? An hour? A week?

Somehow, she found her way home. She didn't notice or care if anyone else was home. She wanted to crawl into bed, pull the covers over her head; forget the rest of the world existed.

"Tyler?"

Go away, Tyler wanted to scream at her mother. She tried lifting her head. She didn't have the energy.

265

"Baby? Are you feeling okay?"

Anita sat on the edge of Tyler's bed. She tested for a fever with the back of her hand, finding nothing but a cool forehead.

"Just tired," Tyler managed to mumble.

"You're never tired. Especially not in the middle of the day."

Not wanting to talk to her mother, Tyler rolled over. It didn't matter how well intentioned, she would never understand. Tyler's heart was broken. What could a married woman with three children know about that kind of thing?

"Rose will be home soon. I'll send her up right away."

Rose. Dani. They knew about Drew. Tyler burrowed deeper. She needed her friends.

Tyler didn't stay in her room the rest of the day. She stayed in Dani's.

She cried, raged, broke a cup nobody cared about. Her friends listened. They were outraged when she needed it. Teary when she was bawling. In other words, they were Rose and Dani.

By the next day, Tyler knew she didn't want to give up or give in. She no longer waffled between sad and angry. She was full on mad. She planned on staying that way.

"We could kill him," Rose suggested. They were living on chocolate cake and diet soda.

"True," Dani nodded. "We aren't eighteen yet. If we get a sympathetic woman judge, we might be out before we're twenty-one."

"Not to mention the sugar." Rose licked the last crumb from her fork. "A good lawyer would say we were hopped up on the stuff. I can see it now; they'll call it the Cake Coma defense. It will be required reading for every law student in the country."

"Now you're being silly." Dani took the plate of half-eaten cake from Rose. "No more for you."

"I'm going to his graduation next week."

"Such a bad idea," Rose said.

"As your best friends, it's our job to stop you from doing anything self-destructive," Dani agreed.

"I'm going." Tyler was adamant.

"Why put yourself through that?"

Tyler's hand went to the key she still wore around her neck. The key to Drew's stupid car. What she foolishly thought symbolized the key to his heart.

"I have something that belongs to him."

"Mail it back," Dani urged.

No. This had to be done in person. Tyler wanted to throw it in Drew's face with all his rich kid friends watching. Then walk away without a backward glance. Once it was done, she never wanted to see Drew Harper again.

The day of the graduation ceremony, Tyler spent more time than usual getting dressed. If this was going to be the last time Drew saw her, she wanted to look her best. Let him see what he threw away.

Tyler owned two dresses. One black, for church and funerals. She refused to attend either. The dress still had the price tag. Seventy-five percent off. Her mother knew how to find a bargain.

Not today, Tyler thought. Black was not right for the image she wanted to project.

Her other choice she bought herself. Drawn by the color, Tyler picked it up for next to nothing at a second-hand store in Spokane. Classic, the owner of the shop told her. She would be able to wear it now and twenty years from now. Tyler was only worried about the dress getting her through high school. Who could worry about twenty years from now?

Tyler stood back, twirling around once in front of the mirror. The ocean blue color suited her, making her gray eyes look almost lavender. The dress showed off her tanned legs, the three-inch heels on her sandals making them look impossibly long.

She decided to leave her hair loose. Thick and shiny, it hung down her back almost to her waist. Drew would lean over her, twirling a strand around his finger. He told her it was like silk.

No. Tyler shook herself. She wasn't going to get weepy again. *Hold on to the anger*, she told herself. *That will get you through.*

A dab of pink lip-gloss was all the makeup she needed. Her skin was smooth, lightly touched by the sun. The color in her cheeks was flattering. Too bad it was caused by thoughts of wrapping her hands around Drew Harper's throat. When she pictured squeezing the life out of him, her face took on a rosy glow.

Tyler grabbed her purse. She wasn't afraid of being seen. Her mother was at church polishing pews or something like that. Her father was out of town — nothing new there. Her brothers could be anywhere. They were the least of her worries.

She let herself out the back door, walking the short distance to the Wilde's driveway where Dani and Rose waited. They insisted on going with her if only to watch her back. This was an invitation-only ceremony. Crashing the graduation wouldn't be difficult. The secret was to act like you belonged. Find a crowd. Flow into the building with them.

Plan B? Pick a lock. Tyler used to do it at Harper High all the time — just for fun. She was a bit rusty. Still, she doubted the doors at Harper Academy would be that difficult to get through.

As it turned out, she never found out. No one gave them a second glance. They walked in like they belonged, blending in easily with the dozens of other girls their age.

"That was kind of disappointing," Dani said as the three of them took seats on the aisle. "I was hoping Tyler would have to do her cat burglar routine."

Rose looked around the auditorium. Not that long ago, she was a student here. On that very stage, she participated in plays, musicals, recitals. Her sophomore year, she had the lead in Grease. Funny, as nice as it was here, she didn't miss it a bit.

The lights flickered signaling everyone to take their seats. The voices quieted, slowly becoming silent. The orchestra began the opening bars of Pomp and Circumstance. The group of gowned students gathered behind them.

This was her moment. Tyler searched the sea of purple and white. Finding Drew was easy. Taller than most of his classmates, his height and build made him stand out.

Turn, Tyler silently urged him. *Let me see how happy you are.*

He would pass right by, an easy target. She opened her purse, her hand wrapping around the key. She took a deep breath, her anger dissipating any nerves. Obliterating the little voice of reason that told her this was a bad idea. He deserved to be embarrassed. He deserved…

Tyler lost her train of thought the second he turned.

Drew looked terrible. Dark circles under his eyes. A slump to his shoulders. It was only a few days since she last saw him. Had he lost weight?

Tyler gripped her chair, every fiber of her being urging her to go to him. He needed comfort — he needed her.

She knew she was kidding herself, seeing what she wanted to see. Drew didn't want her. He certainly didn't need her. If he looked tired, it was because of all the end of school activities. Finals, parties. Girls.

Tyler felt another rush of anger. Only this time, it was muted. It wasn't enough to let her carry through with what was a stupid, immature, reckless plan. Drew was moving on. She was going to do the same.

Soon, she promised herself. If not today, or tomorrow, next week. A month at most.

She glanced at Drew one last time. She closed her eyes, taking a deep breath. As the first of the graduates began their procession, Tyler motioned for Dani and Rose to follow her. They made their way down the row, avoiding feet, apologizing to annoyed spectators.

Tyler pushed through the outer doors, not stopping until they reached the car Dani borrowed from her mother only an hour earlier.

"What happened?" Rose asked, rubbing Tyler's back.

"It was a mistake," Tyler explained, taking a deep breath of fresh air. "I couldn't go through with it."

Dani joined them, her hand taking Tyler's.

"We could egg his car. Not as public but really effective."

Tempting. Then Tyler pictured the car and she knew she could never do it. Drew hurt her, his car didn't.

"Let's go home."

"Home? Are you kidding?" Dani exclaimed. "We are three hot women dressed up, looking like a million bucks."

"Make that *three* million," Rose chimed in.

"Exactly. A car, a full tank of gas. The day is ours. The only question is Spokane or Coeur d'Alene?

God, I love them, Tyler thought. Her heart was broken; no denying it. She was angry, in pain. All that would pass. Men would come and go. Dani and Rose were forever.

"Well?" Dani jiggled the keys. "Where shall it be?"

Smiling, Tyler linked hands with her best friends. It didn't matter where they went as long as they went together.

In the end, they flipped a coin.

TYLER WIPED THE tears from her face.

All the time she spent angry — hating Drew. He broke her heart to save her family. Why didn't she see before now how much he suffered too? She thought he abandoned her when all along he was with her, feeling what she felt. Aching the way she did.

Yesterday she didn't think it was possible to love him anymore. Now she realized love was infinite. It would continue to grow as long as they took care not to be neglectful.

Tyler sighed, pulling the comforter tighter. She needed to take better care starting right now.

She reached for her phone; her only thought to speak to Drew, when she noticed the time. Three o'clock? She could still call. He wouldn't complain if she woke him.

Her thumb hovered over the button. No. A few hours wouldn't make any difference.

Tyler snuggled back down on the couch, too warm and comfortable to bother going to bed. She would close her eyes — drift. Morning would be here before she knew it.

Sleep was almost within her grasp when someone pounded on her front door. Tyler shot up, her heart racing. She jumped up, still wrapped like a mummy. Nothing good ever came knocking at two a.m.

She hobbled over, looking through the peephole. She was right. Trouble. Flabby, dirty, drunk trouble.

"Go away, M.J."

"Need help."

"Are you injured?"

There was a pause.

"Yes?"

Her brother, a proud member of Mensa. If he wasn't sure, she certainly wasn't opening the door.

"I'll call 911. It'll only take a few minutes for the paramedics to get here."

"No." M.J. hit the door again.

"Find someplace to sleep it off." Tyler turned to leave. Halfway back to the couch, she had a terrible thought. She rushed back to the door.

"M.J.," she called out. "Are you still there?"

"You letting me in?"

"No. Did you drive here?"

"Pile of crap wouldn't start. Walking."

Normally, that would be a good thing. He could air out before going home. Unfortunately, the mild fall was finally starting to feel like late November. On top of that, they called for a chance of snow. Guilt would follow her the rest of her days if she let M.J. freeze in some gutter.

"Let me call you a cab."

She heard mumbling and something that sounded a lot like *bitch*. Calling her names was not helping his cause.

"Mom's sick."

"What?"

Tyler had the alarm turned off and locks disengaged in a few seconds. She knew he could be lying. Hell, he probably was. If something was wrong with their mother, Tyler wasn't taking any chances.

"What's wrong? Where is she?"

"And they say I'm stupid."

She didn't have time to react. All she felt was a fist hitting her face. Then nothing.

DREW FINISHED HIS workout hitting the pool for fifty laps. Swimming loosened any tired muscles, refreshing his body after a run and hitting the weights. His brain flowed, smooth like his arms cutting through the water. He could think when he swam. This morning he thought about Tyler.

He grinned, drying his hair. Hell, he thought about Tyler every morning. If he were obsessive, he could calculate the number. Started after he, a seventeen-year-old kid, was lucky enough to run into a smart-mouthed fifteen-year-old siren in the making. He couldn't say every morning since, but it was close.

Not all those mornings were as good as this one. There were times he hated that the memory was burned into his brain. Then there was now when he considered every thought, even the bad ones, a blessing.

It was still early, before seven, when he walked into his office. Neither Jack nor Drew was in yet. They had women keeping their beds warm. They would be fools to leave, especially when the temperature outside was below freezing. Lucky bastards.

He planned on being just as lucky. Before the first of December, if he had his way. Tyler wanted to take it slow. He wanted to speed up. Supersonic. There had to be a place to meet between the two.

Drew booted up his computer before checking his morning schedule. Nothing earthshaking. Plenty of time to strategize. Project *Get Tyler to Move In* was officially underway. How to start?

Smiling, Drew picked up his phone calling the one person he knew got up earlier than he did.

"*Peony.*"

"This is your private number."

Lila chuckled. "I had my calls transferred down here because of an early delivery so I went ahead and opened the shop. You would be surprised how many people need flowers at seven in the morning."

"I might be except you're talking to one."

"The men who love my friends are becoming very good customers."

He liked Alex's little sister. Smart as a whip, pretty. Sweet as can be. He also liked sending some business her way. Today, he was giving her a doozy.

"How many roses do you have in your shop?"

"Lots. How many do you need?"

"Eleven dozen." Drew thought about it. "And a half."

"Well, sure. What would be the point without the half?"

Exactly. Eleven years, six months. That was how long ago he and Tyler met. Roses signified love. So what if it wasn't exactly subtle. He didn't have time for that. Full-on assault. That was his plan.

"I can do it if you don't mind a mixture. Or all red."

"Not red."

Tyler was not traditional.

"A mixture it is."

"Can you call me right before delivery?"

"Want to be there to reap the benefits?"

"Something like that."

"I don't see any reason they won't get there before lunch. Sooner, if my assistant is early."

"Thanks, Lila." Drew read off his credit card number." We need to see about finding a guy to buy *you* flowers."

"Ugh," Lila said. "Don't get me wrong. I wouldn't turn down a hot guy for Christmas. If you meet him first, tell him no thanks."

"Like someone bringing a chocolate maker candy."

"Exactly."

"What does a guy bring you to win you over?"

"Let's just say I'll know it when it happens."

Smiling, Drew hung up. Deciding it was late enough, he called Tyler. When it went to voicemail, he was disappointed. She was probably working. He left a quick message inviting her to lunch. Hopefully, the flowers would arrive the same time he did.

Drew pulled up the latest sales figures for their new software program. Better than projected. His mind wandered as he wondered what it was like to make love on a bed of rose petals.

Chapter Nineteen

IT WAS ALMOST eight hours since M.J. cold-cocked her. Her phone rang five times; the fourth call had M.J. hurling it across the room. That didn't stop it from ringing; it simply muffled the sound.

Tyler moved her jaw from side to side, cursing her stupidity. Don't open the door. No matter what. Her brother found one of the few things that would make her throw out her caution. She should know better. Never trust M.J.

He was a weasel. A thief. He treated women like dirt, including his own mother. In spite of all that, she never thought he would hit her. This was the first time.

The shock of it was wearing off. She woke, tied up. According to the clock on the wall, she was only out a few minutes. In that time, M.J. managed to secure her to the pipes under the sink, tear through the drawers in her desk, and find the two bottles of champagne she was saving for New Year's Eve.

He grumbled his way through the first, complaining that it was nothing but fizzing piss with no kick. By the second bottle, he was still complaining, swaying, and hiccupping the entire time.

When he leaned against the wall, his legs seemed to give out. He slid to the floor giving Tyler hope that he had passed out. No such luck. He slept in fits and starts. The sleep period didn't last long enough for Tyler to work at the ropes around her wrists. Not long enough for her to make much progress.

She needed to try reasoning with him. To do that, he had to be sober, but not too sober. Still sporting a buzz, yet not incoherent. By the looks of him when he came out of the bathroom, he was as close as she could hope for.

"If you want money, M.J. I'll give you my bankcard. There's an ATM over at the grocery store."

"Big, fucking deal. Couple hundred bucks."

"You can withdraw a thousand dollars. I'll give you the pin number."

"Bet you gave Kyle a hell of a lot more than that to get him out of town."

Kyle? That's what this was about?

"He asked for my help."

"Kyle is worthless." M.J. took another drink, most of the liquid missing his mouth and running down his chin.

"He wanted to start over, try something new."

Tyler leaned her head against her arm. She was tired, thirsty — scared. M.J. was unpredictable. His mind didn't work in a logical, straight line. The alcohol didn't help.

"Is that what you want, M.J.? To leave Harper Falls? I'll help. Untie me. We can figure this out."

"I don't want to leave," M.J. shouted. He threw the champagne bottle at Tyler, narrowly missing her head, hitting the sink. The glass didn't shatter, thank goodness. But it did break. She was able to grab a piece, hiding it under her leg. If only he would go back to sleep, or better pass out, she could cut through the rope.

"This is my town." He advanced on her. He poked her in the chest, emphasizing his words. "I was born here. I deserve to have something…"

"What?"

M.J. swayed backward, catching himself on the side of the counter. He glared at Tyler.

"Dad hated you, I hate you. Kyle. I thought he hated you. Now he's gone."

He wasn't making sense. She couldn't reason with him. Her mind raced. Drew. He was bound to come looking for her when she failed to return any of his calls. M.J. didn't have a weapon; she was certain of that. Physically, he was no match for Drew. But her brother did have the element of surprise on his side. There was no telling what a lucky punch might do. She had to get free. Soon.

"Everything would be fine if you were dead."

Tyler swallowed hard. No. He couldn't mean it. The alcohol was taking over.

"M.J., think about what you're doing. Leave now. I won't tell anyone you were here. It will be like it never happened."

"Never happened," his blurry eyes locked on her. "I like that. I can make it like you never happened."

M.J. came at her, still a little unsteady, but the look on his face was determined. Tyler felt a chill run down her spine. Was she going to die? Would Drew know how she much loved him? It wasn't fair. She wasn't going down that easily.

Tyler searched under her leg for the piece of glass. Pathetically inadequate, but it was the only weapon she had. She gripped the shard in her hand, the rope holding her wrists together made movement difficult. If M.J. came close enough, she would make do. She planned on drawing blood.

"Car keys."

Tyler felt a wave of relief. Take the car, you bastard. Just get out.

"In the bowl by the door."

"Let's go."

"What? No!"

Tyler tried to shrink away from him, but there was no place for her to go.

"Take the damn car, M.J. Leave me here."

"Shut up, bitch."

M.J. slapped her. Tyler's head snapped back, knocking hard against the cabinet. Stars swam in front of her eyes, making her wonder if she was going to pass out. Worried what he would do to her if she did, she lashed out with the sharp glass. The satisfaction she felt when she heard his scream was short-lived.

"Goddamn bitch. You cut me."

M.J. sounded surprised. Outraged that she would dare such a thing.

This time when he hit her, she knew it was coming. Unfortunately, that didn't make it hurt any less. She slumped forward knowing this was it.

She was going to die.

"HEY, WHERE ARE you off to in such a hurry?"

Drew tried to swerve around Jack's big body only to have him use one of the moves from his old football days. The guy was deceptively fast. It was one of the things that made his partner an All-American. It also made him a pain in the ass.

Grinning, Jack stayed in front of Drew.

"Want some company?

"Yes," Drew said, faking left before skirting to the right. "But not yours."

Laughing, Jack followed him to the parking lot. Alex was already gone, meeting with Dani. Rose waited for him at home.

"Do you miss the days when we were free to share our lunch with random women?"

"You mean like the pizza parlor twins?"

"They were sweet. A little clingy, but sweet."

"I wouldn't know. You're the one who took them home. I wasn't interested."

"Hung up on Tyler."

"You were soon to be hung up on Rose."

The old friends exchanged looks, grinning.

"Miss those days?" Jack asked again.

"Hell no."

"Me neither."

Drew was still smiling when he pulled his Pontiac GTO to a stop in front of Tyler's studio. *Purple*, he grinned as he shut off the engine, *she would like that. Couldn't have timed it better,* he thought as Lila's delivery van pulled up right behind him.

"Personal service from the owner. How do I rate?"

Drew opened the driver's side door, helping Lila out.

"You and Jack spent most of a day installing that nifty security system at *Peony*. Seems only fair I return the favor." She opened the back, taking out a huge arrangement of white and purple roses in a cut crystal vase.

"Besides, I want to see Tyler's face when you give her these." She looked around, frowning. "I don't see her car."

"In a town this size, she can't be far. If she isn't home, I'll give her a call. She'll be back in five minutes — tops."

She handed the flowers to Drew before pointing to five other arrangements. Picking one up, Lila said, "I'll come back for the others. Lead on, McDuff."

Drew jogged up the steps. He reached to ring the bell when he noticed the front door was ajar.

"Is something wrong?

Drew raised a finger to his lips, motioning Lila to the side and out of the way. His heart raced. Tyler knew better than to leave her door unsecured. He set the flowers down before slowly opening the door, peering inside.

The place was a disaster. Overturned furniture, broken dishes. Papers strewn in every direction. Tyler's work area was the worst hit. Broken pots of paint left streaks down the wall, brushes broken in half. A marble statue was turned over, a crack running across the half-finished face.

Anything that could be smashed, crushed, or broken lay in random heaps.

"Tyler," Drew called out.

His dread was now panic. Rushing to the bathroom, he threw open the door. More destruction, no Tyler.

"Drew."

He looked to where Lila stood. She was pale, her eyes filled with horror. Drew rushed to the kitchen to see what she found.

Blood. Not a lot, but it was sprayed everywhere.

He wanted to yell, punch something. He wanted Tyler. Alive. Unharmed.

He pulled out his phone. Pulling up her number, he chanted under his breath, "Answer, answer, answer."

At the first ring, his shoulders slumped. He watched Lila move across the room and bend down. She held up the ringing phone, tears forming in her eyes.

Tyler wasn't going to answer.

"Son of a bitch."

Drew tried to dial again, his hand shaking so much he kept missing the button. *Stop*, he told himself. *Pull it together. Tyler needs you.* He knew how to do this. His training as a bodyguard prepared him to be calm in pressure situations. Nothing, though, prepared him to deal with this. The woman he loved was in danger. That wasn't in any manual.

Taking a deep breath, his steady finger hit speed dial.

"Drew. *Lunch* over already?"

The sound of Jack's teasing calmed him like nothing else could. He could count on his partner.

"I need you here, at Tyler's. Now. Get Alex!" Drew looked grimly around the trashed room again. "And Jack? Bring guns."

TYLER WAS AWARE of movement.

Disoriented, her head ached something fierce. Whatever was causing her body to bump all over the place needed to stop. As she jostled around, her stomach began to roil, making the bile rise up into her mouth. Keeping her eyes closed, she took deeper breaths. It helped.

When Tyler was certain the threat of vomiting was over, she slowly opened her eyes.

Darkness. Pitch black nothingness. She flashed back to being a little girl trapped in that closet. Hours alone with no light, begging for help that wouldn't come. Panic washed over her, a clammy sweat breaking out on her body. This was her worse nightmare come to life. Closing her eyes again, she curled into a ball.

Breathe. In, out, in, out. You aren't a child. You don't need to give in to your fear. Think of something else. Think of what makes you happy.

Drew's face popped into her mind. The way he smiled. How easy it was for him to make her laugh. The way he touched her — held her. Tyler felt her heartbeat start to slow. Her breathing became less ragged, more natural.

She bounced again. Where was she? When the panic started to rise again, Tyler reminded herself. Think of Drew. Think of how... he loves you.

That did the trick. Her nerves weren't glass-smooth, but she was calm enough to climb over the fear. Drew was with her, she could get through this.

Tyler opened her eyes. Think, she told herself.

M.J. had knocked her out. Tyler listened, hearing a motor and the sounds of tires rolling over an unpaved road. She was in the trunk of her car. Feeling around, she realized her hands were no longer tied. Instead of cutting the rope securing her to the pipe, he got rid of the ones around her wrists. Good. One less thing to worry about.

Tyler braced herself as the car made a sharp turn. They couldn't be in town anymore. M.J. was driving too fast. The road wasn't paved. That eliminated the main highway. She didn't think that too much time had passed. Still, they could be in Canada for all she knew. The chances of Drew or anyone else finding her seemed depressingly remote. She was on her own. If she was going to survive, she needed a plan.

JACK PULLED UP fifteen minutes later. Alex was right behind him.

Drew didn't question the men bringing Rose and Dani with them. Knowing Tyler was missing, there would be no keeping them away.

They gathered in the parking lot. Drew didn't want the women to see the mess inside. Tyler's friends were worried enough without adding that image.

Drew gave them a brief rundown. There wasn't that much to tell. She was missing and so was her car.

"Her car is gone?" Jack asked, pulling out his phone. "Hell, Drew. Why didn't you say so?"

"You have a tracking device on Tyler's car?" Rose demanded.

"Hers. Yours, Dani's." Jack typed furiously. "You can get pissed at me later. Right now, we have to find Tyler."

"Pissed. Jack, I could kiss you."

Not looking up, Jack smiled slightly.

"Later. There," he exclaimed with satisfaction.

Drew grabbed the phone. The signal was clear and strong.

"Not too far. Fuck, I must have just missed the son of a bitch." He looked up at Jack. "Your SUV. We're headed up the mountain."

TYLER'S MIND RACED.

Lug wrench. It wasn't something she ever used, but she knew there had to be one back here. Turning over, she felt around when out of the corner of her eye, she saw a glowing object. Light, any kind, no matter how small was a welcome surprise. She scooted closer. The tab hung from the lid of the trunk, flopping up and down with every bump the car hit.

Tyler reached out. Plastic. She almost pulled before she remembered something Jack once said about every newer car having an escape latch of some kind in the trunk. That must be it.

Feeling a surge of hope, Tyler renewed her search for the wrench. The second the car stopped, she would pull the latch. She wanted to have a weapon with her in case M.J. was faster than he used to be. If luck were with her, there would be someplace nearby to hide. Trees, bushes. Anything.

When her hand finally came in contact with a long metal rod, Tyler almost wept with relief. She gripped the wrench in her hands, kept her eyes on that little glowing lifeline, and waited.

"WHY THE FUCK did he come up here?"

Dani patted Rose's hand. No time for cute little euphemisms. Their best friend was in danger. Rose turned her palm up finding comfort. She rested her head on Dani's shoulder, trying not to cry — willing Jack to drive faster.

"Who has her? And why?" Alex wanted to know. "Ransom?"

They were all piled into Jack's SUV headed up Crossfire Hill. Not towards the H&W complex. No one got in there without clearance. Following the tracker on Tyler's car brought them to the base of the mountain. About half a mile up, they turned onto an unpaved road. If you could call it that. More of a trail barely wide enough for the large vehicle. Branches scraped noisily, catching on the side view mirror. A particularly low-hanging one hit the windshield with such force it was a wonder the glass didn't shatter.

No one commented. Jack handled the vehicle with ease, only cursing when it was necessary to slow down for a sharp turn.

"Not ransom. Though if he had half a brain, that's what he would do. I'd pay any price to get Tyler back."

"Who?"

"M.J."

"Tyler's brother?" Dani cried out. She and Rose exchanged worried looks. "Are you certain?"

Drew took his phone, scrolling to the picture he snapped before leaving Tyler's place. On the inside of the cabinet, next to the ropes he tried to block out of his mind, carved into the wood was one word. M.J.

"Using her brain," Jack said after a quick glance. He couldn't afford to take his eyes off the road for longer than that. Especially now that flecks of white were hitting the windshield.

"He's snapped," Rose whispered, shaking her head in disbelief. "All the petty things he's done to her. Even locking her in that closet. It was cruel, nasty. He never had the balls to go after her face-to-face. Deep down, he's scared of Tyler."

"I don't know his motivation. I don't fucking care. The asshole can spend the rest of his life letting some shrink decipher his twisted brain." Drew's hand fisted in his lap. "If he's hurt Tyler, there won't be enough of him left to worry about."

THEY WERE GOING too fast.

Her car wasn't made for this kind of abuse. Tyler knew by the bumps and swerves, they had to be on a rural road. One that didn't get used enough to warrant upkeep. If she made it out of this… Tyler stopped herself. Not *if*, *when*. There was no other option. *When* she got out of this, she would be bruised from top to bottom.

Another sharp turn sent her shooting to the side, her head connecting with a hard thump. Tyler rubbed the spot. Add a possible concussion to her growing list of injuries.

"Slow down before you kill us both."

The car braked slightly, then accelerated, going even faster than before.

"Shut up. I'm not dying. You are."

Before Tyler could open her mouth to yell back, she heard a curse followed by a sickening thud. The car started to fishtail. M.J. was no longer cursing, he was screaming. The car was out of his control.

Tyler closed her eyes, took a deep breath, and braced for impact. She didn't have long to wait. She felt the car rolling down some kind of incline. *Please, let it be a hill, not a cliff.*

She waited for the feeling of weightlessness as the car fell through the air. Instead, she shot forward, one last insult to her already battered body. Then nothing. The sound of the crash was still ringing in her ears as she inched back to the front of the trunk. She was shaken. It didn't feel like anything serious. She didn't have time to find out.

Somehow, Tyler still held the lug wrench. It would be her luck if M.J. walked away from the crash unhurt. She still needed a weapon — just in case. Reaching up, she grasped the glowing tab and pulled. The whoosh of the opening trunk was the sweetest sound she'd ever heard.

Stiff yet determined, Tyler crawled out. Still light out, she observed, not knowing if that was good or bad. It would be harder to hide from M.J. That meant staying off the road. In the dark, she might have tripped and broken her neck. After everything else, that would be a tragically ironic ending.

Light was good, she decided. Lucky. Now if only that luck held. Hopefully, M.J. was out of commission. Not dead. For her mother's sake, she couldn't wish for that. Unconscious? That she could live with.

Tyler's legs weren't as steady as she might have liked. When she looked out, she found solid ground to be a bit of a hop away. Holding on to the wrench, she jumped, thinking straight ahead had to be better than straight down. Her feet hit the embankment, slipping on the wet surface. If she'd known her brother was going to stuff her in the trunk of her car, drive into hills, then get into a wreck, she would have thought ahead. Hiking boots were much more practical than socks in a situation like this.

When did it start to snow? Not much. A light skiff that made climbing difficult under the best of circumstances. With her beat-up body, the twenty feet to the top looked like a mile.

Tyler wasn't giving up now. Gritting her teeth, she started up, one inch at a time. She slid back, then started again. Two feet, then three. Only to slip back a foot. Climbing wasn't made any easier with a metal bar in one hand. If she dropped it, she might make better progress.

Resting her head on the wet ground, she thought about it. The faster she got to the top, the better. Rocks could be used as weapons. Big sticks. A well-aimed foot to the balls. Right now, she needed both hands. With regret, she tossed the wrench as far away as possible. If she couldn't use it, neither could anyone else.

Taking a deep breath, Tyler commenced climbing again. *Don't think about how icy your fingers feel or how at any moment your toes might break off like frozen shards. Getting to the top is the goal.* Think about that, about finding help. Hot coffee, a steaming shower. Drew. Drew would make her warm again.

She was finally making progress. *Nothing could stop me now,* she thought with satisfaction. Then, all of a sudden, she slid back down, her fingers leaving ten distinct trails in the thickening snow. Feeling something on her ankle, Tyler realized, *I'm not slipping. I'm being pulled.*

"You made me crash, you fucking cunt."

Tyler felt despair crash around her. M.J., his bloody face looming over her, was finally going to get his wish. He was going to kill her.

"Yelling at me. Making me look away from the road." M.J. grabbed her by the shirt, pulling her up then slamming her back to the ground. "I would have missed that deer if it weren't for you."

Tyler felt the air rush from her lungs, the hard ground knocking it out of her. For a second, she let the idea of defeat take root in her brain. *Give up. You're exhausted. You've been fighting all your life. What has it gotten you?*

Tyler's eyes popped open. What has fighting gotten her? Friends, a career, a man to love. Everything. Tyler Jones was a fighter. That wasn't going to change now.

Using her last reserve of energy, Tyler punched and kicked at the same time. Her fist connected with M.J.'s already bloody nose, her foot going for his balls. Neither had much heft behind them. Luckily, it didn't take much. M.J. fell back, clutching his face. It gave Tyler enough time to scoot away. This time she wasn't going up; she was going sideways.

The bushes to her right would give her some cover. If M.J. were determined to pursue her, maybe they would slow him down enough to give her time to put some space between them. She started to crawl away when her hand landed on something hard and cold. Her fingers curled around the metal bar. *Hello, old friend.* If she'd had the energy, she would have cried.

"Die, bitch."

Tyler rolled over, gripping the lug wrench in her hand, to see M.J. coming at her. He was only a few feet away, in his hand a rock. As he raised it, Tyler prepared herself. One more fight. She was ready. He took another limping step, raised his weapon. But before he could strike, a shot rang out. M.J.'s body jerked back, falling to the ground.

Tyler stared disbelieving. A red patch spread across his chest. Blood, she realized. M.J. had been shot.

"Tyler."

She heard her name seconds before she was pulled into Drew's arms. She didn't hug him back. She couldn't. She was too dazed by the sudden turn of events. And she was still holding on to the lug wrench.

"Are you hurt?"

Drew gently smoothed the tangled hair back from her face. Not a pretty picture, she imagined. His vivid curses. Confirmed the fact.

"That mother fucking bastard."

"Cold," Tyler whispered.

Letting out another stream of obscenities, this time aimed at himself, Drew shrugged out of his coat. He carefully wrapped it around her, the lug wrench getting in his way.

"No," she cried when he tried to take the bar from her hand.

"It's okay, honey." Drew gently pried the piece of metal from her fingers. "You're safe. You don't need that anymore."

He gathered Tyler into his arms, starting up the hill without a backward glance at the man who lay bleeding in the snow.

"Need you."

Tyler sighed the words as she finally began to relax. The strong arms that held her so securely tightened.

"You have me, Ty. Always."

Chapter Twenty

TYLER REMEMBERED VERY little after that.

There were a lot of people. Dani, Rose. She knew they were there, holding her hand, fussing. Voices hushed. She was in a car again. This time in the back seat, not the trunk. And Drew. She not so much remembered him holding her, talking, soothing. It was a feeling. Warm. Comforting. Safe.

The next thing she knew, she woke up in a hospital bed. An IV stuck in her arm, a heart monitor beeped somewhere out of sight.

She was achy more than in pain. A pleasant floaty feeling encompassed her body. Drugs. The good ones. Tyler smiled. They didn't make getting slapped around, kidnapped, bruised from head to toe, and almost killed acceptable. They did make the aftermath a whole lot more pleasant.

"A smile. Must be the drugs."

Tyler turned her head. Her smile got bigger when she saw Drew sitting next to her bed. He looked tired. His hair stood in several different directions, a scruffy beard covered his face. He took her hand, raising it to his lips.

"Hey, handsome."

"Not pretty?"

Her gaze moved up and down. From his mud-caked boots to his weary eyes. No, not pretty. But he was the best-looking thing she had ever seen.

"Not right now." She smiled again. "You need a shower. Then some sleep. How long have we been here?"

"A little over twenty-four hours."

He kissed the back of her hand again before rubbing it against his face. Bristly. She turned her hand to cup his cheek. Nice. Something just yesterday she didn't think she would ever be able to do again. Tears filled her eyes when she thought of how close she came to never touching his dear, dear face again.

"Hey." Drew moved to sit on the edge of the bed. "You want to cry, go ahead. I might just join you."

Caught between a sob and a laugh, Tyler felt her tears evaporate. Maybe later. Right now, she needed something else.

"Hold me."

"Oh, Ty. There's nothing I would like more. Honey," Drew swallowed hard. "Thank God you're in pretty good shape. Nothing broken, no concussion."

"I was worried about that last one." Tyler held out arms.

"I'm afraid I'll hurt you. Right now, you're pretty much one solid bruise."

"I could have died."

"I'm well aware."

This time Tyler kissed the back of *his* hand, wanting to give comfort, reassurance.

"I didn't. I survived. I'm here, and so pumped full of drugs the only thing that hurts is your refusal to hug me. Now, indulge me." She scooted over. "Get in bed and take me in your arms."

"Bossy."

Taking time to remove his boots, Drew eased down beside her, careful not to jostle.

"These beds weren't made for two, Ty."

"Depends on how you do it."

Tyler turned, keeping her hand with the IV out of the way. Once her back was to him, she looked over her shoulder, waiting.

"The rest is up to you."

Drew took his time, which was fine with Tyler. In the end, they were spooning. She didn't mind that he was outside the covers. His arm curved around her waist and his warmth enveloped her better than any blanket. Her body finally began to relax.

"Tell me everything I missed. Is M.J. dead?"

"No."

"Good. My mother would have grieved."

"Mmm. If Jack hadn't pointed that out at the last second, things would be different. I was originally going for a head shot."

Tyler let that sink in. Was it terrible that, if not for her mother, she would be okay with M.J.'s death? Who knew? The fact was he had never been a real brother to her. Given the chance, he was going to kill her. She wasn't going to feel guilty. It was what it was. She wouldn't have grieved.

"What about—"

"You first," Drew interrupted. "Start with why you ever opened the door for that bastard."

Tyler was amazed how removed she felt from the events. Something that began less than two days ago already seemed weeks removed. She was able to recount what happened dispassionately. Almost as though it happened to someone else.

"Now it's your turn," she said. "How did you find me so fast?"

She waited for Drew to answer. Waited. Frowning, Tyler reached back, touching his face. What she felt there made her breath catch. He was crying.

"Drew."

"I almost lost you."

He whispered the words, burying his face in her hair. Even with an overcoat of antiseptic and hospital, Tyler's scent was still there. Drew breathed deeply. Savoring. Grateful beyond words to hold her safely in his arms.

"I love you. I always have. Even when I didn't want to. When I was convinced my hatred obliterated every good feeling I'd ever had for you. Even then I couldn't stop."

"Always," he promised. "From that day on the bridge through ten years of self-inflicted misery. Now and forever, Ty. I love you."

Tyler let her eyes close. Sleep took over. She didn't want to fight it. Drew held her; he would be holding her when she woke. Today, tomorrow, always.

"I'LL BE HOME for lunch. One o'clock."

Tyler smiled when she read the note Drew left leaning against a freshly brewed pot of coffee.

Tyler was one week out of the hospital and she felt great. The bruises lingered. The one on her chin was a particularly nasty combination of yellow and green. The rest were fading fast. No headaches, no lingering stiffness. She was doing so well, Dani and Rose booked the three of them in for a hot yoga session the day after Thanksgiving. The day after tomorrow.

After much debate, Bobbie Wilde's wish for tradition won out. If the house was bursting at the seams, all the better. Dani's mother loved having people around, especially during the holidays. She embodied the phrase, 'the more, the merrier.'

Tyler's doctor gave her the okay, releasing her from the hospital one day after all the drama went down. Her mother wanted Tyler to come home. Anita's home. As much as she loved the woman, there was no way she could ever stay in that house again. Bad childhood memories. Bad new ones. Traces of her brother would be everywhere.

M.J. was a subject she and her mother hadn't discussed. Tyler knew Anita went to see him at the county jail in Spokane. The details of the visit would forever remain a mystery she didn't want to solve. She couldn't begrudge a mother for her need to see her child, no matter what he had done. Deep down, she even understood. That was as far as it went. She was glad M.J. wasn't dead. As far as she was concerned, he might as well be.

This time when Drew suggested, or rather insisted, that Tyler move in with him, she didn't hesitate. Being trapped in the trunk of a car? Thinking you were on your way to your death? It had a funny way of knocking out any bit of lingering doubt from a person's mind.

Drew kindly invited Anita to move in while Tyler recovered. An offer her mother quickly refused. She said she wouldn't want to intrude. Tyler suspected the truth was she wasn't very comfortable around Regina Harper's son. She wanted her daughter to be happy. She believed Drew was a good man. The rest would take time.

In the end, Anita visited daily, usually arriving just after Drew left for work, and staying for several hours. A perfect solution for all involved.

Tyler spent all of yesterday with Dani and Rose. Her studio needed cleaning out. Drew wanted to hire someone. Sweep it all away. Start over. She could make a list of anything she wanted to salvage, he would go and supervise. She loved him for the intention. Why go back? Forget the terrible things that had happened there

That would mean forgetting the good too, she argued. She wanted to make peace with the place that was her home, her studio. She was ready to give it up. First, she needed to say goodbye.

It turned out to be easier than she could have imagined. There were a few twinges, a little bit of wistfulness. She was able to walk through the building, pack up her belongings, then walk away. The worst part was seeing what M.J. had done to her work. Luckily, he only destroyed two projects. Everything else was either finished, shipped, or in the planning stages. She had already spoken to her clients. They were very understanding about the delay insisting she take her time and get back on her feet. They were willing to wait for an original Tyler Jones.

An original Tyler Jones. Knowing someone thought of her art that way gave her a little thrill. It might not be the most important thing; everyone liked to be appreciated.

Glancing at the clock, Tyler poured herself a cup of coffee before heading to her new studio. It was almost perfect. The light, the size. She could expand the kind of projects she took on. One side of the room was perfect for the pottery wheel she ordered yesterday. A few tweaks here and there. Soon she would have the kind of studio any artist would envy.

She was just cleaning up when she heard Drew come through the front door. It was becoming her favorite time of day. Five o'clock, ten, one. She didn't care what the hour and minute hands read. Drew was home. That's all that mattered.

Drew set his keys in the little bowl by the door. Tyler's contribution. Handy, too. He liked the little things she added. Every day, the house became less his place. More theirs. And there was the contribution he liked most. Tyler.

She bounced down the stairs, her momentum carrying her across the room, into his waiting arms. He could live to be a thousand — this he would never grow tired of.

"You're home."

"Home?"

Tyler looked into his eyes, knowing what he asked.

"Yes," she said, her gaze a steady crystal clear gray. "The house, my studio. They're wonderful. My heart is where you are. *You* are my home."

Drew felt his heart swell, a lump forming in his throat. So many years. Certain his chance had passed him by. This was his dream come true. Having the right to call Tyler his, to shout it to the world. No one could stop them. This time the future was theirs.

"I've told you, I'm fine. Squeeze," Tyler teased when his hug was too gentle for her taste. "You didn't treat me like I was made of glass last night. Or this morning."

Her first night home from the hospital Drew gave every bruise and contusion on Tyler's body a careful, close-up examination. He gently kissed them with his mouth, then loved her the same way. Last night was the first time she was able to convince him to fully make love to her. A new red lace bustier, garters, and stockings helped. A lot.

"Your naked body tends to turn my brain to mush. I forgot to be careful."

"Forget again."

Tyler trailed her lips across his jaw. Reaching his ear, she used her teeth on his lobe just the way she knew he liked it.

Drew felt his body, his brain included, responding in the usual way. From zero to off the charts in no time at all. He turned his head, giving her better access. *No*, he groaned, reluctantly pushing Tyler to arm's length. *Plans*, he reminded himself. Any more of that and they wouldn't get out of the house for a week.

"Lunch."

"Later."

Laughing when she tried to reach between his legs, Drew did a quick side step.

"Ty, I love your enthusiasm. Later, I promise."

"Party pooper." Tyler playfully stuck out her tongue.

"I have a surprise for you."

Drew took Tyler's hand, leading her to the front door. He got her coat from the nearby closet, bundling her up against the cold November weather. The snow that so inconveniently appeared on the day of her kidnapping promptly melted as fast as it arrived. It was replaced by bitingly cold temperatures.

"Where are we going?" Tyler asked as he wrapped a soft wool scarf around her neck and placed her favorite leather gloves on her hands. "The North Pole?"

Drew kissed the end of her nose.

"Do you want to catch cold?"

"I never catch cold."

"Let's keep it that way."

She might argue. The truth was she enjoyed Drew's fussing. She would set him straight if it went too far. For now, it was just the right amount.

"Since your car was totaled, you need something to drive."

"My insurance will cover it."

"Partly," he said. "It was what, five, six years old? Unlikely you'll get full replacement value."

"If you plan on giving me one of your cars, Drew, think again. They are all way too valuable. Every time I drove it, I'd be afraid of nicking the paint or having some idiot bang their door into mine in the parking lot at the grocery store."

"With a few minor exceptions, they are meant to be driven, Ty. That's why I take a different one out every day. Eyes closed?"

He steered her out the door, stopping at the top of the porch steps.

"This one is yours," he said firmly. Standing behind her, he placed his arms around her waist. "No arguments. Open up."

Almost afraid of what she would see, Tyler slowly lifted her lids.

"Drew," she breathed.

It couldn't be. Sleek. Bright red. A blast from the past she never thought to see again. His nineteen-fifty-five Thunderbird.

"But how? I thought you left it in Harper Falls when you went to college."

"I did. Hurt like hell too. I assumed Regina would turn it into scrap metal."

"So…?"

"My dad," Drew explained. "He put the car in storage. Arranged through his lawyer to keep up the payments even after he died. The terms were if I ever returned to Harper Falls, the car was to be delivered to me."

"And it was."

Drew nodded. "It showed up on my doorstep the next day."

Tyler turned into his arms. Another example of how much his father loved him.

"I know you hate taking expensive gifts, Ty. I thought this time—"

"Stay right there." Tyler raced back into the house. She called over her shoulder, "Don't move."

Puzzled, Drew waited. Less than a minute later, Tyler popped back through the door, a huge smile on her face.

"You're letting me give you the car?" he asked, grinning back. He took the key out of his pocket, holding it out to her.

"No need."

Tyler extended her hand, palm up. There, still on its chain, was the key he gave her ten years earlier.

"You kept it."

Hearing the wonder in his voice, Tyler felt tears form in her eyes. It might only be a key. A small, shiny piece of metal. What it symbolized made it priceless.

"I could never bring myself to throw it away."

"I love you, Ty."

"I love you."

"Come on; let's see if it still fits."

Feeling like teenagers again, they piled into the car. Tyler inserted the key, turning the ignition. Smooth as silk.

"Let's go."

"Where?" Tyler asked.

"Just drive. I'll guide you as we go."

Where they ended up was as surprising as the car. And just as meaningful.

As they got out of the car, Tyler marveled that the path down to the river was still here. Drew thought his Thunderbird would end up on the scrap heap. She thought Regina would have blown this place to kingdom come.

Silently, Drew took her hand, leading her down. Such a familiar journey, yet somehow new. This time they weren't hiding. If someone saw Tyler Jones and Drew Harper together, well, let them look. Kids no longer. Adults, able to make their own decisions. Free to love.

"The last time we were here…"

Tyler squeezed his hand. The worst day of her life. She looked around the cove. So many happy times. For too long, this place represented only pain. Finally, she was able to reclaim the good times.

"We can come back here anytime we want. From now on, I want our lasting memory to be a good one."

Drew released Tyler's right hand, picking up her left. His eyes locked on hers, he slipped a platinum band onto her ring finger. The diamond wasn't large, the setting a bit old-fashioned. In other words, it was perfect.

"It belonged to my great-great-grandmother. My dad showed it to me once. He made me promise to find a woman who wanted me enough to accept a ring whose sentimental value far outweighed its monetary worth."

Drew lightly touched her mouth with his. The kiss sweet.

"Marry me, Tyler?"

Beaming, Tyler nodded. Her answer, simple. After all these years, there was no need for more.

"Yes."

Epilogue

"THE STATUE IS perfect, Tyler."

Tyler thanked the unknown woman. All day since the unveiling of her contribution to the Harper Falls Centennial, people had come up to her like they were old friends. Most were complete strangers. Tyler simply smiled, the glow of success practically beaming from every pore.

The celebration, over two years in the planning, was a party like nothing Harper Falls had ever known. Those who warned about snow ruining the festivities were proven wrong.

It was the second week in December. The weather was unseasonably mild. Crowds of happy people milled around, taking in puppet shows, eating food from booths where vendors served a mind-boggling assortment. Hot chocolate. Spiced cider. The choices were neverending.

"Your book will be sold out by the end of the day," Tyler said to Dani.

The hardcover history of Harper Falls was filled with a mixture of old and new photographs. Dani spent months taking pictures, compiling what she hoped was a proper representation. By the way people snapped it up, she nailed it.

"I'm amazed. There are already plans for a second printing."

"Well, I'm not surprised." Alex took Dani into his arms, giving her a thorough kiss. "You are a brilliant photographer."

"I would say love is blind, except that would be false modesty."

They all laughed. Tyler looked around at her friends, the men they loved.

Rose had something she never thought possible. Love. Jack Winston took the opening she provided and ran with it. The one-night stand that never happened turned into a true love story.

Dani found the love of her life, gave him up, only to get her second chance. She and Alex were perfect together. Both strong, resilient. Their future wonderfully, blindingly bright.

"You did it, Ty."

Drew came up behind her, his arms slipping around her waist. He rubbed his cheek against her hair.

"Everyone finally sees what I always knew. You are brilliant, my love."

He nodded toward the bronze statue prominently displayed in the town center. A man, a woman, and a child. They represented Harper Falls. Family. Opportunity. A place that welcomed everyone — turned away none. It was an ideal. Something to strive for. She wanted generations to come to look at it and understand the tradition being passed to them.

"I thought I needed to prove this town wrong," Tyler relaxed against Drew. "I was going to show them that Tyler Jones was capable of being more than a hot head. I wanted to shove my talent in their faces and say, 'You thought I couldn't do it? Well, look. I'm good. Damn good.'"

"You did just that."

"I've suddenly realized it wasn't the people of Harper Falls I needed to prove something to; it was me. In spite of all my bravado, I've always had a little voice telling me I wasn't good enough. Well, you know what, Drew Harper? I am."

Drew spun her around, kissing the breath out of her.

"Damn straight, you are." He kissed her again, slower. "Mmm, how much longer do we have to stay?"

"Down boy," Tyler laughed.

She took his hand, strolling through the street.

"I'm going to say this, and then the name can be locked away again. Where is Regina?"

The Harper Falls Centennial celebration was Regina's baby. She pushed, prodded, bullied. Micro-managed every detail. Now, she wasn't here to enjoy her labors.

"You didn't really expect her?"

"I know she isn't known to socialize with the common folk." Tyler looked around. Definitely not Regina's crowd.

"I imagine she'll put in an appearance," Drew shrugged. "Let the hoi polloi bask in her presence for a few minutes then return to her crypt."

And with that, as promised, the subject of Regina Harper was retired. She had no place in their happy lives. That shadow was lifted forever.

They joined their friends, everyone getting something hot to drink. Alex's sister Lila, who spent the morning making sure her flower displays were properly set out, accepted a cup of cider from Jack.

"Here's to us." Jack raised his cup with one hand, his other holding one of Rose's.

"To us," the group echoed, tapping cups all around.

They drank, talking, enjoying the company.

When Rose's phone signaled an incoming text, she handed her hot chocolate to Jack. Looking at the message, she gave a bemused laugh.

"What?" Tyler asked.

Rose turned the phone so everyone could see.

"Guess who's coming to Christmas dinner?"

COMING IN OCTOBER

If I Had You

— *CHRISTMAS IN HARPER FALLS*
LILA'S STORY

www.ingramcontent.com/pod-product-compliance
Lightning Source LLC
Chambersburg PA
CBHW071111250626
47159CB00002B/702